THE LIVING AND THE DEAD

A. E. Purvis

Published by Stardust Literary LLC

Cover art by Michael Castro // Danger Designs

Coauthoring, snuggles, and endless moral support by George Bailey Purvis

First edition 2025

ISBN: 979-8-9999847-0-8 (paperback)
ISBN: 979-8-9999847-1-5 (hardcover)
ISBN: 979-8-9999847-2-2 (EPUB)
ISBN: 979-8-9999847-3-9 (Kindle)

www.aepurvis.com

For the girls who feel at once both much older than this world ever was and younger than they truly are, forever waiting for someone to look back and see them.

And for the eldest daughters who would wage wars and lead rebellions for their family—either found or biological.

Content Warning:

THE LIVING AND THE DEAD is a romantic fantasy that follows a Dead girl through haunting a gothic Southern manor alone, finding a place where she's loved, and being ripped from it to be forced on a trek through Appalachia where her very Existence is threatened. Abby's story contains violence and slight gore (the author is very squeamish so don't worry—it's not that bad), kidnapping, a character being forcibly restrained against their will, fear of sexual assault (which does not occur), death of a parent, animal death (a black bear), and vomiting. Swords, daggers, and knives are used and blood is occasionally drawn either by the aforementioned blades or by bare hands. As the book's main characters include a ghost and a Reaper, Death is present and referenced throughout the book and occurs both on- and off- page. Readers who may be sensitive to these elements should read with caution and take care of themselves however is necessary.

Please feel free to reach out to the author for any questions regarding content warning.

1

The enemies are becoming lovers when the giant front doors of Halcyon Hall fly open.

Their resounding creaks echo through the entire manor, booming up the stairs into the library I've tucked myself into.

God the Living owners of this place piss me off. I slam the book I'd been reading closed and tip toe across the room, sliding it back into its space on the shelf so that nothing appears disturbed before slipping into my invisible form.

"I'll get the rest of the boxes from the car," I hear Dave shout from downstairs.

Freakin' Dave.

He's not the *worst* guy, I guess. His wife Bethany loves him, he's always kind and respectful to guests, and any time I've accidentally made a sound when he's here, he's immediately shouted that I'm *"welcome here as long as yer not a demon or somethin'!"*

Don't worry, Dave, I'm just a girl.

They're here to set up for their latest semi-regular paranormal event, which take place every Friday the 13th and most of the weeks leading up to Halloween. They charge an entry fee and offer guided tours through several rooms they've painstakingly decorated to be as historically accurate to the Hall's prime as possible—rooms like a billiards room, a parlor, dining room, and the library I'm currently haunting.

Luckily for me, that careful curation doesn't extend to some of the bookshelves. Bethany is an avid reader and uses Halcyon Hall's library to store her personal collection, so it has a perfect mix of leather-bound tomes she'd found at estate sales for *aesthetics*, all of the expected classics, and Romantasy books about politics with faeries and dragons...one of which I'd been enjoying before I'd been so rudely interrupted.

Unluckily for me, Dave and Bethany have terrible timing—and unluckily for *them*, I'm feeling vengeful.

I slowly sneak down the stairs, mindful of the creaky spots, and wait until Bethany has gone outside to "supervise" the unloading of their car before fully entering the grand foyer. I take a second to scan the room and spot her keys placed neatly atop her notebook that I notice features several checklists for today.

I scoop up the keys and cross the foyer to the stack of boxes Dave has already brought in. I hang her keys gently off of the corner of the top box, which is eye level with me and decidedly *not* a place someone would put their keys.

I've just passed through the open doorway to the *absolutely-not-aesthetic-because-it's-falling-apart-and-no-guests-would-ever-be-allowed-to-set-foot-in-here* kitchen when Dave and Bethany return bickering. At least from here I can watch my prank unfold.

"I don't know *why* you insisted on parking so far down the lane, it's not productive," Bethany is saying as she walks backwards towards where she'd left her keys.

"I don't know, honey, but you were right," Dave responds. "I should have backed up to the door like you suggested." Dave, Bethany, and I all know he's just saying that to appease her and avoid an argument, but the car's location is quickly forgotten when Bethany turns to pick up keys that aren't there.

"Did you take the keys?" she whirls toward Dave.

"I haven't touched the keys since I handed them to you to unlock the doors," he promises, hands up defensively.

"I know I left them here," she points at her notebook. "They were right here. I put everything down while you got the first boxes, and circled the room to open a few of the drapes to let some light in, then I came out to you." Her tone is starting to rise; she's panicking.

"Let's just retrace your steps," Dave steps into Bethany's space, grabbing her hands. If I had to guess, they're in their mid-fifties, so they've been married awhile and likely know how to soothe each other in stressful situations. I'd almost feel bad for causing Bethany anxiety, but I know they'll find the keys in 3...2...

"There they are!" Dave spots them from over Bethany's head. He drops her hands and spins her by the shoulders, pointing at the box where I'd hung the keys.

Bethany shivers. "I didn't put them there," she whispers and Dave rubs her arms up and down.

"Don't go getting soft on me now," he encourages. "You know she won't hurt you."

I bristle, because it'll never *not* be uncomfortable for Livings to talk about you in a room you are sitting invisibly in.

"I know," she says, nodding, "but it's just unsettling." She snatches up her keys and places them back on top of her notebook. "I like things in their place and I don't like it when they're moved."

"Then tell her that," Dave raises both arms to gesture vaguely around the foyer. Bethany sighs.

"Please don't move my things!" Bethany calls shrilly. She's

exasperated but willing to humor her husband.

"Atta girl," he croons, kissing the top of her head as he takes the keys from their *right place* and begins to back towards the still open front doors. "I'm going to go move the car and bring in the last bit of merch."

"I'll start setting up the *Haaaaag*!" Bethany calls back in an deep and overly dramatized voice meant to sound spooky.

I can't help the sigh that crawls from the depths of my chest to escape my mouth.

The Hag.

The Hag of Halcyon Hall.

Me.

2

The Haaaaag is apparently a Life sized *mannequin*...of me.

Or, a Life sized mannequin of what they *think* I look like.

I can't even blame them when I see that they've painted the mannequin's face to be pale and gaunt, or when Bethany adds a wig of stringy, dull brown waves that is riddled with knots. She's in a dull gray gown and honestly, they've done a good job matching the ghost they *think* is here to the Hall itself.

Halcyon Hall is a sprawling gothic monstrosity in the low country of Georgia, set well off the beaten path. The miles and miles surrounding the building are swampy marshlands and waist high grasses that are home to all manner of reptiles I don't want to associate with. The manor stretches up out of the ground, almost as if it is made of the marsh itself: a grey brick behemoth that is so covered in twisting roots and Dead vines that the house looks to be entirely made of earth. Its front doors are huge wooden panels that easily weigh over a hundred pounds each, and are so swollen from weather and disuse that they never close properly. On one side of the structure is a garden, overrun with every form of plant-Life imaginable. On the other side, a *porte cochere* juts out, a Spanish-moss laden reminder of the bygone era when horse-drawn carriages delivered and collected many a reveler after a masquerade at the manor.

Those days of revelry are gone. The inside of the manor was ransacked by looters long before I settled here, but I don't need much: just somewhere to sleep, running water, and some food. Regular ghosts don't *have* to eat, but *I* do, and even if I didn't, eating like a Living makes me feel normal and gives me a routine.

Thanks to an upstairs bedroom that Dave and Bethany haven't renovated, a mattress that was mercifully left in tact, the well on the property, and the overrun garden, I have all I need to survive.

But, back to my being *the Hag of Halcyon Hall*. Being a huge, scary looking old mansion, Halcyon Hall is a beacon for bored teenagers looking for thrills and paranormal investigators looking for *more*. After a decade of little-to-no contact with anyone else, I decided that *I*, needing some thrills of my own, would give the people what they wanted. I spend many a night stepping through a wall and immediately shifting to my solid form in front of the young, doe-eyed Livings that are brave enough to break into the Hill. They always leave with the same stories: they'd seen the Hag, but she'd vanished before they'd gotten it on video. They'd seen the Hag, and she looked so sad: a dull, grey knee-length dress, shabby like her soul, once-golden hair that hung, loose and limp, around a sallow, pathetically sad face, and eyes whose pain haunted them. They'd seen the Hag, and they felt her loneliness—and they'd never go back to Halcyon Hall again.

Maybe Dave and Bethany's mannequin isn't that far off at all.

I hate that visitors leave with some of my pain wearing them down, but I...I'm so lonely, and I can't perk up just because someone is in front of me asking me to do parlor tricks. I know that, as much fun as an evening entertaining Halcyon Hall's trespassers may be for me, they always go back to their Lives as the Sun rises, leaving me alone once again.

It's early-September, a full moon, and Friday the 13th. After Dave and Bethany spent the afternoon setting up, Halcyon Hall is filled to the brim with supernatural enthusiasts. Ever since they'd decided to capitalize on spooky occasions and started selling tickets for late-night tours through the sinister estate, they'd advertised with the most cringe-worthy slogan I've ever heard: *"Spooky season's in the bag, get your tickets to see the Hag!"*

Mortifying, right? But somehow, it does the trick, because they sell out all of their dates within minutes.

Visitors come in droves: solo investigators and groups, families, *meeeeediums*, with gear, without gear; you name it, they are here in the halls of Halcyon. The moonlight seeping in from several broken windows reflects off every surface of the massive foyer as the owners and guides wait for every visitor to sign a waiver. "We don't want *you* to become a ghost here," they guffaw at each person as they hand them a Halcyon Hall branded pen.

Tonight, as I often do for entertainment during these events, I'm posing as a guest. Thanks to Ma, whose Existence is somewhat integrated with Living because of her work in hospitals, I have a small but decently modern wardrobe. Tonight I've donned black leggings and an oversized grey sweatshirt, something demure enough that I hope the ticket-takers won't notice me as someone who hasn't already checked in.

Dave and Bethany go all out for these events, not only providing attendees with a tour of the facility and the chance to hunt for, well... *me*, but they also provide a spread of hors d'oeuvres so elaborate that it's impossible to ignore. The guest experience is a place where Bethany truly shines, and the food is no exception: on a black-table cloth laden table in the *Grand Foyer* (as she calls it), peppering in a French accent when in front of the guests, there's a grazing station covered in smoked meats, an array of cheeses, and more crackers and dips than I can count. They've placed the grotesque mannequin in the doorway to the kitchen, essentially blocking guests from entering, and beneath her sightless gaze stands a sea of stacked sandwiches: turkey and ham with Swiss, pimento cheese, BBQ pulled pork sliders, and egg salad. The sweets table is no less grandiose: assorted bite sized cakes, candies, and treats are there for the taking.

And I take.

I can't help it. I generally survive on the overrun garden on the property, which means I haven't tasted salt, butter, or any flavor past raw vegetables in...well, I don't know how long. Normal ghosts are so much luckier than they realize; I can't imagine how it must feel to be able to eat if you want to, but to not *have* to. What is it like to not know hunger, but have the ability to eat and enjoy something if you feel like it?

I'm lost in thought, once again puzzling over the injustice that is my particular Existence and wishing I was the girl in the book I'd been reading earlier when I'm knocked into from my left. The force nearly sends me to the ground, but two strong hands grasp my arms and hold me upright.

"My apologies," a deep male voice rumbles. I turn and barely get a glimpse of him before he's lost to the crowd, but he was tall and bearded, with auburn hair, bright blue eyes, and soul-crushingly handsome.

Gods, what a loss.

I pop an olive into my mouth and sigh, resigned to know that I'll never be that girl in the books I love so much, with a male lead that looks like *that* and loves me desperately. No, I'll Exist for however long I have, then, like all souls, I'll go into the Unknown.

And just like that, my mood has soured and it's gotten far too *people-y* in here to remain visible. I make my way up the sweeping staircase, careful to take my time so as not to attract attention. I turn the corner and do a final scan of the room, noting that Dave and Bethany are about to officially start the tours with their normal speech. Once in my bedroom where I *know* there aren't any snooping guests, I snap into my invisible form. I desperately want to hide out here, in the safest space I have in the house, but I know that I can't actually pass up being around people—even if I'm invisible. I'm absolutely an introvert by both nature and circumstance, but it could be months before I see another human—either Living or Dead—and I spend too much of my time alone.

Most of my days are filled with wandering the rooms of Halcyon, either picking through Bethany's library stacks to occupy myself, or Trancing (the ghostly version of REM sleep), for a small respite from hating how my Existence has come to this. I can't even let myself go visit my Ma, or allow her to come to Halcyon, because I can't possibly let her see what I've become. She'd worry, which I don't want for her, so I've condemned myself to step fully into being *the Hag of Halcyon Hall.*

That is, until Zelie the Medium steps through the Hall's front doors.

3

I should probably take this opportunity to tell you that everything that you think you know about Mediums is a crock of *shiiit*.

Not all Mediums, but you know the type I'm talking about. They have to announce to the world that they're a *meeeeedium*, complete with all the theatrics and the expectation of fanfare you'd expect. They're all wriggling fingers and grandiose displays of false knowledge of the ghostly world, "*I don't care what the historians say, I'm a meeeeedium*"s and drawn out (and completely fabricated) stories about people and places. Most of their claims end up being proven false very quickly, because they're in it for the attention and not the abilities they claim to have. And if, out of sheer luck or prior research they happen to spout out a name or scenario that is actually correct?

Exhausting.

Wannabe "mediums" are exhausting. Every paranormal group and online forum seems to attract at least one, and the ones that come into Halcyon Hall are the worst. They sweep through the halls of the house, suddenly stopping at random locations to press their eyes tightly closed, flare their nostrils, wave an overly bejeweled hand in the air, and breathily shout about, "*Sarah, the child who Lived here and Died from influenza,*" or "*Ezra, the happy haunt who Died in his nineties but loved this property so much he stayed on to grin at meeeeediums, and only meeeeediums.*" As the sole ghost for miles, I can confirm that every single one of the "mediums" that has come through Halcyon Hall has been full of it.

Until Zelie. I know Zelie is a legitimate Medium the second I meet her.

How?

Because she sees me when I'm invisible.

Once I've given myself enough of a pep-talk, I return to the event in my invisible form. I spend a few minutes talking through a Spirit Box for a particularly handsome ghost hunter with brown hair, a slightly scruffy beard, and sea blue eyes, here searching for a reason to believe and using what he'd called the Estes Method to talk to me. He moves on quickly, though, muttering something about a beacon to his also-bearded business partner.

They, at least, weren't obnoxious, which is more than I can say for the rest of the groups that pass through Halcyon.

I'm lifting my foot to not-so-gently stomp it on the toes of an overly rude jerk who has been loudly proclaiming that everyone needed to shut up, that he's a *meeeeedium* who is channeling Hannah, the Hag, who Died in Halcyon in 1832, when Zelie walks in.

She is absolutely radiant, but effortlessly so. Her rich, brown skin glows subtly, as if she has gold glitter peeking out from beneath her pores. A gold nose ring glints in the minimal light in the room, and her full lips have been painted a beautiful berry pink. She is tall and curvy, and her clothes are unremarkable but stylish: a pale blue zip-up hoodie, dark denim jeggings, and combat booties that I would steal in a second if I could figure out how to get them off of her feet. She wears a simple gold wedding band with a dainty engagement ring on her left hand. She's wrapped her long, brown and amber box braids into a bun on the top of her head, securing it with a clip shaped like an oversized safety pin, and I chuckle when I see her earrings: two tiny, perfectly fraternal iridescent crystal ghosts. Her eyes shoot to me as the giggle escapes my lips and our eyes meet for the briefest of seconds.

Before I can gasp, she looks away, making me question whether I'd imagined it.

I'm invisible, there's no way she could've seen me.

"Hi! Don't be afraid," a bright, friendly voice suddenly whispers inside of my head, catching me so off guard that I actually *do* drop my foot onto the toes of the insufferable guest.

Of course, he takes that as his cue to leap back in horror, theatrically screaming that he'd been attacked, and that Hannah the Hag is shouting threats to curse everyone in the room.

If I wasn't so taken aback by the *phantom voice in my head!* I might double over in laughter, but instead I stumble backwards, my eyes widening as I scan the room for the fastest escape. I could simply fall through the wall behind me, but the newcomer keeps meeting my eyes and immediately looking away.

It's as if she wants to draw *my* attention, but doesn't want anyone else to notice.

"I'm sorry!" the voice cries. *"I know I probably startled you. My name is Zelie. What's your name? If you think your answer 'at' me, I'll hear it."*

Her deep brown eyes sweep back into my direction and her lips quirk up in the slightest smile. There is no way that voice is meant for me, because I'm not a telepath, but just in case...

"Uh...Abby. My name is Abby."

"Well, it's nice to meet you, Abby. Are you staying in this place by

yourself?"

So obviously I'm losing my mind. Cool. Who is this Zelie, and how is she talking in my head?

And how am I talking back?

"H...how are you talking to me? No offense, but your voice was suddenly in my head, which has never happened before, so I'm pretty sure that I've reached some level of hag where I'm just certifiably crazy."

She chuckles in my head and her smile broadens.

"I'm a Medium—not like these clowns," she cuts herself off quickly, clarifying. *"I'm a true Medium. I don't gallivant around chasing ghost stories to point them out and call attention to myself."* She has a very slight French accent, so slight that it's barely there, but it draws me to her. It reminds me of my Ma, who has a heavier French accent. I can hear Zelie talking in my head, but can also see her, apparently deep in conversation with the *meeeeedium*, who had been identified as a podcaster named Rich Walters. How—

She glances in my direction for another second, noting my dazed expression, before turning back to whatever she'd been saying to Rich.

"Oh, true Mediums communicate very differently than ghosts and the Living. We are able to see ghosts, even in your invisible forms, just as clearly as we can see the Living. We can commune with the 'Dead' while having full conversations with the Living, never missing a beat in either conversation."

"But...how? How can you see me? How do you know I'm here?" I ask around my fingers—when I'm anxious, which I definitely am in this moment, my go-to coping mechanism is nail-biting.

"If you're asking me how I became a Medium, I'm sorry to tell you that I was Born this way. That's it. I've seen ghosts since I was an infant, and have been able to communicate with them since I learned words. True Mediums don't know why we are gifted with this ability."

Rich's histrionics have escalated to near hysteria, and everyone in his group is starting to fall for it. Shouts of, "Hannah, we're so sorry you're stuck here!" and "Hannah, go to the light!" start to ring out, and I see Zelie shaking with restrained laughter.

"I'm going to have to get him out of here, but...would it be alright if I came back to visit you? You seem..." her eyes soften then, and I see the pity.

I stiffen, drawing back my shoulders and training my face back to an expression of feigned indifference.

"I'm fine. I don't need your pity," I think at her coldly. Who does she think she is?

"I don't mean to offend. You just look...lonely. And, well, being the weird girl who is afraid to tell anyone that she can talk to Dead people —I thought we might be friends."

Just as quickly as I'd seen the pity, I see what lies underneath it, and what's underneath the beautiful facade: she's lonely, too. She has a spouse, or at least a wedding ring, but she feels alone. She is lonely on the same level that I am—an outcast, a sideshow, never allowing herself to have friends. Something people gawk at when it is on television, or during the month of October when it's cool to be scared, but that is never actually loved or cared for. I soften then.

I see myself in her, and I know that she is right.

"I guess that would be alright," I sniff, trying to sound casual, as if I get visitors all the time and that I'd just pencil Zelie right into my very, very busy schedule. *"When will you come by? I'll try to be available."*

Ha.

"I wish I could come back tomorrow, but I'm sure there will be cleanup from the tours. Do you think the weekend will be enough time for the owners to forget this place exists, again?" she asks.

Next weekend.

That is *days* away.

I've gone from being perpetually alone, to being starved for friendship, which is what Zelie is offering, in a matter of seconds and I speak before I have time to talk myself out of it.

"Next weekend would be fine," I say, only then remembering that she isn't the enemy—my circumstance is—so I smile warmly and ease up on the 'tude. *"I'm really looking forward to it. I'm glad I met you, Zelie."*

She's sweeping out of the room after Rich, waving him through the doorway with shouts about having heard somewhere that Hannah leapt from a window on the third floor, but I know she hears me.

She shoots a wink in my direction, and as she closes the door behind her, I hear, much more faintly now that she isn't in front of me, *"Me too, Abby. I just know that we are going to be best friends."*

Once Zelie is gone, I hear my mother's voice in my head. *"You can't trust Mediums, Abby. Not when you are what you are. You can't trust anyone, but Mediums...Mediums could sense you and what makes you different. And if others know you're different, we don't know what could happen."* I wring my hands in the same way she always does when she's worrying about me before shutting down that train of thought.

I can't Exist in that fear, even knowing that I can't have lasting friendships, *especially* with a Medium. Every instinct I've ever learned from my mother screams at me that this will end badly. That others can be around me only briefly before they know. Before they see I'm aging when ghosts are decidedly *not* supposed to do that.

Because I was Born Dead.

4

No one was more shocked than my mother when she, in *Death*, started experiencing symptoms of pregnancy.

Can you blame her? Ma's form had been all but frozen in time for two hundred and sixty eight years. She'd survived passage from Marseille in the early 1700s after her wealthy shoemaker father put her on a boat to save her from a deadly Bubonic plague *and* Life with a Puritan family in Boston, eventually succumbing to smallpox in 1721. She was nineteen at the time of her Death.

Ma stayed in Boston as a ghost, not quite ready to go into the Unknown. She haunted abandoned cabins and churches, occasionally befriending other ghosts but doing everything she could to stay away from the Living.

Then suddenly, she had a baby bump. My father immediately split, accusing her of, "trapping him into something that shouldn't Exist."

Apparently, a Puritanical way of thinking was still alive and well in the late 1980s.

She was changing, and that was something that she'd never seen another ghost do. It terrified her so much, this impossible situation, that she went into hiding. She was afraid: afraid that other ghosts, even ones she considered friends, would notice and ring some mysterious alarm over her head, afraid that she'd meet some never-before-heard-of Eternal End (one worse than going into the Unknown), afraid that she'd be found out. But most of all, she was afraid because, stronger than any fear she might have felt, from the millisecond she realized that I Existed, she loved me more fiercely than any other emotion she had ever felt in her Life—and in her Death. The idea that, through whatever circumstances she couldn't guess, she could lose me only motivated her to protect me that much more.

She took up residence in a weathered old barn that had once been used to store hay for local livestock but, with the advent of cars since her Death, had fallen into disrepair and been long forgotten. It stood under the shelter of a grove of black cherry trees that provided shade to cover a gaping hole in the roof. Not that Ma needed shade. There were windows along both sides of the barn, all of which were cracked, hole-riddled, or busted in some way. The place *looked* haunted, so it was the perfect place for a ghost to hide.

Once she was settled, Ma went into the Trance. During a Trance, a ghost seems to cease Existing. Neither the Living nor other ghosts can see them, and they are, for all intents and purposes, not there. It's as if the ghost vanishes from all senses to any being nearby. For the ghost, it feels like a long nap one might have during their Life; the Trance is like an extreme ghostly hibernation. We *can* sleep like Living do, but a Trance is far more energizing. Ghosts Trance to save up their energy in case they need to cross the Barrier and be seen or heard by the Living.

Oh, yeah: we can be seen or heard when and if we want to be. Ghosts have energy much like the Living do, and just like the Living, we have to "recharge." Sleep and the Trance are very similar—they both charge metaphorical batteries, they both typically make the body wake up feeling refreshed, and they're both needed regularly for survival. The biggest difference between sleep and the Trance is that ghosts aren't fussy; we don't need a bed, or a couch, or to lie down to Trance. We can Trance anywhere, seeming to blip right out of Existence when it happens. Oh, and we can Trance for much longer than the typical Living sleeps, and we can go much longer, sometimes days or weeks, *without* the Trance; far longer than Livings can go without sleep.

Anyways, back to my mother and her pregnancy in the barn. Any time a Living—usually an inquisitive, brave child on an adventure (or a dare)—got close to Ma's shack in the cherry grove, she'd rattle a plank in the wall, toss a rusty nail across the room to ping off of a broken window pane, or let out an "otherworldly"—*ha, we love these*—moan. Even the biggest of the bad, toughest of the tough, bravest of all the kids (and even some adults summoned by said children) would turn tail and bolt the second she made a peep. These moments, terrifying (but *never* actually endangering) Living kids out of their wits while trying to hide, were a bright spot in an otherwise nightmare period for my mother. She was scared to Death—pun intended—and making that little shack groan to give the local children thrilling stories to tell for the rest of their Lives helped her to cope.

Then, one day a few months after she realized she had a baby bump, I was Born. Dead. But we've already established that. And everything Ma thought she knew about ghosts and Death went up in smoke.

My childhood was spent in hospitals.

Not because I was sick in any way, although I did grow up bearing witness to an endless stream of sick kids. It always seemed so unfair that the Living kids could go through such awful, painful, devastating illnesses while myself and other ghost kids always remained the picture of health...but I guess when you're already Dead, there's not much use for an immune system to fight to keep you from Dying.

No, I grew up in hospitals because my mother worked in them.

Once I was old enough to be trusted to stay home alone, and after having spent hundreds of years doing not much of anything of note, Ma realized that she had an actual stake in the future of the world, especially when it came to ghosts. She wanted me, the only Born ghost she'd ever heard of, to have the best possible future, and she hoped that nurturing new ghosts through the transition into Death would encourage a better pool of ghosts for her daughter to end up around if I ever (her fingers were always crossed) stopped aging.

Luckily for her, when I was about seven a ghost acquaintance mentioned that she sometimes volunteered in the morgue, doing just what Ma wanted: holding the hands of new ghosts as they left their Lives behind. Counseling them through the decision of staying here as a ghost, or proceeding into the Unknown.

From then on, we moved constantly. Ma didn't want to stay in any single place long enough for anyone to notice that I was aging, which was fair given the amount of growth spurts I regularly hit. She was absolutely terrified for me to be noticed in any capacity, so we never spent more than six months in one place before she'd make up a story to tell her volunteer friends then uproot us to migrate across the country.

At nearly every hospital we went to, there was a little old ghost lady who watched the kids of volunteers. I guess the ghostly community acknowledged that parents and children sometimes Died together, and that sometimes the parents needed time away from their children, so "babysitters" in any area where adult ghosts might commune with each other weren't that uncommon. No clue why it always seemed to be little old ladies, but I digress...

At least in these hospitals, I got to also spend time with ghost kids, which was more than I could've ever hoped for as a lonely kid who had to keep a major part of her Existence a secret from...pretty much everyone. When I was nine, at a hospital in San Jose, I met Autumn Crawley. She was Filipino-American, obsessed with Lisa Frank, and also nine. She was my first ever friend. We moved the day before my birthday. Then when I was ten, there was Laney Cole in Libby, Wyoming. After only being there six weeks, we left in the middle of the night. I never got to return the Spider-Man comic I borrowed from him. Cameron Sykes held my hand in Phoenix as I cried my heart out over fear that Y2K would bring the end of the world as we knew it. We were eleven, holed up in a broom closet while our parents dealt with far too many new ghosts as a result of New Year's Eve drunk drivers. And my thirteen year old heart broke leaving Shaina Halstead in Lexington, Kentucky. She introduced me to ER, which I immediately got Ma hooked on as well. Every Thursday night, without fail, Ma and I planted ourselves on the couch to find out what happened in Cook County General that week.

Since I was a minor and subject to the whims of an overprotective mother, I never had a say in when or where we moved. But I always let myself believe that I was the problem.

That Ma wouldn't have to move so much if it weren't for me.

That I was incapable of having, and keeping, friends.

5

I won't bore you with the details of the week it's taken Zelie to come back. We'll just say that there has been a lot of Trancing, a lot of pacing, and some frantic cleaning so that she doesn't think I live like...well, a hag.

Finally, *finally*, it's Friday evening. I spent the day trying to clean myself up some, because the hag persona really was getting easier and easier to fall into. I'm in my solid form since no one else is in the house. It will be easier to talk out loud than pretend to be a telepath—and the talking in my brain was weird.

What are we going to do, sit here in silence all night *thinking* at each other? Gross.

Once I've worn a new path in the already shabby flooring, unable to stop myself from pacing, I start letting the intrusive thoughts in. They're telling me that she isn't coming and that I'd been a fool to think anyone would want to hang out with me. I'm starting to believe them when I hear the telltale creak of the huge front doors followed by soft footsteps in the foyer. I pad down the stairs and find her beaming at me.

"Hey bestie!" she calls out, holding up a bottle, a bouquet of chrysanthemums, and several grocery bags. "I brought wine and cheese!" The fact that she knows that ghosts can eat puts a lump in my throat; she obviously cares enough to learn about the people—people that aren't like her—that she is communicating with.

My phone buzzes with a call from Ma, but I quickly silence it. I'll call her back later.

"I thought you'd never get here!" I tease, guiding her towards the pretty decrepit kitchen before stopping in my tracks.

I feel my cheeks heating, and I rush to explain, "With Halcyon Hall, I take what I can get. The kitchen is in terrible shape, but since I'm alone here and don't *have* to eat to survive..." I trail off, kicking myself for not thinking about the fact that *Zelie is a Living, you absolute moron*! Why didn't I consider that she might find the cobwebs, holes in the floorboards, and overall dingy nature of this room off-putting?!

"I...I cleaned the rooms I typically stay in, but didn't think about the kitchen." Gods, I am *such an idiot.*

"Girl! No worries!" she brushes away my excuses—and the "problem" of the grimy kitchen—with a wave of her hands. "I brought everything we'd need—I don't need a kitchen. Guide the way to your quarters, milady!" she adds a very exaggerated British accent at the end, making me giggle.

I lead her upstairs, past the room where Rich Walters had his epic meltdown, and down the hallway to what I consider to be "my" room.

Zelie brought a feast fit for a king.

Or, a feast fit for two thirty-somethings, Life status be damned. She makes her way to a dressing table that is surprisingly sturdy for being as old and neglected as it has been all these years. Today, she's wearing a lilac t-shirt dress with a denim jacket and white Converse, and she's traded her safety pin clip for a heart clip. She still wears the crystal ghost earrings. My outfit pales in comparison: I'm in some old beige sweats and a Hozier t-shirt I'd brought when I moved here. Both are as shabby as the rest of my small wardrobe, but being Dead doesn't exactly come with a huge clothing stipend—thrift stores are my jam.

From her bag, Zelie pulls out a variety of cheeses, cured meats, and pickles, with crackers and several spreads to choose from. From a second bag, she produces napkins, red plastic cups, and a bottle opener. Then, comes the dessert bag: chocolates, cheesecake, and even cotton candy.

"I wasn't sure what you liked, so I got a variety," she sheepishly explains. "Charcuterie is typically universally beloved, and you can't go wrong with sweets. Plus, I made the mistake of going to the grocery store hungry, so..." she laughs, gesturing at the smorgasbord and while I've never had that experience myself, I totally get her point.

"I'm so glad you did. I love food!" I make quick work of stacking a wheat cracker, a smear of pepper jelly, brie, prosciutto, and a pickled green bean before I devour it all in one bite. I have to stifle a moan; that was the perfect charcuterie combination and the flavors burst on my tongue.

"I also brought Rosé, because it's my favorite." She wiggles the bottle as she pours before handing me a plastic cup. I take a sip, relishing in the tiny bubbles tickling my nose.

"And, I brought you flowers, because, well," she blushes, "I wasn't sure if anyone ever had."

"You were right," I smile, taking the bouquet and inhaling their sweet scent, "No one has ever gifted me flowers, *and* mums are my favorite."

She beams before I demand, "Okay, tell me everything. Where did you grow up? What's your family like? What are your favorite things?" I try to stop myself from asking so many questions, but I'm so excited to have a friend that I want to know everything there is to know about her.

"Well, I was Born and raised a couple hours from Atlanta. My parents were wonderful, and incredibly supportive. They knew I was a Medium, and never tried to make me hide it." My chest tightens at that.

As wonderful as Ma is, she was almost too careful, always hiding what I was to protect me.

"They passed in a car accident a few years ago and chose to go into the Unknown, so I can't communicate with them, but it's okay. I talk to enough ghosts to know that I'll see them again." She dazes off for a second, clearly thinking fondly of her parents. "Um, what else? Oh, I'm married," she says, holding up her left hand absently, "or...I was married. My husband, Jess, passed eleven months ago."

That explains how she could seem so lonely, even with a spouse. My heart aches for her; she's been through so many tragedies at such a young age.

"I'm so sorry," I say before I can stop myself. Maybe she doesn't want my sympathy. Sometimes "I'm sorry" is the least helpful thing you can say. I feel my cheeks burn again.

"No, no, it's okay," she promises. Jess was diagnosed before we met. He had a rare form of cancer. We were lucky to get the time that we got and cherished every second." Her eyes go misty, and I'm not sure what to do. I don't want to ignore her pain, but I don't want to call attention to her tears and put her on the spot. Our friendship is so new and I'm terrified to ruin it with my utter lack of social skills.

"It sounds like he really cared about you," I muse, settling on tossing the emotional ball into her court and trying not to be jealous of the fact that she'd had a partner that loved her so much.

"He did, very much. He wanted to stick around and help me adjust, but I knew he didn't truly want to be a ghost. So, we talked about it a lot before he passed and when he did, he went *on*, too."

We sit in silence for a few minutes, both lost in thought, but it isn't uncomfortable. Being around Zelie, even in total quiet, is somehow effortless. She's a comforting presence.

"Anyways, enough about me! Tell me about you!" she perks up, plucking herself out of her reverie.

"Unfortunately, I'm boring. I just hop from place to place until I get...bored." Hey, it isn't technically a lie. I was bored of every place we stayed when I was a child.

She quirks an eyebrow then.

"What?" I ask. I swipe at my face, sure that I must have crumbs on my cheek—something has to have triggered her curious expression.

"You're not like other ghosts I've met," she says simply.

"What do you mean?"

"You seem like...I don't know. There's just something different. It's almost like," she closes her eyes, and a breeze rustles through the room. Her eyes fly open. "You did *Die*, right?"

I'm suddenly frozen in place. I'll have to move again. If she's already picking up on my being Born, I can't stay here. I'll have to flee, never speak to her again, and hope that it's enough. I'll have to hope that she doesn't come looking for me...that she doesn't think I'm some specimen to be studied. If I can get her to leave soon, I can pack and be gone tonight, but I'll hate to leave the quiet sanctuary that Halcyon Hall has provided me. How could I be so stupid stupid *stupid*?

Panic rips through me and I try to recover my features quickly—I pray she doesn't notice the terror that's wreaking havoc on my mind.

"I...w—what?" I flounder. "What do you mean? I...I'm a ghost. Of...of course I'm Dead."

A technicality.

I've grown very precise with my words so that they can be not-lies, even if they aren't the truth. They are still not lies.

"I know you're a ghost, but...there's something else. Normally, I can sense how someone Died. But with you, it's not there. But, I guess some people have traumatic Deaths that they need time to unpack." She eyes me then, as if she's waiting for me to reveal my cause of Death. Which I obviously can't do and *why* hadn't I thought to make up a story before now?! I could have rehearsed and had it all ready.

All the glory be to all the gods there ever were that at that moment, a sudden clap of thunder booms, shaking the entire house and everything inside it—us included. Immediately, a torrential downpour starts, complete with rain pouring through the holes in the ceiling and lightning flashes that make the room look like it's daytime well into the night.

We collapse into a fit of giggles at how badly that thunderclap had made us jump and fall back into easy, albeit superficial, conversation. We talk for hours about pop culture, things we like, things we hate, and all the reasons why *meeeeediums* are the worst. She tells me about the new apartment in Midtown Atlanta she's just moved into with two roommates, who she is getting to know and like, so far, and how she works with law enforcement investigations, using her abilities as a Medium to help solve cold cases. She is in town for a couple weeks for one of those cases before she will return home. The thought of losing the first chance at a friend I've had in over a decade so quickly stings more than I'd expected.

The fact that she let me off about my Death so easily is a quiet comfort that whispers that maybe I don't have to flee tonight. Maybe I can consider trying to trust her. Maybe I can change the way I react, so instantly, to letting someone get close. Maybe I can have faith that Zelie is the truly good person that she seems to be.

She gets up to leave around midnight, swearing she'll be back after her meetings at the local police precinct the next day. I'd never understood the term bosom buddies before, but I am certain, with every fiber of my being, that Zelie and I were destined to be best friends.

A. E. Purvis

Too bad I'm terrible at keeping those.

6

I was in my bedroom picking at a hole in the shabby comforter when Ma came home and said the words that would change my entire Existence.

To be able to afford things like a secondhand bed, clothes, her reloadable pay-by-the-minute flip phone, and food for the ghostly child she'd birthed and quickly found out actually required regular sustenance, Ma moonlit as a Living waitress five nights a week throughout my entire childhood and teenaged years, getting paid under the table so that she could skirt the IRS. Between shifts at the restaurant and all of her volunteer work, I rarely saw her anymore. She'd come home to prep food for me and catch a Trance, but then she'd be gone again. Taking care of other people.

I was fifteen and angsty.

"He decided to teach his girls about *Possession*," Ma whispered to whoever was on the other end of the call. "*Oui*, I guess they 'ave to learn about it eventually, but they're so young..." she trails off. A sigh. "Anyways, I 'ave to go. *Au revoir*." A click.

I was, of course, *not* planning on leaving my room, because I was angry at the world and feeling neglected and what better way to prove that than be a jerk, right? I'd been watching a carpenter bee weave lazily into and out of a hole in the grimy windowsill above my bed and wishing I could be anywhere but there. But that sentence—I *felt* it. It wasn't like the earth split open or the sky shattered or anything, but when I heard, from my own mother's mouth, that Possession was *real*, something that could be taught, it sent a charge through the air and I knew that *this* moment...it was going to be important.

"He decided to teach his girls about Possession."

I barreled out of my bed and through my open doorway, only stumbling a little over the mess littering the floor. (I was a teenager with a messy room, leave me alone about it.)

"Possession?" I demanded, Ma whirling to face me from her place by the rundown, but still functional, kitchen stove. "What's that about?"

I could tell by her expression that she hadn't wanted me to overhear that conversation. A flush crept up her neck before peppering her cheeks with pink splotches and she gnawed at her lower lip. Unfortunately for her, I was never one to leave well enough alone.

"There's no chance of you forgetting you 'eard that, is there?" she asked.

"None," I agreed. "So you can tell me now, or in a few weeks once I've spent every minute asking you about it."

She smirked, but the sour look on her face confirmed that this was something she didn't *want* me to know.

We sat for a few moments in agonizing silence before she sighed again. She'd raised a mercilessly stubborn daughter and she knew it.

"Alright, *mon coeur*. I'll teach you about Possession...soon."

I raged.

Soon?

Soon?

When is soon?!

"Soon" turned out to be a few days later, once Ma had talked to another ghost volunteer at the hospital—the one who'd apparently been planning to teach his girls about Possession. "His girls" were his twin daughters, who were conveniently my age, and our parents had agreed to teach us about Possession together in an old forgotten break room at the Middletown General Hospital in Middletown, Ohio.

On the walk over, Ma reminded me for probably the *millionth* time that she and I were *sisters*.

Ah, yes, the ever-present reminder that my mother who Died at *nineteen* and has been all but frozen in time since, couldn't possibly be mother to my fifteen-year-old self.

Middletown General was, on the outside, nothing special to look at. It was a massive gray brick behemoth with tall windows spreading evenly across the entire height and width of its facade. There was a main Visitor entrance and an Emergency Room entrance, plus several access doors around the building for staff. We bypassed the Visitor and Emergency Room doors, Ma instead guiding us to a staff access door at the back corner of the hospital, almost fully hidden behind an overgrown cypress tree.

She guided me through the door and into a dark hallway that led into the heart of the hospital. The floors were bright white with little flecks of silver in them, and they shone brightly as if they'd just been waxed to perfection. The walls, which were just exposed cinder blocks, were also painted white with a silver strip running horizontally across their length. My nose wrinkled as the smell hit me: that unnerving blend of disinfectant with subtle notes of body horror you expect from every hospital. I stuffed the lower half of my face into the collar of my plain grey sweatshirt as we passed several wood doors, all closed, with boards on the outside of each listing the patient's last name.

I spotted Samaya, one of Ma's ghost friends, in her scrubs, power walking down the hall behind a team of doctors and nurses that surrounded an old man in a hospital bed. When she'd started volunteering in hospitals, Ma had quickly found that no one questioned a ghost in solid form, in a hospital, if they were wearing scrubs, so ghosts always nicked a few pairs so that they could roam the halls of the building unaccosted while on shift; in them, everyone just assumed they were one of the hundreds of nurses that the hospital officially employed. She glanced up and waved, blowing two kisses our way before following the group around a corner and out of sight.

Ma continued down the hallway, ducking down a short flight of stairs and past a thin sheet of hanging plastic sporting a **NO ENTRY, CONSTRUCTION ZONE** sign. A few paces further, she stopped in front of another nondescript wood door with a tattered scrap of paper once printed with "Break Room No Longer In Use" hanging by one last piece of tape at my eye level.

The wood paneled walls of the break room were a callback to the 1970s, and the drop ceiling had enough mildew stains that it had to be hazardous even Existing inside of a functioning hospital—room forgotten or not. A thin layer of dust coated every surface, dust bunnies floating in the air with any move any of us made. It made me scrunch my nose again as I waited for the impending sneeze, giving me time to be thankful that the room somehow still had that clinical antiseptic smell that Ma assured me was "l'hôpital smell" and not the smell of decades old mold or bodily fluids like the stench a few floors up.

The twins turned out to be Eya and Wana Byrne. Like me, they looked to be around the same age as normal fifteen-year-old Livings. They had the most gorgeous almond skin tone you'd ever see and dark brown eyes. Both seemingly preferred to wear their thick and curly ash brown hair back in high afro-puff buns, and both preferred leggings, oversized tees, and sweatshirts as their regular wardrobe. They were the epitome of cool comfort, and I was naturally drawn to them in a way I hadn't been with anyone else I'd met.

"The first thing you should know," said Ma, catching my eye in apparent shock that I was actually paying attention for once, "is that Possession can be very, very *dangereux* if not done correctly. Possessions gone wrong have caused irrevocable 'arm to Living victims, landing them in mental turmoil, long-term physical pain, and even Death in the most extreme cases—to say nothing of what the ghost will face."

I shuddered at that. I was an angsty teenaged ghost, but I never wanted to see anyone *actually* harmed, especially not because of me.

"I don't say that to scare you, because those situations are uncommon, and most Possessions are completely safe. They cause no 'arm to the ghost or the Living involved. Successfully Possessing a Living just gives the ghost a jolt of Life."

Her last sentence made my eyebrows knit together. A jolt of...*Life*?

It...it didn't make any sense. Sure, ghosts didn't exactly *need* to breathe, but out of habit or some weird elemental, evolutionary response, we still did. Unless we'd died horrifically and needed to stay for our souls to heal (which often took hundreds of years), we weren't bound to one singular location. We could move freely through the world, just like the Living, and could even appear in a solid form if we chose to. Many Living interacted with ghosts every single day and had no idea. What more Life could we experience by Possessing a Living?

"What do you mean experience Life? We already do experience Life...what more is there?" I asked, cutting Ma off in the middle of the sentence that hadn't even made it to my ears over the thoughts racing through my mind.

"Oui, oui, yes, we ghosts experience Life in our own way," she started, stepping around one of the tables in the room to take a seat across from us, "You can make your chest rise and fall with breath, and you can smell rain kissed grass and chimney smoke. Oui, you can pluck an orange from a tree and taste its pulp, and feel the Sun shining on your skin. But a jolt, and 'ow jolts work, is something that we 'ave yet to be able to explain. A jolt of Life quickly energizes a ghost to levels that an ordinary Trance might not allow. Possessing a Living for one minute, just sixty seconds, will give the same energy level that a month long Trance might."

"What does it do to the Living?" Eya asked, although she looked almost scared to know the answer. She thumbed nervously at the sleeve of her sweater, which featured a penguin reading a book—which I would later learn were two of her favorite things. "Does it jolt them, too?" Eya wasn't the only one anxious; a quick glance to her other side proved that Wana was also horrified at the thought of Possessing someone.

But not me.

"Goodness, no," Mr. Byrne laughed, catching Ma's eye with a knowing glance as I noted his Jamaican accent. He was tall and broad, with slightly darker skin than his daughters and their same dark brown eyes. "Possession of a Living by a ghost, when done correctly and safely, doesn't hurt the Living at all. Actually, when Possessed correctly, the Living experiences nothing more than a daydream. If the daydream is realistic enough, the Living may even feel refreshed once the Possession ends, like they've had a power-nap."

Eya let out a sigh of relief and Wana relaxed back into her seat, lifting the hood of her pink tie-dyed sweatshirt over her bun and returning to the doodles she'd been working on on her forearm. They both seemed perfectly at ease while I was back in mental turmoil, my brows reaching towards each other again. A...*daydream*? What on earth was a daydream? My heartbeat quickened, and I wasn't sure if I could ask what a daydream was. I was *never* around other ghost kids, and I wasn't like the rest of the ghost children in the room. I felt the familiar pang of shame and loneliness start to creep back in—and realized that I hadn't felt it in the minutes I'd actively been paying attention to our parents.

"We all remember daydreams from being alive," Mr. Byrne continued, while I silently thanked all the gods that ever were that he was going over this since I'd never actually *been* a Living, "those weird visions that happen to Livings during times of boredom. They're dreams that happen while you're awake, visions that show up in Living minds to distract from a tedious task. Like a little movie that plays out in their heads."

"Er...right, of course. I remember daydreams." That had been a close one—I *had* to get faster on my feet when someone made a reference to Life. Who knows what could happen if someone found out what I was? It could be...catastrophic. The pit that had taken up permanent residence in my stomach seemed endless. For what had to be the billionth time in my Death, I wished that I hadn't been Born Dead, and the injustice of my situation felt like it might overwhelm me, but I pushed those feelings down so that I could focus on Ma and Mr. Byrne, who was explaining exactly *how* to Possess Living.

"To successfully, and safely, Possess a Living," Ma started, pulling out and unfolding a paper diagram of the human body she'd likely swiped from an exam room, "you must first locate the teres major muscle underneath their left arm." She points to a spot under the model's arm for emphasis.

"Ewww!" Wana yelled out. "The Living have sweaty, smelly armpits! Why do we have to start there?!"

"Because that's where their consciousness can most easily unzip—it's nearest to their heart, which is the portal to their soul," her dad explained.

"UNZIP?" Eya screeched. "We have to *unzip* Livings?" I would swear that she started turning green.

"Relax, relax," Mr. Byrne chuckled, trying to regain all of our composure. "It isn't as gross or as sinister as it sounds."

"Coulda fooled me, this sounds nasty," Wana muttered under her breath in my direction as I tried, and failed, not to giggle. Wana was clearly the more outspoken of the twins, quick to speak her mind while her more timid sister Eya lived between the pages of books about mafias and had little time to worry about being extroverted.

"The teres major muscle is, as I was saying, a muscle that runs under the armpit of the Living. To Possess a Living, a ghost should simply reach into the Living's left side, and feel for that muscle. If you close your 'and around it, it feels almost like a strap. If you pull gently down on the muscle, it will form a small opening that you can lean into." Wana made a quiet gagging noise and covered her face with her hands.

"Dad, all due respect, but this is sounding more and more like something I will never in my Death have any interest in doing, ever," Wana bleated. I couldn't help but agree with her. The thought of grabbing a Living by the armpit, un. zipping. them. and then

MORPHING INSIDE? That sounded like the way the word "moist" makes both the Living and the Dead feel: creepy, and violated, and unsanitary.

"I really wish there was a better way to explain this to you all," Mr. Byrne chuckled, "but yes—I have to agree that it sounds pretty disgusting. I promise you that it isn't, at all. Possessing a Living feels like simply taking a step. Once you've opened their side through the teres major, you just lean towards the Living and then, voila, you have successfully Possessed them."

Eya timidly raised her hand, and asked, "So, how is this different from all of those scary movies that the Living make? Is it not a violation of the Living to Possess them without their knowledge or consent?" Wana nodded in agreement.

I knew that I didn't even *know* them yet, but the fact that the twins questioned the Living's ability to consent felt so purely *them*. Like I could tell, even being in the same room with them for no more than five minutes, that they were thoughtful and caring and would never violate someone against their will.

I really hoped Ma would let me see these girls again.

"Excellent question, Eya!" Ma beamed. "There are actually several differences between a ghostly Possession and those depicted in the Living's films. First, we are not Demons. We do not, as a general rule, Possess a Living for any malicious reason. If we Possess a Living, it will be to obtain a jolt of Life for ourselves, to allow them a brief daydream, or both. Second, we cannot control the Living's body, mind, or spirit during a ghostly Possession without their immediate, knowing permission. Without their consent, we can only temporarily trigger them to daze off and imagine a scene that isn't actually taking place in front of them. Third, ghostly Possessions are always very brief: no longer than two to three minutes. Once the Living snaps out of their daydream, the ghost is automatically ejected from the Possession, whether the ghost was ready to leave—fully energized—or not. And lastly, the Living is, without knowing it, completely in control of their Possession at all times. Any Living with even the most minute aversion to being Possessed simply cannot be Possessed. The ghost will either be unable to find the teres major muscle, or will be unable to open the portal to Possess that 'uman."

"So, we can't Possess anyone who doesn't *want* to be Possessed?" I asked.

"Precisely. The Living doesn't even have to have the conscious thought of '*I do not want any ghosts to ever Possess me.*' Their subconscious is just aware of whether they are open to ghostly Possession or not. "

A knock sounded to my left and we all glanced at the break room door as Mrs. Bowers, one of the few of Ma's volunteer friends I'd actually met, poked her head into the room. She had curly brown hair, a bright smile, and a warm, friendly demeanor.

"Were you guys planning on starting your shifts today? It's almost 4:00..." she teased, jerking her head towards the clock over my shoulder.

"Well, time flies when the teenagers are actually listening for once," Mr. Byrne joked while playfully squeezing Eya's shoulder.

"I need to get you 'ome," Ma said to me as an idea formed.

"Wait, can we stay here?" I ask, gesturing to the twins. "I mean...if you guys would want to hang out?"

Gods I felt so lame.

Ma went slightly pale at the request and I knew everything that could go wrong was flying through her head: what if I sprouted a grey hair right in front of their eyes? What if I told them I was Born? What if they're secret agents, working for an underground agency with the sole mission of apprehending the world's only Born ghost?

She'd let me hang out with the occasional ghost kid out of necessity, but I'd been younger and more easily manipulated by a "because I said so." Now, I had the teeth of a pissed off and somewhat resentful teenager and she knew it.

"We would love that!" Wana squealed. "Oh Dad, please say we can hang out here! We won't leave the room, we swear!"

Eya nodded along, clutching her dad's arm.

He and Ma shared a look, having some unspoken conversation before they both begrudgingly nodded and started laying down ground rules that included not leaving this room, not speaking to anyone else, and going invisible if anyone happened upon the room.

After that first night, the twins and I were nearly inseparable.

Once Ma realized that I was smart (and old) enough to have friends without spilling that secret, she relaxed a bit, but still gave regular lectures about how no one could know I'd been Born. As if I'd jump onto the nearest rooftop to let everyone know how different I was. No, I desperately wanted to be like every other ghost I knew.

Seeing the twins and I becoming close prompted other ghost volunteers to bring their kids in until we had a gang of misfit teenagers —all of whom happened to be ghosts. The core group was the twins, Ethan Matheson, Anabel Yung, Latrell Lee, and Kara Wilde. Occasionally another ghost kid would pop in, but for the most part, we were the friend group.

Ethan was tall and lanky, with white skin, sandy hair, and a bright smile. He was always the first to crack a joke and kept us all laughing. Anabel was Chinese-American, with jet black hair in a sharp bob around her chin. She was the designated mom friend, always making sure we were being safe and cautious of everyone's actions at all times. Latrell was a short Black boy, with a smooth fade and short locs secured in a top knot. What he lacked in height, he made up for in strength and agility. He dreamed of being a pro wrestler before he became, well...a ghost. And last but not least, was Kara. She was

Pakistani-American with warm brown skin and a dancer's build. She was an absolute fashionista and gave Eya a run for her money for who was the most artistic in the group.

Our parents quickly realized that sequestering us to a dingy old break room was just asking for us to be caught by a runaway patient or doddering old janitor, so they eventually allowed us to roam our small town, posing as Living kids, in groups. They figured we could get a small taste of freedom, but have power in numbers.

Little did they know that we loved to go haunting.

It was Wana, of course, who had the idea to mess with the Living. We'd been lounging on the floor at the twins' house: an abandoned fire station a few blocks from the hospital. Unlike my current digs, the twins' house was cool...mainly because it had a fire pole. Okay, it was only cool because it had a fire pole. We spent hours running up the stairs only to jump and grab onto the pole, slide down, and bolt to the stairs to do it all over again. The day we started haunting, though, even the fire pole had lost its appeal.

Ma would never have approved of haunting, but she'd taken on even more volunteer shifts than usual. She was there most days from noon to at least midnight, sometimes later. I guess she really was convinced that I was old enough to be trusted with my secret—which I was—and to take care of myself, and stay out of trouble, for a while.

My poor, sweet, naive mother.

Most days our parents allowed us out of the hospital, the three of us (and anyone else in the friend group who was around at the time) would pick a favorite spot of the Living kids. Sometimes it was the town playground, sometimes the library, and sometimes we'd just find a gaggle of kids walking home. The location didn't really matter. Once we found our target, it was time for some happy haunting.

Every time, at least one of us would ditch our solid states, opting for invisibility. We'd sneak up behind the unsuspecting Livings and whisper nonsense into their ears.

"Psst, you smell like a slug."

"Your Momma's a hag!"

"Hey, did you hear that?!"

And, of course, old faithful: "BOO!"

At first, they'd think it was their friends messing with them, but we always escalated our hijinks, terrorizing the poor Living kids until they were all in tears. Now as an adult, I'm not proud of what we did...but it was a lot of fun at the time with the best friends I'd ever let myself have. We didn't consider haunting to be malicious, and thought that once the Living got over the initial shock, they'd have a cool "ghost story" to tell.

We were thoughtful like that.

For what it's worth, we tried to seek out mean kids for haunting. In those days, I didn't think about the fact that some of those kids might not have been so bad, and would probably grow to need therapy because of us.

I was just happy to have friends that seemed to genuinely want to spend time with me.

A few weeks after our original lesson on Possession, Ma and Mr. Byrne decided that we were ready for a more practical Possession experience. I know how much it terrified my paranoid mother, but she must have talked herself into it knowing that if she was present for my first Possession, it would be under a controlled environment, with her right there to step in and spin some damage control if anything went wrong.

If my being a Born ghost impacted my ability to Possess someone.

We came to the end of the long, main hallway, and Mr. Byrne opened another wooden door marked "Stairs." We passed the construction zone and our secret break room before being led us up one flight and out another door onto the second floor. The floors here were the same smooth, white-and-silver-flecked tile, and the walls, still exposed cinderblocks, were the same dull grey. This hallway was brighter thanks to the wall of windows that lined one side of the hallway. A few twists and turns led us to our destination: Palliative Care.

The empty nurses' station was cheerily decorated with bouquets of bright, happy flowers in every color you could imagine: vivid yellow sunflowers, deep magenta Dahlias, dazzling blue cornflowers, and timeless white and yellow daisies. A small Zen fountain sat on one corner of the large desk, cascading water over a stack of smooth black stones before pooling in a round, wooden basin. There was a string of white twinkle lights that stretched around the front of the desk, no doubt to bring even more light to what must often feel like a dark and dreary corner of the hospital. It was clear that the staff of this ward wanted their patients to feel at peace with their surroundings, at least as best they could.

Mr. Byrne, who had positioned his back to a door marked 217, gestured for us to gather in closely before whispering, "Ladies, please go invisible so that we don't disrupt the nurses that will be returning from their rounds any minute now." We followed his directions until only Ma and Mr. Byrne, who like my mother worked among the Living every day without their realizing he was a ghost, remained in solid form.

"Alright, as you can see, we are at Palliative Care," Mr. Byrne said, pointing to the sign above our heads. "This is a place for Living who have limited time left before they pass into Death. As we will all remember from our own Deaths," he held each of our eyes for a moment, "the Living has the choice to remain as a ghost or move on to the Unknown. At this stage of their Life, the veil between Life and Death is thin, and the Living can see beyond." Wana sniffed behind me as Eya fidgeted with her hoodie sleeve.

"You all know this," he continued, "but for most of my volunteer shifts, I work in this ward, helping the Living make the choice of how they'd like to enter their Death. If they plan to be a ghost, they work with Abby's sister to learn the ins-and-outs of Death as a ghost." My cheeks reddened briefly at being the center of attention, even knowing I wasn't embarrassed of my mother in the slightest. "If they choose to go on to the Unknown, I stand by for moral support, and to remind them of their wish to move on, as it is often hard for them to witness the pain their passing causes their Living loved ones."

Eya and Wana were a mirror image, both swiping at their eyes with the ends of their sleeves. They were both, of course, likely remembering their own Deaths, which we'd never talked about. Oh, right! I quickly threw up a mask of morose despair so that I would blend in with my friends as we obviously mourned our own passings.

"Many times, the Living in Palliative Care knows what is coming, and are able to communicate with me, or other ghosts. They see us as clearly as they see their Living loved ones. Since this is a place where it is understood that the Living go to pass on, if the patient starts speaking to ghosts, their loved ones assume that it is only hallucinations and pay the conversations no mind. Since I am here to provide comfort to the Dying, I often tell them a little about myself. This kind gentleman offered to help us with our lesson." Mr. Byrne paused then, looking around at all of us to signal that the practical part of the lesson was coming.

"Offered to help?" Wana asked quietly, her lower lip quivering gently. "Like a sacrifice?"

"Baby girl, no!" Mr. Byrne's words came out in a whoosh, his face crumpling slightly at what his daughter had thought must be coming next. "No, nothing will be sacrificed. The gentleman in the room behind me is Mr. Prentice Winstone. Mr. Winstone is 98 years old, and has been battling Parkinson's disease for decades. Over the past few months, Mr. Winstone developed pneumonia, which hasn't improved. He was hospitalized, and eventually moved here to the Palliative Care wing as he no longer wished to continue major Lifesaving treatments. Mr. Winstone has had a long and happy Life, and he is ready to move on. He plans to enter the Unknown, because he knows that his beloved wife Jeanine and his favorite dog, Spot, are waiting for him there."

We all smiled, then. Ghosts, of all beings (myself excluded), knew what it was like to leave a loved one behind, and the thought of their coming reunion cheered us slightly.

"Mr. Winstone has also had to spend a good chunk of time with 'Ol Dad over the last few weeks, and knows that we are learning about Possession," he went on, smiling at his daughters. "He has agreed to be a "practice" vessel for all of you, so that you can learn how to safely Possess a Living in a controlled setting under the watchful eye of your favorite teacher." Mr. Byrne's eyes twinkled at his own joke, even though he *was* a great teacher—both he and Ma.

"We do 'ave a few ground rules, or things that you should keep in mind," Ma stepped in. "One, this man is sick, and probably in pain. You must be gentle and kind to 'im every moment. Two, 'e has volunteered for the three of you to Possess 'im, of 'is own free will, just to 'elp you learn. Thank 'im, genuinely. Third, since the veil is thinning for 'im as 'is Life comes to a close, 'e will be able to see you even in your invisible form. There will be no need to go solid. Lastly, remember what we taught you: feel for the teres major under 'is left arm, grasp it gently, and pull slightly. Then, you'll lean into the opening, and you'll be Possessing 'im. Take 5-10 seconds to get a sense of what it feels to Possess a Living, then again feel for the teres major, and lean back out of 'is body."

"Ready?" Mr. Byrne asked us, noting our nerves.

We all nodded slightly, and he turned to gently knock on the door before easing it open slowly.

"Good afternoon, Mr. Winstone. It's me, Adrian. How are you feeling today?"

None of us heard Mr. Winstone's response as we took in the sight before us. His room was painted a bright blue. A fluorescent light above the bed flickered, casting a whitish yellow hue across the whole room. There was a window on one wall that was filled with gifts from his loved ones: little potted plants, balloons with every version of the words "I love you" that you could think of plastered across them, cards propped up against the window, both store-bought and handmade (clearly by young children), and even a few small stuffed animals. There was a small couch that likely folded out into a bed, and several chairs were scattered around the hospital bed in the center of the room. The faint *blip-blip* of a heart monitor kept the room from being silent, as did the ticking of a clock on the wall opposite the bed, and the airy sound of oxygen being pulled from a tank behind the bed, through tubes, and directly into the nose of Mr. Prentice Winstone.

He had a beautifully sweet face, pocked as it was with age spots and lined with wrinkles. My heart warmed slightly as I noticed that most of the wrinkles on his face were laugh lines—he spent a good part of his Life laughing. He wore large bifocal glasses in thin wire frames, which gave him an almost owlish look. He smiled feebly up at us, but it was obvious that the gesture was taking a toll on his waning energy.

After some brief introductions including all of our names and quick asides about each of us from Mr. Byrne, it was time to begin.

Eya and Wana were first to try Possession. I stood there nervously tapping my foot and trying—and failing—to think about anything but the fact that I was going to learn to Possess another person. I still couldn't figure out why learning about Possession was so important to me, but it just felt...different. Like it was vital that I know this.

Finally, after what felt like seconds and lifetimes, Wana eased out of Mr. Winstone's side and it was my turn.

I never wondered if ghosts could throw up—or what throwing up *even felt like*—until it was my turn to Possess a Living for the first time.

"It's okay to be nervous, *mon coeur*," Ma murmured softly, sensing my anxiety.

I stepped up to Mr. Winstone, smiling down at him shyly. He returned the gesture, and, like with the twins, took my hand in his own, patting the top of mine with his. This action, somehow, calmed my nerves completely. It was like he was telling me, without words, that he was at peace, and that I should be, too.

I reached towards his arm, which was mostly skin and bone and covered in the purplish bruises of age, and, just as Ma and Mr. Byrne said, found the teres major that stood out very clearly to my fingers. I wrapped them around the warm muscle and tugged very gently. A small opening formed and I was immediately taken aback: he glowed! From the opening, I could see swirls of green and yellow that reminded me of a warm, summer day on a lake. I could almost feel the Sun on my cheeks and the breeze rustling my hair, and I could hear the water gently slapping against the bank.

I leaned forward slowly and then, all at once, I was looking through Mr. Winstone's eyes. I could see my friends, Mr. Byrne, and Ma around me in varying stages of shock, discomfort, pity, and awe. I could feel Mr. Winstone's emotions, too. He was afraid of what was to come, even knowing he was ready to embrace it, and he didn't want me or my friends to be affected. He wanted to comfort them—us—all. He wanted to embrace us and assure us that all would be fine, and that the Circle of Life must be followed. It was the natural way.

Mr. Winstone's eyes fluttered shut, winking my vision of the hospital room out of Existence. I could still hear the beeping of the monitors, but it faded into the background as the rushing, lapping sounds of the lake got louder. I looked down to see what I expected to be Mr. Winstone's body, but it was drastically different. The bruised and weathered hands that had held mine moments ago were young and strong, free of any of the markings of age. He was seated in an Adirondack chair on the porch of a cabin overlooking a lake with lush, green mountains surrounding it on all sides. The sunshine I'd started to feel intensified, and it was clear that it had to be mid-summer— underlined by a cacophony of birdsong that joined the sounds of the lake.

As the scene came into greater focus, I noticed a young woman approaching from the shore. She was strikingly beautiful, with bright red hair pulled back into a curly ponytail and bangs that immediately reminds me of the first ever Barbie doll. She was wearing a black 1950's style one-piece bathing suit with white polka dots, and little white heeled sandals to match. A Jack Russell terrier puppy bounced playfully at her heels, bounding along behind her.

A gasp caught in my throat, and I couldn't decide if the tears pricking my eyes were mine or Mr. Winstone's—not that it mattered. I knew who I was looking at.

Mrs. Winstone and Spot.

I felt guilty, as if I was intruding in Mr. Winstone's private thoughts, and pulled my focus back to the Possession itself. Almost instantly, I felt my energy level increase. It was a pleasant sensation, as if I'd started to awaken from a nice, long Trance. I wondered, briefly, if the lake that I'd imagined as I started the Possession, the daydream that Mr. Winstone was experiencing, was real. I hoped that his wife and dog were there, at that lake, so that he could tell them that he would join them soon. I gently leaned back toward Mr. Winstone's side, slipping back into my own invisible form, and that was that.

Later, when we were home, Ma told me that the images that we had seen were the combination of Mr. Winstone's aura and soul...which didn't surprise me at all given how profoundly beautiful it was.

He seemed like a beautiful man.

7

Zelie returns to Halcyon Hall several times over the next few weeks.

By now, it's late September, so she has to be careful—Dave and Bethany have started planning their October Halcyon Hall event schedule, and Bethany wants to go all out. She's talking seances with *meeeeediums*, vendor events on the weekends, and even paying some paranormal reality stars to promote the hall.

Anything to get people to come pay $85 for a chance to *see the Hag*! This place is soul crushing.

Zelie, however, is not soul crushing. We spend afternoons digging through boxes in the attic, placing bets on which of us will find the creepiest artifacts. We take walks through the messy garden on the cool, crisp fall evenings. One night, she shows up with hot chocolates and thick blankets and we sit on the front porch, wrapped up and gazing at the stars.

While I can't tell her *all* of my secrets, I confide in Zelie more than I've ever been able to with anyone else—even Ma. I tell her how lonely I've been, and how isolated I feel out here. I admit that I've found myself Trancing more and more, barely Existing unless Dave and Bethany have an event that rouses me. I whisper that I can feel parts of myself slipping away, like they're lost from me. Like they've stashed themselves away to become part of the house...little pieces of myself that I'll never get back.

She listens intently and doesn't offer any words of comfort or advice, which is odd for Zelie. Usually, so far, she's known exactly what to say. But all she can do now is furrow her brow.

Eventually, it gets late, and she returns to her car.

"Hey, it's Friday night, so I don't have anything to do tomorrow. I'll come back and we'll hang out some more."

She comes back, as promised, the next day with a wild and crazy plan to get me out of Halcyon Hall.

8

"Move in with you and your roommates? Your...*Living*...roommates? And just how would that work?"

I've just cracked open a can of the caramel apple flavored hard cider Zelie brought, and can't wait to hear how she plans to tell her roommates that she wants a *ghost* to move in.

We're sitting in the garden on two wrought iron benches that may have once been white, but are now the same dull grey as the manor itself. It's late September, but we're still in Georgia, so the air is muggy with a crisp breeze sporadically rustling the vines around us. I'm looking the part of a hag in an old Norma Jean sweatshirt and jeans I snagged at a Goodwill years ago, and Zelie is as effortlessly perfect as all of the other times I've seen her: today, she's donned a white V-neck t-shirt, pink cardigan, grey leggings, and black and white Chucks. She's wearing her brown-and-amber micro braids in a loose braid around her shoulder today, and she still looks like glitter sparkles just under her skin.

"Just hear me out," she begs, putting her hands together in front of her chest.

"Fine...I'm listening." I take another sip of the cider, which might be the best drink I've ever had.

"So, we have a four bedroom, fully furnished apartment in Midtown, and there are three of us: Amarie, Em, and me. We each have our own room and more than enough space, so that fourth bedroom is just... there. We all work during the day and travel regularly for our jobs, so other than being invisible when they're around, you could have free run of the place. I'm not knocking Halcyon Hall, but..." she gestures around at nothing and everything, all at once. "Abby, it's not healthy to confine yourself to a place like this. You are young, and vibrant, and this place will drain it all out of you so fast. And I've talked to a lot of ghosts in my Life but I've never heard of a mental institution for ghosts, so if you let this place drive you mad...I'm afraid you'll be stuck here."

Her last sentence touches a nerve, because she's right. I'd already felt the spiral starting before the last Friday the 13th event when we'd met. This place is too depressing, and I've been here alone too long. If I stay much longer, I could become part of the house—one of those ghosts that can't leave, and can't go on. I'd become what Rich Walters shrieked about.

I'd become a Poltergeist.

I can't let that happen.

"But...you'd be okay to lie to your roommates? To just not tell them someone else is in the apartment all the time?" I ask, trying to navigate any potential problems while desperately hoping she'll have a solution for them all. I hadn't known how desperately I needed to leave Halcyon Hall until Zelie's offer.

"I look at it like this," she leans towards me conspiratorially, "Any place they make their home could be haunted without their knowledge, right?" I nod slightly, because it's true. Some ghosts spend decades in homes and never make their presences known to the Living. "They know I'm a Medium, but they don't know the intricacies. If I choose not to tell them you're there, it'd be no different than if the apartment came with a mild-mannered ghost that didn't want to communicate with me. And Abby," her brows knit, "I can't just leave you here. It isn't ethical."

"Okay." I breathe before I can think any longer and talk myself out of it.

"'Okay,' what?" she asks.

"Okay, I'll do it. I'll be your fourth roomie."

I truly can't believe how little convincing it took, but the thought of becoming a Poltergeist is enough to get me to do something—anything —to stop that from being my fate.

I don't have much to pack two weeks later when I move out of Halcyon Hall: just a few bags of tattered, old clothes that probably should have just gone in a dumpster. I hope that once I rejoin society, even in the limited capacity that I will staying with Zelie and her roommates, I'll eventually be brave enough to venture out and find an under-the-table paying job waiting tables or babysitting kids or something—anything to earn some tax-free (lest the government find out that the Dead are out here and try to tax us, too) money to update my wardrobe. Being a sitter? Is that not the next family-friendly adventure movie in the making? *Don't Tell Mom the Babysitter's Dead*!

My phone buzzes in my pocket and I pull it out to see Ma's face. I swipe to answer the FaceTime, strategically maneuvering so she's not able to see the few small bags of clothes at my feet.

"Hi, Ma!"

"*Bonjour*, kid! 'ow's it going?" she asks, and I note that she's wearing scrubs, walking down a tree-lined path beside a bland concrete building.

"It's going," I reply, "another day in paradise. Are you on the way to work?"

A fold creases her brow. "I am, but *mon coeur*, why do you insist on staying in that place?" She squints, and I can tell she's inspecting my surroundings. "Why don't you just come stay with me in Wilmington?"

I roll my eyes unconsciously. "Ma, I'm fine. This place is...charming." I struggle to cover the grimace. "And I'm happy. It's...er—a fixer upper."

"I do love that show," she muses and I know I've said the right thing. My mother LOVES a home improvement reality show. Now, instead of picturing her daughter in an abandoned manor with holes in the roof, she'll romanticize it into her daughter, lovingly restoring a historic landmark room by room. "I'll 'ave to come visit and see what you've done with the place."

I know she's expecting an invitation, but I obviously have to hold her off. "Not until I'm done!" I playfully chastise her, waggling my finger.

"Alright well, I just wanted a Confirmation of Existence," she explains. "I'm walking into l'hôpital now. Talk soon?"

"Definitely," I promise. "Love you, Ma."

"Love you, too, *mon coeur*."

She ends the call and my stomach drops. I *hate* lying to her, but she absolutely cannot know that I'm about to move into an apartment with three Livings. She'd never understand, and she'd insist that I come stay with her, in hiding, for the rest of my Existence.

I drop my phone into one of the bags and take a moment to collect my thoughts.

I'm moving into an apartment with three Livings.

It doesn't seem real.

I'm standing on the second-floor landing looking out at the grounds of Halcyon Hall one last time while waiting for Zelie to pick me up and mulling over the months spent here when a slight movement on the horizon catches my attention. I squint my eyes to see better, and his shape comes into clearer focus. It's what appears to be a Living man. He isn't exactly sneaking around, but I can tell by the swiftness of his movement that he doesn't want to be seen: he moves quickly to one spot, then stands rooted there until he all but becomes part of the landscape, then he moves again.

He's *very* tall, at least six-foot-five or -six, with curly, shoulder length reddish-brown hair. He doesn't seem beefy, exactly; instead, he looks thin but muscular—someone you wouldn't want to brawl against but also doesn't seem so huge that he's overly threatening. But the most odd thing about this man is his outfit: he looks to be dressed in some sort of fighting leathers, or battle garb, black from the armor—armor?!—on his shoulders to the boots on his feet. His sleeves are pushed up, and—I squint harder—I think I can just see the edges of a tattoo snaking down one of his arms.

And that is the precise moment that the hand I'm leaning against the windowsill slips, slamming my top half against the window and creating a crashing sound that ricochets off of every surface in the hall and across the grounds.

I train my eyes back to the mystery man, who stands out in the open now, no longer trying to hide. I see his top lip curve into a snarl before he starts running towards the manor. Towards *me*.

What in the hell?! What is his problem?

I'd been so focused on the man that I hadn't noticed Zelie pulling up in an older Honda Civic. The quick *thunk* of her car door closing pulls my eyes away from the man, who seems to have also noticed Zelie. When I look back, he's vanished, as if he'd never been there at all.

I meet her at the door, shaken but deciding that either the Hall had finally gotten to me enough to make me hallucinate, or that was a ghost of some soldier who didn't want to be seen, gone invisible before sinking into the tall marsh grasses.

"Zelie," I teasingly scold. "You're a Medium. What are you doing in this old beater?!" I giggle and she laughs.

"What?" she shrills playfully. "I haven't been invited on a TV show yet," she puts her hands up defensively, "those Mediums could probably afford a nicer car. The rest of us? We're making due in ten-year-old Hondas."

9

I take one single step into the apartment I'll share with Zelie and her roommates and know that Existing alone in that decrepit old mansion had been one of the biggest mistakes I've ever made.

The apartment is in a high rise in Midtown Atlanta. It's technically on the thirteenth floor, but the building's architect had apparently been superstitious, so the elevator's buttons skip from twelve to fourteen. The hallway leading to our door—*our door!*—is clean and bright, and smells subtly of cinnamon. As we approach it, Zelie explains that Amarie is spending the weekend with her brother Tristan in Charleston, and Em is visiting her parents for her mom's birthday.

The apartment door opens into a small white-walled foyer, which the girls have filled with a bright blue console table, full length gold mirror, and a coat rack. Stepping through a small archway across from the door, Zelie leads me into the apartment's common areas. To my left, there is a Living room featuring a wall-to-wall assortment of built-in bookcases, a flat screen TV over an electric fireplace, and a very cozy looking brown leather sectional which sits opposite the television, creating a natural divide between the Living room and eating areas. Several throw blankets are casually tossed on the couch at random, and a round concrete coffee table holds a stack of books and a vase full of fresh peonies.

The kitchen is equally as breathtaking: top cabinets in white and lower cabinets in a complementary grey, with a huge island, topped with a white-flecked-with-silver slab of granite and lined on one side with dark walnut and grey metal barstools. Just past the kitchen stands a six-person wood dining table in the breakfast nook surrounded by six cerulean velvet dining chairs.

"Okay, but I didn't know you guys were millionaires," I mumble in awe. Zelie chuckles.

"Em's dad owns the building. He's a day trader, so he's been buying and selling stocks for years. But don't let that put you off when it comes to Em though," she clarifies. "Em is *amazing*. Even though 'Daddy owns the building,' she still pays her share of the rent. Granted, rent is *waaaaaay* less for us than it would be for anyone else, but... 'Daddy owns the building.'" she winks.

As gorgeous as these rooms are, however, the real focal point has to be the wall-to-wall, floor-to-ceiling windows that span the side directly opposite the foyer. From here, you can see the city skyline, which comes alive in the moonlight. I imagine that during the day, these windows keep the entire apartment bright and cheery. Along that wall of windows, leading in both directions, I can see the reflections of hallways that I assume lead to bed and bathrooms.

I'd assumed correctly, as Zelie lets me take in our surroundings then guides me to the left, down the hallway that lead to the rooms behind the wall of bookcases. The first door we come to is a powder room, then Zelie points out her own bedroom. The last door at the end of the hallway is closed, and as we approach it, Zelie makes a show of opening the door and gesturing me in while formally saying, "your humble abode."

My room—*my room*—is stunning, like something out of a magazine. The wall of windows from the hallway extends here, and the rest are painted a hunter green, with elements of wood and gold. The bedding is all white and oversized, giving it the appearance of a cloud I can't wait to sink into. There is a wood dresser with a round, gilded gold mirror above it, and two additional doors: one leading to a closet and one to a full bathroom.

"So..." Zelie starts. I tense, because I've seen enough television to know that 'so...' is *rarely* a good thing. I watch her tentatively, waiting for the rest of her thought.

"You know you're here and I know you're here, but Amarie and Em don't yet, right?"

"Yet?!" I choke.

She can't be thinking of telling them, can she? Not many Living are exactly open to sharing their home with ghosts—in fact, many are taught to fear us.

"I'm just saying, that...I think they're cool. And I think they'd love you, too. I just...I need a little time to figure out how to...broach the subject of you with them. *Ugh*, this is weird," she wrings her hands. "I just—I don't want you to feel like I'm hiding you from the Living, or that being a ghost is anything to be...*ashamed of*."

Ah. There it is. She's feeling guilty that I'll have to Exist in secret, and is trying to find a way to make *me* more comfortable here by introducing me to Amarie and Em. I beam at her, touched by her concern.

"Zelie, what you've done for me by bringing me here is incredible, okay? *Incredible*. I don't feel like you're locking the crazed poltergeist away. I know that not all Living are thrilled about ghosts. Honestly," I point at the cloud masquerading as a bed, "if I can just wait out the rest of my Existence laying there, I'll be more than fine."

Her worry breaks then, and she smiles back at me. "Any chance you want to go out as a Living in public tonight? Because I am starving and I feel like the Skull is calling my name."

I'd been in my solid form since no one but Zelie was here, but the thought of going out causes my stomach to do a couple somersaults—but *no*.

No, I will not allow myself back into that headspace. I need to stop hiding away.

Am I a ghost? Yes. Do others have to know that? No.

Who cares if a few Living—who I will never see again—see me in solid form in a restaurant?

"I'm not sure what the Skull is, but I really could use an actual shower. Can you wait to starve for like, an hour?" I'd found ways to keep semi-clean using the running, but freezing, water at Halcyon, but I haven't had a hot shower in—goodness I can't even remember.

"Of course!" Zelie pushes me into the bathroom and throws open the white and gold lined shower curtain, pointing at a shelf inside.

"So you should probably shower when Em and Amarie aren't home for the time being, but I went ahead and stocked up your shower. You have shampoo and conditioner, body wash, a jar of scrub if you want to exfoliate, shaving cream and a razor if you're into shaving, and," she swiftly turns back to the white marble sink, which sits upon a deep green cabinet with counter space on each side, "lotion, leave-in conditioner, random skin and hair products, and a wet brush. Oh! And my extra hair dryer. If you need anything else, like a curling iron, or straightener, just let me know and you can borrow mine. As far as the products go, we keep a stockpile on hand in the hall closet," she gestures to Em and Amarie's side of the apartment, where I guess this closet must be, "so do not ever worry about running out of anything. Just help yourself—we all collectively restock it frequently and everything in it belongs to all of us...we don't have an '*I bought it so it's mine*' mentality around here."

"Zelie, I—" I can't find the words. Her generosity is overwhelming, far more than I deserve, and I can't help but let that little voice in my head creep in, whispering, "*she'll leave, she'll leave, she'll leave.*"

She smiles and places a hand on my shoulder. "Girl, this is nothing. Don't even mention it."

I nod, forcing my anxiety away, knowing it for what it is: a liar that wants me alone, slowly losing myself and my sanity, until I really am a hag haunting the halls of somewhere like Halcyon.

I have to stop listening to it, stop letting it dictate my every move.

"This is your home now, too, Abby. And once I broach the topic of our apartment being haunted with Em and Amarie," she winked, "things will get even better."

Her words are a dream that I can't wait to experience.

I'm ready to go an hour later.

I could have been ready in twenty minutes, but I spent a solid half an hour letting the blissfully hot water pour over me. I felt, in a way, like I was being baptized. Like I'm leaving my past self, the one capable of being a hermit, behind and moving into a new Existence with more than just Ma to care about me. I know I'm eventually going to have to tell Ma about this major "Life change," but I'm not ready for that conversation yet.

For now, I let myself relish in the luxury of shampoos and soaps, exfoliators and razors. By the time I step out of the shower, my fingers and toes are pruny.

I'm well past drying off and moisturizing when I suddenly realize that I don't have any clothes other than the rags I brought from Halcyon, which I really don't want to be caught Dead—*ha*—in in public. I wrap the fluffy white towel around myself and throw open the bathroom door, planning to—I don't know? What do you do when you've Existed in a tattered, stained wardrobe for years and suddenly have a need for actual, going-out-in-public clothes?

A small pile on the bed catches my eye before I have time to gnaw on a fingernail or start pacing.

"Hey girl!" Zelie calls from down the hall, "I left some clothes on your bed—I hope they fit! You can borrow anything of mine that you'd like for now, and we can go thrifting this week for you to have your own clothes. I hope that's okay!"

I can tell from her voice that she is moving around, likely getting ready herself. I close my eyes, thanking the universe for the absolute angel I've found in Zelie.

"Zelie, you are too wonderful for *words*!" I yell back at her.

I was once a self-conscious teenager, worried over every inch around my waist and what those inches meant—as if somehow, those inches measured my value. Now, I am grateful for my curves, because neither Zelie nor I have small frames or figures—we share similar shapes with thick thighs, tummies that are not exactly flat, and medium chests. We're in that middle ground that makes it almost impossible to find clothes that truly fit. Since neither of us could be sure that we wore the *exact* same size, Zelie has opted to leave me a stretchy black maxi dress and a denim jacket. She's also left out socks and taupe booties to complete the ensemble.

"Oh, by the way!" Zelie calls out again, "I just made a trip to update my bras and panties last week, so what I left out for you is yours and has never been worn—just washed!"

At this point, I would be absolutely fine to "go Commando" given how much Zelie has already done for me, but I pull on the deep green undergarments gratefully. I don the dress, jacket, and booties (which are a size too big but still comfortable enough to walk in), and throw my damp hair up into a ballerina bun with one of the elastics Zelie had stocked the—*my*—bathroom with.

I step into the Living room to find Zelie waiting patiently.

"Are you ready to have the best burger in the city?"

I absolutely am.

The Skull, as it turns out, is a bar that specializes in eclectic, gourmet hamburgers.

To enter, we walk through the mouth of a giant skull with burgers for eyes and grab a table by the bar.

My phone buzzes and I glance down to see a text from Ma: **Hey mon coeur, just checking in. Call me when you have a few. Love you.** Guilt twists my gut but I shake it away, promising to call Ma later, and turn my attention back to deciding what to eat.

After spending a few minutes scouring the menu and a few heated rounds of "Eeny Meeny Miny Moe," I settle on the "Good Morning, Atlanta" burger: two half pound burgers with your choice of cheese, smushed between two cinnamon rolls. It sounds just bizarre enough to work without being outright gross. I opt for tots and a pumpkin flavored hard cider to accompany my burger. Zelie goes with a pimento bacon burger, complete with bacon jam, fries, and the same cider.

As the waiter leaves to put in our order, yet another shortcoming hits me: I don't have any money.

Oh, shit.

Zelie notices, of course, because she notices everything. "Abby, girl, you have got to relax!"

"I just...I shouldn't have come out with you. I don't," my cheeks heat, "I don't have any money," I admit in barely a whisper.

The shame hits me like a wave, crashing over me and leaving me feeling sick in its wake.

Why did I think this was a good idea?

"What?" Zelie sucks in a breath and clutches a hand around her neck, feigning shock. "You mean that in the months you were Existing alone in an abandoned mansion, you weren't drawing a paycheck?!"

She smirks at me, the look reminding me that while Zelie is the nicest person I'd ever met, she is also an eternal smart ass.

"I know you don't have cash. Driving a ten-year-old Honda has its perks—like no car payments. I've got this."

"Zelie you shouldn't have to be financially responsible for me. That's not fair to you." I know arguing about this, in this moment when our food is already being made, is futile, but I can't have her signing on for this long-term. "I'll find a way to make some cash to contribute. Maybe I can wait tables, or..."

"Actually..." Zelie cuts me off. I can see the wheels of her brain turning behind her eyes, "That's a good idea. Not waiting tables, I think that would get too risky. But...we are in the age of technology. There are *tons* of online, work from home jobs available. You'd have to have a Social Security Number, which you can't have, but..." she pauses for a second, to think before I can almost see the light bulb light up above her head, "you could use mine! It would look like I, a frequently-unemployed-contract Medium, took a side hustle to make more money on nights and weekends, and between Mediumship gigs."

She gnaws at the inside of her cheek for a moment and stares up at the ceiling, deep in thought. "You'd have to have pay sent to my account, so I get it if you're not comfortable with that...because it's a lot to ask for you to trust me with your money..." She seems suddenly embarrassed, which confuses me.

I reach across the table and take her hand in mine.

"Zelie, my friend, you opened your home to me when I had nothing. I would *give* you every dollar I could possibly make and do so gladly."

How does she not see how Existence-changing her coming into Halcyon Hall has been for me?

"Well, I would never let you do that, but it would give you some money to get your own clothes and contribute around the apartment—but only if you want to." Her eyes bore into mine and she takes on a stern, almost bossy tone. "You are not obligated to pay rent or for anything in the apartment. I offered to let you stay there knowing you wouldn't have money."

"I definitely do. Want to contribute, that is." I assure her.

Our meals come and we spend most of the rest of dinner in pleasant conversation about potential online jobs that a ghost could do from home, posing as her Medium roommate. Or...the rest of *my* dinner.

I notice much too slowly that Zelie has been pushing most of her food around on the plate the whole time, and her eyes are shimmering, full of unshed tears. I reach for her hand again.

"Zelie? Zelie, what's wrong?" I whisper, low enough that I don't draw attention to her. I know enough about normal Living people to know that *no one* wants an entire restaurant staring at them if they're emotional about something.

"I'm sorry," she breathes, pressing the tips of her ring fingers into the inner corners of her eyes to try and quell her tears. "It's just that Jess and I used to come here a lot."

I have next to no experience with the grief after a Death—how could I? All of the people I've ever cared about, until Zelie, have been ghosts.

But I can empathize. I give her hand a gentle squeeze.

"Will you tell me about him?" I ask. Maybe she just needs someone to listen, someone to hear her. I think I've made the right call because she smiles and nods.

"Jess was...incredible," she grins through her tears. "He was so strong, even in the face of everything he went through. I never knew him before he was sick, but he had such a joy for Life. He never, not once in his Life, met a stranger." She stops for a sip of cider then pauses, lost in her memories. "He was a practical joker, too. I found waaaay too many fake spiders in my shower, lost several bars of soap to clear nail polish so they wouldn't make suds, and I've eaten too many Oreos with toothpaste instead of creme filling. Once," she guffaws and quickly covers her mouth as an ornery couple at a nearby table glares at us. "Sorry!" she whispers and waves at them, "once, he even swapped the milk carton in the fridge for a cake!" My eyes go wide.

"What? A cake?"

She giggles, nodding theatrically, "yes, girl! I don't know how he did it, but I went to grab milk for my morning coffee and came back with a handful of cake where the 'handle' had been! I still don't know where he got it—it looked *just* like a milk carton! That ended in a food fight," her eyes go misty, "we were both covered head to toe in cake. We wore more of it than we got to eat."

He sounds like a dream, and I tell her as much.

"He really was the absolute best. He was so kind and supportive of anything and everything I wanted. If things had been different, if he'd been given a longer Life, we would have been completely unstoppab—," she gasps on a sob. "I'm sorry," she repeats. "I didn't expect to word vomit all of this out on you, or to become a blubbering mess at our first dinner out. You probably think I'm crazy," she looks up at me then, eyes so vulnerable and I know that how I respond to her truly matters.

"Zelie, please don't ever apologize for feeling. Not to me, or to anyone else. You went through a terrible loss, especially at such a young age and so new into your marriage...it's okay to be sad about it, and to miss what you had. And it's okay to talk about it...about him."

She flinches slightly at my words, and I fear that I've said something terribly wrong.

"You're right, it's just..." she takes a moment to collect her thoughts, and I give her the time she needs without pressing her to continue. "It's just that I feel so *disloyal*," she breathes before dropping her face into her hands.

"Disloyal? How so?" I'm trying to remain empathetic and not let my curiosity get the better of me, but I'm stumped.

"Because lately," another pause. "Lately, I've been feeling like I'm ready to move on. Like I could see myself taking my rings off, and dating again, and accepting the fact that he is gone and not coming back, and that he wouldn't want me to have this half Life of missing what I had and never trying to find love again. But then other days I'm so overcome by missing Jess that I can barely get out of bed, let alone trying to start anything...romantic with someone else."

"Oh, Zelie," my heart aches for her. "That's such a hard situation to be in."

She smiles sadly again. "Yeah, it really, really sucks."

"Well, I didn't know Jess, nor have I ever lost anyone I've loved," this isn't exactly an admission, but she's still got that wistful smile so I continue, "but if Jess was great enough to get to love you, and to earn your love back, then I think you're probably right about him. He wouldn't want you to suffer, or spend a moment being sad if you could find ways to be joyful instead. You're always going to miss him. That weight isn't ever going away," my words are blunt, but thankfully she nods, because she knows it's true. "But if you could find someone to help you carry it...I think Jess would want that for you. It's what I would hope that the love of my Existence would want for me, if I was in your shoes."

"You're right," she agrees. "I feel like I'm being silly." She looks down at her lap.

"What?!" I gasp. "No! You're not being silly at all!" I pause, waiting for her to look at me, and hold her eyes with mine. "You lost your husband so much younger than most people do. Even though you both knew going in that this would be the outcome, it doesn't negate any anger, sorrow, or any other feelings you feel. It still doesn't make it fair."

"I *am* glad that we knew," the tears are falling less freely now. "It forced us to really focus on each other and our love. We knew from the start that every second we had together was precious, so we were able to cherish our relationship in ways that most people don't."

"That's beautiful, Zelie." Damnit, she's going to make *me* cry! I blink them away, because it would be selfish of me to cry—it might make Zelie feel like she needs to console *me* for *her* grief.

"Wait...," Zelie leans forward suddenly, on high alert, eyes bright and as sharp as knives. "*Who is the love of your Existence?!*" She's playfully glaring at me as if I've been holding out on her.

I grin.

"Harry Styles, of course."

The joke is a gamble—not everyone copes with trauma through humor. I sit in anxious silence waiting to see if it was a mistake.

The grin that splits her face could put the Sun to shame.

"Thank you," she whispers, squeezing my hand back before letting it go to actually eat her food.

Once both of our plates have been cleaned, our table cleared, and the waiter brings Zelie's card back, the mood in the entire bar changes infinitesimally.

None of the Living seem to notice, but it's as if all the air let out of the room at once. There is sudden, mind-numbing quiet, even though the noise level in the bar hasn't changed—I've just suddenly been tuned out of it.

Zelie is in the middle of a polite but heartfelt conversation with the waiter, Julian, because his recently-passed grandmother had appeared to us and asked Zelie to pass him a message—but to me, everything feels like it's moving in silent slow motion.

I scan the room for anything out of the ordinary and don't see anything strange, until my eyes lock onto another pair that are... *glaring?* back at me.

They belong to a man with dark, curly red-brown hair that lands just above his shoulders. He is utterly, devastatingly *gorgeous*, but the glaring is...unnerving and unnecessary. I blink, startled, and glance at Zelie to see if she's noticed anything odd. She clearly hasn't, as she is cheerily wrapping up talking to Julian, who is wiping his eyes and thanking her profusely.

I swing my gaze back to the eyes, and they're gone. I jump as the exit door slams shut with such force that it rattles the whole bar before my senses catch up and the bar resumes its normal volume and speed.

We make it home without incident, but as I sink into the bed that is even *more* comfortable than I'd imagined, I can't help but think back to that stranger's apparent rage. And how similar it was to my last moments at Halcyon.

Twice now, a broody (strikingly handsome, but broody) man has appeared, seemingly out of nowhere, with hate in his eyes and a snarl on his lips.

Twice now, that gaze has been trained on me, and twice now, that gaze has been full of Death.

10

I settle into the apartment as smoothly as the single ghost secretly sharing a space with three Living women can.

Em turns out to be a Living angel. She has fine, almost white-blonde hair, pale skin, and bright blue-green eyes that catch the light and give the appearance that her eyes are always dancing with laughter. Em has a sweet face and a—usually—gentle disposition that draws me to her in a way I can't quite explain. She also turns out to be a bookworm who spends her downtime between the pages of anything *with* pages. She devours fantasy novels, non-fiction tomes, fairy-tale retellings, and horror filled true-crime stories. This works out to my advantage—I spend many days hovering silently over her shoulder, soaking up every page along with her. Thankfully, we share a particular soft-spot for fantasy novels with bright young heroines, brooding villains cloaked in our favorite color: morally grey, faraway lands, and the glimmers of magic. I know that I could read ahead of her when she leaves the apartment during the day, but I never do—I love feeling close to her while we read together.

I just wish that I could gush over the stories we shared *with* her, rather than be the silent spectre looming over her shoulder.

Amarie, on the other hand, has deep, olive toned skin, amber, almost gold eyes, and bright purple hair. She has the most enigmatic style I've ever experienced: one day, she'll walk out of her room in head to toe black, complete with Doc Martens, fishnet hose, and a chain belt, and the next day, she's in the frilliest pink dress looking like your favorite fairy tale princess. She loves her signature black lipstick, but even that can be replaced with bright colors as her mood sees fit. Amarie is a boisterous soul with a penchant for baked goods and a successful YouTube channel she shares with her younger brother, Tristan. They are collectors by nature, so they create videos showing off hauls of action figures, vinyl records, comic books—anything that can be collected. I steer clear of the area any time she is filming content, always terrified that my presence will end up on some sort of "caught on camera" ghost show. She spends hours every weekend in the kitchen baking cakes, pies, and cookies for her small business, Cake in a Cup, which, with the help of her YouTube, has amassed quite a following. She spends hours on *Baldur's Gate 3*, lost in her love for Astarion (not that I can blame her), and has played through so many different scenarios that I've lost count of how many storylines she's perfected. Amarie has a cat, Luna, who—if cats could talk—would give me away in an instant. Her eyes follow me (always in my invisible form) anytime we are in the same room, and I just know that eventually one of the girls will notice and my cover will be blown.

All three of my roommates are reality TV junkies. We spend countless hours sprawled around on the sectional in front of housewives and celebrities, the staffs of bars and pawn shop shenanigans. Well...they sprawl on the sectional. I sit, invisibly, on the kitchen island, part of the fun but not included in the fun—unless you count giggling telepathically with Zelie.

Occasionally, Zelie will place her palms together in front of her chest and level a pleading look in my direction, her way of asking me to give her just a little bit more time to broach the subject of haunted apartments with Em and Amarie. I can tell that my being here in secret bothers her, not only because she knows it bothers *me*, but because she also hates lying to Em and Amarie.

All three roommates spend their days outside of the apartment, which means I have mostly free run of the place. I stay out of their bedrooms, of course, because they all have a right to privacy. I also steer clear of Luna the cat, because whether I am solid or invisible, I don't trust her to not find a way to tell Amarie that I'm here before Zelie can. When Em and Amarie are out, I'm able to do all the things that would make it very easily clear that there are one-too-many beings in the apartment: I can shower without fear of the water being heard, use the kitchen without apples appearing to float along in midair, and I can wash the clothes I've been able to buy with the online job Zelie found for me.

We'd no sooner made it back from the Skull before Zelie had found me the perfect job:

"Virtual assistant?" I'd never actually assisted anyone with... anything.

"It'll be easy! You'll be working for a photographer: Xeta Hayes. She's incredibly talented at what she does, and her business has taken off. On top of being one of the most sought after photographers in Georgia, she has young children now, so she's looking to off-load the administrative side of her business so that she can have more time with her kids."

"So, what exactly would she need me to do for her?" I was hesitant—torn between the need to make some cash and the paralyzing fear that I'd somehow be found out.

Zelie didn't seem concerned at all. "Mostly you'll be responding to emails for her, and setting up photoshoot times that work for both her and her client. She may also have you send out invoices and instruct clients on how to pay them, but she will have to train you on all of that. You'll have to use my name and Venmo, like we talked about, but..." she trailed off nervously. "Is that still okay?"

"I want to be ready to contribute, and even have back-rent from the day I moved in, ready when you tell Em and Amarie—so they can see that I'm not just here to mooch off of you guys."

I'd landed the job a few days later, and have been slowly but surely learning Xeta's ways. It's an interesting way to interact with Livings without having to be face to face. While it's super slow, Zelie's old laptop is a workhorse, so I have everything I need to support Xeta through the rest of autumn.

She'd prepared me for a drop in workload during the holidays, and I've hoarded every penny I've made, with the exception of a tiny Goodwill haul to keep me clothed without having to raid Zelie's closet daily. When winter comes, my schedule goes from working forty hours a week to working no more than three hours on Tuesdays and Thursdays, but I don't mind.

It gives me spare time to plan for Ma to visit for Christmas.

11

I can't lie. I'm dreading the conversation that I know I have to have with Ma.

The one in which I tell her that I am sharing an apartment in the middle of Atlanta with three Living girls...two of whom don't know I Exist.

Ma had settled in the small, coastal town of Wilmington, North Carolina at the same time that I was starting to call Halcyon Hall home. She obviously can't know about my roommate situation, so Zelie reluctantly agreed to drive me back to Halcyon so that Ma can come there to stay for a few days.

"I really don't want to leave you there," Zelie whines on the drive down to the low country. "It seems cruel."

She pouts, leveling a glance in my direction.

"I know, but I don't know what else to do!" I throw my hands up in the air, exasperated. "She wants to see me, but she can't know you guys Exist. Ugh, this is so convoluted," I press the heels of my palms into my eyes, thinking that maybe if I rub them hard enough all of this will go away.

"Hey, it's okay," Zelie grabs my hand, gently tugging it away from my face. "That place is just awful, but it's only a few days, right? Plus, I packed some supplies that will make it not so awful."

"Do I even want to know what your supplies are?"

She only returns a mischievous grin.

I genuinely don't know what I did to deserve Zelie.

She's brought an arsenal of cleaning supplies, bedsheets, an air mattress, and enough food that I won't even be able to think about being hungry the entire time Ma and I are at Halcyon.

After we both do a scan of the property and deem it free of any new ghosts, we spend the entire day cleaning and setting up the hall. It looks like Dave and Bethany have made some repairs and started doing some renovations, which will help underline the lie I'd told Ma about this place being a fixer-upper project I'd undertaken.

The kitchen has been updated slightly, but mercifully remains in the style of the rest of the house, so there are no flashy new appliances or decor that would make it unbelievable that a ghost girl with no job or income could have cleaned it up on her own. We clean dust away and load the fridge with the food Zelie brought, concocting the alibi that the couple who owns the house were planning a major Christmas event here before being coerced into visiting family instead. I'd "overheard them saying they'd send someone to take all the food to a nearby shelter after Christmas," so they wouldn't notice if any of the food was missing.

Thankfully, "my" room has gone untouched, meaning there's still a nice bed with a mattress and no construction chaos in sight. We make up the bed with the sheets Zelie brought so that Ma can stay in this room in relative comfort.

I insist that we set up the air mattress for me in the library—the one room at Halcyon that I truly miss. Sleeping among the books I've loved so much will be cathartic for me, I think. I step over to the nearest shelf, running my fingers along their spines and smiling to myself. Bethany has added quite a few titles since I've been gone, and I can't wait to tear into them.

Once the manor looks less like an abandoned monstrosity and more like reasonable accommodations for two ghosts, Zelie checks her watch. "She said she'd be here around five?"

"Yeah," I nod, not sure of what else to say. Suddenly, I feel awkward, and resort to chewing on a cuticle.

"Okay, then I'd better go. You'll call me if you need anything at all?" she makes me promise, which I do, thankful for the phone Ma provided me years ago and insists that I keep so that we can contact each other.

Ma arrives in a sea of cheek kisses and worried glances a few hours after Zelie leaves.

It's clear near-immediately that she isn't exactly thrilled with Halcyon. From the time she steps out of the taxi she'd taken from the nearest bus station, posing as a Living the whole journey, she's darting glances around at the state of the place and trying to make the best of it...until she gets to the library. Ma is as avid a reader as I am, so the room takes her breath away and she asks if we can arm wrestle for who gets the bed here. I assure her that I won't let her have this room, because it's an air mattress and she's old, to which she lovingly responds that her nineteen year old body can handle an air mattress far more easily than my thirty year old body.

"Yikes, that hurts!" I cry out, my pride mortally wounded. I finally give in, agreeing to give her the library. I do, however, make a dash and snatch the books I want to read before she can claim them.

Over dinner of her famous spaghetti she'd brought with her, Ma tells me about Wilmington. She's begun volunteering at their local hospital, just like she did in Middletown and every other town we moved to, and has continued her goal of helping as many Living transition to Death as she can. It's honorable work, but I know that she is always exhausted.

I hope that the next week will be just what she needs: rest and relaxation with her daughter.

The house Ma has settled on is under construction, with its owners staying in Florida while renovations are underway. There is still, thankfully according to Ma, electricity and running water, and plenty of furnishings in the bedrooms. The house itself is a quaint little Ranch-style, pale blue-grey with dark wood accents. There are window boxes interspersed across the front of the house that would have been overflowing with flowers had Ma snapped the photos she's showing me in spring.

We pass the rest of the evening in pleasant conversation, Ma recounting some of the more interesting Life-to-Death transitions she's helped on and me regaling her with Halcyon Hall's Halloween tourists...conveniently leaving out Zelie and anything that has happened after. She muses about her options once the homeowners return to her current house, and how she's been eyeing some new constructions that haven't quite been able to sell yet, and a spooky mansion set on a hill just outside of town that can't be sold no matter what. She wants to check it out, but doesn't want to unwittingly sneak up on another ghost alone.

She also admits that a ghost friend she made at the hospital helped her hack into the security cameras that the homeowners set up before leaving on their vacation. Ma overheard the owners talking about disabling the app on their phones because of all of the motion they expected from the construction crews, so she knew they wouldn't actually be watching the cameras at all over the next several months. I download the app on my phone. She promises all the silly faces and goofy dances any time I want to check the app, and I promise that I will check in on her occasionally.

We clean up the kitchen together then make our way through the grand foyer. Apparently, Ma found a tree that I can only describe as a Charlie Brown twig, but she's decorated it with ribbons, baubles, and multicolored lights that glow so vividly that even so late in the evening, the room is as bright as midday. The floor around the tree is littered with gifts that I know could only be for me. My heart warms.

"When did you have time to do this?" I ask, mystified.

"I didn't really need you to cut every single vegetable of the salad into 'alf inch pieces because that's what Gordon Ramsay says to do," she admits. Her eyes twinkle with mischief. "I just needed a second to spoil *mon coeur*."

"Well I have gifts for you, too!" I squeal, darting to my room to grab the few packages I'd stashed in my bag. I return, lovingly scattering them around the gifts she'd placed for me.

I show her to the bathroom before we say our goodnights.

Even though I'm keeping a secret from her, I sleep better than I have in months...all because I am under the same roof as my Ma.

The week passes in the blink of an eye.

Ma and I exchange gifts on Christmas Eve, as is our tradition. Even though I've been pinching pennies to be able to offer Em, Amarie, and Zelie repayment for rent and food and utilities once the two former roommates know I'm there, I'd let myself splurge a little for Ma. I brought her two new sets of scrubs, a fuzzy pink bathrobe, and a new pair of tennis shoes to make the walks to and from the hospital easier. She gives me two outfits, a fuzzy blue bathrobe, and a cute new pair of ankle booties. We break into a fit of giggles when we realize that our gifts mostly matched, and immediately don our robes.

Christmas day, Ma digs a sea of hors d'oeuvres out of the fridge, and we spend the entire day snacking and watching all of our favorite Christmas movies on the TV we rescued from Dave's storage closet—which he uses to play a loop of not-me-at-all "*Captured Evidence of the Hag!*" during Halcyon events. We laugh when the Griswolds' "*shitter's full,*" we weep when George Bailey discovers that he is the richest man in town, and we recite every word of "A Christmas Story" by heart. I fall asleep with my head nestled in my mother's lap.

Before I know it, it's the night before Ma is set to return to Wilmington, and I still haven't told her the truth. I'm sitting on my makeshift bed in PJs and my cozy new bathrobe when I hear Ma puttering around downstairs. I pad down the stairs and into the kitchen before forcing out a breathy, "Ma, I have something to tell you," before I lose my nerve.

Then, the words flood out of me.

"I've been staying in an apartment with Zelie and Em and Amarie and I know you will hate it but Zelie showed up at the Halloween thing here and she was so nice to me because she was a Medium who could actually see me and we became friends and she is a Living and invited me to move in with her and her roommates and I couldn't say no because I was losing every ounce of myself to that place and I needed... *I needed,*" I begin to sob uncontrollably and press my face into my palms. "I'm so sorry that I lied to you, Ma, but I needed my situation to be different. I...I couldn't keep running or hiding, especially when I found a friend who truly *saw* me. The other two don't know I'm there yet, but I just...*I needed a friend.*" I heave a breath, exhausted.

I slump onto the counter behind me.

Tears pool in Ma's eyes and my stomach clinches. "That...terrifies me, mon coeur," she whispers as she falls into the spot beside me.

"I know, Ma. I know. And I didn't want to tell you, because I knew what you'd say. But I can't keep Existing in fear of being found out. I...I can't do it anymore."

"So, this isn't your 'ome anymore?" she asks, eyes darting around as if we'll be caught trespassing at any moment.

"No, I haven't lived here since October," I admit sheepishly. "But since Halloween is over and there isn't another Friday the 13th for months, the owners won't even know we were here."

Ma has a lot of questions, which I answer as best I can. By the end, she's shaking with anger and disappointment, which kills me—no pun intended.

"I can't believe you would do something like this," she whispers. "After *everything* I've taught you, about all of the *risks*, you chose to throw it all away and move in with a Medium?! I raised you better than that, Abby Gale."

"I know that, Ma," I grunt through my teeth. "But Zelie isn't like that."

"'ow do you know that, Abby?!" she shrieks. "You can't know that!"

"But I do!" I shout back. "She hasn't given me a single reason to think that she can't be trusted!"

"Yet!" Ma seethes.

Hot tears burn as they fall down my cheeks. "I'm an idiot. I thought for a second you'd be happy for me."

"'ow can I be happy when you're making choices that put you, *my child*, at risk?"

"That's just the thing! Ghost or not, I'm not a child anymore, Ma! I'm a thirty year old woman who can make decisions for herself!"

She doesn't respond, just stands there glaring at me like she did when I was a smart-mouthed teenager with a snarky comeback.

I take a deep breath, trying to reel in my anger. "This isn't how I wanted Christmas to end," I whisper, rubbing my eyes.

"This certainly isn't what I wanted, either," she sniffs. "To be clear, I don't agree with the choices that you're making. I'm in no way going to support you on this. I think you're being foolish in trusting these outsiders."

"Do you just want me to Exist completely alone?" The tears come much faster now and I scrub my face to try and clear my vision. "Is that what you want? For me to be so *miserable*, so lonely, that I become a Poltergeist? Because Ma," I meet her equally teary gaze, "that was happening. Zelie quite literally saved me from myself."

"Non, I don't want you to become a Poltergeist!" She draws back as if I've slapped her. "But you don't 'ave to be lonely, you could come stay with me in Wilmington!"

I roll my eyes. "Yes, because *Grey Gardens* is every girl's dream." I amend my tone, because I don't want to hurt her feelings. "Ma, I love being with you, and being around you, but I also need an Existence of my own. I can't be with you every minute of every day—I need more than that. I need *friends*."

We go back and forth for what feels like hours, with no actual resolution. Ultimately, though, the conversation ends with—maybe not agreement—but mutual respect for one another, like disagreements with Ma always end.

Ma isn't ready to meet Zelie quite yet, so we say our goodbyes the next morning before she arrives.

"I need you to know 'ow much I love you. No matter what happens, being your 'Ma' has been the greatest 'onor and privilege I could 'ave ever been granted, both in Life and Death." Normally Ma isn't the heartfelt type, so this pronouncement is...odd. "I am so blessed to be your Ma, and I will love you for the rest of time and then some, *mon coeur.*"

"I love you too, Ma," I laugh nervously, smirking to alleviate the semi-awkwardness of her proclamation. "I'll call you when I get...er...," I stick on the word, because I'd started to say, "home." It puts a lump in my throat, one of sadness for my Ma but also innate joy for me—I have a *home.* I have a place where I feel safe, with people that I love, even if they don't know I'm there yet.

I finish the sentence lamely with, "To Atlanta. I'll call you when I get to Atlanta."

She pulls me in for one more hug then before I know it, she's gone and Zelie is pulling up.

"Ready to go?" Zelie asks as I plop into the passenger seat after loading my bags into the trunk.

"I am," I sigh.

We pull away from Halcyon, Zelie happily chirping about a new case she's taken on, but none of her words register.

I'm still reeling from the fight with Ma, and how, fifteen years later, my mother *still* doesn't care about the seemingly endless loneliness I feel.

12

We'd only known each other a couple weeks, but when the twins left to visit their ghost grandmother in Jamaica, I didn't know what to do with myself. I spent the weekend at home, reading books and watching DVDs of "The Office," which Shella, a Living girl in town, had loaned me. Shella was another person in my world that I had to lie to regularly; the twins and I had befriended her on the town playground, settling on telling her that we were all homeschooled together. We all hated to be dishonest, but it was the only way to be a child, in a small town, that didn't attend the public school, without drawing much attention to ourselves.

Ma had taken on even more volunteer shifts at the hospital morgue that weekend, so I had been home alone which made time go by that much more slowly. She checked in on Saturday evening for a quick Trance and what she referred to as a "Confirmation of Existence": Ma's term for making sure that I was safe, intact, and if not happy, at least still Existing. She threw some pizza rolls in the oven for me and I sat down in my solid form at the small table in the farmhouse's large but very shabby kitchen. For the first time in a while, I looked at my Ma, also in her solid form, and could see exhaustion lining every inch of her perpetually nineteen year old face.

"Ma," I said quietly, pulling my knees up to my chest. I was freezing in this drafty old house, so I'd donned some thick grey sweat pants, an oversized teal sweatshirt with the word "homebody" across the chest in artsy calligraphy, and fuzzy polka dotted socks that stretched up to my knees. My hair was in a messy knot on top of my head and my solid form was in desperate need of the shower that I'd been putting off because the "hot" water in this place was lukewarm at the very best.

Ma started at the sound of my voice, which made me even more nervous about her current state.

"What, *mon coeur*?" Ma asked, turning to start a pot of water to boil for tea.

"Are...are you okay?" I asked anxiously. "It's just...you've been at the hospital a whole lot lately, on top of the random cash gigs you take to make Living money, and you look really, really tired. I mean—" I cut myself off, worrying over how rude that last bit had been. "You're always beautiful, I just..."

Ma chuckled quietly, and I knew she hadn't been offended.

"Well, *merci* for that, but I'm fine. We've just 'ad more people Dying in l'hôpital lately than usual. There's been some staff turnover, which would normally be fine but we lost power briefly Thursday night which shut down some Life support machines when the generators malfunctioned."

I sucked in a breath.

"That's awful, Ma. Those poor people—gone just because of an accident."

"That's what I'm there for, *mon coeur*. Most of the new ghosts 'ave been excited to be out of l'hôpital beds and able to move around again, but they also don't understand why they can't just walk into their 'ouses now. I know you've never Died," her voice dropping to a hushed whisper, as if the ancient refrigerator she had stopped to prop herself against might hear and alert the news media, "but Death is a very confusing thing. You still feel mostly like you did when you were Living, but if you, as a ghost, just barge through your front door, it will cause lasting psychological trauma on those you left behind: your parents, your spouse, your children...they won't be able to understand how you are standing there, knowing that your body is in the local morgue."

"Wouldn't seeing the person that they loved make them happy, though?" I asked, seriously curious as to why that could be a bad thing.

"*Ma chérie*," my mother breathed, smiling warmly at me as she pulled her tawny sweater tighter around herself, "I know that it seems like 'aving your family member in any capacity seems like the best thing in the world after thinking you'd lost them, but...it's different for the Living. They are going through unspeakable grief over the Death, and their loved one being a ghost just reminds them that they're...not part of the same world anymore. Not really. So it's cruel to appear to them after Death unless there is a desperate need."

"What would a desperate need be?" I asked. "Like, telling them where you left a buried treasure or who killed you?"

"Not exactly," Ma chortled, knowing that I hadn't meant that as rashly as it had come out. "Non, typically after their Death, a ghost will only appear to one of their Living loved ones if they think that their Living is in immediate danger, or in very rare cases, and only when they are certain that the Living can 'andle it, to say goodbye. Normally, if they're saying goodbye, they do so from a distance, and only for a second...so briefly that the Living would think that they imagined it."

"So basically you're teaching the new ghosts all these rules?"

"That's exactly what I'm doing. Again, thankfully you've never Died, but it's a difficult transition to make...so I'm there to ease them along, as long as they need 'elp. I give them the basic rules that they need to Exist until they can get set up in their new Existence. There's a corridor off of the morgue that the Living think is an old broom closet, where new ghosts can stay until they're ready to leave and be on their own." Ma quirked an eyebrow then, amusement sparking in her eyes as she smiled even bigger at me.

"What?" I asked, feeling that contagious smile spread across my own face. "Why are you looking at me like that?"

"You've just never really asked about what I do at l'hôpital before. I know you've been there to learn about Possession and to see your," she all but chokes on the word, "*friends*. But it's nice to talk about my work with someone that isn't also a volunteer, or a new ghost."

"Well, I think that what you do is really cool, Ma." I admitted, now that I knew how hard the countless hours that she spent there had to be, and how thankless the work could be for her.

"If you ever want to volunteer—" she started. The tea kettle on the stove let out a sudden, shrill whistle to let us know that the water was boiling. Ma turned back to making tea, shaking off whatever she'd been about to say.

"Hey, Ma," I said softly, watching her pull the cooked pizza rolls out of the oven. She looked back over at me with the remnants of her earlier enthusiasm still fading from her face.

"I think I'd like that, sometime," I smiled, knowing that she'd been thinking that I was a teenager who wouldn't want to spend time with her mom when she could be spending time with her friends.

She left for the hospital a few minutes later, more energized than I'd seen her in weeks.

After Possession lessons, I quickly developed an interest in the transition from Life to Death and took Ma up on the offer to accompany her on some of her volunteer shifts at the hospital.

To say she was over the moon would be an understatement. Ma was absolutely ecstatic that I was showing an interest in her work, and that we'd be spending extra time together.

The night of my first volunteer shift, I paced my room anxiously. Ma had loaned me a set of her scrubs: a solid, bright pink ensemble with a red heart over the breast pocket. I pulled my hair up into a messy top knot and donned my favorite black and white tennis shoes, since I knew most of the night would be spent on my feet. I could hear Ma still getting ready in her room, so I flopped back on my bed and practiced some breathing techniques I'd seen on some talk show earlier in the week. It didn't help—I was still nervous. What would the new ghosts be like? Would I say or do something wrong? How do you talk to someone newly Dead?

Finally, Ma knocked on my door and I sat up.

"You ready to—ugh, goodness Abby you have got to clean up this room!" she said, glancing around the room disapprovingly.

She was right, my room was a disaster zone. In my defense, the farmhouse was already shabby, and my room was no exception. Random sections of the yellow wallpaper had been torn off, their remnants hanging in small strips. There was a small bookshelf in the corner that was overloaded with books of varying shapes and sizes, and a purple inflatable chair in the corner that you could barely see over the clutter of a teenaged girl—ghost or not. Clothes, shoes, jewelry, and assorted papers littered every possible surface of the room. The drawers of my dresser hung open at odd angles, more clothes spilling over their fronts.

"Seriously, I don't know how you Live like this," Ma fussed, stepping into the room and bending to pick a discarded blanket up from the floor before stopping herself, remembering our upcoming shift. She didn't give me the time to throw out a sarcastic, "*I don't 'Live' like this, I'm Dead*," before she let out a sigh and asked, "Are you ready to go?"

"Yeah, let's go. I'll clean up some when I get back," I promised, knowing full well that it would take a miracle for me to actually clean my room to her standards.

"*D'accord*. On our walk over, I'll give you a run down of things that will 'elp your first night go smoothly."

We approached Middletown General, my head still reeling from Ma's information-dump. On the way over, she'd dropped several nuggets of knowledge that felt like a gold mine to me:

"First thing's first, you 'ave to remember that the people we'll be working with tonight 'ave just Died," Ma started. "And I know that you don't understand what that feels like, but it is a very confusing time for a person. You are stuck between missing your loved ones and 'ating to leave them, relief at no longer feeling the pain and anxiety that often accompanies Death, and curiosity and apprehension at what Life as a ghost may be like."

"What about the people that choose not to be ghosts?" I asked. I'd always been curious about the Unknown.

"Those souls go through the Reaping before we see them—so you won't encounter anyone who isn't sure that they want to remain on Earth as a ghost."

"The...Reaping? What is that?"

"That is when a Reaper comes and asks the person, upon their Death, what choice they've made. If they've decided to become a ghost, the Reaper leaves the new ghost in our care. If they've decided to move on, the Reaper collects—or Reaps—their soul, to carry it into the Unknown."

"What is a *Reaper*?!" I asked, panic rising in me. I'd never heard of any of this before.

Ma laughed, sensing my anxiety and said, "The Brotherhood of Reapers is a group that, like I said, is responsible for ferrying souls from this Life to whatever comes next. But since both the Living and ghosts cannot know what is beyond this realm, the Brotherhood of Reapers is a very secretive organization, and only a few in their ranks can actually travel between 'ere and the Unknown."

"So are they ghosts?" I asked, unsure what I wanted the answer to be.

"Non, Reapers are generally 'uman. For the most part, Reapers Live normal 'uman Lives until they come of age. For whatever reason—be it strength, or faith, or exceptional knowledge, or powerful force of will—they are invited to join the Brotherhood, which is 'ow they refer to themselves even though there are just as many female and non-binary Reapers as there are male Reapers. Many of them were Born, and many of them 'ave the same average Lifespan as Livings do."

"Many, but not all..." I let my voice trail off, knowing that Ma would pick up on the question that went unspoken.

"Some of the 'igher-ranking Reapers were created in the Unknown, at the dawn of time, to lead the Reapers because the Creators knew that Death was to be a part of Life. Those Reapers are incredibly powerful, and control who joins the Reapers. They're also the Reapers that guard the final leg of the journey to the Unknown, and are the last portion of this realm that souls see before passing through the barrier."

"They sound scary," I said, wrapping my arms around myself.

"They can be...intimidating," Ma agreed, "but they're necessary. Imagine what it would be like if there were millions of lost souls just floating around the world, not wanting to be a ghost but 'aving nowhere to go. The Brotherhood's job is often thankless, and they're regularly associated with goofy, greeting card 'alloween characters that wear long black cloaks and carry scythes. In reality, they're more warrior than grim spectre, because the weight of a 'uman soul is not small. To be a Reaper, one must be incredibly strong—strong enough to carry a soul's memories, joy, fear, anguish, and all of the other emotions over moving on."

"You'll like this, *mon coeur*," Ma continued, leaning in to whisper conspiratorially. "The Reapers get cool tattoos when they join the Brotherhood."

"They have tattoos?" I asked, perking up slightly.

"It's kind of their 'thing,'" Ma laughed. "You'll know a Reaper if you see one, because they 'ave a tattoo that sweeps between the elbow and shoulder of their right arm. Some of it is just filigreed swirls, but the focal point of every Reaper's tattoo is an 'ourglass. The top 'alf of the 'ourglass is a skull, which blends into the proverbial sands of Time at the 'ourglass' center, and the bottom of the 'ourglass is different, and personally chosen by each Reaper when they join the Brotherhood. It becomes their sigil."

I shuddered. What a creepy tattoo!

"But enough about Reapers," Ma said abruptly, realizing that we'd spent half our walk talking about Reapers and not about what I should expect going into my first volunteer shift. "There are a few things that you should be ready for. I can't *believe* I'm letting you do this," she worried, "but I'm trying to be better about not being such a worry wart —so I'm letting you come with me because you'll be *with* me. If any Reapers show up, we will leave immediately, got it, my *'little sister'*?"

I nodded, even though the thought of seeing a Reaper up close sent a thrill up my spine.

Ma went on to remind me that tonight would be emotional, because Death was hard on ghosts, but most of what she said went in one ear and out the other as I mulled over the Existence of the Reapers.

We entered Middletown General through the same doors I'd walked through with her when we'd had the Possession lesson. Ma instructed me to stay in my solid form since I was with her, and since she was a familiar presence in the hospital, no one would question me.

We made our way down the same long, sterile hallway as before and entered the same stairwell. This time, though, instead of stopping at the construction zone, Ma led me down to the basement. The lower level still carried the sterile environment you'd expect from a hospital: the flooring was a dull grey concrete, and the painted cinderblock walls matched. Unlike the floors above, there were no windows; the only lights here were the bright fluorescent lamps that hung from the ceiling. Ma stopped outside of a heavy metal door with a "MORGUE" plaque overhead.

"Are you ready?" she asked me, gauging my mood.

I took a deep breath and steeled myself before nodding. Ma pulled the heavy door open, and I gasped. It was...*empty*?

"Where is everyone? Where are all the ghosts?" I asked, craning my neck to peek around the room, wondering if all the ghosts were hiding behind the huge stainless steel exam table in the middle of the room. I could see that one side of the room was lined floor-to-ceiling with cabinets, and another wall was lined with drawers that I knew held the bodies of those that had passed on inside the hospital recently.

Ma stepped into the room and twisted around a plant and coat rack that were placed so haphazardly in a corner that I hadn't even noticed they were there. Behind them stood a wooden door that was all but invisible unless you were actually looking for it.

"I know I told you this before, but most of the Living that work in this area forget about this area of l'hôpital entirely—they think it's an old broom closet." Ma explained as she pushed open the door and led me in.

I'm not sure what I expected, but what waited on the other side of that nearly hidden door was definitely not it.

The room we entered was...bizarre.

It was bigger than I expected, and home to at least fifteen beds that looked to be a few decades old; they were probably stolen away over time when beds in other wings of the hospital were replaced. They were shabby but clean, all neatly made up with—again, outdated—hospital linens. There was one dingy window along the very top end of one wall, so covered in grime and hidden behind so much overgrowth that it was clear that no one remembered that the window, or this room, Existed.

The strangeness of the room was, however, completely overshadowed by the *ghosts* here. There were ten of them that I could see off the bat, not including Ma or me. There were ghosts of various ages, races, and genders: a middle aged man looking outraged at everyone, a young girl in pigtails who, heartbreakingly, looked relieved to be up and about, a thirty-something who had a "they/them" button proudly displayed on their chest, and—my heart dropped—Mr. Winstone smiled at me sadly from the corner.

"Oh, Mr. Winstone..." I started before sharply cutting myself off. I hadn't asked Ma what you *say* to new ghosts. *'I'm sorry you Died'* didn't seem wildly appropriate, nor did, *'so how are you liking Death?'*

"I know," Mr. Winstone again took my hand, patting it gently. He had the most comforting presence I'd ever encountered, his gentle voice calming my nerves. "And I thank you, but I'm okay," he said.

"I'm just...sorry you're here," I admitted, "and I'm a little nervous. I'm not exactly sure what to do. This is my first volunteer shift." I stared at my feet as I shifted them uncomfortably, unable to look him in the eye.

"I'm sure you'll be great at this, and wonder if you wouldn't mind starting by helping me? I'm a bit nervous myself," Mr. Winstone mused as he stage whispered, "I've never been a ghost before!"

I knew that he was asking for help not for himself, but for me, so that he could be the ghost that experienced my *inexperience* in helping others. That knowledge brought tears to my eyes, but I blinked them away and smiled at him.

"I'd like that very much, Mr. Winstone. Thank you."

"Where do we start?" he asked at the same time that I noticed that he was in his invisible form.

"Let's start with invisibility. Look around the room for me," I directed him. "Do you see that little girl, or the person sitting on the foot of their bed chatting with the man in the suit?"

"Yes, I can see them all...it would appear that Death cured my pesky cataracts," Mr Winstone joked. I smiled before continuing.

"Well...technically, they're all invisible right now." Mr. Winstone's shock was evident, but he reigned it in quickly.

"How in the...why in the...*what*?" he asked, bewildered.

"Look at one of them a little more closely. Do you notice anything strange about them?"

Mr. Winstone squinted his eyes and leaned forward towards the man in the suit, not at all subtly. The man made a strange face before continuing his soon-to-be-yelling match with a tall blonde man who was clearly a volunteer in deep navy scrubs.

"Well, other than his being angry about Dying," Mr. Winstone rolled his eyes, "it almost looks like he has a haze around him? As if the edges of his body are a little...smoky?" He looked down at me and I knew he was expecting me to call him crazy.

"Yes! That's exactly it! Since you are a ghost, you will be able to see other ghosts, even if they're in their invisible forms, if they want you to. Other ghosts will, of course, be able to see you, no matter what form you're in, if you allow it. The difference with ghosts, is that we have multiple invisible forms, and the Living can *only* see us when we want them to. Ghosts can see you in your visible *and* invisible forms, but you also have an invisible form where no one can see you. It's kind of confusing, I know," I admitted lamely.

Why was I so bad at this?!

"Like I was able to see you and your friends when you visited me before I..." he cut himself off, and I could tell that, as much as he tried to cover it, he was truly devastated to have Died.

"Well, no. We were invisible, but you were so close to," I hated the words as they came out, "...*passing*, that you could see us—we were in our invisible-to-Living-but-visible-to-ghosts forms."

"Ah...I...that makes sense." I watched as he wrung his hands, and knew that he needed a moment to collect himself. I busied myself with re-tying one of my shoelaces, taking much longer than I actually needed to. When I straightened back up, he was ready to continue our conversation.

"Do you want to learn how to switch between invisibles and solid? It's really easy!" I tried to put as much pep into my voice as I could.

"I think I would like that very much," Mr. Winstone said, smiling.

"Okay, so...basically, all you need to do is just think about whichever form you want to be in. You just say, in your mind, 'I want to go invisible,' or 'I need to be solid,' and your body just kind of...follows suit." I explained, flipping between my forms as I said the two phrases out loud. "Oh, and you don't have to say those exact words. Any thought that means that you want to go solid or invisible will work. Your body will follow whatever your brain tells it to...then eventually your body will sense what you need and you won't even have to 'think' the words. Do you feel comfortable trying it out?"

He nodded and closed his eyes, fists clenching in laser focus. I had to stifle a giggle, not because anything was funny, but because Mr. Winstone was trying so hard and it was adorable. I truly hoped that Mr. Winstone and I could remain friends forever, before ice-cold reality caught up to me. I don't get to have friends for eternity...I barely get to have friends for a moment.

Before I could wallow in that ever-present pit, Mr. Winstone popped into his solid form, and let out a proud, "Whoop!"

"You did it, Mr. Winstone! You did it and I am so proud of you!" I beamed at him.

Mr. Winstone looked down at himself in disbelief, then popped in and out of his solid form several times before breaking into a wide, toothy grin.

"This is so strange, but wonderful! I never thought that I would get to experience being invisible!"

Then he tried, successfully, to wink out of vision for me, and flipped in and out of that form several times, until it became a sort of game.

"Eventually, you'll be able to walk through solids in your invisible form," I stage whisper to him conspiratorially. "But that's a lesson for another day." He winks at me in acknowledgment and goes invisible again.

After that, we spent the next few hours going over some of the ground rules of being a ghost. I explained to him that, as much as he might like to see them, his sudden appearance in front of any of his loved ones would cause them additional grief. We went over secrecy and the reality that, while we can appear in solid form in front of and interact with the Living, they must believe, at all times, that we are also Living. That he cannot just change forms in front of a Living, or confirm in any way that we do Exist. That rule seemed to confuse him, so I stopped to give him the break to ask a question.

"So...if we aren't allowed to let the Living know that we Exist...how do ghost hunters on TV shows work?" he asked, genuinely curious.

"We are *allowed* to do mundane things while we're invisible, like knocking on a wall, casting a shadow, or making a light flicker, but most of the time, it's Poltergeists that interact with ghost hunters. Most ghosts tend to want to either blend in with the Living, or Exist completely separately from the Living...there isn't really an in between very often."

"What is a Poltergeist?" he asked.

"The best way that I can explain a Poltergeist is...well, you and I are ghosts, right?"

He nodded, brows furrowed because he couldn't tell where I was going with this.

"So, we are ghosts, and we are still in our human forms, able to eat if we want to and breathe if we want to and move around and we're aware of our surroundings, conscious of every decision that we make. Poltergeists don't have that anymore. They've been ghosts for so long that they've become more energy than consciousness. Even though the energy of a Poltergeist can appear to make conscious decisions, like knocking on a wall or rolling a ball across a floor or making a sound."

"Like an energy that doesn't know it's a ghost anymore?"

I shivered at the thought of not knowing your own consciousness anymore.

"Sort of...and poltergeists don't have the same rules as we do. We can see any ghost, no matter what form they're in, whether solid or invisible—but we can't see Poltergeists. Or, if we do see a Poltergeist, it's no different than what the Living see: a quick shadowy figure just at the edge of our vision."

"Ghosts have ghosts...noted," Mr. Winstone joked.

I laughed, and we spent the rest of the night with me answering his questions about finding a home, Trancing for energy, and setting him up with a network of other ghosts that could help him until he was fully on his feet and settled in his new Existence.

"Mr. Winstone, can I ask you a question?"

"Of course you can, dear," he nodded.

"It's just...you were so excited to be reunited with your wife and Spot. I just...I wondered why you decided not to go into the Unknown. Why are you learning to be a ghost?"

He took in a long breath while he thought of how to answer, finally settling on, "Because I am afraid."

I furrowed my brow. "Afraid of what?" I asked.

"Going into the Unknown is...an unknown experience for me," he admitted, taking my hand in his wizened one again. "And while I can't wait to see them both," his lip quivered, "I'm afraid to...cross over. So this old man just needs a little time first. I know I will go to them soon, but I want to have this short experience first."

Before I knew it, Ma appeared behind me and gently put her hand on my shoulder.

"You ready to go, *mon coeur*?" she asked, and I glanced at the window. The Sun was coming up! I'd spent the entire night talking to Mr. Winstone. I flushed, embarrassed and ashamed that I hadn't devoted any time to the other ghosts. I said my goodbyes to him and left the room behind Ma.

"I'm sorry," I said quietly once we were in the stairwell. "I was just working so hard with Mr. Winstone that time just...got away from me." Ma smiled.

"Oh, *mon coeur*, don't be sorry. Your being there 'elped, because Mr. Winstone was one less person that needed my attention. You did beautifully."

I couldn't wait to see the twins and tell them all about my first volunteer shift.

Until the next morning, when Ma found out that they'd decided to stay in Jamaica.

They left me behind, without a call or backwards glance.

She dropped the news like one might tell the weather, casually destroying my entire world. Later, when she found me in my room sobbing, she told me that this was for the best—that it was wisest to steer clear of others who might find me out.

I felt like a person on the gallows. I felt the noose of loneliness gripping my throat, ripping into my skin and stopping any breath from escaping. I felt the floor fall out from under me. I felt the free fall of knowing that my entire Existence would come and go, with my never having anyone but my mother to truly care about me.

13

Before we know it, it's springtime, and Amarie and Em still have no idea that I'm in the apartment almost twenty-four seven.

We do, however, have one scare around Valentine's Day, because of the damned cat.

Zelie isn't home, and Em and Amarie (and me, unbeknownst to them) are watching reruns of the *Real Housewives of Somewhere or Other*, when Luna the cat suddenly jumps up and slinks towards me where I'm perched invisibly on the kitchen island. She saunters right up to me, looks me in the eyes, and *hisses*. I swear to the gods, she HISSES. Thankfully (or not—at this point their knowing that I Exist might be a blessing) a knock that signifies pizza sounds from the foyer, so the girls chalk it up to Luna hearing the delivery guy and showing off how ferocious of a protector she is.

After that, I quickly lose interest in the *Housewives* and retreat to my bedroom where I will hide out, in my invisible form, until they both go to sleep.

Then maybe I'll find that cat and give her a swift kick. (I would never *actually* do that—I love animals and would never hurt one—but I won't lie and pretend that the thought doesn't at least bring me some comfort.)

Stupid cat.

Why couldn't it be a dog? Dogs, at least, are friendly as long as your...aura, or whatever, is pure. But cats...*ugh*.

I while away the days when the apartment is empty working full time for Xeta, and spend the nights being as silent as possible. Even Zelie can't keep me company as much as I'd like, because her Mediumship had piqued the interest of a Paranormal Investigation Research Center in Virginia, and she's been working with them nonstop to start a program that helps new Mediums (not to be confused with *meeeeediums*) foster their abilities in a safe, controlled environment.

When she isn't actually *in* Virginia, she's on the phone with Virginia.

Existence has gotten pretty lonely for me, but I'm not sure how to change my lot. Being around the girls fulfills my need for social interaction better than being the sole, well...*soul*, at Halcyon, but there aren't any actual interactions.

I've grown fond of two people who have no idea I Exist.

I have two "friends" that don't know I'm here.

I've considered just popping into my solid form on the couch one night and shouting out, "hey, ladies! Don't be scared! I know you haven't seen me before but I've been here for months and I freaking love y'all and want us to be actual real besties!" but I know that that would just end with me being promptly evicted and Em and Amarie both in therapy.

I'm sitting on my bed one April morning, trying to Trance just for something to do, when I hear Zelie call, "bye!" before she pokes her head into my room.

"Hey, The Squares are gone, wanna go get brunch?" She jokingly refers to Em and Amarie as "The Squares" sometimes, insinuating that they are drags because they don't know I Exist—because they aren't Mediums, or because they aren't, "in-the-know," I'm not sure.

I dive off the bed, desperate to get out of the apartment. "Ugh, yes, please, I am literally DYING in this place!"

"You're...'literally' Dying? How does a Dead girl 'literally Die,' again?" Zelie's laugh is cut short when she's forced to duck, avoiding the throw pillow I chuck at her head.

We walk to Jittery Java, a nearby coffee shop and Zelie's and my preferred brunch haunt. I love it for their house-made bagels. Zelie loves it for Sam, the cute barista with lime green hair and glittery cat-eye glasses that she'd been low-key flirting with. I hadn't wanted to call attention to it: she'd so recently moved her wedding rings from her finger to a chain on her neck. I know that she still misses Jess with every breath she takes, and I don't want my teasing to spook her out of trying to find happiness wherever she can.

It's unseasonably hot for Atlanta in April, so we're grateful for the *whoosh* of the AC as Zelie opens the Jittery Java door and ushers me inside. The vibes in this place are, as always, immaculate. There's a cozy group of couches set in a square around a low, obviously custom made coffee table. The couches are worn, plush brown leather and the table is perfectly weathered, as if it's spent years as a surface for endless indentions through math homework, paint splatter from craft projects, spilled coffee, and overflowed candle wax. There's a vintage record stand and suitcase turntable in the corner by the front windows, underneath which sit a sampling of records that patrons can choose from to play. Under the coffee table, an endless array of board games waits for the next friend group to dig through their stacks. There are hanging plants everywhere, an eclectic blend of chairs surrounding tables of various sizes, and rugs scattered across the floors haphazardly.

I absolutely love it here, and that's even before the first scent of roasting coffee beans reaches my soul.

Sam is working the counter today, and we both order strawberry bagels with fresh blueberry cream cheese and cold brews. She hands over our cold brews and tells us that our bagels will be out shortly.

"Do you think she knows I'm flirting with her?" Zelie asks as she plops down into the seat across from me. I'd snagged a table close to the counter so that we could be in Sam's radius.

"I mean...maybe?" I wince. She's my best friend, but I have to admit...Zelie is an *awkward* flirt.

"*Ughhhhhh*. I'm hopeless!" She covers her face with her hands, sagging deeper into her seat.

"You're not making your situation any better, Zelie...she can see you slumped in your chair like a weirdo."

Zelie immediately straightens, throws her head back, and guffaws as if we'd been deep in conversation and I'd just delivered the punchline to a *very* funny joke. I furrow my brows and widen my eyes, overwhelmingly uncomfortable.

"Too much, too much, *too much*," I whisper through my teeth. "Just be normal! You are out to brunch with your best friend, so just...do that."

She suddenly gasps, eyes wide, and throws a hand over her mouth. "You don't think she thinks that we are...*together*, do you?" She whispers, "together" as if it's a curse, the dirtiest of dirty words.

I clutch my chest, feigning offense. "I'm gonna pretend like you didn't just insinuate that I'm not a catch!" I quietly shriek, throwing a balled up straw paper at her. "Unfortunately I, unlike you, am only interested in men. It's tragic, I know, because falling in *love* love with you would be so easy," I tease, "and you're my soulmate, but...not romantically."

"Yeah, yeah, you know that and I know that, but...does *she* know that?!"

"Oh...," I hadn't thought about this. Did Sam think we were a *couple*? "Oh, Zelie that's a good point. She may *not* know that we're not together...I obviously only ever come here with you..."

"...and I only come here with *you*! Oh my gods she thinks we are a couple!" Zelie leans forward, braces her elbows on the table, and hangs her head down into her hands. I'm not convinced she's not about to start hyperventilating.

Before I (or more importantly, *Zelie*) know what I'm doing, I'm on my feet. "I know how to remedy that! I'll be back!" I call over my shoulder. Her feeble protests fade into background noise as I saunter up to the bar, slyly grabbing a napkin from a dispenser as I approach Sam.

"Hey there, do you have a pen?" Sam barely glances at me before nodding towards a cup full of pens on the other side of the register.

"Thanks," I smile lamely. "You see my best friend over there? Zelie?"

I nod and jab the pen in Zelie's direction as she frantically turns away, suddenly very deeply contemplating the ingredients in a packet of Splenda.

Sam perks up immediately at the "best friend" part as I scribble quickly on the napkin.

"Well, she's too shy to say it, but she's into you. If you're into her, too, then use this," I hand over the napkin with Zelie's phone number. "If you're *not* into her...well, we will probably be finding a new brunch spot or I will be finding a grave because she's going to kill me—or both."

Pretending to be a Living is getting easier and easier.

"Okay, well, anyways, can I get our food to-go? Because no way is she going to allow us to stay here after this."

Poor Sam is dumbfounded, but beaming, as she hands me our bagged up bagels.

"Call her. She's amazing," I smile at her knowingly before before turning to Zelie.

"Let's eat in the park, shall we?" I call to her, holding up the to-go food as I make a beeline to the exit.

Zelie scrambles up behind me, not daring to look back towards the bar. "I am never showing my face here again. I am never *speaking* to you again."

"Sure you are. In fact, you and Sam could be end-game, and could have your wedding right here in this very coffee shop, with me, your matchmaker, officiating." I hand over her coffee and link my arm through hers as we step outside and let the warm spring air wash over both of us. Silently, I hope the slight breeze that's finally breaking the heat will also calm Zelie's nerves.

We barely make it to the park two blocks away when Zelie's phone buzzes.

I'm still riding the high of playing matchmaker when we make our way back to the apartment.

Em and Amarie aren't due back for a few hours and Zelie and Sam set up a date for *that night*, so naturally she wants ample time to get ready. This will be her first date since Jess passed, so I can feel the bittersweet edge to her jitters. She loves the butterflies, but is also feeling guilty. I know that the guilt will pass with time, and so does she. Her departed husband would want her to be happy. I don't bring it up, knowing that she'll talk to me about it if she needs to vent. I help her get ready and we spend the whole time giggling, tearing her room apart so that she can pick the perfect outfit: a sage green knee-length and sleeveless sundress, leather sandals that I don't tell her looks like they might have been borrowed from Moses, and a matching leather crossbody bag.

Even rocking her Moses 3000s, Zelie looks beautiful.

She leaves around four with a call of, "see you later!" and several air kisses. I yell toward the closing door that I promise not to wait up.

I spend some time in the kitchen, absentmindedly staring in the snack cabinet for something to eat, even though I'm not truly hungry. I finally give that up, admitting to myself that I'm just bored, and make my way to my bedroom where I'm absently staring out the window at the street below—my favorite pastime—when I see something... *impossible*.

Two women, with almond-toned skin, identical (from here) are walking along the sidewalk opposite my building. Two women, with ash-brown hair that they've both accentuated with long box braids that flow in perfect patterns from their heads.

Two *women* that couldn't be anyone other than Eya and Wana Byrne.

14

I'm taking the stairs three at a time and sprinting down the road after them before I know what hits me.

I'm not even sure I'll find them; they could have gone into any building on the street or gotten into a car and driven off, but I don't care. My lungs burn and my legs scream, but I have to keep going.

It's *impossible*, but I have to know...had that actually been Eya and Wana I'd seen?

Am I wishful thinking?

Since I was Born, Ma had made it very clear that ghosts did not age; that my Existence was unheard of. We'd moved constantly to avoid anyone noticing that I was aging. She'd discouraged my getting close to anyone, ever after the twins left, for fear that they might see that I was different. I grew up mostly alone, save for Ma, because ghosts don't age.

If that were true...how had I just seen Eya and Wana Byrne, the *adults*, strolling along my street?

I'm almost to the point of giving up and chalking it up to my mind playing tricks on me when they come into view. They are stepping out of a deli, each carrying a bag of food. It *was* them...but...*how*?

"Hey!" I call out, coming to an abrupt stop in the middle of the street. I double over, suddenly winded.

They turn simultaneously and two pairs of chocolate brown eyes land on me.

Recognition slams into both of them in an instant, and they look to each other frantically. I can tell by their expressions that they are just as surprised as I am at this unexpected reunion. Wana's mouth forms a perfect "O" while Eya wrings her hands—something I remember that she's always done when she's nervous.

"How?" I ask, feeling the ridiculous prick of tears starting to form at this obvious betrayal. A bubble grows in my throat, but I go on. "How are you...adults?"

"How are *we* adults?! How are *you* an adult?" Wana bellows, almost accusingly.

She takes a step towards me and I flinch, suddenly worried that she plans to...what?

Hit me? No.

Instead, she wraps her arms around me in a bear hug, surprising us both. I return the hug, then reach for Eya, who, like me, is now letting her tears flow. We embrace as I state the obvious: "I don't think I'm as rare as I thought I was."

They choke on identical sobs.

"Can we...talk? Do you guys have somewhere you have to be right now?" I don't know where they were headed, and I don't know if they even want to talk to me, but I can't just let them walk out of my Life again. Not when I've found them after all these years, and definitely not after the revelation we've all just had.

I'm not the only ghost who is aging.

Wana leads the way to Jittery Java of all places. I send up a silent prayer of thanks that Zelie is on a date with Sam, who wouldn't want to come to her workplace on her night off. We wade through a sea of tables and order our drinks before settling into a booth at the back of the shop.

"Explain," she instructs me once we're seated with our lattes.

I give the briefest rundown that I can: I was Born in Boston, moved every six months or so, especially after Ma started volunteering, and once I'd grown to adulthood, I'd found a huge abandoned manor to haunt before my best friend had found me and invited me here.

I leave out the part about Zelie being a Medium, because I'm not sure how the twins feel about Mediums, and I don't know if Zelie wants her abilities advertised to every ghost I meet.

Eya and Wana silently take in my story before tag-teaming theirs. Both of their parents were ghosts. After they were Born, their mother, afraid of repercussions once she realized they were aging, went immediately into the Unknown. Their father was a military ghost, and they'd stayed with him. They, like me, moved regularly.

"We lived in Japan for a little bit when we were really young, but mostly stuck to the U.S. after that," Eya explains. "Dad wanted to be state-side in case...in case anyone found out what we were."

"Yeah, then we just moved to random towns that he knew had bases or hospitals he could volunteer in once we were old enough, and that's how we ended up in Middletown." Wana looks at me sheepishly. "We never wanted to leave, just so you know."

I feel all the feelings of abandonment rushing back at once and my stupid eyes start leaking again. "You...you didn't?"

"Of course we didn't, Abby," Eya takes my hand in both of hers. "We loved you, and when we got to Jamaica and Dad told us we weren't coming back, we begged, pleaded, and fought."

Wana nods her agreement. "Middletown was the first place where we ever actually felt at home. Hanging out with you and Anabel and Ethan and the others..." she looks out the window, clearly trying to shake the wistful expression from her face. "We barely spoke to Dad for weeks after we left."

"Why did he make you leave?" I'm both afraid, and Dying, to know the answer.

They share another nervous look. "He..." Wana starts, "he was nervous about how close we were getting to our friends there. He said it was only a matter of time before we let it slip that we'd been Born, and that that could have dangerous consequences that he wouldn't risk."

I'm not exactly surprised, because that was Ma's attitude too. "So, you didn't *want* to go? Because when you left, I...," my cheeks warm, "I blamed myself a lot. I thought you left because you hated it there."

"Hated it there? Are you crazy?!" Eya chuckles, a soft, semi-sarcastic noise, "that was our favorite place we've ever been."

"So, what have things been like for you since Middletown?" I ask. They haven't said anything about their adulthoods yet.

I can't believe we are all experiencing *adulthood*.

Wana answers my question as Eya excuses herself to go get us another round of coffees. "Honestly, we've kept up with the routine of moving regularly, even though we haven't stayed with our Dad in a long time, other than for short visits. We came to Atlanta because we hadn't been here yet. There's a hotel down the street that's closed for renovations, but they're only doing a floor at a time—so we have completely furnished hotel rooms that no one ever checks."

Eya returns, handing out the coffees. She's opted for caramel macchiatos, and the hot drink warms my hands through the cup. Over the next few hours, our conversation is light, but not meaningless. We're making up for lost years, relearning each other's personalities. They'd had significant others over the years, but never anything too serious, because of the aging.

Aging ruined everything for them, just as it had for me. They'd taken jobs that paid under-the-table to have spending money, but were always prepared to run at a moment's notice.

I confess that I'd never gotten close enough to anyone to have ever had a romantic relationship, and how much that hurts me. Leaving out the part about how I read over a Living's shoulder, I tell them about my love of books, and how all I want is to be the Main Character in some fantasy novel, with a morally grey warrior who is completely obsessed with me—after we spend some time as enemies, of course. We all laugh at that, and at how we each have our own alternative reality we'd accept, fully, the second it was offered if we could: Eya wants to Exist in a mafia manga, and Wana would rather be part of a Netflix dramedy.

Before I know it, the sky is that hazy grey that falls just after dusk, when it's not quite dark yet but the Sun has fled for the other side of the world. We all know that we eventually have to part, but we purposefully drag our feet as we exit Jittery Java. "I'm really glad I ran into you guys," I tell them nervously.

"So are we," Wana reciprocates as I hug them both tight. "We aren't going anywhere, by the way."

I unclench my jaw—I didn't even realize that I'd clamped it down, or that my shoulders were so tense until she says they're staying.

Eya squeezes me one more time as we make plans to meet up for dinner a few days from now. We exchange numbers, and I leave thanking the gods that I looked out my window when I did—I might have missed them, and might never have found out that I am not actually alone.

What the *hell*?

I'm not actually alone?

I walk down the long, bright hallway towards the apartment, musing over the new mystery ahead: just how many Born ghosts are out there?

And what were our parents so afraid of?

I gnaw my lip as I think over all that I'd learned I'd been wrong about, and am readying myself to tell Zelie everything when I approach the apartment door and realize it's slightly ajar. *That's odd...* I think to myself as I toe the door open before choking on a gasp.

The entire apartment has been ransacked. From the door I can see that the foyer table had been broken in half, and there are strange reflections glittering across the wall; the gold mirror has been shattered, its pieces littering the floor and casting a sinister glow around the room. I can see the couch cushions tossed about the room, as if they'd been thrown haphazardly.

I rush in on tiptoes, knowing that if the burglars are still there, I can go invisible and they won't be able to find me easily. I silently thank the gods that none of my roommates are supposed to be home yet, but I hear a strange, mewling sound coming from the kitchen. Tripping over the wood shards of what were once the stools set beneath the kitchen island, I stumble towards the cabinet that is the source of the crying, and find that it's being held closed by a 10 pound bag of flour. I kick the bag out of the way, sending a spray of dust into the air as the door flies open, a frantic Luna leaping out and leaving nothing but a hiss in her wake.

I don't see the paper until I turn, my gaze following Luna. She skitters around the room and past the couch, where a piece of paper has been skewered into a couch cushion with a kitchen knife. I approach it slowly, feeling the cold prick of fear sliding down my spine and landing like a stone in my gut.

I pick up the page, which holds only a photo of me during one of the Halloween "seances" at Halcyon Hall. Impossible. I'd been in my invisible form the entire time...how could anyone have gotten a picture of me?

My fingers start to tingle and my vision blurs at the edges as I scan the rest of the page, which only holds three words:

Abby Gale. Born.

I flip it over, trying to make sense of what I'm seeing, when I notice—too late—the arms coming around me in my peripheral and feel the knife point at the base of my throat.

"I know what you are. If you want to see your roommates again, you'll do as I say."

15

"Who are you?" I grunt through my teeth. "What do you want?"

The voice—male, deep and husky—chuckles next to my ear, so close that I can feel warm breath tickle the back of my ear.

It's utterly revolting, violating.

My back is pressed to his hard chest, and I can feel solid muscles everywhere my body touches his. I'd never been able to get close enough to trust anyone else to be *this* close to my body. I feel bile rise in my throat as he replies.

"You don't need to be afraid. Or, maybe you do, I don't know." The fantasy reader in me notes his faintly English accent and the combined scents of leather, sandalwood, and the tang of sweat.

"What do you want?!" I scream, hoping that it might rouse a neighbor...anyone who can either help me or call the police. He only chuckles again, tightening his grip around me and pressing the knifepoint deeper into my neck until I feel my skin tear ever so slightly beneath it.

"Look," he breathes against my neck, "I have my orders to bring you in. So you can scream. You can cry. You can fight if you consider yourself brave; although you'd lose very, *very* quickly. You can beg a little if you think it'll help you—I might even enjoy that." My stomach twists at the implication. "But this will all end the same way. You, coming with me. Me, handing you over."

"Handing me over to who, exactly?" Talking presses my neck deeper into the knifepoint, but it's worth the risk. Maybe if I keep him talking...what? Zelie will come home and be in danger, too? I balk at the thought of Zelie being here, being in this same danger.

I don't want that.

I won't allow that.

"You'll find that out soon enough." He takes a step back, but his grip around me hasn't slackened. I strain my eyes downwards and choke back a sob as I realize that there are ropes binding my arms to my torso.

"Who are you?" I ask again, resigning myself to the fact that he clearly has the upper hand; acknowledging to myself that I will have to find a way to talk myself out of this. I'm certainly in a fight-or-flight situation, but physically fighting is impossible, and would lead to nothing but more of my blood being spilled. This fight will have to be psychological if I have any chance of finding a way out of this.

I feel the hot, angry tears flowing down my cheeks, even as he pulls the knife from my throat. "Ryden Pengrave. Lieutenant of the Brotherhood of Reapers." I spin quickly on my heels, stunned at his words, and promptly stumble. He sticks out a hand and catches me by the arm, around the ropes, which bite into my skin roughly.

"Reapers? You're a Reaper?"

"Yes," he slides the blade back into a sheath on his chest, "now it's time to go."

He steps into a sliver of moonlight to grab what I assume is his pack and I fall backwards again, blessedly landing against the couch and regaining my balance.

He's the man I'd seen at Halcyon...the man I'd found snarling at me from across the Skull. Up close, even in the moonlight, I can see that his eyes are a startlingly deep shade of blue, with slight flecks of gold around the irises. He has an oblong, but slightly heart shaped face with a strong nose and angular jawline that is speckled with stubble. His reddish brown hair is curly, clearly trained over time to sweep away from his face.

He snatches the page up from where it had fluttered back to the couch and holds it up to me, comparing my face to the printed likeness. He knows it's me; he's only doing this to mock me. Clearly, I can't deny it's me even as my entire being is screaming for me to do something—anything—to get out of this predicament. He steps towards me again and I stiffen instinctively.

I try to dig my heels into the floor, try to make myself as heavy as possible, bracing myself. Even though I'm not exactly a small girl, he appraises me with a predator's confidence.

"Go where?" I finally get the courage to ask.

He sighs. "Twenty questions isn't going to save you, love."

A sudden, fleeting idea comes to my mind; a glimmer of hope in the bleakness. I have rights. I can't just be taken into custody without a word of explanation. I haven't done anything wrong...I'd just been *Born*. That was more out of my control than anything else I've ever experienced...right?

"Shouldn't...shouldn't I get a phone call? Before I'm...taken in?" I flinch at how shaky my voice is.

He pauses, eyes meeting mine, before he barks out a sarcastic laugh.

"I'm serious...I," oh gods I'm going to lose my nerve. Or my lunch. Or both. "I want my phone call."

"Oh, darling," he croons. "I am not some common human cop, hauling in petty criminals and gnawing on donuts. I am a *Reaper*.

There are no 'rights' to be read when it comes to..." he falters imperceptibly, "to oddities and abominations," he finishes as his eyes sweep over me from head to toe.

His disgust at my Existence is palpable.

My blood turns to ice at his admission even as he continues.

"You can either walk out of here, or I will drag you," he promises.

The tears continue to leak from my eyes as the gravity of my situation hits me full on. No one is coming to save me from this. No one *can* save me now that the Reapers know I Exist. He steps up to face me, not quite looking me in the eye.

"Are you afraid?" His grin is menacing as he whispers, "because I would love it if you were afraid. I need you to be so, *so* afraid, Abby." He reaches up to cup my cheek in his hand, the lightest of caresses, so at odds with his words.

"*Please*," I whisper, seeing the window of opportunity to get out of this situation closing on me.

He responds by stepping towards me and hoisting me over a shoulder as if I am no more than a ragdoll, and that window slams shut.

"Why are you doing this?!" I plead, defeated, his shoulder jutting uncomfortably into my abdomen. "What did I do to you?"

"That's enough questions for now," he commands, sounding almost pained, and I know that he won't be giving me any more information.

I know two things as this lean, powerful *creature* drops me in the backseat of a waiting vehicle before slamming the back door and climbing into the driver's seat.

One: he has all but admitted to not being human. "*I am not some common human cop.*" Then what *is* he? I'd always assumed, maybe stupidly, that what Ma had told me was right. That Reapers are humans like the rest of us—just a different variant: Living, ghosts, Reapers. I kick myself over my own ignorance; I know that Death is an entity all to itself, but it's glaringly obvious now that Death's minions wouldn't be entirely human. How could they be, if they're called to ferry souls from this Existence to the Unknown?

Two: I am utterly terrified. In the span of mere minutes, I've found my home ransacked, released that hellish cat from the cupboard, been kidnapped, and called an *abomination*. I am physically exhausted and traumatized when I have another fleeting thought. I am a *ghost* for goodness' sake—what am I doing in a crumpled heap in the back of a car being driven to the gods know where for the gods know what? In my invisible form, I could easily manipulate solids to travel through them—walls, doors, I'd stepped through them all.

Why should this scenario be any different?

I close my eyes, trying with all my might to keep from laughing out loud lest my captor notice too soon, and go invisible. Or—I try to.

I am...still solid?

"*What the hell?*" I whisper to myself, baffled as I try, and fail, to go invisible again.

"Oh by the way," my captor calls from the front seat. "The ropes are warded. There's no getting out of them by switching your form." He chuckles to himself as if he's a career comedian.

"Well, that's just fantastic!" I yell, causing him to laugh again. I relax all my muscles; fighting against my restraints has only made them feel tighter. There is nothing I can do as I await my fate...whatever that's going to be.

Minutes or hours later, I'm not sure, I feel the vehicle pull to a stop. I shoot up, only noticing then that my restraints have loosened slightly, and peek out the window. We're outside of what appears to be the shell of an empty warehouse. I can see huge steel beams that frame the structure, holding up thin metal walls that have all seen better days. Rust coats almost every surface in my line of sight, and the roof and walls are covered in jagged holes that expose the glistening night sky above.

The door I've been leaning against is suddenly opened and I tumble out, landing with a thud on the gravel. The tiny rocks bite into my skin through my clothes and bindings, snagging as I struggle to sit upright.

Somehow, miraculously, my bindings feel even looser, as if I could wriggle out of them if given the chance. I only have one shot, and I have to make it count. My Existence may very well depend on the choices I make in the next few moments. As much as my mind is screaming for me to *run, run, RUN*, my gut tells me to wait until my captor—Ryden—is distracted.

I will not let this man force me into the Unknown.

"Where are you taking me?" I ask again, putting as much venom into my voice as I can muster as I look up at him from my position on my knees in the gravel.

He sighs and steps towards me as I scream. "Don't touch me!"

"Relax," he sighs as he places a hand on each of my arms, pulling me to a standing position just as a "hey!" rings out from behind me.

"Damnit," Ryden mutters as his eyes land on the source of the noise, just over my shoulder. I can hear heavy footsteps rushing towards me and I pray that they are the steps of a friend and not another foe.

"Hey! What the hell are you doing?! Let her go!" the unidentified voice growls.

I twist, taking in the newcomer: he's about six feet tall and hugely muscular, easily double Ryden's bulk while being a good half a foot shorter. I note that his clothing is at odds with the spring weather: he's bundled in all black, a beanie pulled down low over his ears, and a scarf wound around his face so that only the skin of his hands and around his eyes show a deep, warm, sepia brown.

"Are you okay?" he calls to me in a heavily Southern accent as Ryden approaches him, his stance clearly that of someone preparing for a fight. The newcomer apparently isn't one to back down from a challenge, because he also braces to brawl.

My savior throws the first punch, uppercutting Ryden, who shocks me by remaining standing. This newcomer is *huge*, but clearly the corded muscles I'd felt earlier aren't just for show: Ryden's lithe, muscular frame is somehow equally matched with this brute's.

Ryden returns a fist, this time sinking a punch into the newcomer's stomach. The air whooshes out of his mouth in a gust, then he is back up and returning blows.

Forgetting my bindings, I turn to run and they loosen even more, cascading from my arms to land in a loose tangle around my waist. I take a second, one singular heartbeat, to stare in confusion at the ropes that fall to my feet before I'm in motion, tearing as far away from this cursed warehouse as I can possibly get.

I have no idea where I am, or where I'm going, but I know I have to put as much distance between myself and Ryden—a non-human Reaper—as I can. I can still hear the two men brawling, but it fades as I run, the only sound becoming my shoes slapping against the pavement.

Ice-cold dread shoots down my spine as I remember that Ryden is *not human* and a *Reaper*...and I'd just left my unwitting savior in his sights. I have an all-consuming survival instinct, but I would also go to the Unknown before I could leave an innocent Living to whatever fate had awaited me in that warehouse. I skid to a halt, spinning on my heels. I take a few steps back towards the warehouse and am sucking in a breath preparing to scream out a warning to my savior, but the scene before me steals that breath from my lungs.

Where Ryden and the newcomer had been sparring only moments before, there now stands...*nothing*?

The warehouse is there, as is the car, but both fighting males are gone.

I run, lungs screaming, until I find an open convenience store.

Thankfully, we hadn't actually driven far from the apartment, but I call an Uber to avoid being out on the streets—just in case Ryden is out looking for me.

Has he gone back to the apartment?

Is he there now, waiting for me?

Does he have one, or all, of my roommates?

Fear holds me in its grip as the minutes pass waiting for the driver.

On the way back to the apartment, I start to formulate a plan. First and foremost, I am moving out immediately. I cannot, I *will not*, risk Zelie, Em, and Amarie. I will not allow whatever problems could come from my being Born put them at risk. It isn't fair of me, especially since Em and Amarie don't even know that I Exist. Zelie has done too much by being my friend and offering me a home, and I will love her forever for it, but it isn't their fight. Even if I have no idea what—or why—I'm fighting, I'll do it alone.

But *why* does Ryden, why do the *Reapers*, care that I was Born?

Dread coats my bones as the word echoes through my brain.

Born.

Ryden has come for me because I was *Born.*

Will Eya and Wana be next?

I have to warn them the second I get back to my phone, which had been lost in the melee of our—their—Living room. I laugh humorlessly at the irony of the common term: "Living room." Why did I think that I could ever Exist in a space that had a "Living room" when I was not—nor have I ever been—a Living?

I climb out of the Uber, using Zelie's account and the driver's phone to pay. I'd set up a digital bank account in her name to hold all the money I'd earned working for Xeta, and I'll need to send her all of the information she'll need to access the money I'd been saving to help with rent and expenses for the apartment.

I won't need it where I'm going...back to somewhere like Halcyon.

Back to somewhere that my Existence doesn't put anyone else in danger.

16

Zelie's relieved shriek could wake the Dead.

"Abby!" she cries as she slams into me in the apartment building's lobby, wrapping me in the tightest embrace.

"Oh, thank the gods you're okay!" She pulls away, scanning me up and down for injuries. "I got home and found the apartment ransacked and a photo of you," she lowers her voice to a whisper, "with a note about you being Born. Luna was out of her entire mind and you were gone and I just..." she whimpers before a sob rattles her entire body. "Abby, I was so worried about you."

I tut-tut and there-there her as we make our way upstairs to the apartment, doing what I can to help her calm down enough for me to fill her in on what happened, which I do quickly. I tell her about finding Luna locked in a cupboard, about Ryden being here, and the knife. I instinctively reach for my neck, and can feel a patch of dried blood where the pinprick cut had been. In a few days, there won't even be a scar.

I tell her about how I'd been tied up and thrown in the back of a car and taken to a warehouse, and I tell her about the mystery savior showing up and quite possibly saving me from...what, I didn't know. I tell her that my ropes loosened with my movements and I was able to run.

I tell her about how I'd remembered that Ryden was a Reaper and that I'd turned to warn the stranger, only to find them both gone.

We pad down the long hallway back to the apartment, and I take it in one last time. Even though I've obviously never met any of our—their—neighbors, I still know about them. There's crotchety old Mrs. Crabapple who hates everyone but her poodle, Mitzi. I'll miss hearing the roommates ranting about how she's reported them to Em's dad *again*, because she's forgotten that *Em's dad is her landlord*. Then Nadira is across the hall. She's a labor and delivery nurse who works long hours, and has a hijab to match every outfit. I've always envied how effortlessly put together she always seems, even when I know she's in such a demanding line of work. The Brouchards are next door to Nadira, and are Canadian transplants who migrated south one winter and couldn't bring themselves to go back to the climate in Winnipeg. They're the kind of neighbors you borrow sugar from, where you borrow spite from Mrs. Crabapple and have a charcuterie night with Nadira.

The apartment across from the Brouchards' is a mystery. We know someone lives there, but he comes and goes so rarely that it's like he isn't there at all. Zelie and I assume he's some international super spy, but she's only seen him once and can't actually remember anything about him.

I'm yanked from my reverie when Zelie opens the apartment door and Luna bolts towards us, unleashing a shrieking hiss before winding her way through my feet and...purring?

This cat *hates* me...why is she purring?

"She was as worried as I was," Zelie explains, scooping Luna up and cradling her close.

It hits me then: there is no one in the apartment other than Zelie, Luna, and me. "Wait...there aren't any police here. Did you not call 911?"

"I didn't have a chance! I got home, found all this," she gestures around as we step into the ravaged remains of our once stunning Living room, "and went running downstairs to see if I could see where you'd gone."

I puzzle, gnawing on my lower lip.

"Do we call the police?" I decide that I'll defer to Zelie's wishes, but I can see both pros and cons for involving Living law enforcement. For one, we would have to remove the paper with my photo and name, and I'd have to either go invisible or leave while they were here—which I don't want to do: I can't leave Zelie alone to deal with the mess before I leave for good.

We also can't exactly tell them that a Reaper had come in looking for a ghost who was Born a ghost, so it would have to be a common break in. It would be a lot of time and resources wasted when we know there isn't some petty thief to blame.

On the other hand, however, Em and Amarie may *want* law enforcement to be involved since they don't know anything other than the world of the Living. To them, this would be a random break in. My stomach hurts to think about their space—their home—being violated... not only by a Reaper, but by *me* in the first place.

"Leeeeet me talk to the other girls, first," she pleads. "I just texted them, and they'll both be here any minute."

"I'll be in my room," I sigh.

This will give me an opportunity to pack what little things I can take with me—clothes and shoes, and half-used toiletries.

"Abby..." she calls as I cross the threshold to my bedroom. I turn, the exhaustion of literally being kidnapped crashing over me like a wave, promising to draw me under any second. "It's going to be alright."

I smile at her, half heartedly, wondering how on earth that could ever be true.

I know when Em and Amarie are home by the surprised shrieks at the destruction they find.

I must have fallen into an exhausted half-Trance, clutching my knees to my chest on my—their—bed, because I vaguely hear muted voices before a shrill, "what?!?" rings out, followed immediately by footsteps pounding down the hallway towards my door. Panicking, I snap into my invisible form just as Amarie flings the door open. Em and Zelie follow closely on her heels. Em's face is a mix of awed curiosity and Zelie's is nervous apprehension, but Amarie?

Amarie is *furious.*

"Where?" Amarie demands, crossing her arms and turning to scowl at Zelie. Even in my invisible form I am frozen, paralyzed with fear... again.

"Abby, it's okay," Zelie says, meeting my eyes, the only one in the room who could actually see me. "They know. You can let them see you."

"What are you doing?!" I think frantically at Zelie.

"I'm doing what I should have done months ago, Abby," Zelie responds out loud. To Amarie and Em, she explains, "Abby can't believe I told you. She's," she pauses briefly and I know she's gauging my emotions by the look on my face. Curse her for knowing me so well.

Curse me for letting her.

"She's terrified. She's been through a lot tonight, and this is only going to add to her stress, but...it's necessary. It's overdue, and it's necessary. Abby, let them see you." Her eyes haven't left mine.

"Yes, please come out," Em calls, much louder than is actually needed, her eyes flickering back and forth across the ceiling wildly, "if we are friends, I'd like to be a part of it, too." A dimple appears above her lip, her bright blue-green eyes twinkling with a mischief that is entirely Em. I can feel her sincerity; she is genuinely ready to meet me, and is open to friendship with a ghost.

Amarie, on the other hand...

"I just need you to know how *ridiculous* this entire thing is," Amarie has a bit of a temper, and she's letting it show. "You could have told us that you were here from the start instead of *lying* to us. And now, if you're going to be our roommate, the *least* you could do is have the guts to face us."

I let out a sigh. She's right.

I brace myself, preparing to shift back to my solid form when Luna winds her way through their legs and leaps up onto my bed, curling herself into a perfect round ball atop my legs.

I shift to my solid form and Amarie's and Em's eyes shoot to me. Em's face lights with childlike delight while Amarie's gaze is more careful, more appraising. We all sit together in stunned silence, each waiting for one of the others to break the silence.

"Well," Amarie's cool tone slices through the tension without breaking it, "you certainly don't *look* like a ghost." She smiles, tentatively at first, and I know in that moment that my response matters.

If I say something cutting, it could lead to a larger rift than the one we all currently stand across...the one Zelie and I had created in the apartment the moment I agreed to move in without telling the others I was here.

"I..." I stammer, "I'm sorry...to disappoint?" At the last second, I shoot up my tone on the end of the phrase, turning it into a question.

She laughs then, genuinely. "I mean, it's kind of disrespectful. If we're going to have an apartment ghost, I'd have wanted it to be someone dripping in blood and communicating only in shrieks or something." She sniffs dramatically and surveys her black coffin shaped fingernails. "I guess you'll do."

Em pounces on the bed then, laying her head on the pillow beside me. "Hi roomie! I'm Em!"

I launch myself out of the bed, upsetting Luna who hisses as she scrambles to land on her feet. I shake my head and wave my hands like a maniac. "No. No, no, no...*no*." Em jumps back like she's been shocked.

"*No?*" Amarie asks. "No...what?"

"Did I spook her?" Em eyes Zelie warily.

"No," I go on. "No, we aren't roomies. We *were* roomies. I'm so sorry that Zelie and I lied to you, and I'm sorry for mooching off of you, truly. I have saved every penny that I possibly could to repay you for rent, toiletries, any food I ate, and utilities while I was here. It's all yours, and it's in Zelie's name already so getting to it won't be a problem."

All three of them are looking at me as if *now* is the weird thing, and not the thing that happened moments ago, when I appeared from thin air sitting on a bed in their home with Amarie's cat purring gently on my lap.

Em shoots a nervous glance at Zelie. "I'm not computing here, Zelie. What is going on with her?"

Zelie crawls onto the bed beside me, putting her hands on both of my shoulders and meeting my eyes. "Abby, talk to me. What's going on? What are you saying?"

"I'm saying that I can't be your roommate anymore."

Don't cry. Don't cry. Don't cry.

"Why in hell not?" Zelie asks, her tone sharpening. Zelie doesn't get angry often, so this is surprising.

"Did you miss the part where our—your—apartment was ransacked because of *me*? What if one of you had been home when...when he..." I crumple, falling to the ground in a sobbing heap of tears and snot.

As if it's one fluid motion, all three of them are on me in an instant:

the second group hug I'd ever experienced in my entire Existence. They sit with me in silence for a moment, allowing me the space to feel what I need to, and that unexpected support lifts my mood strangely quickly. When I've calmed down enough to regain control of my mind, Em, head resting on my shoulder, says, "I'm not sure what you mean by this being your fault, but girlfriend, I don't think you are the only one of us with secrets."

She lifts her head, meeting Amarie and Zelie's eyes, each for a brief moment, before turning to find mine. "I think it's time for a roomies tell-all."

The digital clock on the stove flashes 12:15 AM as we clear the dining table of debris and take seats around it.

Em busies herself in the kitchen making us mugs of English Breakfast tea, joking that "if we're all going to spill the tea, we might as well drink some, too." While she pours, Amarie unearths a plastic container full of sugar cookies she had left over from a vendor event the previous weekend. We don't bother with plates or napkins; we'll be cleaning up the mess of the apartment soon, and a few cookie crumbs will be the least of our worries.

I'd decided that I would leave as soon as the apartment was cleaned up, and everything broken was replaced. I can't in good conscience leave before that, knowing that their home being a disaster zone is my fault. I sigh quietly, resigning myself to be the Hag of Halcyon Hall forever, and feel the pit in my stomach grow at the thought.

I'm going to become a Poltergeist.

I shiver as the terror traces its talons down my spine.

"Okay," Em starts. It's clear that she's to be the peacemaker. "I'll start." She takes in a deep breath, letting it out in a long whoosh. "I... am an Empath."

Amarie lets out a sarcastic snort. "That's it? That's your big 'secret'?" She seems almost offended, as if Em's admission had called her out in some way. "Sorry to break it to you, Em, but we are all empathetic."

Em shakes her head, smiling softly. "I didn't say I was *empathetic*. I said that I am an *Empath*. A true Empath."

Zelie gasps, her hand covering her mouth. "Oh my gods, how did I not see it? You totally are!"

"What's an Empath?" I ask, feeling stupid for not knowing.

"I feel others' emotions," Em starts, eliciting another eye roll from Amarie, "but it's more than that. I can...manipulate those emotions."

Amarie's jaw drops then.

"*What?*" she breathes.

Em nods emphatically. "So, if tensions are high, I can kind of... alleviate it. Or if someone is overly excited and stressing everyone out I can...level out everyone's moods."

I nibble on a cookie, too anxious to add to the conversation.

"You're so full of it," Amarie laughs, a little too loudly, as if she thinks her laughter will make Em's words untrue.

"Am I, though?" Em asks, raising her brows. "I just did it in Abby's room ten minutes ago." She brings her mug of tea to her lips, sipping gently.

"*No!*" Zelie whispered, her features blanketed in awe.

"What did...how did you...what?" Amarie stutters.

"You were big mad when Zelie told us Abby was here, and it was giving me a headache. So I just..." Em looks away slyly. "I toned down your anger when Abby appeared."

Zelie nods in agreement. "You know, now that you mention it, her anger did go from here," she holds her hand up above her head, "to here," she drops her hand in front of her chest, "really fast."

"Ya," Em winks. "You're welcome."

"So can you do that with anyone?" I ask timidly.

Truth be told, I'm fascinated. I've never met an Empath before. Granted, I haven't met a lot of people, but...Em is someone with abilities that I could *actually* talk to.

"I mean, I need to be in a close proximity to them, but yes," Em beams, quickly rubbing her fingers together to clear them of sugar cookie dust. "And it's not a person-by-person basis...I can manipulate all of the emotions in a small room if I want. It helps a lot if I'm in a bar and a fight breaks out, or when I find out that I have a secret extra roommate. I don't like to do it without permission, but...desperate times called for...well..." She smiles down at her tea.

"I'm a Medium," Zelie pipes up, "but everyone here already knew that," she teases, playfully elbowing me in the rib before turning her gaze on Amarie. "Alright, Amarie. It's your turn. Tell them your secret."

Em's incredulous eyes dart from Zelie to Amarie as Zelie's words registered. "Wait, you know Amarie's secret already? What the heck, guys?" she whines. "Has *everyone* been keeping their secret from just me?"

"To be fair," Amarie raises a defensive finger in the air, "I didn't think Zelie would believe me, and only told her since she's a Medium. I figured she had one foot in the paranormal world, so at worst she'd laugh me off."

"What is it?" Em is hanging on the edge of her seat in anticipation. "Oh, tell me, c'mon Amarie!"

"Fine, fiiiiine," Amarie giggles. "I'm a witch."

It's Em's turn to sigh and roll her eyes. "Really, Amarie, what is your real secret?"

My eyes dart between them like I'm watching the most riveting game of ping pong to have ever been played. (No shade to Forrest Gump.)

"I'm really a witch! Scout's honor!" Amarie raises three fingers in the air to show off the sincerity in her words as Luna jumps onto the tabletop in front of her. She lovingly scratches behind the cat's ears for a moment before continuing. "I am a witch, and Luna here is my Familiar." Luna purrs her agreement.

I gape.

"No possible way," I say. "There is no way that cat is your Familiar, and you also didn't know I was here. She's known I was here from day one, and has hated me up until...well, today."

"I don't know what kind of weird TV you've been watching," Amarie turns to me, still not fully on board with me especially after learning that Em's power had forced her to tone her anger down, "but we don't communicate with words. It's not like she could have said, 'hey, there's a strange invisible girl down the hall,'" she says, giving Luna a comical, sing-song voice, "we can just sense each other, and are very protective of each other. So, if you thought Luna hated you, it's because I didn't know you were here and she was trying to keep you...at bay, to protect me."

I have to admit, it makes sense. "Why, then," I have to ask, "did she circle my legs and purr when Zelie and I got back to the apartment this evening? And you were mad when you came into my—" I choke, "the spare room where I was, but she jumped right into my lap and fell asleep."

"I guess she's learned enough about your aura to trust you. And maybe the lap thing was her way of telling me that I can." Amarie sniffs.

She isn't exactly sold yet—which is fine.

Em raps on the table, startling us all. "I'm going to need more information about this whole 'being a witch' thing. Can you fly? Do you have a broom?"

Amarie scoffs, "No, I don't have a broom, Em. I just have some abilities. I can't like, use my witchy power to kill people," she says sarcastically, "but if there's something that can be done magically to make Life easier," she winks, "then I can pretty much do it. I don't need a wand or anything," she says quickly, before Em can ask it, "but I can do magic. It's why my baking business goes so well—because I perfect everything with actual magic."

"I say this in the most loving way possible," Em's eyes have that mischievous, totally Em gleam again, "but *prove it*."

Amarie sighs, leaning back into her chair with a soft *plop*. "Fine."

She twists her wrist lazily and the apartment erupts into motion. Em and I dive from our chairs, Zelie and Amarie collapsing instead into a sea of giggles at our reactions.

From every corner of the open space, things are moving. Books that had toppled from the bookcases during Ryden's destruction are flipped back onto the shelves, organizing themselves neatly. The shards of glass from the shattered foyer mirror sparkle before forming a perfect mirror once more. Dishes that had been flung from cabinets whiz through the air, landing neatly back into their cupboards, and the bag of flour I'd kicked to free Luna refills and seals itself. The couch cushion, once maimed by Ryden's blade, stitches itself back together.

Em and I clutch each other as we peer out from beneath the table.

We would have aced "Duck and Cover" lessons if we'd been Born a few decades earlier.

My stomach drops again at the thought of my being Born.

In a matter of seconds and the flick of a single wrist, Amarie has set the apartment back into perfect order, as if Ryden hadn't been there at all. Despite my roiling stomach, I am awestruck.

"Whyyyyyy did you never tell me you could do that?!" Em whines, reclaiming her seat at the table. "I have been cleaning around this place the old-fashioned way since we moved in!"

"I'm sorry," Amarie apologizes, clearly chagrined. "It's just...humans aren't supposed to know about me, or what I can do. It's—I'm— supposed to stay a secret. The paranormal *world* is supposed to stay a secret." She hangs her head, and I feel my resolve land even as a lump forms in my throat.

I can't have them baring their souls before me and not do the same in return.

"Okay," I call out assertively. "My turn."

17

I tell them *everything*.

"I was Born a ghost," I whisper. "And for my entire Existence, literally up until today, I thought I was the only one."

Zelie bristles in her chair beside me. "You've never told me that," she whispers. Her tone is both hurt and slightly accusatory.

"I know, and I'm sorry." I turn to her, taking her hand in mine. "You've done so much for me, and I should have trusted you with it. I just...I was raised to never trust anyone, other than my mom. She was so afraid of what I was that she never let me get close to anyone. We moved a lot, and any time I made friends, we left."

I suddenly feel the overwhelming need to defend Ma.

"It wasn't her fault," I explain quickly, "she thought she was protecting me, but my childhood was...lonely. My entire Life has been lonely, up until I met Zelie and she brought me here."

I can't help it when huge tears start leaking from my eyes, dripping onto the newly cleaned table. I release Zelie's hand to dab my eyes with the end of my sleeve, buying myself time to think.

I weigh my next words carefully, because learned behaviors are not easy to suddenly forget. From the first second of my Existence, I'd been taught that my birth was a rarity, that I was the only one.

That I needed to run...hide...lie.

I feel, to my very core, the absolutely overwhelming urge to protect that notion—even if the logical side of my brain knows that I'm not actually the *only* one anymore. Could this next revelation be a betrayal? Could there be repercussions? I settle on giving the girls a half-truth.

"Earlier today, I—I learned that I may not actually be the only ghost to have been...Born." I glance at my hands as I wring them in my lap. "I don't want to say any more about that," I put my palms up in the air, feeling defensive again, "because it's not my story to tell. I just...ran into someone from my childhood that wasn't a child anymore, like me."

Em reaches across the table, tapping it gently in front of me, forcing me to meet her eyes. "Hey—that's allowed. You don't have to tell us anything that you don't feel comfortable saying—you just met us. It's okay not to trust us yet."

My stomach plummets as a sad, wistful smile forms on my face.

"That's the thing, Em. This situation is completely screwed up, because I *didn't* just meet you. Not really. You just met me, sure...but I've been here for months. I've slept in that room every night," I point down the hallway to my—the spare bedroom's—door. "I sat right there," I gesture to the kitchen island, "and binge watched *Housewives* with all of you. I read books over your shoulder, I ate your food, I..." I trail off as more tears fall, tracking huge and hot paths down my cheeks. "I've fallen in love with all of you, and you and Amarie had no idea I was even here and it's just so fucked up and I..." I pause to catch my breath, my nose leaking as Amarie flicks her wrist and a tissue appears in front of me.

None of them say a word, but the silence isn't exactly uncomfortable. They know I have more to say, and wait patiently for me to let my thoughts form the rest of what I need to get out.

"So today," I continue, finally, "I found out that I'm not actually the only Born ghost, and when I got back here, a Reaper was waiting for me." Amarie sucks in a gasp, her hand rising to cover her own mouth instinctively.

So, Zelie had told them about me, but not what had actually happened in the apartment.

"Yes," I confirm meeting Amarie's gaze, "a Reaper destroyed the apartment and locked Luna in the cupboard, because *I* was here. And I keep replaying this scenario over and over again in my head...*what if you'd been home?*" I'm sobbing now, and can't stop the flooding from my eyes.

Amarie snorts. She actually snorts. "Well, I know with certainty that if some Reaper had showed up when *I* was home, he'd rue the day he ever even saw our building." She grins at the table for a moment, lost in some daydream.

"Wait...*what*?" I ask, not sure I'd heard her right. It's clear she's never been on the receiving end of a Reaper's wrath.

"Abby," Amarie leans forward to place her elbows on the table, pursing her lips as she rests her chin on the tops of her interlocked fingers, "I mean this with all the love in the world that someone who just met you could have, okay? But have you ever once thought that your situation might not be universal?"

"What do you mean?" I ask her. I'm not sure what she's implying, but it stings nonetheless.

"I mean," she pulls one knee up to her chest, wrapping her arms around it, "you were this Born ghost whose mother all but hid her away, Rapunzel-style, right?"

I nod, which is her cue to continue. "So did you ever, for one teensy second, consider that a girl who was Born a ghost and hidden away for her entire Existence *might* not be a—" she swirls her hands in front of her, looking for the right words, "a *wealth* of information when it comes to the paranormal world?"

Em and Zelie nod their agreement.

"What are you saying?" I ask, still not grasping how this is relevant. A Reaper destroyed our apartment and kidnapped me—how does my knowledge of the paranormal come into play?

"Girl, what I'm saying is that Reapers are a dime a dozen." I stiffen and she rushes to recover. "I don't mean that what you went through wasn't terrifying," she clarifies, "that was absolutely traumatic, I'm sure. I'm just saying that Reapers, to *witches*, aren't exactly scary. They're like..." again, she pauses to find the right words, "oh! They're like Mediums or Empaths!" She gestures to Em and Zelie, who look as confused as I am.

"Wait so we are like Reapers?" Em asks indignantly.

"No, no, *ugh*," Amarie is clearly growing more frustrated by the moment. "I'm saying that to me, Mediums, Empaths, ghosts, and Reapers aren't strange. They're just...another paranormal entity, like me. Some of them you love, like I love you guys, and some of them you just—have mutual respect for. That's it. Witches and Reapers, and other supernatural beings, for that matter, have...mutual respect for each other. But back to Abby's original fear. If I had been here when the Reaper showed up, the situation would have been drastically different, because I am more...*evenly matched* with a Reaper. I could use magic to protect myself against them. Em could manipulate their mood to protect herself, too. You and Zelie would be the ones I'd worry about, far more than Em and me...and even then, Em and I would have been perfectly fine to protect both of you." She falls back against her chair, grinning at finally having made her point.

"Well, that isn't something that you'll have to worry about for much longer," I sniff, "because I'm leaving tonight."

Zelie rolls her eyes, loosing a long, dramatic sigh. "Abby, why? Why do you feel like you need to leave?"

"Because, Zelie! Because the Reaper was clearly after me! Because, ability to protect yourselves or not, you shouldn't *have* to protect yourselves in your own home, especially if my not being here could one-hundred-percent prevent it!"

"But see, that's the thing," Amarie says, pointing at me, eyes like fire, "say you do leave. Who will be there to protect *you*?"

I am admittedly moved by her concern, because I can't be concerned for myself. "That's sweet, Amarie, really. But I am not your, or Em's, or Zelie's problem to deal with. I'll hide out somewhere, move frequently, whatever I need to do to keep Ryden from finding me again."

"Wait," Amarie's head snaps toward me and she leans forward rapidly. "Did you say 'Ryden'? Like, Ryden Pengrave, Ryden? Super tall guy, reddish brown hair and blue eyes, ridiculously hot and overly rude and sarcastic?"

"Yeah..." I can feel my forehead creasing. "The Reaper said his name was Ryden."

This time, Amarie's indignation is palpable.

"Oh, I am going to *kill* that man and make him Reap himself!" Amarie hisses.

I believe her, too. Amarie doesn't strike me as someone to cross.

"Wait, you know Ryden?" I ask, clutching the table like a lifeline.

"We've had a few run-ins over the years." She arches a brow, making it clear that she is plotting her revenge. "The last time I saw him, he'd been assigned to Reap a ghost that was on the verge of becoming a Poltergeist. I was asked to be there to keep regular humans from suspecting that anything was going on. I basically had to ward the house so that, from the street, it looked and sounded vacant."

"You can do that?" Em asks, awestruck.

Amarie smirks. "This particular Poltergeist didn't exactly make it easy. I kept having to reinforce my spells to silence the screaming to anyone that wasn't inside the house."

I shudder. "The...screaming?"

"It was awful," she nods. "The Poltergeist in question was just coherent enough to remember that they were afraid of the Unknown, but so far gone that they were pretty feral. I'm amazed the house is still standing." She inspects her nails, something that is clearly a habit of hers, then pops a piece of sugar cookie into her mouth as if talk of feral Poltergeists is a normal, everyday topic of conversation.

"Wait," I interject, dread building deep in my gut. "I thought you had to *choose* to go into the Unknown. I didn't think that Reapers, or anyone, could *force* you to go."

Was that what Ryden planned to do to me?

I feel the bile rise in my throat and it takes every ounce of my willpower to force it down.

"For the most part, that's true. Most people spend a century or two as a ghost, then get tired or bored. They've been around to watch all of their loved ones Die, and they're ready to embrace the Unknown and go on to the next adventure. But some ghosts stay too long, and become...lost," she explains for Em's benefit. "That's the best way I can describe it. They're lost, aimless, merely Existing. And they've been that way for hundreds, even thousands of years until their humanity is gone. That's when Reapers of Ryden's caliber step in."

The pool of dread in me is cresting, and I know it will overflow soon if I don't focus on something else. Literally *anything* else. "So Ryden is..." I trail off, hoping Amarie will finish my sentence.

She does.

"Ryden has climbed up the ranks of Reapers, which is impressive for his age. He's got to be like, thirty-five at the most. He's one of the elite. So he doesn't only get assigned petty passings, like a little old lady choosing to go on to find her husband in the Unknown. Ryden also gets called for the difficult cases—the ones that don't want to go. The ones that might be dangerous."

I balk. "Then why is he after *me*?!"

It's silent for a beat before Zelie calls out the elephant in the room.

"It sounds like he's been called to Reap you," she whispers.

"But *why*?" I can't stop the tears that fall, and begin openly weeping. "What did I do? What *do* I do?"

Em has been silent for so long that I'd almost forgotten that she's here until she says, "It doesn't matter, Abby. Because we are simply not going to let the Reapers get you." Amarie and Zelie nod their agreement.

"And, I'm going to have a talk with Ryden," Amarie determines. "I'm going to let him know, that you are under the protection of a witch, an Empath, and a Medium, and that we are not to be trifled with."

It's really going to hurt to leave them.

"I can't stay here, Amarie. Not anymore." I sniff, tears still falling freely even as I dab at my eyes.

"Look, I understand your need to be all noble, Abby. I do. I understand why you feel like you need to go. But I need you to think, okay? Can you hear us out for a minute?" Zelie asks gently.

I can tell from her demeanor that her question is genuine. Her eyes are wide and hopeful, and she's reached back out to cup my hand in hers. She truly wants me to hear them out before making a decision, and I certainly owe her that much. I nod meekly and whisper out a feeble, "Fine."

"If you go back to somewhere like Halcyon," she says to me, then quickly turns to Amarie and Em, "a decrepit, falling apart old blight, might I add," she points out sharply before returning her gaze to me, "it is you versus a Reaper and it is only a matter of time before you *will* be found and forced into the Unknown—or worse." I feel utterly hollow at her last word, and its unspoken promise. Yes, I can imagine that there could be things vastly worse than going into the Unknown.

I study my lap, picking at the frayed end of my sleeve.

"But if you stay here," Em's voice is cheery, breathing Life back into the room, "we can help you."

"I can't put you all at risk."

Why don't they understand?

"At risk of what, exactly, Abby?" Amarie asks.

"Of him coming back! Of him taking you, or hurting you, or threatening you, to get to me!"

"Girl, we are all alive," Amarie says, trying her best not to sound condescending. "There isn't much a Reaper can do to us. Sure, he can try to overpower us physically, but what Ryden—or any Reaper—may have in strength, we have in our own abilities. We'd be pretty evenly matched. Well enough to confidently protect ourselves, and you. And before you go on with that whole '*you shouldn't have to protect yourselves or me*' tirade again, let me stop you. I am *begging* you to stay with us, because our Lives have been soooo boring. Adding the intrigue and drama of a Reaper after our roomie is just the kind of thing we need to...liven up the place."

Em agrees emphatically while a maniacal gleam shines in Amarie's eyes.

"You guys are sick, you know that?" I say, feeling the ghost of a smile.

Do I dare to stay?

"Besides," Zelie says cooly, "you're my best friend, Abby. I'm not just going to send you off to be slaughtered. I'd worry myself to Death, then *I'd* be the one dealing with Reapers!" A tiny giggle escapes my lips, which was her intention. "Seriously, Abby. Please stay with us. We all want you to."

"Really?" I whisper, afraid to hope. "You guys really want me to stay?"

"All in favor, say 'aye!'" Em jokes, but they all yell, "aye!" unanimously.

"That settles that. You're stuck with us." Amarie announces.

We sit around the table for a bit longer before finally deciding to retreat to our bedrooms just as the first hints of sunrise begin to watercolor the sky. As I fall into bed and immediately into a Trance, giving in to the exhaustion of the day, I can't help but wonder if my staying is the right thing to do, or if I am dooming us all.

18

I wake from the Trance the next morning, drenched in cold sweat. Visions of Ryden, the wrecked apartment, and the Living I left behind plagued me all night, and not even the light of a beautiful spring afternoon can untie the knots in my stomach.

No matter what Amarie, Em, and Zelie said, I'm still not sure I made the right decision by staying.

What if they aren't as strong as they think? What if they aren't a match for Ryden?

I'd seen, and felt, firsthand how powerful he is.

I fling off my comforter and retreat into the bathroom, thinking that maybe a shower will help. I catch a glimpse of myself in the mirror and wince. As I'd suspected the night before, the pinprick point where the knife tip pressed into my throat is nearly gone already, barely a blemish on my skin. A tiny scar that wouldn't Exist much longer isn't what takes me aback, though.

It's the sheer desperation in my eyes—they look haunted in a way they haven't since before I left Halcyon Hall.

That's why I chose to stay: because I am desperate to not be alone anymore.

I follow that train of thought as I shower, hating myself over it. *How can I be so selfish?* I am willingly risking the Lives of three people that I love, simply so I don't have to be alone.

Before I know it, I'm choking back sobs, gasping for air around the despair that traps me here in the shower. My stomach rolls, wave upon wave of nausea threatening to bring me under.

It isn't fair. None of this is fair.

I'd spent most of my Existence as a recluse, always taught to shy away from any contact, and now that I have actual friends, I can't let them go.

Selfish, selfish, selfish.

When every inch of me is pruny, I climb out of the shower and towel off, throwing on an old *Walking Dead* t-shirt (which I'd snagged at a

Goodwill because the irony of me wearing it had cracked me up) and some pajama shorts Zelie had given me in the weeks after I'd moved in. I go through the motions, slathering moisturizer on my face and brushing tangles out of hair because I know that as deeply sad as I am in this moment, future-me will appreciate the extra seconds of self-care.

I walk out of the bathroom, deciding that I'm going to get back into bed and wallow in self-pity some more, when a soft knock sounds at my door.

"Abby?" Em calls. "Can we talk?"

Em piles up beside me in my bed while I try, and fail, to avoid eye contact.

"Do you want to talk about it?" she finally asks. Her voice is soft, but I still jump.

"I don't know what there is to talk about that we didn't cover last night." I hate my tone, how cutting it sounds, as if I'm lashing out against her.

Maybe I am. I'm just *so* tired. Soul tired.

Em doesn't even flinch. "Abby, I can feel everything you're feeling and it's crushing. You've got to cut yourself some slack." Her eyes are earnest, and I trust that she speaks the truth, but her words add another layer of emotion to my mania: guilt.

I feel *guilty* that my depression is impacting her.

She screws up her face in confusion, and sighs. "You don't need to feel guilty about that. It's not your fault—I can feel *everyone's* emotions, all the time. I learned a long time ago not to let others' feelings impact *my* feelings. Don't worry—I'm fine. But I *am* worried about you." She sits up, grabbing a pillow and clutching it to her chest.

"Why?" I demand, again with the defensive tone. I take a breath and wait a beat before amending. "Why are you worried about me?" I ask more gently.

"Because you have been through so much in the past twenty-four hours. I would be near catatonic if I'd been through half of what you have. I can feel your fear, and your anxiety, and your grief, and your rage, and your guilt, and I want to help you sort through it all."

I bristle as a sudden thought crosses my mind. "I don't want you to use your abilities on me."

"I wouldn't do that without your permission—other than last night which was a high tension situation. You're allowed to feel your feelings, even if I wish you didn't feel some of them." She smiles softly, wistfully. "I'm not trying to take pain away from you...we *need* to feel pain to know that we are alive; we have to experience lows to fully appreciate the highs, just as much as we need to remember the highs to know that the lows are temporary."

"I just...I...I..." I feel the sob clawing its way out of my throat and try as I might, I can't stop it. Em doesn't bat an eye. She reaches out and gently presses her hand to my shoulder, firmly trailing it up and down my arm as if she can force the sobs out.

Damn if it doesn't work.

I wail, beating my pillow and crying hysterically for what feels like hours. Em stays, never leaving my side. Occasionally, she whispers *"that's good, let it out"* or *"it's all going to be alright,"* but otherwise, she does just what she'd promised: she lets me feel what I need to feel, without judgment, shame, or expectations.

Finally, once my voice is all but gone and my eyes are so swollen I can barely see, my crying ceases as quickly as it had come on.

"I am so, so sorry," I breathe, suddenly mortified.

Gods, I literally threw a tantrum in front of someone who hadn't known that I Existed until yesterday.

"No, no, that was great!" Em squeals, eyes bright. "You're already feeling better!"

She's right.

I still have all of my issues: I'm still terrified of what could have happened during my kidnapping, angry at Ryden for kidnapping me and also angry at Ma for conditioning me to be a recluse. I'm ashamed that I'd lied to Em and Amarie, and guilty for Em's having to feel my emotions. I'm lonely, I'm emotional, and I'm tired. All of that is still there, heavy in my chest, but it's no longer breaking my back. I'm not being dragged to the ground, the weight of my shame and fear and anguish so heavy that I can't bear it.

It's all still there, but I can stand, and I can breathe.

I use that breath, and the breaths that follow, to spill my entire heart out to Em. I tell her *everything*. I'd given the roommates my history the night before, but I hadn't told them about all of the broken parts of me: the abandonment I felt when the twins left, the betrayal I felt at my mother raising me to Exist completely alone, the empty loneliness I'd felt at Halcyon Hall, and how afraid I was that I would be Reaped now that I finally had a shot at *friends*.

She listens, and once I've told her the secrets only Zelie knew, she sits up abruptly.

"Now that you're feeling even better," which I am—she is *amazing*, "I think it's time we had a normal roomies night where you *actually* get to participate."

We eat pizza and watch old movies.

And they know—and are *happy*—that I'm here.

19

My roommates and I quickly settle into routines. We all have our different jobs, interests, and in Amarie, Em, and Zelie's cases, friends outside of the apartment, but we also spend plenty of time together.

We are couch potatoes on Monday nights for *This is Us*, sobbing hysterically every episode and relying on each other for moral support. We religiously observe Taco (and margarita) Tuesdays, and Thursdays are always pizza night. Weekends are a free-for-all, depending on who is working a shift, or has an event, or has to jet out of town. Even when that happens, there is always at least one other roommate around.

I haven't worked up the courage to introduce them yet, but in between working for Xeta and spending time with the roommates, I see Eya and Wana regularly. We meet up for coffees, walks through the park, dessert—anything we can do to blend in with the Living, even temporarily, we do, and we relish it. Together, we feel safer, as if there is power in our numbers; there are three of us, so a Reaper ambush is less likely.

Of course, I'd filled Eya and Wana in after Ryden's attack, so they are also constantly on their guard. We can't know that the Reapers aren't also trailing them.

Apartment Life is as close to bliss as I've ever dared to hope for, even with the looming threat of Reapers always hovering over me: a cloud that I can sometimes, for the briefest of moments, almost pretend doesn't Exist.

I'm also introduced to my roommates' friend Nels, who instantly becomes another one of my favorite people on earth.

They have soft brown hair that is close-cropped on the sides and back, with longer locks atop their head that sweep back away from their face in a loose pompadour style. Their deep tanned skin is flawless—it's clear that they have a rigorous skincare routine—and their sense of style is immaculate: seventies bohemian meets chic in a whirlwind of high waisted, brightly colored linen trousers, printed satin shirts unbuttoned dangerously low, and jackets of the finest faux-fur no matter the weather. They are the Life of the party, the very *soul* of the party, always leading the crusade to start a dance-off or Conga line.

Even though they are the most sought-after person in the room, Nels is also warm and inviting to have a conversation with—and not just a small-talk, surface level chats. Nels is a scholar, and relishes deep conversations about politics, history, and the arts. They always make me feel like I'm the only person in the room; the effect on, and respect they show to, everyone they encounter. Their impish grin is utterly infectious, and I take to Nels immediately.

I don't think I'll ever deserve the amount of people that I *finally* have in my corner.

It's a sweltering Friday night in early June, and Nels and I are in the corner of the Living room nearest mine and Zelie's bedrooms discussing all of the ways that Marvel's Cinematic Universe is superior to DC films. Nels is animatedly waving their arms in that energetic, *joie de vivre* way that is so utterly Nels, making their point, and I'm close to doubled over in laughter.

For this fête, Em, our Party Planning Queen, has outdone herself.

The theme? Prohibit Prohibition.

All guests were instructed to come dressed as if they were attending a Gatsby-level soirée, and she's spent all week gilding the apartment; every surface of the apartment shimmers, from the dining table covered in a sequined gold cloth to the black and gold glitter backdrop she's placed over one of the window panels for selfies. The food doesn't disappoint—Em spent the entire day making hors d'oeuvres. We have everything from Oysters Rockefeller to deviled eggs, Caprese skewers to crudités with dip, and everything in between.

She's even managed to build an honest-to-gods champagne flute tower, with a plan to fill them from the top as the evening's showstopper.

Nels and I move on from bashing DC's attempts at filmmaking to marveling at Em's party-throwing prowess. We stand in awe, truly taking in our surroundings and ooh-ing and ahh-ing together in good measure.

"We need a selfie!" Nels proclaims in their heavy English accent, wrapping their hand around my wrist and dragging me towards the photo wall. They snatch up a deep blue feather boa, wrap it around my shoulders and mutter that it's perfect with my silver flapper dress. They're right—the dress, which fits my curves perfectly, is just the right tone of silver that the blue boa was almost made for it. They select a gold cape for themself, tossing it haphazardly over their black-suited shoulder with a flourish. We take a few test photos, trying to find the perfect combination of angle and lighting.

Nels lifts their phone over their head to take a shot from above which opens my line of sight to more of the room. Out of the corner of my eye, I notice the apartment door open and a new figure enter the foyer just as all of the air leaves the room.

It's Ryden.

Ryden is here.

Ryden is here in my apartment.

Ryden is here in my apartment *full of Livings*.

Nels' face clouds with worry as I all but collapse into myself. They grab my arm to keep me from tumbling to the floor and loop an arm around my waist. "Abby?" they call, the cape falling from their shoulders into a heap on the floor as they glance furiously around the room. When they find no obvious threat, their eyes fall back to me. They shake me gently and demand, "Abby, what's wrong?"

"I need to get out of here," I whisper, feeling the sting of tears in the corner of my eyes. "Now."

I'm going to have a panic attack, I can feel it.

Within what feels like seconds, I'm in my bathroom, sitting on top of the toilet tank with my feet on the lid and my head in my hands. Nels is leaning against the wall opposite me, their hands in their pockets but with that same impish, totally Nels grin on their face.

They study me curiously.

"Boyfriend drama?" they ask conspiratorially as they waggle their eyebrows. "Want me to get rid of 'im?" A pause, while they come up with their game plan. "I can drag you out there right now, kiss you until you're delirious in front of everyone, drive 'im insane with jealousy, and introduce m'self to 'im as your devilishly gorgeous partner."

They wink, but I know they're waiting on me to explain why I had such an instant reaction to the stranger in the foyer.

Before I can come up with a story to tell this Living who, to my knowledge, has no paranormal abilities, there is a brisk knock at the bathroom door. I suck in a breath, releasing it in a whoosh as Amarie slides in and shuts the door quickly behind her.

"He's gone, and I've got some *friends*," she eyes me carefully, in a way that tells me she means some other witches, "that followed to make sure he won't come back."

"What was he even *doing* here?" I ask, defeated, letting the tears fall slowly.

"He...," Amarie is clearly contemplating her words, taking care to not say the wrong thing in front of Nels, "thought he had friends here. And, he might. But he knows now, in no uncertain terms, that he is not welcome in this building."

"He must have done a number on you then, eh darling?" Nels asks. I can tell that their interest is piqued, and that they would love nothing more than for Amarie and I to spill the tea.

Even though I know that Nels means no harm and clearly doesn't know the gravity of the situation, I can't stop the cringe as it passes over my features.

They lean over me then, stooping to meet my eye level and gently taking my chin in their black polished fingers. They pull my face up until I meet their hazel eyes. "Hey. S'not my business, so you don't need to worry about telling your ol' pal Nels a thing. Just remember: there are plenty of people that love you, and if some loser doesn't, that's 'is problem. He can only hurt you emotionally if you let 'im. Screw him!"

Bless them, they're trying.

And oddly, Nels' pep talk *does* help, even if it isn't in the way they intended. I *do* have people that love me: Amarie springing into action to immediately handle Ryden. Nels immediately getting me to a safe, quiet place when I needed to escape.

I nod and force a slight smile.

"Alright then, c'mon," they shout, grabbing me by the hand and pulling me out of the bathroom. "I think it's time for a CONGA LINE!" And with that, I'm swept back into the joy that is being in Nels' orbit.

20

The morning after the Prohibit Prohibition party, I wake with a pounding headache. You'd think being a ghost would have its benefits like, I don't know, *not having to experience a hangover*, but alas I have no such luck. I was *Born*, so once again I toe the line between the Living and the Dead, my body in this case acting more Living than Dead.

I hiss as I hear a car horn blare on the street below and it shoots an electric wave of pain between my temples. My stomach roils and I barely made it to the toilet before I lose everything that had remained in my stomach the night before.

Fabulous.

Once I'm sure I can't possibly throw up any more, I chance a shower hoping that it will help me feel better.

It does, if only slightly. The heat of the water seeps through my pores and helps loosen muscles that had been tensed in my discomfort. I get out more quickly than I would have preferred, but I can feel the swirling in my stomach twisting from nausea to hunger. I brush out my hair and massage SPF moisturizer onto my face and neck, since in the shower I'd settled on running out to pick up brunch and coffee—and maybe a *little* hair of the dog. I wish for the trillionth time that I could be like other ghosts who don't have to use SPF, but I'm aging...it's necessary. I don't want to look like an old crone at forty.

I throw on a thrifted white *Ghostbusters* t-shirt, a denim jacket, grey joggers, and a pair of Converse that has been with me since I was a teenager and slink out of the apartment without seeing a single roommate.

They must all be in varying stages of misery, too.

As I step outside into the already sweltering Georgia morning, I decide to bring back a big bag of greasy cheeseburgers and some Bloody Mary mix to pair with the bottle of vodka I'm sure is still nestled under the kitchen sink for *emergencies* like this.

I make it a few feet towards Jittery Java before the mix of hangover and humidity starts to catch up to me. I feel weighted down, as if there's lead in my shoes. I can feel my heartbeat in my ears, and the nausea is returning with a vengeance, bringing with it vision-blurring exhaustion. Every step is a feat, and as I all but crawl into Jittery Java, I know that desperate times are going to call for drastic measures.

Once I finally get inside Jittery Java, I will my eyes to stay open as I peer around the room. The cafe is booming, owing the Saturday morning rush to the Emory University Hospital staff clocking out of their night shifts, students desperately trying to salvage an enjoyable weekend by knocking out their homework while their friends still sleep, and several caffeine hungry individuals that look just as bad off as I feel. I'm about to give up hope and collapse in the doorway when I see my opportunity. There, in the corner of Jittery Java, is a woman.

Other than the fact that she is breathtakingly beautiful, there isn't anything out of the ordinary about her. She has brown hair, cut in a fashionable curly bob at chin length, soft green eyes, and a prominent cupid's bow on her dark tinted lips. She's gazing out the window, occasionally sipping tea and staring at what appears to be...*nothing*.

"Oh thank the *gods*," I whisper to myself as I fall through the nearby bathroom door, check that I'm alone, then shift into my invisible form. I slip through the door and approach her.

I haven't Possessed someone in so long that I'm afraid that I might fail, or reveal myself somehow, but I reach my hand towards her torso and felt the teres major muscle warm in my palm as I close my hand.

It's like no time has passed, and I'm back in Mr. Winstone's room in Middletown.

Before I can reminisce further, I'm pulled in. Her aura is stunning, swirls of gold and burgundy, sage and burnt orange; it reminds me of a crisp autumn day, a warm mug of tea, and a good book. I lean further into the Possession and can see through her eyes—just like it was with Mr. Winstone. I don't see the cafe before me, or the window the woman had been staring out moments before. She's still gazing outside, but instead I see her daydream.

There are two children, a girl and a boy, laughing up at her as they stroll through the streets of...where are we? The children are walking at her side along a cobbled street in a very old city. There are other adults in her party, too, pointing at buildings and fountains, laughing along with the woman and children. As the children dart ahead to round a corner in front of her, a sign comes into view: *Campo de' Fiori*, with an arrow pointing ahead. It's *Rome*! The woman is daydreaming about taking her children, her family, to Italy.

The joy she feels at that someday trip is overwhelming.

It only takes a few seconds until I have enough energy to function and I ease out of the Possession. I take a moment to center myself, and watch as she shakes herself out of the daydream, a smile quirking the corner of her lips. She drains her mug of tea and eats the last few bites of her lavender scone. She pulls a few bills out of her cell phone holder/

wallet combo and leaves them on the table for the busser who will be along any moment to clear the table for another guest. I step aside as she makes her way out of the cafe, moving at a leisurely pace to her next destination.

I slide back into the bathroom, this time behind another patron, slither into a stall, and shift back into my solid form.

I step back out into the cafe and approach the counter, ordering four coffees—black, since we have all the necessary accoutrements at home —to go. I speak briefly to Sam, making a mental note to ask Zelie how things are going in that department as I leave Jittery Java and stop by the food truck alley at the corner of the nearby park. Mercifully, a burger truck is on rotation, and I order four with all the fixings and French fries. I hope that they're all so greasy that the bag will be soaked through by the time I get home.

I make one more quick stop into a bodega down the street from our building and snag the Bloody Mary mix before rushing back home.

The paper bag full of burgers breaks, tearing around the massive grease spot, just as I approach the kitchen island.

Since they land on the island and not spilled about the floor, I smirk, knowing how much better we will all feel once we've devoured the cheeseburgers and Bloody Marys.

I'm already feeling much better after the Possession at Jittery Java, and bend down to pull the bottle of vodka out of the cabinet beneath the sink.

A low, groaning *unnnnnnngggggghhhhhh* sounds from nowhere and I nearly hit my head on the underside of the cabinet as I straighten. I round the other side of the island and find Zelie, wrapped in a blanket and lying on the kitchen floor.

"What happened to you?" I laugh as I lean down to help her up.

She pulls away from me and sinks further into the floor. "Em. Em and her parties happened to me. Is there an axe in my scalp?" she asks, making feeble attempts to reach her arms to the back of her head. "Because I feel like there's an axe in my scalp."

"You are, thankfully, axe-less," I assure her. "C'mon, let's get you vertical."

I pull on her arm in a game of tug-of-war as she tries to maintain her position on the ground.

Eventually, I win, and she settles onto one of the island's barstools still wrapped in her blanket. I unwrap a burger and fries, passing both to her with strict instructions: "Don't think, just do. Eat."

Zelie groans again but takes a bite of her cheeseburger as I turn to mix up a Bloody Mary.

As the spoon I'd chosen to stir the drink tinkles against the glass, a pile of blankets shoots up from the couch. It's Amarie, who I hadn't even noticed had clearly fallen asleep on the couch last night after the party.

"*How* can you possibly be eating right now and *why* are you making that hellish sound with that spoon?" she demands, pressing her palms into her temples.

At the far end of the apartment, I hear Em's bedroom door open with a *whoosh*. I brace myself for a third roommate needing to be cared for, but my jaw drops as she steps around the corner of the hallway and into view. She looks...*perfect?*

"You *biiiiiiitch!*" Amarie yells, then winces at the pain as her shout clearly ricochets through her skull. "How do you look like *that* this morning?"

She's right. Em is bright eyed and bushy tailed. She's showered, put on light makeup, and donned a chic matching baby pink sweatsuit. Her hair is pulled high on her head in a sleek bun, and she looks for all the world like she's never had a drop of alcohol in her Life, let alone gotten raging drunk last night with the rest of us.

I'd seen her drinking all night, so unless she, in addition to being an Empath, also has magic anti-hangover powers, she has somehow totally avoided the hangover the rest of us are suffering through.

Since I'm sure that there is no magical cure for a hangover or Amarie the witch would have found it, I press Em on Amarie's behalf. "Yeah," I scrunch my face into an exaggerated frown, "how are you not miserable?"

"I've been telling all of you to take activated charcoal before drinking, and to hydrate, hydrate, *hydrate* by also drinking *water* while you're drinking. If you don't want to listen to me...then you deserve your hangovers!" She giggles, moving playfully around the room making just enough noise that we know she's trying to, without it being so much noise that it causes genuine discomfort.

She helps me unpack the remaining food and hands out Bloody Marys as we all sit at the island.

"So, great party, huh?" Em asks, elbowing me for compliments.

"It was awesome," I agree, "but what about Ryden showing up?"

The thought of him coming here, *again,* after abducting me from this room, sends shivers trailing up my spine while it also drops a stone through my gut.

"Oh yeah, about that..." Amarie cuts in, finally showing signs of Life after a few bites of her burger. "He text me this morning. He wants to talk to you."

21

"How did I let you talk me into this?" I glower at Amarie from my spot on our sectional. Ryden is set to arrive at any second, and my nerves are on high-alert.

She smirks at me, but I can tell that she's almost as nervous as I am. After she'd dropped the bombshell that Ryden wanted to talk to me, it had taken endless effort on her part to get me—and Em and Zelie, who are also seated on the sectional, both looking as nauseated as I feel—to agree.

She'd refused to tell us why she was so willing to let bygones be bygones with Ryden and invite him into our home. All she would tell us was that we needed to hear him out, and that she'd ward the apartment to keep us safe in case anything got out of hand.

A sharp knock sounds from the apartment door and the hollow pit in my stomach magnifies tenfold.

I'm going to be sick.

Amarie bolts to the door, checking the peephole before loosing a relieved sigh and opening the door to...*not Ryden.*

"Jaali! My favorite Reaper...it's so good to see you!" Amarie squeals as she throws her arms around the man. He's easily six feet tall and very muscular, his warm brown skin crinkling around golden eyes as he smiles down at her. He has locs that fall between his shoulder blades, the pieces that would frame his face pulled back into a twist at the base of his skull. He seems vaguely familiar somehow, even though I know I've only ever met one Reaper, and this definitely isn't Ryden.

"It's good to see you too, my friend!" The newcomer, Jaali, beams back at Amarie.

"Come in, come in! Let me introduce you to my roommates!" She leads Jaali into the Living room as I stand. I need to burn off some of the nervous energy that has built up inside of me. Since Ryden hadn't appeared behind the door, the energy has nowhere to go and I feel my skin begin to crawl as Amarie proudly announces, "Roomies, this is my friend Jaali. He's a Reaper—one of the best in the Brotherhood."

"I don't know about that," Jaali seems almost shy. Given my limited experience with Reapers, I'd thought they were all cocky brutes, so Jaali's reaction surprises me. "I just do what I was called to." I note that, much like Ryden, Jaali has a bit of an accent. Unlike Ryden's, which is clearly English, I can't quite place Jaali's, but it's lovely nonetheless.

I mentally file the "called to" comment away to think about later, as Zelie approaches Jaali.

"It's good to see you again," she says shyly, and suddenly all eyes in the room are on them.

"Wait," Amarie nearly shouts, "you two know each other?!"

"Jaali was Jess' Reaper," Zelie admits quietly, and tears start to form in her eyes.

"Oh, Zelie," Amarie whispers as she reaches for Zelie's hand. She squeezes it for a moment before letting go. "I'm sorry."

"Don't be," Zelie gracefully waves off the well-meaning sympathy and meets Jaali's eye, head held high, "Jaali was the best Reaper I could have asked for, and made Jess' passing that much more... peaceful." There's a sheen in his eyes now too. He's next to clasp Zelie's hand.

Zelie turns then, to allow Em to introduce herself. All of my roommates seem markedly more at ease than they'd been two minutes prior. I wonder idly if Em has altered our moods before pushing that thought aside—Em wouldn't do that without our consent unless the situation was absolutely dire.

I realize that while I'd been musing, the room has gone silent. Everyone is staring at me, and it's clear that Jaali is waiting on me to introduce myself, too. "Oh! Sorry, I'm Abby. Abby Gale." I cringe, realizing I'd just given my last name.

If Jaali is a Reaper, would he know that I am apparently a fugitive? Will my full name ring a bell to him, and will he immediately Reap me right here in front of my roommates and Luna? I can feel sweat pooling on my brow as I wonder if these are the last moments I'll Exist.

If he recognizes my name at all, he doesn't show it. Jaali shakes my hand gently and says, "It's a pleasure to see you, Abby Gale." Some of the tension in my shoulders relaxes as Jaali asks, "May I sit?" and Amarie ushers him to a spot on the couch. We all reclaim our places, making ourselves comfortable for what is likely to easily become an *un*comfortable conversation.

I wouldn't dare bring up Ryden for fear that speaking his name would somehow summon him, but Zelie apparently doesn't have the same qualms. "So, no offense to you Jaali, but you are not who we expected to meet tonight."

"Ah, yes," Jaali nods. "Ryden sends his...regards. He was called for a Reaping last minute and asked me to meet with you on his behalf. Which," he glances in my direction, "he thought might be preferable, given the...*awkwardness* of recent encounters."

I can't help but scoff.

"Awkwardness," I bark, crossing my arms in front of my chest. "That's one way to describe my being abducted from my home." The words are harsh, but I don't care. Let him explain to me why abducting a woman—ghost or not—is justified.

Jaali's eyes are full of sympathy and something else...almost pity, as they meet mine. His entire demeanor is sympathetic at first, then suddenly, I see resolve break in his eyes. He quickly straightens, looking to Amarie, and asks, "This apartment is warded?"

"Yes..." she replies, suddenly suspicious. I assume that means that she can cast magical protection spells around herself and others. Noted.

"Against what, exactly?"

"Anyone who isn't the five of us," Amarie's eyes are wide, "well, six if you count Luna." She points to Luna who is purring gently from her perch on the coffee table.

"How was I able to approach if you were expecting Ryden?" Jaali presses. "Shouldn't the wards have held against me?"

Amarie bristles, clearly irritated that her abilities are being called into question. "Because," her words come out in a harsh breath, "I sensed that the being in the hallway was friend, not foe, and allowed you to approach. Should I regret that decision?"

"No," Jaali raises his hands in front of himself in a defensive gesture before lowering his voice. "No. I am a friend. But I want to be sure that there are no loopholes where we could be overheard by anyone who is not sitting in this room."

"Consider me intrigued," Zelie interjects, giving a voice to what we'd all been thinking. "Don't keep us waiting, Jaali. Do tell."

Jaali still looks anxious, but agrees as we all lean in, hovering on the edges of our seats. He speaks barely above a whisper.

"There is a new Commander of the Brotherhood of the Reapers: Raelle. No one is quite sure how she gained control, but she has, and the Brotherhood is in chaos."

Amarie leans even closer to Jaali, concern written all over her face. Since she is the only other person in the room familiar with the hierarchy of Reapers, his words clearly impact her more than the rest of us. "What do you mean chaos?"

"Can we turn on some music?" Jaali asks. It's admittedly an odd request, but Amarie points at the TV and Em's Spotify playlist appears, "Cute Without the 'E' (Cut From the Team)" by Taking Back Sunday roaring to Life through the surround sound speakers. When Jaali continues, I realize that the music is another layer of protection from any supernatural eavesdropping; I'm all of three feet away from him and have to strain to hear him.

"Raelle has taken over and is changing up the Brotherhood's code—one we've maintained for hundreds of thousands of years."

"Can you please just get to the point?" Em cuts in. "You're giving these tiny nuggets of information that aren't actually telling us anything at all. What do you mean she's 'changing the code'? *Elaborate!*"

Zelie snorts. She loves when sweet, gentle Em's feisty side makes an appearance.

"Sorry," Jaali apologizes. "It's difficult information for me to share, not just because of it being hard news to deliver, but also because I am a Reaper, honor bound and sworn to the Brotherhood. There are things I cannot readily divulge because of the oaths I've sworn. I'm trying. Please have patience," he pleads, but his tone isn't admonishing.

Em visibly relaxes and nods at him. "That must be hard." Trust the Empath to be...well, empathetic.

"Thank you, it is. I'm torn between the code of my Brotherhood and my own moral code. But Raelle's orders are unlike anything I've ever heard of."

We let the words hang in the air, somehow knowing that we don't want to hear what comes next. No one presses him for more, but Jaali continues anyways.

"Raelle wants to rid the world of ghosts entirely," he looks pointedly at me. "She says she wants you all Reaped, by any means necessary."

22

"Excuse me for a moment," I whisper, rising from my spot on the couch and walking briskly towards my bedroom.

I pass through my room and into my bathroom, my knees screaming as they slam to the ground around the toilet. I retch, even though there is nothing in my stomach. I haven't been able to eat since Amarie told me Ryden was coming to our apartment. It doesn't matter—my body still feels the need to purge. Maybe it thinks that if it keeps going, I'll rid myself of the knowledge that an entire Brotherhood of supernatural beings will actively be hunting me soon—if they aren't already.

Once I truly have nothing left in me to throw up, I slump back against the wall, utterly exhausted. I need to get up. I need to march back into the Living room and demand answers from Jaali, I need to flee, I need to warn Eya and Wana. I need to get out of here before Jaali does what he came to do and reaps me.

A shadow flickers across the shower curtain in my periphery and I glance toward the door. Jaali leans against the frame with his hands raised, again, defensively. I can see Amarie peeking at me from behind him, and I feel slightly more at ease. I know that he wouldn't try to Reap me right in front of her, at least. Even knowing that Amarie will keep me relatively safe, I still use my feet to slide myself as far away from Jaali as I can. I press my back into the corner of the shower, using the pressure to push myself into a seated position even as I cower into the wall.

I am, personally, defenseless and I know it.

Jaali sees the terror on my face and takes a step...*backwards*? "Abby, I told you that I was a friend and I meant it. I swear to you that I am not here to Reap you. Nor will I try to Reap you in the future. You are safe now."

Ha. Now. I scoff. I'm ready to unleash all of the tension I've been trying, and failing, to reign in. "I'm safe *now*. What about when you leave tonight? What about tomorrow? What about every second for the rest of my Existence? You've just told me and my roommates that your leader wants me, and everyone like me, to stop Existing, so forgive me if I'm a bit on edge." The energy that my anger costs takes its toll on my already exhausted body and I sink back to the floor.

Amarie, bless her, pushes past Jaali and falls to her knees on the floor in front of me. "You may not know that you can trust Jaali yet, but I hope you know by now that you can trust me...right?" I nod imperceptibly at her, but she knows that I trust her. "Good. I swear to you, Abby. You are safe. You trust me, and I trust Jaali. Jaali is *good*, okay? If Jaali says he will do you no harm, he means that he will literally Die before he hurts you. Okay?"

I nod again, but can't reach my voice yet.

Amarie glances over her shoulder to Jaali and says, "Tell her the rest of what you told us."

Jaali approaches slowly, clearly worried that his proximity to me may cause me to retreat or blow up again. I let him sink to his knees in front of me so that he can meet my eyes. "Raelle may have given orders to Reap all ghosts, but there are many Reapers who are opposing her—both openly and in secret."

"What do you mean?" I choke.

"I mean that there are just as many Reapers who will refuse to Reap you as those that would follow through. The struggle now is knowing which Reapers will side with Raelle, and which Reapers have defected."

"Why would you—they—defect?" I ask, truly curious. "Why does it matter to you? Isn't a soul a soul?"

Jaali's reaction is genuine shock followed by overwhelming, soul deep sadness. "*A soul is the most precious thing to ever Exist, Abby,*" he whispers, almost reverently. "Every single soul is just as important as the next."

"But why does it matter to you? Why defy Raelle? Why not just do your job and Reap people?" I can feel my cynicism filling the small room.

"Because consent is *critical*, Abby. Sure, there are cases, typically Poltergeists," he glances at Amarie who nods in confirmation, "where the soul is too far gone to consent, and the humane thing to do is to Reap them so they'll be out of their misery and in the Unknown quickly. But if you think that those situations don't weigh on Reapers, haunting us, you're wrong. It is a devastating thing to do, to Reap a soul that hasn't willingly chosen to go. That act, even done with the best of intentions, stays with the Reaper, always." He shudders and presses his hand to his heart, closing his eyes. The weight of truth is written all over the soft lines of his face. "I hate myself for Reaping them," he opens his eyes and there is a blazing intensity—a furious regret—in them. "Most of the time they're completely terrified and I feel like a monster."

I understand his aversions, and he's right. No sane ghost should ever be Reaped against their will. This Raelle, whoever she is, is Reaping people who still need time here. Maybe they have unfinished business, or aren't quite ready to leave the places they knew in Life. Or maybe, gods forbid, they just aren't ready to go yet.

"Okay then," I stand, my anger renewing my energy, "how do we stop her?"

We move back to the couch and, after Em passes out cups of steaming hot tea, spend the next few hours with Jaali learning everything that we can about the current state of the Brotherhood of Reapers, which starts with a brief history of the Brotherhood for my, Em, and Zelie's benefit.

"The Brotherhood formed when the first prehistoric humans emerged, and became the bridge between this world and what's beyond," Jaali begins. "Our mission is a simple one: to guide souls from here to there."

"Wait," I interject, a thought coming to me. "Why are you all so... big?" I asked.

Amarie snorts. "'*Why are you all so big*?' You can't ask people why they're big, Abby."

I blush as I realized how the words had come out. I'm mortified and quickly backpedal. "No! That's not how I meant it! I just meant that if you are just ferrying souls, why do you all look like warriors prepared for battle? Every Reaper I've seen," my blush deepens as I realize my ignorance—I'd only seen *two* Reapers, which hardly made me an expert on their physique—but I finish the sentence, "you've all been big enough to like, rip a car in half with your bare hands."

Jaali chuckles. "Well, thank you for the compliment, but there's no actual requirement that a Reaper be...muscular," he laughs again. "Most of us are because of the nature of our responsibilities. Souls can be a lot heavier to bear than you'd think. They're not just light wisps of mist flitting through the air. Your soul carries your every thought, every experience, your entire Existence. We need to be able to hold that weight as the soul passes through. Some of us, like Ryden," my stomach tightens reflexively, "are stronger than others. He's one of the strongest Reapers I've ever encountered—maybe in all of our history. Others may appear to you as small, but even they are stronger than they look." I nod and quickly mumble for Jaali to continue.

"For hundreds of thousands of years, we have Existed alongside humans, both Living and ghosts," Jaali goes on.

"Wait again," I interrupt. "You aren't human?" Em and Zelie lean in, also intrigued. Amarie glances toward Jaali and it's clear that even she doesn't fully understand what Reapers actually are.

"That's a difficult question to answer," Jaali hesitates, "but I'll try. We are very similar to humans in that we have solid forms, hearts that beat, and a lifespan very close to that of a human's. If you cut my skin, I'll bleed, and I can Die just as easily as you can," he blindly gestures towards Em and Zelie. "But we also are decidedly *not* human. Once we get our sigils, we become generally—because of what I just explained— quite a bit stronger than humans, and we are privy to knowledge that most humans will never know. Also, to state the obvious, an average human can't transport another's soul."

I have so much to mull over, but again gesture for Jaali to go on. He toys with a hole on the leg of his joggers before continuing.

"Since the Brotherhood came to be, we've done our job diligently. We've helped billions of souls cross over, and have done so mostly peacefully. That was until Raelle took over when our former Commander went into the Unknown himself." His voice becomes husky. "Parker Knox was the best Commander the Brotherhood has ever had, and the fact that his successor is destroying all that we stand for is just..." I think for a moment he is going to cry, then the mug shatters in his hand. He jumps into action both apologizing profusely and trying to clean it up until a sweep of Amarie's hand makes the mug pieces and spilled tea disappear.

"Anyways, I've been working with a few of the Brotherhood that I know won't stand for Raelle to grow our ranks so that we can stand against her and right all that she's forced our Brotherhood to wrong."

Amarie cuts in, "But even that is difficult, because you never know which members of the Brotherhood support her."

"Exactly," Jaali agrees as he waves an approving hand in Amarie's direction. "She has a blind following now. Even if she's taken out, the poison has already taken root. It'll take generations to weed out her followers and the views she's infected them with and get the Brotherhood back on the path we should be on: the one where we ferry souls that are ready to pass from here to the Unknown."

"So Ryden is the strongest of you, right?" Amarie whispers, bringing the subject back to Ryden. "Is he with you, or against you?"

Jaali's mouth tightens into a grim line and he winces, almost like he's in pain.. He glances my way, clearly warring with himself.

"I...I don't know."

The words hang in the air, a dark omen over the rest of us. Jaali opens his mouth to say more when a loud knock sounds from the front door.

23

Amarie, of all of us, is the most surprised at the knocking coming from our door.

Jaali leans forward, gently grasps her arm, and quickly whispers, "I thought you said your wards would hold against foes?!"

"They should!" she cries back. "A foe shouldn't be able to get within 20 feet of our door; they'd suddenly remember something urgent they'd forgotten to do if they tried."

"And when I got here, you sensed that I was a friend?" Jaali asks softly. He's lethally calm, which makes the rest of us anxious. Is he preparing for a possible fight?

"Yes," Amarie replies.

"That's good then, right?" Em cuts in. "That means that whoever it is is a friend?"

"Theoretically, yes," Amarie breathes, "but I can't sense *anyone* on the other side of the ward at all."

Jaali swiftly makes his way to the door, holding one arm behind him in a gesture that tells us to stay put. His surprise is evident as he peers through the peephole, rocks back onto his heels, and glances over his shoulder at us.

"It's Ryden," he mouths and I feel cold fear wash over me. I stand, fully prepared to exercise the "flight" portion of my fight or flight reflex.

"Sit back down and act natural," Amarie commands in a hushed whisper. "Jaali is still over here because we are friends. He hasn't gotten to Ryden's message because we have been catching up. We haven't discussed the Brotherhood at all. We know nothing. Understood?"

Em, Zelie, and I all nod in agreement. Their faces are masks of horror that match my own. Suddenly, Amarie jolts towards the door and cackles loudly, startling us all. She waves Jaali towards the couch, gesturing for him to reclaim his seat.

"Yes! She didn't share *any* of the activated charcoal with us, so we were all miserable and she was as fresh as a daisy!" Jaali guffaws as he lounges back on the couch, the picture of someone casually relaxed while hanging out with friends.

Amarie swings the door open mid laugh and feigns shock. "Ryden! What a surprise!" She ushers him into the foyer, ever the gracious hostess. "Come in! Jaali stopped by and we've been catching up. We didn't expect you to be here because of your unexpected Reaping tonight, and since the last two times you were here were not exactly ideal circumstances—and you shouldn't have been able to get past my wards..." her voice takes on a stern tone as she chastises him.

He steps fully into the room and my mouth goes dry.

Gods above.

I'm pretty sure he's my enemy but the man is breathtaking. Every other time I've seen him, he's either been in those odd fighting leathers or I hadn't had time to notice his clothes before fleeing. But this time, with Jaali and Amarie here, I let myself take a moment to appreciate the beautiful Reaper in front of me.

Tonight, he wears a simple white v-neck t-shirt, a navy blue hoodie, grey joggers, and black running shoes. Every inch of him is modestly covered, but it's still very apparent that he's strong. The sleeves of his hoodie are pushed up to mid-forearm, and the cords of muscles are visible...and delectable.

He drops a nondescript black backpack at his feet before speaking in that robotic, monotone way that comes with a rehearsed speech someone absolutely doesn't want to make.

"Yeah," he smirks at Amarie," I've learned a few new tricks about wards." Oh, Amarie is *seething*. "I'll show you sometime."

This man has a Death wish.

Amarie looks on the verge of blowing a gasket when he continues. "I wanted to come...apologize for not being here when I'd asked you to meet with me," his eyes dart around the room before landing on me.

I'm going to throw up again, I can feel it.

"My assignment decided that they were ready for their Reaping a bit earlier than planned, so I was called to...assist."

In any other scenario, that slight English accent might have been the Death of me—pun intended—but instead I feel bile rise in my throat. Had he Reaped an unwilling soul tonight?

"Ah, was it finally old lady McGillum?" Jaali asks jovially. He turns to us to explain, "Old lady McGillum has been haunting an old townhouse nearby, and has been flirting with the idea of the Reaping for years. Honestly, I think she was just a lonely old lady who wanted the attention of my dear friend Ryden here." Jaali rises and claps a hand on Ryden's shoulder.

Ryden smiles shyly—the first time I'd ever seen one on his face. I hate the way that it lifts my spirits in the midst of the silent breakdown I'm having, but he has *dimples*.

Christ, what am I, fourteen?

"It *was* old lady McGillum, actually. She finally decided she's ready to go find that poor husband of hers."

I relax, if only slightly. She'd gone willingly.

"Poor bastard has probably been enjoying the peace of the Unknown until now," Jaali laughs, as does Ryden, for a moment. Then, the room falls silent.

After what feels like an eternity, Ryden coughs and sits down on the sectional across the room from me.

"So," Ryden starts. His eyes meet mine and I'm struck again by the blue depths. "I owe you an...apology." He coughs again. Clearly, apologies are not something Ryden makes regularly. There's no warmth at all in his words or his demeanor.

"*What?*" I ask.

"I...I know what you are," he admits almost coldly.

"A ghost?" Amarie cuts in, her tone deadly. "She's a ghost. Big deal. There are millions of ghosts out there."

"You can pretend that she's just a ghost all you like, Amarie," Ryden sighs, leveling a glare in Amarie's direction, "but I know she's not just a ghost. She's *Primo Natus Exspiravit*."

There's a beat of silence as we all take in his words. Amarie and Jaali are both taken aback, their cries of "what?!" and "what are you talking about?" coming together. I, on the other hand, can't help myself.

I throw my head back and laugh.

"Okay, did you guys pay this guy?" I use the sleeve of my sweatshirt to wipe the tears from the corners of my eyes as I continue giggling. My relief is palpable; there's no way this is real. "You guys are *assholes*, though, because I've genuinely been *so scared* of him!" I wail, pointing an accusatory finger at Ryden, still giggling like a madwoman.

"I can assure you that there is nothing funny about your situation." Ryden stares at me, his annoyance written all over his face. "You are *Primo Natus Exspiravit*, whether you like it or not. That puts a price on your head that most members of the paranormal realm would gladly trade you for without a second thought."

"What does that even mean?" I sneer. He's being so obnoxious in what is more and more obviously a practical joke one of my roommates has dreamed up. Except for the fact that none of them look anything but totally panicked.

My heart stops, yet again.

"Why are you calling her that?" Amarie demands sharply at the same time that Jaali says, "She can't be. Look at her, she's no more than thirty years old. It's not possible that the *Primo* would be that young."

"What the hell is a *Primo Natus*...whatever?" Em wails, successfully silencing Amarie and Jaali's protests so that Ryden can answer her.

"The *Primo Natus Exspiravit*: The First Born Ghost."

24

"What are you even saying?" I ask coldly, all sense of humor drained from me in an instant.

"*Primo Natus Exspiravit*. The First Born Ghost," Ryden repeats. "It has been prophesied that your Birth would bring about a new era: a new generation of ghosts powerful enough to bring the Brotherhood of Reapers to its knees. Ghosts that were Born, and aged, and maybe even Died. But how can something *Die* if it's already Dead?" he muses.

Jaali stares, open mouthed at his friend. "Ryden, you can't truly think that she's the *Primo*. She's so young."

"Sure she is," Ryden agrees. "But how is that relevant? The *Primo*, the First, has to be just that—*first*."

"How could I be the 'first' Born ghost?" I interject. "As far as I know, I'm the *only* Born ghost." The lie rolls off my tongue easily enough—I will not betray Eya and Wana. I'll willingly hand myself over to be Reaped before that happens.

Ryden scoffs and rubs his hand across his face in exasperation, chuckling for a moment before resting his hand on his chin. "Oh, love. If only that were true."

"Am I not the only Born ghost?" I can feel my voice rise, infinitesimally, and am powerless to stop it. I quickly school my features into those of a curious and ignorant lamb. *Others? I had no idea there were others! I've just been here alone, praying.*

"You insult me, Abby." His eyes meet mine. His grin is positively lethal, as wicked as the Devil himself. I shudder involuntarily but can't look away as he continues.

"Do you really think that I don't know about the twins?"

I only thought I'd known true fear before.

Being kidnapped was nothing. It was as meaningless as an awkward first date with someone you don't plan to see again. My abduction was insignificant in the wake of the millstone that Ryden has just dropped. A bomb that is shattering my world.

"Where are they?" I stand and make my way towards him. I'll gouge his eyes out myself. I'll tear him apart. I'll—suddenly, arms circle my waist from behind and pull me backwards. *Jaali*.

"Don't do anything rash," he whispers as he returns me to my seat and rests on the couch arm beside me. The threat is still there, though, and Ryden narrows his eyes as he notices it. Jaali will fight to protect me from Ryden if he needs to.

"Wait, who are the twins?" Amarie asks almost accusingly, glancing my way. Unfortunately, I don't have time for twenty questions, even if Amarie is the one needing answers.

"Where are they?" I scream. I will end him for this. The gods as my witnesses, if either twin has so much as a hair out of place, Ryden will pay with his Life. "What have you done with them?"

"*Who are the twins*?!" Amarie commands and I glare at her.

"When I was a child, Living in the middle-of-nowhere Ohio, I had some friends that were also ghosts, about my age at the time. They were children. They relocated then I relocated, before they could ever tell that I was aging. End of discussion." I cut the air with my hands, hoping that that will end any further discussion.

Ryden makes a *tsk-tsk-tsk* noise and laughs again. "You lie to the few friends you have?" He sucks in a breath, reveling in the discord he's sowing between my roommates and me. "For shame, Abby." He glances around the room, surveying his audience and I know he's about to deliver the blow.

They're gone.

Reaped into oblivion.

My tears feel like fire, silently scorching the skin on my cheeks.

I revel in the pain.

"Our dear friend Abby here has a bit of a secret," Ryden rises from the couch as he pauses for dramatic effect. "It seems that she has had contact with the twins, quite regularly in fact, over the past several weeks. And they are definitely not still children. Isn't that right, Abby?"

Zelie, who has been quiet up until that point, hisses. "Why should that matter to us? Abby is allowed to have things that she keeps to herself—as we all are. She's allowed to have friends that we don't know about."

I reach out and squeeze her hand, a silent gesture of thanks, and she smiles back at me.

"That's right," Em agrees. "You're trying to make out like Abby kept some big secret because she didn't trust us. She does, I know she does. She would have told us eventually, but it wasn't her secret to tell."

I truly had found the most wonderful people on earth when Zelie brought me here. No matter where this Hellscape ends, I know that I will be eternally grateful for having loved, and been loved by, the three incredible women in this room.

"Where are the twins?!" I scream one last time. If he doesn't answer me this time, I'm leaving. I will scour the earth until I find them or the answers I seek.

"I'd hoped to do this differently, but apologizing and making nice clearly isn't going to work. Your friends are safe for now," Ryden admits, "and they will remain safe as long as you, ah, assist me in a little venture I'm working on."

Oh, so we're going with blackmail?

"Assist you with what?" I ask. It's a stupid, irrelevant question. It doesn't matter what he asks of me, I'm going to do it.

"You'll be coming with me on a little...," he pauses for dramatic effect, which is infuriating, "trip. Pack a bag and be ready to go in twenty minutes."

I laugh bitterly again. "You think I'll just drop everything and come with you based on what? Your word? As if *that* means a thing to me."

He bristles slightly and it's obvious I struck a nerve. His reaction passes before anyone else can notice it and he's back to business, stepping around the couch to snatch up the backpack he'd left at the door. From it, he pulls two identical file folders, each marked with a twin's name. He drops the folders into my lap before perching on the armrest beside me, much too close for my comfort.

I theatrically scoot as far away from him as I can. It's a ruse—less about trying to force as much distance as possible between us and more about taking a few precious seconds to control my racing heart, my shaking hands, the boundless fear that had overtaken me the instant he mentioned the twins.

Once I think I can move without him seeing my trembling hands, I pick up one of the folders. It's Eya's. A pile of photos fall out and I can't help the gasp that escapes. They're all, unsurprisingly, photos of her, but they're photos of her from *all* ages. There are photos of her as a toddler in Japan, some from when I knew her in Middletown, and photos of her in what has to be Jamaica.

Bile rises in my throat when I unearth the bottom photo: it's one of Eya and Wana, taken from the top corner of an empty, sterile room. They sit huddled together. Their faces are obscured by the haze of what I assume is the security camera that provided this still, but their hair is the same as it was when I'd had a quick FaceTime with them a few nights ago: hip length box braids.

"What have you done to them?" I scream as I lunge at him. Jaali catches me around the waist, *again*. "Jaali, let me go!"

He only releases me once he stands between Ryden and me.

"Nothing," Ryden croons. "And nothing *will* be done to them if you come with me."

"Fine," I seethe. I stand and stomp towards my bedroom as my roommates begin screeching in unison.

Twenty minutes goes by much faster than I'd ever thought possible when it's the last twenty minutes I'll have in the safest home I've ever known.

That reality washes over me. Even with my own mother, I hadn't felt as safe as I did with Zelie, Em, and Amarie—likely because they had become my family by *choosing* me. The love of chosen family is often just as—if not more—sacred than the love of blood. I love my Ma endlessly and I know she loves me just as fiercely back, but I'm just as honored to be loved by my beautiful roommates.

"Abby, please, you've got to listen to reason," Em begs. "You can't just leave with that...that...*monster*."

Zelie is wild-eyed behind her. "Em's right. We can find a way out of this. We can find your friends. You do not need to go with him."

"Yes, I do. It's my fault he found them in the first place," I glare at him through the walls separating my bedroom from where I know he waits in the Living room. He'd all but banished Jaali, who'd tried to protest on my behalf. Since Ryden is such a high ranking Reaper and given the current fracture within the Brotherhood, Jaali had no choice but to obey; had he not, Ryden would know he'd defected.

"He's been stalking me since Halcyon. He literally abducted me. I was stupid to think he'd just...stop. I led him right to them. *Me*. Whatever happens to them now is *my fault*." I want to collapse, but there's no time. Not when Eya and Wana's very souls could be hanging in the balance.

Ma's face lights up my phone screen; she's trying to call me. I can't hear her voice right now or I *will* break, so I send the call to voicemail. Thankfully, she doesn't leave a message.

I zip up the backpack that I've haphazardly filled with clothing that could be easily layered. It's June in Georgia and the temperatures are soaring, but I have no idea where we'll be going; I want to be prepared for anything. I throw some travel sized toiletries into a front pouch and pull it closed. I'd been barefoot earlier, so I rifle through the few pairs of shoes that litter my closet and settle on a pair of running shoes I'd picked up at a local thrift store. Once I've tied the laces I stand, unable to prolong the inevitable anymore.

"Do me a favor?" I plead, turning to Em. "If you haven't heard anything from me in a month, call my Ma and tell her that I love her?" I press a slip of paper with Ma's number and most recent address into her palm before drawing her into a bear hug.

Em promises, and I turn to Amarie who hasn't said a word—only glowered—since we'd entered my bedroom and she'd perched on the end of my bed. She stands and takes one step towards me. "Give him hell, every single second," she urges as her eyes bore into mine. Oh, she's on fire. "I will find a way to burn him to the ground. Just hold on for a little bit and I swear to you, we will come for you. It's all going to be okay." Her eyes shine, but not with any tears or sorrow. No, Amarie doesn't have time for any sadness or fear. Her rage will guide her, more powerful than any other emotion in the room.

I shudder involuntarily; despite Ryden's unspoken threat that I wouldn't be returning, *I believe her*. Amarie will come for me, damning anyone who gets in her way.

"Remind me never to get on your bad side," I tease as I pull her in for a hug. Amarie doesn't laugh, only glares at me as Zelie begins openly weeping behind me. I turn to her: the hardest goodbye of the night for the best friend I've ever known.

"I don't even have any words," I whisper as tears finally begin to leak over my face.

"You don't need any," she smiles sadly through her own tears. "I'll see you soon. That's a promise, okay? And you can't break a promise to your best friend."

"Deal," I try to grin at her, but it's definitely a grimace. "This will not be the last time I see you. I promise." In my peripheral I see Amarie slip something into my bag, but Ryden calls, "it's time" from the Living room at the same moment, pulling my attention away from Amarie before I'd fully registered what I'd seen.

I hug Zelie one last time then turn to meet my Fate, in the form of a tall, brooding Reaper that I can't wait to be rid of—however that may come to pass.

25

Ryden rolls his eyes as I reenter the Living room covered in the tears and snot of leaving your best friends behind, but doesn't say a word; he simply turns his back to me and leads me out of the apartment.

Once we've made our way downstairs and out of the building, I stop Dead in my tracks. "I'm not getting on that."

Ryden turns from the small, sleek black motorcycle, that devilish grin back on his face. "Oh, I think you are." He holds out a helmet to me but I'm frozen in place.

"I don't do motorcycles," I argue, taking tiny baby steps backwards towards my apartment and the safety of not finding out what happens to a Born ghost when her body meets concrete. "There's nothing to keep my brain from painting the sidewalk if we crash."

"We won't crash," he promises, but I have no reason to trust a word he says.

"You can't know that."

He sighs dramatically. "Have you forgotten that you are a ghost, Abby? Even if we were in an accident, it's not like you can Die. And even if you could, you're in the company of a Reaper. You won't go into the Unknown until it's time."

I go cold all over.

"T-t-time for *what*?" I ask, hearing (and hating) the stammer of fear in my voice.

"Just put your helmet on, for the love of the gods." He turns away, resting his own helmet on the top of his head. He straddles the seat and turns back to me, reaching one hand out towards me.

I hesitate, and he flips the visor up so that I can see his blue eyes. "Your friends are waiting..."

That threat is all I need, and I'm on the back of the motorcycle and stuffing my head into a helmet before I even realize that I've moved. Ryden's brief grin over his shoulder is absolutely feral as he whispers, "*Hold on to me, love.*" Then he's slamming down his own helmet and we're off.

We tear through the streets, Ryden expertly weaving in-and-out of traffic at break-neck speed. I hate myself for it, but my fear of crashing overcomes my loathing of the man in front of me almost instantly and I wrap my arms around his hard, lithe torso. I can't hear over the roaring of the winds our speed creates, but I feel a rumble beneath my hands, deep in his chest. Of course he's laughing at me.

Mercifully, the drive isn't long before we pull up to—an apartment building?

"What are we doing here?" I ask timidly as I loosen my grasp on Ryden's chest and climb off the motorcycle.

"We'll be staying in my apartment until the morning. Then we'll depart." He peels off of the bike and approaches me.

I don't want to know, but I still ask, "Depart for where exactly?"

"All in good time, love," he winks at me and my stomach turns over.

"I am not your love," I seethed, "so you can stop calling me that."

"Don't flatter yourself," he sneers down at me. Gods, he's tall. "I'm English. Using the word 'love' just happens to be in my nature...*love*."

I'm going to end up getting myself killed if the fury I feel is any indication. Every instinct in my body screams for me to slap that stupid grin off of his face, but I have to regain control of my emotions.

He's baiting me...*why*? Is he trying to force my hand so that I can be Reaped sooner rather than later? I have to be more careful, before I lash out and get myself, and Eya and Wana, forced into the Unknown.

I snap out of my reverie and realize that Ryden is no longer standing in front of me. "Are you coming?" he calls from the building's entrance, "or were you going to stand out here all night?" I wonder idly if he'd actually allow that.

I trudge up the sidewalk, hefting my backpack up onto my shoulders as I walk. We step into a lobby that is surrounded in glimmering white tiles, all flecked with gold marbling and polished to perfection. The tile spreads across the floor and climbs up the walls before meeting a dark gold ceiling and a massive gold and glass chandelier. There's a doorman's desk, but it's empty, its occupant likely gone off to relieve himself or take a scheduled break. A gilded clock above the desk reads 1:45am. I sigh as the exhaustion of the day sets in.

Ryden hears my sigh and glances over his shoulder before returning his attention to waiting on the elevator he'd led me to, clearly disinterested. Which is fine...I don't exactly want to have a conversation with my captor, either. The elevator snaps open: even more white and gold tile glitters from within. We step inside and Ryden thumbs the "7" button. I roll my eyes; *lucky number seven.*

I don't feel lucky in the slightest.

We leave the elevator and make our way to apartment 713. Ryden unlocks the door quickly and pushes it open, holding it for me to enter. And they say chivalry is Dead.

The apartment, while tastefully decorated, is much less spacious than I'd expected. It has a small kitchen immediately to our left, with dark brown cabinets and granite countertops. An island stands in the center, wide enough for two barstools. Everything is neat and tidy, not even an apple in the fruit bowl on the counter out of place, and the wax warmer plug in glowing above the sink makes the whole place smell like cinnamon.

Opposite the kitchen on my right is a door that stands slightly ajar; inside it I can see a stacked washer and dryer. Directly in front of us is a Living room with a plush brown leather sectional, a wrought iron coffee table, and a flat screen TV on the wall. Along the same wall as the laundry room is a door leading to what I assume is the single bedroom.

"There's a bathroom through that door," Ryden nods towards the bedroom door I'd just noted. "Feel free to freshen up if you'd like. You can take the bed." He drops onto the sofa, grabbing a throw pillow and placing it under his head. He closes his eyes as if he's about to drift off to sleep.

"I'm sorry...what?" I ask, utterly dumbfounded.

"You do *sleep*...right?" Ryden asks, intentionally speaking condescendingly as if I'm an idiot. "So, go in there," he points to the door, "use the bathroom however you need to, find the bed—you can't miss it—and sleep."

"Why would I want to sleep in your bed?"

He sits up and begins rubbing his eyes with his fingertips. "Are you always this maddening?" he asks, and for once it feels like a genuine question. "I don't particularly care if you sleep or if you don't. Just go in that room and do whatever you want. Sleep, build a pillow fort, jump on the bed, or rip all of my clothes out of the closet and toss them out the window. I. Don't. Care." He falls back onto the sectional and closes his eyes again.

When I don't move from where I stand beside the kitchen island, he opens one eye. "You're welcome to sleep here on the sofa with me if you'd like," he smirks wickedly, scooting himself closer to the back of the couch and patting the space in front of him. "You can be the little spoon."

That gets me moving; I flee into his bedroom, slamming and locking the door behind me. I swear I hear him chuckle under his breath as I go.

Ryden's bedroom is both lavish and plain. The king-sized bed takes up most of the wall opposite the door, and there's a nightstand on either side, each holding a lamp. There's also a dresser that houses another flat screen TV beside the door. To my right is a pair of double doors that I assume means his closet is behind them, then a single door that leads to the bathroom. A wall of windows lines the wall across from the bathroom and closet, and as I stare at them I have a fleeting thought.

I rush to the windows before I can think myself out of it. I throw open the curtains and curse. Of course they don't actually open. *Asshole.* He knew these windows were for aesthetics only.

If they had, could I have escaped? Could I have shimmied down a drain pipe or something and run?

No...*no*, I couldn't do that.

Even if the windows opened, my fleeing would doom Eya and Wana. Even though I desperately want to leave, I can't—I *won't*, and Ryden knows it.

Sighing, I stalk to the bathroom deciding that I'll at least grant myself the luxury of a shower. I flick on the lights and lock the door behind me. The locked doors bring me a small comfort for some reason, even though I know that if Ryden wanted to get in here, tiny metal locks would certainly not stop him.

I turn on the shower and peek through the cabinets in search of a towel. I find one; the cabinets are empty save for a stack of towels and a few extra rolls of toilet paper. The countertop is equally as bare: a toothbrush, a tube of toothpaste, and a hair brush are meticulously placed in a perfect row together, the only items in sight save for an electric beared trimmer plugged into its stand on the wall. In the shower, there is a bottle of 3-in-1 shampoo, conditioner, and body wash, with a loofah hanging lazily from the shower handle.

I step into the shower and grab the 3-in-1 bottle. I have no idea how long we will be off on this mysterious "journey," so I'm not about to waste the tiny bottles of shampoo, conditioner, and soap I'd packed for myself. And if running low on this garbage liquid inconveniences Ryden even slightly—all the better.

I pour half of the bottle down the shower drain before I snatch his loofah and make quick work of bathing. I work the greenish liquid into my hair and cringe. It smells terrible, an overly harsh, fake beachy scent. I can't understand how Ryden uses this junk, because it's nothing at all like the delicious scent of hi—

I stop that thought before it can form. It doesn't matter that he's hot and smells nice. It's a farce; a front put up to throw others off; a cruel, cosmic joke.

He's beautiful, yes. But he's also a Reaper.

26

I awake the next morning to Ryden throwing open the curtains to the harsh morning light. I hiss, covering my eyes from the blinding rays.

"Get up and get dressed," he crosses the room and stands in the open doorway. "We're leaving in ten minutes."

I sit bolt upright in the bed. "How did you get in here? I locked the door." I knew that the locks wouldn't stop him, but if he'd broken in and I hadn't woken up...

"This is *my apartment*," he replies, almost puzzled. "I do have keys to the doors..."

"What is a Reaper doing with an apartment, anyways?" I ask as I crawl out of the bed and grab my book bag. "Shouldn't you sleep in like...a lair or a dormitory or something?"

"I'm not even going to dignify that asinine assumption with a response," he scoffs. "Tick tock...you have eight minutes."

I scramble to the bathroom and throw on a pair of denim shorts and a grey-blue v-neck t-shirt. I'd planned to scrub Ryden's toothbrush around in the toilet a few times, but it's gone—packed away for wherever we are going next.

I quickly swipe on some deodorant, slather on some SPF moisturizer, brush my teeth, and stick my toothbrush and the small travel toothpaste back in my bag. I put on the running shoes I'd brought with me and pull my hair up into a messy bun. I don't have anyone to impress, so I take one final glance in the mirror and begrudgingly walk back out to the main part of the apartment. Ryden is standing at the kitchen island with a huge camping backpack and sleeping bag strapped to his back.

"You're in luck," he tosses an apple at me. "You have two minutes left for breakfast."

I slump down onto one of the barstools. "What's the rush?" I bring the apple up to my mouth to take a bite before my brain catches up with my body. I drop the apple and throw myself backwards, knocking the barstool to the floor as I stand.

"I'm not going to poison you, Abby," Ryden sighs, reaching across the island to pick it up and take a bite before rolling it back to me. "See?"

I scowl at him but bite into the apple as he pours a mug of coffee. He exaggeratedly takes a sip before sliding it across the island to me. "Drink up, you'll need energy for today."

"W-what are we doing today?" I ask as the bitter coffee reaches my soul.

"You'll see," he glances at his watch. "Time to go."

"Thank you, thank you, *thank you*," I whisper my gratitude to the gods above. By some miracle, Ryden doesn't make his way to the dreaded motorcycle when we exit his building. Instead, he guides me to a black SUV.

My steps falter as I realize that this is the same vehicle I'd been tossed into when he'd abducted me from the apartment...the first time. My breath lodges in my throat.

I've been abducted *twice.*

By the same person.

Gods above, I have terrible luck. I stand, rooted, waiting for Ryden to bring out ropes to tie me up, or to hoist me over his shoulder again before tossing me into the trunk.

He surprises me by opening both the passenger and backseat doors. "You can have your choice of where you'd like to sit. You may sit up front with me, or you can sit in the back seat." He steps closer, reaching towards me and I flinch. He falters for the briefest moment before gently pulling my bookbag from my shoulder, strolling to the back of the SUV and placing it gently inside.

Deciding that I want to be as far away from Ryden as humanly possible, I choose to ride in the back. I slide into the seat, slam my door, and lock my seatbelt before he's even had time to shut the passenger door. He makes his way around the front of the car and climbs inside.

I'm thrown forward when he backs out of the parking spot—apparently Ryden is a fast driver in general. We peel out of the parking lot as he meets my eyes in the rear view mirror and says, "Best to get comfortable, we'll be driving for a while," before tapping on the radio until what sounds like a podcast starts playing. We listen in silence for a few moments until—

"Are you seriously listening to a podcast that is just obituaries being read?" I ask, somewhat appalled.

"Yes."

I hate him so much.

I grind my teeth. "Why? Is there nothing else more entertaining to you than to hear that Merida Spence leaves behind three loving grandchildren?"

His knuckles turn white on the steering wheel and he takes a moment to answer. "Obituaries are my job, Abby."

Ha. "Your 'job.' Is that what you call what you're doing here? Your *job*?" I scoff.

"No," his hands strain even more, his voice carefully controlled, "this situation is different."

"How so?" If I'm going to be Reaped against my will, I'll at least go out arguing about it.

"Because it is," he growls. "Now if you'll excuse me..."

He starts the episode over and I fall back into my seat, defeated. I stare out the window, watching the Life that goes on outside of this SUV.

People are up and out for the day, heading to work, taking their kids to school, and running errands. None of them have any idea what is going on inside this car. To them, we're just another car, with other people inside, and another destination. If only they knew the truth. Would they try to help? Or would they choose to continue on about their Lives, comfortably, unconcerned with the soul of a helpless ghost?

I must have fallen asleep at some point, because I awake as the car rolls to a stop. I blink my eyes a few times then glance around. We're at a service station, decidedly outside of the metro Atlanta area. Other than this building and the interstate, I can't see another thing in any direction I look. Ryden has his back to me, leaning against the driver's side of the car as he pumps gas.

Knowing that there's no easy escape for me, and that I couldn't even try to get away if I wanted to, I unbuckle my seatbelt and reach over, tapping gently on the window. "I'm going to go inside and use the restroom," I call, and he nods.

"I'll be in in a moment."

I step out of the bathroom a few minutes later and find Ryden waiting casually outside of the door. "If you'd like anything to eat, get it now. We'll be driving a bit longer still."

"Where are we?" I ask, even though I know it isn't likely that I'll get an answer.

To my surprise, he responds. "Somewhere in the middle of nowhere Tennessee right now."

"I need to go back out to the car. I left my cash card in my bag."

"Just...just get whatever you want." he barks.

I start to object and tell him that I don't want to be indebted to my captor, but logic strikes. If he's going to hold me hostage, the very least he can do is pay to feed me. I push past him, so closely that my arm brushes his, and rip open a cooler. I grab a bottled water and a Fruit Punch flavored Body Armor, turn on my heels, and pick up a few assorted bagged snacks. I also grab a few Tony's Chocoloney bars because if Ryden is paying, I'm springing for the pricy chocolate. Ryden, armed with several bottles of water, stomps up behind me and scoffs. "Are you seriously only going to buy junk food?"

"What do you care?" I glare at him as we walk toward the cashier.

"I don't," he shrugs, but snatches several sealed cups of fresh fruit from a waist-high cooler as we pass it. He quickly pays for our groceries and leads the way back to the car. He opens the door for me and I roll my eyes as I reclaim my seat in the car, still as far away from Ryden as I can be. Once he's comfortably in the driver's seat, he reaches back to hand me two of the fruit cups he bought. I pointedly ignore him, causing him to sigh and place them in the cupholder nearest me.

We don't speak again for hours. The Sun begins to dip lower in the sky, making all of the trees look like they've been set on fire. I'm admiring the eerie glow when the car again comes to a stop. I look around and note that there's nothing but trees in sight.

My whole body goes rigid. "Is this where you kill me? In the middle of nowhere?"

He lets out an exasperated huff. "I can't kill you, Abby, you're already Dead."

Oh. *Right.*

"So then where are we?"

"We are at the end of our journey by car. We'll go the rest of the way on foot."

"On foot?!" What is this, some kind of Medieval quest?

He quirks an eyebrow at me, pausing as he pulls our bags from the back of the SUV. "You'll survive," he responds with an unfamiliar gleam in his eye. "A bit of hiking won't kill you."

My mouth goes dry. *Was that a threat?* The hike won't end me, but something else will? Before I can respond, he tosses my bookbag at me and I noticed that it's quite a bit heavier than it had been when we'd left his apartment. "What's in this?" I ask as I pull it open.

"We'll be hiking for...a while," he responds, "so I added some travel-friendly snacks and water to our packs. I'll be able to get us more food as we need it, but I wanted us to have a little stockpile to start with."

"Just exactly how long will we be *hiking?*" I ask, although I'm certain that I don't want to know.

"Depending on how well you can *keep up*," he grins evilly, "we could be there in as little as a week or two."

A week? *Or two*?! I'm going to throw up.

"Where could we possibly be going that will take *two weeks* of hiking in the mountains?"

"I want to show you something." Fear pricks up and down my spine. I'm absolutely certain that I do not want to see whatever it is that Ryden wants me to see.

I open my mouth to say so, but close it quickly. Eya and Wana can't afford for me to get too mouthy, or for me to argue with Ryden. I heave a breath and nod, pulling my backpack onto my shoulders.

"Also, I found your phone in your bag," Ryden admits, and there's a nervous, almost sheepish tension about his words as he idly rubs the back of his neck with one hand. A brief memory surfaces: Amarie slipping something in my bag. Gods bless her. She'd tried to sneak me my phone and, by default, a tracking device. "You don't have to hide it...although we will be without cell reception for the majority of our—er...journey. If you have any last minute communications to make, you have five minutes."

I'm surprised for several reasons: one that he'd allow me to keep my phone *and* reach out to others while I'm literally his captive, but also that he'd gone through my things. Maybe I should be moved by the kindness of letting me have these precious few minutes to contact my mother and roommates, but all I feel is rage.

"You went through my things?" My voice is ice: the cold fury that ricochets through me startles me, but I hold my ground. "What gave you the right to go through my things?"

"I didn't go through your things. I opened the front pocket of your bag to add a water bottle and your phone was the only thing in the pocket." I'd thought that pocket was empty.

"That still doesn't give you the right to go through my bag," I seethe, even as I snatch my phone out of the pocket. Amarie had powered it off to conserve the battery, and had even snuck in a battery backup. I'll have to use it as little as possible, and keep it turned off when I'm not using it, to make the batteries last.

I turn my back from him as my phone lights up. There are dozens of messages in my group chat with the roommates, all various ways of saying, **"check in with us/are you safe?/where is he taking you?"**

I shoot back a single text to them: "**Just found my phone, okay for now. We are hiking somewhere in northern Tennessee. Not sure of destination. Turning phone off to conserve battery. Love you all so much. xoxo**"

Just before I shut it off, I check the security cameras at Ma's current house. The most recent motion is from a few hours ago: Ma, dressed in lavender scrubs, leaving through the front door. The pang that tears through my chest is agonizing. I want to text her, to call her, to have her here to tell me it's all going to be okay. Before I do something rash like reach out and tell my worrisome mother what's going on, I hold down the power button and the screen goes black.

"Ready?" Ryden asks as I put my phone back in my bag.

"As ready as I'll ever be, I guess," I begrudgingly reply.

Can you ever be ready to cease Existing?

27

I've never trusted people that are outdoorsy.

Living or Dead, it doesn't matter to me. They enjoy crawling out of bed before the Sun, slathering on layer upon layer of sunscreen and bug spray, and going out into *nature*? It makes absolutely no sense to me. Brunches on midtown-Atlanta rooftop patios with my roommates are all the outside I will ever, in my entire Existence, need.

It makes my hatred for Ryden burn that much deeper to see him take a deep breath, inhaling the fresh mountain air, and smile almost exultantly, reverently, at nothing in particular. Looking at him, it would be easy to assume that this was a planned outing. A guy and his girlfriend (I shudder at that thought) out for a hike and maybe a picnic. A day of climbing before returning to this car and going home.

This is certainly not going to be a picnic.

While he's cosplaying as Henry David Thoreau staring at Walden Pond, I take the opportunity to take in our surroundings. We are literally in the middle of nowhere. Ryden's car is parked on the near non-existent shoulder of a two-lane highway that looks like it'd been carved between the mountains with a giant potter's rib a millennia ago. The mountains themselves are eerie, covered in soaring hickory, pine, and oak trees and coated in a thick layer of smoke that casts an ominous haze over everything, especially coupled with the fiery reds and oranges that the sunset casts on the scene. It's the middle of summer and I still find myself chilled by the sight, idly wishing that the lone sweatshirt I'd packed wasn't buried in the depths of my backpack. I'm struck by this bone-deep, *soul*-deep knowledge that these mountains must have borne witness to eons of history. The secrets that they must hold...I shudder again, the motion catching Ryden's attention from his periphery.

He turns back to me, the smile fading from his lips as he gruffly mutters, "ready?" before hefting his camping pack up onto his shoulders and stepping into a slight gap that I hadn't noticed in the treeline. It's barely two feet wide and, I'm quite certain very few even know it's here at all. We are quite literally sneaking head-first off the beaten path.

I sigh, resigned, and follow him, because I have no other options. The ground is seemingly flat as far ahead of us as I can see, but I take no comfort in that. We're in the middle of two mountains; I know that an upward climb is coming much sooner than I'd like.

"Why are we starting now?" I whine. I can't help myself—this *sucks*. "Was tomorrow morning taken?" The fact that it's so late in the day isn't helping my mood.

"Because getting you here proved more difficult than I'd originally anticipated," he shows no emotion at all. "So now that I have you, I don't want to waste any time." Before I can argue, or point out how sinister that sounded, he adds, "We'll be making camp in an hour or two. Just far enough into the forest that you won't find your way out if I fall asleep."

"What about your car?" I have to shout because *gods* is he fast. He's a good twenty paces ahead of me and we'd barely set foot on this...I don't know what to call this because it's not a trail. Brush scratches my ankles and I increase my pace, jogging to catch up to him. I can only imagine how many ticks are lying in wait, ready to latch into our skin at the first chance.

That sets my skin crawling.

"I have someone coming to handle it," he responds over his shoulder.

"Handle what?" I ask, visions of blood sucking insects still dancing in my head.

"My...car?" He swivels around and looks at me like I've grown a third eye.

"Oh, right. Your car." I should have packed bug spray. *Why didn't I pack bug spray?*

Thankfully, we come to a gravel path after about five minutes of walking. I turn around, surveying the trees and brush we'd just stepped out of and sigh. Ryden shouldn't have worried about bringing me out here before the Sun set—I already couldn't point out where we'd come from. Everything looks the same: trees, brush, leaves, and grass.

He continues walking ahead of me and I'm left with nothing but my backpack thoughts.

I feel hollow. As if my own Existence, my own destiny, is no longer mine. I'm no longer able to think or make decisions for myself—I'm at the mercy of Ryden...and so are Eya and Wana. I have to remember why I'm here...I have to remember them. I brush away the tears as they form.

The path eventually gives way to damp, earthen soil and moss. Ryden leads us through what feels like miles of trees, weaving around them and making sudden, twisting turns that prove he knows exactly where he's going, even when there are no indicators of a path at all anymore. Finally, after what feels like several hours, he pauses in a small clearing, places both hands on his hips, and announces that "this will do."

I'm drenched in sweat and gasping for air—the outdoors are no joke —when the Sun finally sets. Ryden, of course, looks perfect. He'd tied a strip of a blue bandana around the top of his head to hold his hair back and looks like he could be on the cover of *Hot Outdoorsy People Weekly*. He sweeps an arm around the clearing as if he's proudly showing it off.

I'm remarkably unimpressed. There are a few small boulders that could be suitable for seating with a rare bit of flat ground about the size of a trampoline set in the middle of them.

I collapse onto one of the rocks and cradle my head in my hands. We've only been hiking for an hour or so, but every inch of my body feels it. I ache from my head to my toes and back again. I groan, completely over all of it and press my hands into my throbbing lower back. My backpack, I decide, is going to end me before Ryden can. I'm sticky and gross and hungry and uncomfortable and it shows.

Ryden rifles through his pack for a moment then presents my dinner: a snack sized bag of beef jerky, a few sticks of string cheese, a protein bar, and one of those damned fruit cups from the gas station. After another moment of digging, he unearths a bottle of water, passing it to me with a sarcastic smile.

If I wasn't so ravenous from all of the exertion of the hike, I would probably make some show of defiance, tossing all the food onto the ground and stamping my feet on it. But I'm in the middle of nowhere, could never find my way out alone, and can't afford to starve out here. While mosts ghosts don't need the energy provided by food, it's a necessary part of *my* Existence: another quirk of being Born and all. And I *especially* need food after literally climbing (part of) a mountain. I devour the meal in what feels like seconds then glance around, finding the bottle of water where I'd dropped it at my feet and gulp it down. I wipe my mouth on my sleeve and only then do I remember that I'm not alone.

I chance a look in Ryden's direction and he's staring at me. Of course. *Perfect.*

I clear my throat daintily and sit up straight. I'm annoyed, tired, hot, in desperate need of a toilet that I know I'm miles away from, and in no mood to deal with Mr. Manners, but I decide to let it go.

I'm going to let it go.

I will let it go.

Until he *smirks* at me.

"Uh, what was that?" I ask accusingly.

He feigns ignorance. "What was what?"

"That *smirk*. What was that about?" Who does this guy think he is?

He just stares at me, amused, as if this whole situation is a joke.

"Did you have something to say?"

I'm *not* going to let this go. He's so irritating that I could scream.

"Nope, nothing at all," he smirks *again* and I finally let out the screech I've been holding in since I climbed on that godsforsaken motorcycle.

"I don't know who you think you are, but I do know one thing: you do not know me," I can feel my blood all but begin to boil. "I may be at your mercy, and you may have my friends, but that doesn't mean I have to tolerate your disrespect." I spit the words out and feel lighter, somehow.

He bristles. "Disrespect?" He barks out the word, but seems genuinely puzzled.

"Yes! Disrespect! This entire thing," I stand up and gesture wildly at the air, at the clearing between us, "is the most disrespectful, mortifying, demeaning experience I've ever had in my entire Existence!" I can feel my cheeks heat and I hate myself for feeling suddenly embarrassed. "I came with you willingly because you have my friends, and I cannot—I will not—let you harm them. But I do not have to like it, I do not have to like *you*, and I do not have to pretend like this is in any way normal or pleasant."

Two strides.

It takes him two strides before he's in front of me. His nostrils are flared in anger as he glares down, capturing my eyes with his.

"What a threatening little speech," he croons. "Allow me to set the record straight. I do not *care* if you like me. I do not *care* if you're particularly happy right now. All I care about is my mission, which I intend to see through to the end."

My heart hammers wildly. "And what exactly is that end? What is the mission?"

"That is not for you to know at this time," he huffs.

"Well that's just fantastic!" I scream. I don't know where this courage is coming from—I typically cry if someone yells *around* me, let alone *at* me.

"Look," he utters, taking a breath before continuing far more calmly than before, "this can be easy, or it can be difficult. It's entirely up to you. If you are pleasant, I will be pleasant. I will do what I'm able to make this, er, *excursion* more bearable for you. If you want to act like a spoiled little brat, that is your prerogative, but just know that I will also not be accepting *disrespect*."

I stare at him for a moment. I'm not sure what I should say, so the silence stretches on until he breaks it. "So?" he asks. "Would you like this to be easy, or shall we take the hard way, *love*."

It's the "*love*" for me.

"We'll see how I feel by the moment," I smirk.

I nearly instantly regret my words.

I don't regret putting Ryden in his place. And I don't regret standing up for myself. I do, however, regret that there is so much tension in the air now that nature is calling—no, *screaming*—at me. I have to pee so bad it's blinding, and I'm in the middle of nowhere and have never, ever, in my entire Existence, had to *go* in the wilderness.

I may be a ghost, but I have standards.

I'm back on the boulder I'd claimed when we first appeared in this clearing, except now I'm teetering on the edge, rocking backwards and forwards like a lunatic.

Ryden's eyes had turned maniacal, almost wild when I stood up to him. He'd leveled an infuriatingly charming crooked grin down at me before letting out an "alright, love," turned his back on me, and has successfully ignored me since. He's cleaned up all of the remnants of our dinner, scattering anything biodegradable around the clearing and putting any trash in a side compartment of his pack, and now he's strategically placing a few small collapsible LED lights around the area. I stand up and start practically hopping from foot to foot; I'm to the point of no return—either I have to break the silence or suffer the disgusting consequences.

"So..." I roll my eyes. "If I needed to use the restroom?"

He doesn't even look at me, just points at nothing in particular. "There are more trees around you than you could possibly count. Take your pick."

I blanch. "I'm supposed to go...out *here*?" I'm mortified.

"We're on a mountain, Abby. Where else would you go?" Again with the not looking at me at all.

"I just would've thought that since you dragged me out here, you'd have some sort of plan. I didn't ask to be here, you know."

He finally looks up then. "I'm fresh out of portable outhouses, so use a tree or don't."

"But what if...we're in the middle of nowhere. What if there's like, a wild bear or something out there?"

"I'm quite certain that there are definitely wild bears out there."

"I. Don't. Want. To. Be. Their. Dinner," I grit through my teeth.

"If you happen to see a bear in the fifteen seconds you need to," he coughs, "relieve yourself, just call out and I'll handle it."

"You could fight a bear?"

"Don't you have to...*you know*." Ah. His English sense of propriety. He's getting embarrassed. I hide my grin before I remember that *I'm* embarrassed.

"I...you're...you're *right here*." I am not going to pee in front of this man. Or...I'm not going to pee in front of this man *willingly*, at least. My bladder is quickly letting me know that I'm about two seconds away from losing any say in the matter.

He sighs. "I'm not going to look, Abby. Just step around a tree, do what you need to do, and be done so you can go to sleep and I can get some peace."

"Sleep? We're sleeping out here?!" I try not to get hung up on his words—on the implication that I'll sleep and he won't. Surely he has to sleep...*right*?

Or do Reapers not need sleep?

In response, he unrolls his sleeping bag with a snap. I remember noticing it in the apartment, and it'd been on his back the whole time we'd been walking, but somehow this is still news to me.

I begrudgingly trudge a few yards into the trees. It's close enough that I am still bathed in the glimmer of the LEDs in the clearing, but far enough away that Ryden shouldn't be able to easily see. I slip around the opposite side of a tree and go quickly. I mutter under my breath about how disgusting it is that there is no toilet paper in the wild, and stomp loudly back to our makeshift campsite.

When I return, Ryden is wrapped cozily in his sleeping bag. I freeze.

"Oh...um." I'm not sure what to do, because I clearly don't have anything remotely resembling a bedroll.

Ryden sighs loudly, again, and pinches the bridge of his nose, closing his eyes tightly. "I know, I know...you didn't bring a sleeping bag."

"Why, in any scenario, would I ever have assumed I'd need a sleeping bag? You're a Reaper, and I'm a Born ghost, or a *Primo Natus* or whatever...I figured you'd take me somewhere, do unspeakably awful things to maybe try and torture some information out of me, then," I run my finger across my throat and click my tongue.

He almost looks offended as he sits up swiftly, leaning towards me. "*Jesus*, Abby," he breathes. "I'm not...I don't plan to..." then he closes his eyes and shakes his head as if he's clearing his mind, killing the words that are on his tongue before they can escape from his lips. He rises out of the sleeping bag and points to it. "I just got in there to mess with you. You can...just sleep in that. I'm not tired."

Then he stalks off into the woods without another word.

Ryden is, apparently, an early riser.

I don't know if he even slept. All I know is that, much to my dismay, Ryden's sleeping bag was more comfortable than most beds I've slept in. I'd debated on whether or not to climb into it after he'd disappeared into the treeline, but finally settled on absolutely taking it. He dragged me out here without so much as a whisper about my needing something to sleep in, so it was only fair that he have to hand his over.

I slid into the pack—still warm from his body heat—and fell asleep almost instantly, drunk on both exhaustion and the not unpleasant scent of the pillow: that leather, sandalwood, sweat smell I'd grown to associate with Ryden. Before crawling into the sleeping bag, I'd expected to be up all night worrying over being out in the middle of nowhere with no shortage of wild animals to come make me their dinner in my sleep.

I wake to sunlight, birdsong, and the smell of smoke. It's so pungent that even in those few hazy not-quite-awake-yet seconds, I almost feel the warmth of a fire. I sit bolt upright, the top of the sleeping bag falling into my lap and exposing my arms to the cool morning air. My eyes dart around before they land on Ryden, sitting on a stump, poking at a small fire with a cast iron camping pan full of...*bacon*?

"Good morning, love," he smiles—that devilish grin. "Shall we try to *do better, be better* today?"

"How did you—were you carrying bacon on you this whole time?" I know I should still be angry, and I am, but...my stomach rumbles and my mouth begins to water.

He laughs, but it doesn't reach his eyes. "No. I ran a few errands while you slept. I collected some supplies: this bacon and pan, some coffee, and..." he trailed off but gestured to a brand new, giant camping pack of the palest green. Atop it, tightly rolled for the day's travel, sits a new sleeping bag in the same color. "I picked the color because it..." he hesitates, "I thought it matched your eyes quite well."

I'm amazed that I hear any of what he's saying—that I can hear anything at all over the rage roaring to Life in my ears.

"I'm sorry," I grit out through my teeth. "Did you just say you *left*? You left me here in the middle of the night to go...to go...on a *Costco run*?!"

He straightens. This clearly isn't going the way he'd thought it would. "I—I thought you'd be pleased?"

"Pleased? Pleased that you left me alone in the woods? Are you out of your mind? Any number of things could have happened to me!"

"Do you truly think," he bristles, "that I would just leave you out here without protection?"

"I mean...*yes*?" I sigh, slumping back down into the sleeping bag. "How would I know otherwise? You don't communicate, at all. You're quiet and moody one minute, then chatty and wannabe sociable the next. You've given me absolutely no information on what I'm doing here at all, other than that my friends' fates require me to be here lest you do gods-know-what to them."

"I can assure you," he says, very formally, "that you were not left unprotected last night, even for a moment. Nothing would have happened to you while I was gone."

"Can you like...did you...are you able to cast wards or something?" I'm genuinely curious, even though I can still feel the embers of my anger smoldering just under my skin.

"Reapers have some magical abilities, yes. But I also had a colleague sit with you while I..." he sighs and pokes at the bacon idly.

Oh, my anger totally reignites in an instant. "A colleague?! So, like, a stranger."

"Not a stranger at all. Someone I know well. Someone I trust with my Life."

"Someone that *I don't know*. You trusted *my* 'Life,'" I use my hands to mime air quotes, "with someone that *I* don't know. What if I'd woken up to this stranger here?"

His lips curve up then, that impish smile stoking my fury. "Are you telling me, love, that you trust *me*?"

Icy mortification douses my anger. "I—that's not what I...I just meant..."

"I understand what you meant perfectly. You'd have been totally comfortable to awake in *my* bed and find *me* here, but would not have been keen to find anyone else. Interesting..." he grins at the fire before him. Again with the dimples.

I balk. "I was in the sleeping bag you brought with you, not your *bed*," my cheeks heat, "but how did you even get to a store so fast?" I ask as I move closer to the fire, my hunger winning out over anything else I was feeling moments ago. "It took us hours to get here last night, both hiking and then driving before that."

"Ah," he pulls a face. "Well, about that. It's some of the Reaper magic I mentioned. Since we have to be able to Reap a soul at any given moment, transitioning a ghost into the Unknown the moment they decide that they're ready," he coughs awkwardly—I think we'd both prefer to not discuss ghosts being Reaped if we can help it, given our current predicament, "we have to be able to travel to them with a second's notice. We are able to, uh, flit from one location to another easily. So, I flitted to the nearest large store's restroom, purchased what we needed, returned to the restroom, and flitted back here." He says it as if this is the most natural thing in the world, this flitting that he can do—that he does.

I am *fascinated*, and I can't even try to hide it. "So can you go anywhere? At any moment?"

"I could if I wanted to," he admits as he passes me a plate of bacon and an English muffin from a package I hadn't noticed before. He turns to the small percolator he'd hung low over the flame and begins to pour us each a small metal mug of the thick, dark liquid. "When I first passed the exam and proved I could flit safely, I went all over. I had breakfast on the Eiffel tower, lunch on the Great Wall of China, and dinner," he blushes, "beneath Cinderella's Castle in the Magic Kingdom at Walt Disney World."

The thought of a Reaper sitting among Disney-goers should absolutely terrify me, but the image of Ryden there, in mouse-shaped ears devouring a churro, is one I can't let skate by. I double over in laughter. Once I realize, I quickly stifle my giggles, cough, and school my features.

There should be no laughter here. This is a captor/prisoner relationship, and I can't forget that...even when my captor says something funny or smiles that stupid grin with his stupid dimples or does something stupidly charming. Even if he's heartbreakingly handsome. I shake my head and gulp down my mug of coffee. "So why are we doing all this, then?" I gesture around at our makeshift campsite.

"All...what?" he asks, truly confused again.

"If you can just...flit places, why are we hiking? Why did we drive hours to get here? Why did I have to ride on that godsforsaken motorcycle? You could have just..." I let the thought go because would it have made a difference? If we had—flitted—would I still be here? Or would Ryden have gotten what he needed and sent me into the Unknown by now? The thought sends a shiver up my spine.

"Oh, er...we can't flit other people. We can only flit ourselves and whatever items are on our person at the time."

"Ah," I say lamely. We fall into silence as we eat our breakfast. Ryden had also picked up some slices of cheese so that we could have breakfast sandwiches: English muffin, bacon, and cheese. Once we're finished, Ryden douses the fire and ensures that it's completely out. He circles the campsite, searching for any trash, collecting it all and stuffing it into a pocket of his pack to be disposed of properly later. I step around a tree again to relieve myself, and when I come back, he's strapping his freshly-rolled up sleeping bag to the top of his pack.

Without a word, he slowly picks up my backpack and unzips the new green pack, placing the backpack inside before zipping it closed and handing it to me. As it nestles onto my shoulders I have to admit, begrudgingly as I follow Ryden out of the campsite and on to whatever is next, that it is really a pretty shade of green and since it was made for hiking, will likely be much less murderous on my back than my ratty old backpack was.

What I won't allow myself to admit, at all, even for a second, is that I can feel the tiniest beat of disappointment in the knowledge that my shiny new sleeping bag will smell like big box store and the dye of new fabric, and not at all like the insanely hot but incredibly irritating Reaper, walking steadily in front of me on the narrow trail, when I climb into it tonight.

28

The next day, we hike. Again.

We take a break for a lunch of beef jerky, string cheese, Craisins, and water. It's not much, but we're both ravenous from the gradual incline we've been climbing all day. I know that I'm Dead (ha!) weight, and that Ryden could easily cover far more ground without me, but that's his problem, not mine.

We round out the afternoon with more hiking, only stopping once the Sun begins to set. Ryden finds another clearing, this one slightly larger than last night's and covered in a soft moss that will make our sleeping bags that much more comfortable—we won't be lying in them on top of hard ground.

When he'd flitted to the store for a sleeping bag and breakfast the night before, he'd also bought grilled chicken meals that he could warm over the fire—he hadn't wanted to waste them on lunch, so we eat them in silence for dinner. With our bellies full, we unroll our sleeping bags and prepare for the night.

I realize, tragically, that I'm not even a little bit tired.

"Ryden?" I ask timidly. "How old are you?"

"Older than you," he mutters through gritted teeth.

"How old?"

He raises a hand to pinch two fingers around his nose; he's clearly annoyed with my prodding already. "I'm thirty five."

This takes me by surprise.

"Oh..I thought you'd be older."

He snorts. "What, did you think there was some 500 year age gap?" My cheeks burn because yes, that's exactly what I was thinking. "I'm thirty five, and I've been thirty five since last May, when I was previously thirty four for a year. Not everything is one of your books, Abby."

We sit in silence for a moment, nothing but crickets chirping and the wind rattling through the treetops to keep us company.

"Ryden?" I continue with my interrogation. "Where are you from?"

"I spent most of my early years in London."

"Ryden?" I ask again. "Where are we going?"

A sigh. "Go to sleep, Abby."

I fidget in my sleeping bag. "But I'm not tired."

"Fake it until you make it, love."

"Ryden?" He looses an annoyed breath. "Where do Reapers come from?"

Silence, filled only by the chirping of crickets.

"Ryden?"

"Fine, I'll tell you that story, but then you have to leave me alone and go to sleep. Agreed?" His tone isn't as admonishing as his words are.

"Okay," I agree, nestling back down into my sleeping bag.

"Death themself created the first—"

"—wait."

He sighs. "Already? You have something to say already?"

I feel chastised. "I was just going to ask," I say softly, "why you said, 'themself' for Death? Is Death not...like...a man?"

"Why on Earth would Death have a gender?" He sounds, and looks, truly baffled.

"I mean, I don't know...people just..."

"Yes," he cuts me off. "*People* just. Not Death. Nor God for that matter. Do *people* truly think that these all-powerful, all-knowing entities would debase themselves so much as to confine their entire beings into one of the two boxes that Exist solely because of the social constructs of one planet? One planet out of trillions of planets in billions of galaxies that God and Death and the like oversee, mind you." He scoffs. "*Death having a gender,*" he continues to mutter under his breath. "Unbelievable."

"I mean, when you put it like that..." I say by way of apology.

"As I was saying," Ryden continues, brushing off his annoyance. "Death *themself* created the first Reapers in the same moment that God created the first Living beings, or the moment of the Big Bang—whatever you care to believe."

"So, like, '*let there be light*', right? Or like, when God created Adam and Eve?"

"Abby," he's annoyed again. He rubs his hand over his face before scratching the scruff that has grown there over the last few days. I can't say I don't prefer him like this—bearded and wild looking—but that's irrelevant and takes my attention away from his words. I refocus. "There are planets far older than this Earth...and God, Death, and Life have all Existed longer than this or any other planet."

I nod, not daring to cut him off again lest he refuse to continue his story.

"In terms of Earth, sure. You can say that Reapers have been here since the day God uttered the words, "let there be light," for this planet. It's part of why we are here, actually." He looks up at the soaring hickory trees around us, almost reverently, before leveling a gaze at me.

His blue eyes pierce through me, but I say nothing, so he proceeds.

"I thought surely you'd ask why that is..." he seems almost disappointed.

"I wanted to," I whisper, "but didn't want you to stop telling your story."

He grins at me and starts over. "Death themself created the first Reapers in the same moment that God created the first Living beings; Life requires balance, of course. Life requires Death, Death requires Life. When it was time to create this Earth, God did so, and once it was time for Life to Exist on this planet, Death created us, the Reapers, here, as the two have done billions of times both before and since. Reapers have been on this planet as long as Life has Existed on this planet, but it was not easy—especially in the beginning. While we can appear human easily enough, we are not exactly human anymore."

My stomach tightens reflexively, that ever present fear stretching its limbs inside of me, even though this isn't entirely new information. Jaali already told me that Reapers aren't fully human.

His eyes sweep away from mine and I know he noticed.

"Anymore? Wait, were you Born?" I ask.

He huffs a laugh. "Yes, Abby. I have parents. Human parents. Human parents," he sighs, "who have no idea what I do for work."

"How does that work out?" I'm intrigued—I know people have to lie to their parents occasionally, but Ryden and I could win awards for *Biggest Lies of Omission When Talking to Mom.*

"I just tell them that I travel a lot for work in what they think is consulting," he admits, "and make it a point to be there for birthdays, holidays, and the like. They know I'm busy, although my mother in particular loves to remind me that if I don't slow down I'll work myself to Death."

"I'm sure she just misses you," I say, thinking of my own mother. I wish I'd gotten to see her one more time before...this.

"She does," he agrees. "But it's hard to be around her with her not knowing about such a major part of my Life. She doesn't know that her son isn't fully human anymore." He sighs.

A thought jogs my memory, and I shudder. I don't want to revisit the night he'd kidnapped me, but I have to know. "So is that why you told me that you weren't a human cop?" I ask.

His brows furrow while he tries to find the memory, then I almost see the light bulb moment when it clicks. "Ah, that. While I *am* mostly human," he pauses, "I don't know how to describe it other than once you come of age, something inside you awakens," he explains. "Then, typically, another Reaper approaches you to recruit you, if you choose to become a Reaper. Then you go through training and testing and get your sigil," he gestures to his tattoo, "then *voila*, you're officially part of the Brotherhood."

"Can you say no?" I'm *transfixed.*

"You *can*, but most don't. Who would turn down a Life with magic? The ability to travel anywhere on Earth at a moment's notice? To be able to create wards to protect those you lo—the people around you? And," he jokes, "people are always going to Die...so job security."

"Do you get paid?"

"Yes, Reapers are paid very handsomely for the work we do. And don't ask me where the money comes from because I don't know, nor do I particularly care. Anyways," he sniffs. "Back to our origins, unless you've decided you're bored of the story?"

I mime locking my lips and throwing away the imaginary key.

We sit in silence for a beat before he continues.

"Even in the days that predate written record, there were shamans in most areas that could sense our...*otherness*." His face is wistful, sad even, as he idly twirls a small twig between his fingers. I give him a moment, as I can tell he's grieving for those of his kind that came before him; for the loneliness that they must have felt. The loneliness that *he* must feel—must have felt his whole Existence.

After another minute he shakes himself out of the reverie. "We were never able to fully acclimate into normal societies, because our not being 'one of them' kept us isolated, and isolation became our norm. Did you know," he pauses, those eyes laser focused on mine, "that you are currently lounging in one of the oldest mountain ranges on this continent?"

"I..." I try to speak, but can't, so he carries on.

"These mountains were formed before Life came to be here. They may seem small now, and unassuming when compared to other ranges, but the mountains beneath you right now are *ancient*. They're older than the oceans that formed when they separated from their other, now European half, hundreds of millions of years ago. Older than the dinosaurs, and other great beasts that once walked the Earth. These mountains are older, even, than *bones*."

I shiver.

"In the earliest days of our Existence, once we knew that we would not be able to coexist with the Livings after accepting our roles as Reapers, we fled. We were called to the oldest corners of the Earth. These mountains, the Makhonjwas in what is now South Africa, the Hamersley Range in what you know as Australia, and modern day America's Black Hills, among some of them. We carved out spaces in these mountains, Existing in plain sight of the Livings—but not *with* them. In these very mountains, we all but hid, only coming out when a soul was ready to cross over."

"As the populations grew and technology advanced, we were both needed more often and better able to blend in with society, and these mountains became more of a headquarters than a home to us."

My mouth has turned to sandpaper. "So, you're taking me to Reaper headquarters, then?" I ask, choking on the taste of the lead as it drops in my stomach.

"Not exactly. Some of the HQs, like the one here, have been long abandoned, forgotten to time, but others, like the Hamersley Range, are still very actively inhabited by Reapers."

"So, you're *not* taking me to Reaper headquarters?"

He sighs dramatically. "Nevermind. Go to sleep."

"No, I'd much rather mind. I mind a lot, actually, seeing as how my fate is in the balance and all that." I realize I'm chewing my fingernails, but don't stop myself.

"Please can you just...can you just trust me, Abby?" He rolls towards me, then, eyes full of hope. "Can you trust that what you think *is*, may not actually *be*?"

"I..." I whisper. I have to tell the truth, even if it's uncomfortable. "I'm sorry, Ryden, but I *don't* trust you. I mean," I stumble to add, "I trust that you will do what you can to keep me from being eaten by a panther or kidnapped by some wild Mountain Man, but I fear that that's temporary—like you're keeping me safe...*until*."

"Until *what*?!" He's exasperated. I don't blame him. I honestly wish that I *could* trust him, but that's impossible.

I shake my head. "I can't let myself think about what 'until' might mean. It's...it's too scary. I just want to keep my friends safe, so my being here willingly-ish, every breath I take, is in pursuit of that."

"You love them enough to Die for them?" he asks, almost awestruck.

"I thought you said I can't Die, because I'm already Dead?" I whisper before rolling away from where he sits, pretending to fall asleep as I allow the anxious tears to finally spill from my eyes.

29

We spend the next day hiking mostly in silence.

At midday, Ryden stops by a river and announces that it's time for lunch. The ground is mostly stone so close to the water, but the river offers a cool breeze that is welcome in the heavy, sticky humidity of the South in summer. It takes seeing the water for me to realize just how sweaty I'd been, and I down a bottle of water that had been tucked into the side of my pack.

I, immensely out of shape and exhausted, all but tumble to the ground to rest my legs. I groan as I let them stretch, feeling the tight muscles from the arch of my foot up to my thigh finally get some relief. Once I've had my moment, I glance around looking for Ryden, and, more importantly, food.

I pull another bottle of water out of my pack and down it in three gulps.

"So, what's for lunch?" I ask.

"About that..." he drags out the word and I know bad news is coming. "You see, I just ah—I need to...I need to flit and grab us lunch," his words speed up, "unless you'd like another day of beef sticks and cheese."

He's sheepish, and I know that if I say so, he'll stay here and eat what is a miserable excuse for a lunch for two people hiking in the mountains in the middle of nowhere.

"I don't, but—can you just ward the area? I don't want some Reaper I don't know hovering just out of sight."

He pauses.

"You trust my wards, then?" He doesn't look at me, and his words are stilted; clearly last night's admission that I don't trust him wounded him to some degree.

I don't understand how that could be a great surprise to him.

"Yes." What else could I say?

"But not me?" His gaze is earnest.

My cheeks redden, but I shake my head.

No, I don't trust Ryden.

"Alright," he forces a sad grin. "Give me a moment to cast my wards. I'll come tell you before I go."

I nod. I can hear him circling, giving me a wide berth and muttering under his breath. One gentle but swift breeze is the only indication I have that the wards have fallen into place, unless the breeze is just a coincidence. I can't be sure, but I hear Ryden returning and glance in his direction.

"All set," he says, that sad grin still in place. "The wards will hold until I return and bring them down. No one, Living or Reaper, can enter this area until I return and remove the wards. Unless—" an idea comes to him, "may I have your permission to include Jaali in my wards?"

I chew on my tongue, thinking his question over. Jaali being able to get to me couldn't hurt. "Sure," I begrudgingly nod. "That would be fine with me."

He pauses, studying me. "Are you sure this is what you want? You'll be alright?"

"Mhm," I say, but for some reason I can't meet his eyes. The awkwardness makes the air around us heavy.

"Okay, then. I shouldn't be more than a half an hour or so." He turns to go. "Oh, and love?" he turns to call back over his shoulder, "I wouldn't lie still for too long—it'll be that much harder to get up and moving after lunch."

I turn back to toss a middle finger in his direction, but he's already gone.

He's right, and I know it. I have to get up...if I let my muscles get too comfortable, they'll make the rest of the day even more miserable.

I sit up, begrudgingly, and survey my surroundings before rising fully to my feet. I brush the loose dirt off of my back as I silently bemoan how gross I am. My shower in Ryden's fancy bathroom feels like it was weeks ago, and not just three days. I'm mourning all the showers I've ever willingly skipped in my entire Existence when the glimmer of Sun on the river's glittering water catches my eye.

Before I can even register what I'm doing I'm rustling through my pack, grabbing the small bottles of toiletries. Then, I'm making my way towards the river, leaving a trail of my disgusting, sweaty clothes in my wake.

I decide at the last minute to leave my bra and panties on, because you never truly know who is out in the woods and I have enough modesty in me to care about not being seen naked by total strangers or the elusive Bigfoot.

I know that I could go invisible, but I don't want to. I want to *see* the cool water on my skin, to see my legs wiggle beneath ripples of the splashing crystal waves.

The water is cold enough to make me gasp, but I acclimate quickly and wade further into the stream. The water comes up to my waist when I stop and dip my head beneath its surface. I'd be lying if I said that it isn't heavenly to feel the grime that is multiple days of hiking melt away from my skin. I quickly shampoo and condition my hair and scrub over my body with soap—thankful that the travel sized bottles float. Once all that is done, I let myself float on top of the water, eyes closed, soaking up the Sun and fresh air. I only move to occasionally kick my feet, being mindful to stay near the campsite and not drift away on the water's current.

I lose all track of time. All that matters in these precious moments is my clean skin, the sun's warm rays, and this beautiful water. It's blissfully peaceful, and I can temporarily forget my friends' perilous situation, my kidnapping, my supposedly being *Primo Natus...* whatever it was. Nothing exists outside of this perfect bubble.

Eventually, I come to my senses. I know that I need to make my way back to the shore and get dressed before Ryden gets back with lunch. I take one more deep, soothing breath and stand up. I'm about twenty feet from the bank, and enjoying watching the distortion of my feet as I approach it. Once the water is down to my mid thigh, I lift my eyes to the shore...and stop in my tracks.

Ryden is standing there, utterly frozen. Behind him I can see brown paper bags, likely full of our lunch, that he's clearly forgotten, but he's staring at me. His eyes are darker than I've ever seen them, and for a moment I can't figure out why. Then, they track slowly downward and mortification, hot and swift, follows in their wake.

I am nearly *naked* and *soaking wet.*

Gods, this is so embarrassing.

I glance down and see every flaw: the dimpled skin of my stomach that falls in a soft pooch, the stripes of stretch marks that I'd been cursed with in my teenaged years dappling my thighs, my stupid muffin top that makes my body so awkwardly shaped. I see legs that have thick thighs that somehow taper into chicken leg shins, polka dotted with random splotches of purple spider veins. I see arms that are too much softness and not enough muscle.

I wish I could dip back down into the water but I've made it to the shallows by now—falling into the water here would just make me look like a wallowing hippopotamus.

So I stand here, frozen.

We're just staring at each other. His lips part as his gaze rakes over my body, back up to my face, and he clenches his fists by his side before swiftly turning his back to me.

"So sorry," he calls. "I, ah, didn't realize you'd be...that you were..." he sputters. "I'll just...give you some privacy to..."

He practically runs off into the trees and I frantically step fully onto the bank and use the closest piece of fabric, my dirty shirt, to dry off. I snatch clean clothes out of my bag and hastily pull them on.

"Are you decent?" I hear Ryden's strained voice call from a distance a moment later.

"I—yes," I call back. I have no idea how I'm going to face him after this. I think at this point I'd gladly go into the Unknown right now rather than sit across a clearing from him and eat lunch like nothing had happened. Like he hadn't just seen *everything*. I consider asking—no, *begging*—him to just let my soul cross over from his position in the treeline.

He steps back into the clearing, coughs, and says, "I brought rice and protein bowls, I hope that's okay." He passes me a bag, refusing to make eye contact, which is fine because I can never look him in the eye again.

"That's perfect." I say, my face feeling completely on fire, and we eat, not acknowledging each other again for hours.

During my—now cursed—swim, Ryden had not only gotten us lunch, but he'd also picked up burritos for dinner. He kept them in the insulated part of his pack, and when we stop to make camp for the night, he passes me one without a word.

We eat in silence, neither daring to break it or be the first to make eye contact. I'm mortified, and he's...I don't know. Disgusted? Outraged?

I've only ever seen Ryden and Jaali, but I assume that all Reapers are their level of...attractiveness.

Maybe Ryden has a partner out there: one with a flat, muscled stomach. Someone toned and beautiful, without an ounce of cellulite. He's probably counting down the seconds until he can get back to that person, whoever they may be.

"Abby," Ryden's voice startles me out of my daze. I look up to meet his face, and am surprised to find genuine concern there.

"What?" I ask, trying to seem nonchalant.

"You were clenching your jaw so hard that I could hear your teeth grinding. Are you alright?' he asks.

"I'm fine," I pretend as I pick at stray pieces of rice in my burrito's foil wrapper. It's good, but the part of me longing for normalcy found myself searching the bags for the single lime slice that had been thrown into a tiny container as an afterthought.

"Is this about...earlier?" His eyes bore into me—piercing right through me.

"I would quite literally rather go into the Unknown right now than talk about it." I'm all bravado, but I hope that my sharp tone is enough for him to change the subject.

He surprises me, then, by responding not with agreement or a sharp retort, but with sheer confusion. "Why would you possibly feel that way?"

I say nothing, because what is there to say? *Sorry you had to be subjected to my every physical flaw earlier? At least you didn't go blind!* But his brows are furrowed and I know he's not letting this go easily.

"I...am...*mortified*," I admit, letting my hair fall around my face—a mask so he can't see my cheeks as they catch fire.

"You're m—*mortified*?" he asks, truly seeming dumbfounded.

"Why wouldn't I be?" I squeak. "You basically saw *everything*."

"I mean, I never want to see a woman in any state of undress without her express consent, but...I can't fathom how you'd feel *embarrassed*." He looks completely and utterly confused.

"Please stop," I beg. "I don't want to talk about this." I want my face to keep burning until my entire body is consumed. Until I become nothing more than dust on the side of this mountain.

I don't want to Exist in this conversation.

"I'm truly flummoxed here," he stands and stalks towards me before taking a seat beside me, our shoulders touching. I can feel his breath tickle the side of my face as he leans down towards me and says, "I'm just trying to understand you. That's all. Why do you feel embarrassed about earlier?"

"Because...b-b-because," oh gods. The floodgates...they are about to open and I can do nothing to stop them. I make one final, fleeting attempt to escape this conversation: I snap into my invisible form.

It works.

Well.

It almost works.

It would have worked...had Ryden not reached down and, even in my invisible form, found my hand. He wraps it in his own, and says, so quietly I might have made it up, "Abby. Please don't hide from me, love."

I *should* hide.

He's given me every reason to hide, to fear.

At least, he *had* given me those reasons before.

Since we've been on this journey, though, he's been a completely different person entirely. He's been mostly patient and kind, protective, and willing to teach. And while he hasn't outright said it, a part of me is beginning to notice the subtleties in the things he says. Things about him taking me to an *abandoned* Reaper headquarters. About what I *think* may not actually be what *is*.

I have to wonder if my attitude, and my total unwillingness to trust him, were the reasons that *he* hadn't been able to trust *me*. And if he trusts me, would I, in turn, get more information out of him?

I'm definitely not fully committed to the idea of truly trusting Ryden yet, but I'm beginning to realize that my Existence may depend on him *thinking* that I do.

It's time for me to change my strategy, and lean into the possibility that he may not actually be as bad as I've thought.

I reappear and look up, finding his eyes full of concern. He reaches up tentatively and tucks a stray strand of my hair behind my ear. "Tell me why you're embarrassed," he pleads quietly, his blue eyes capturing my own again.

"Because," I heave in a breath before it becomes a sob. "My body. It's...pretty gross."

He stiffens beside me, dropping my hand.

"*Gross*?" he demands, his tone accusatory, almost angry.

I nod. "My stomach isn't flat and my legs are covered in stretch marks and lumps of cellulite, nothing is toned or tanned or pretty and I should've become a gym person years ago but I was drowning in loneliness and didn't care about myself and I—" I want to continue, it feels surprisingly good to get this all out, but Ryden raises a hand up, a silent gesture for me to stop.

Now it's my turn to don the mask of confusion.

"What?" I breathe.

"Your body looked absolutely perfect from where I was standing, Abby." His eyes are pure fire, the bluest part of a flame, and I know, I *know* that he's telling the truth.

"I—*what*?"

"I flitted back to the campsite and saw you out there, making your way back to the shore, water and light glistening off of you like you were the godsdamned Sun itself. It took my breath away. *You* took my breath away, Abby," he takes my hand in his again. "Your smile, when you thought no one could see. You were unabashedly happy for the briefest moment—even in the middle of what you feel is an existential threat. And those *curves*. It took every ounce of strength I have to turn towards the woods, to give you the privacy that you deserve, and not dive into the water myself...to not wrap my arms around you, drag you back into deeper water, and never let you go."

I can't do anything but gape at him. I want to accuse him of lying, of just saying something nice so I keep cooperating on this ridiculous journey, but his face is so earnest that there's no way he's being anything but honest. He truly does find me, at least physically, attractive. Or at least, he did in that moment.

Maybe it was a fluke.

"I shouldn't admit any of that to you, because of what you are, and what I am. And you can trust that I know that nothing would ever happen...between us," my whole body warms, matching my flaming cheeks, "but I'm sorry, love. I can't have you thinking that there is anything at all *wrong* about you."

"I...I don't know what to say," I admit, sheepishly, "but I think you look pretty perfect, too." I don't know what made me admit it out loud, other than the vulnerability floating in the air between us. Like he offered up a bare part of himself, and I needed to reply in kind. A call and response that I couldn't deny even if I'd wanted to.

"Bah," he waves a hand at me, brushing off my compliment, but he meets my eyes again, dimples on full display, and rasps out a, "thank you, love."

He taps his hands on his knees and says, "Well, now that that's settled, I think it's time we set up this campsite." He smiles at me, and it's more friendly than I've seen from him before. Maybe this whole *building-trust-then-deciding-if-I-can-trust-him* will be easier than I thought...

We set up the campsite quickly and I notice that he set our bedrolls up slightly closer than we've had them in the past. They aren't touching —still about an arm's length apart, but if one of us reached out...

I jolt awake in the middle of the night.

I'm not sure why I'm awake. I scan the clearing and the surrounding trees, but everything seems utterly peaceful. I'm sure that Ryden has warded the area so nothing that would do us any harm could get near us. I don't feel uneasy, either. I'm tired down to my bones; the exhaustion of hiking the past several days weighs on me heavily, but it's clear that my mind, or my body, or both, don't want to be asleep right now.

I turn towards Ryden and am stunned to see that he's actually sleeping. Any other time I've woken on this journey, I've found him sitting watch, pacing through the trees, or in his bedroll, blue eyes wide open as he gazed wordlessly up at the stars. I'd marveled, in those moments, about how the stars reflected so perfectly in the blue of his eyes. I've seen him in all manner of awake, but I've *never* seen him sleep.

A small part of me is pleased when I notice his arm, reached out in my direction, his fingers barely an inch from the edge of my sleeping bag. I stamp that idea down—he'd probably just rolled over. He could be a wild sleeper.

It has nothing to do with me.

I'm staring up at the stars, doing a pretty fair impression of Ryden, when a memory forms—something I haven't thought of in decades.

When I was a child and couldn't sleep, I had a system, a habit that would always end in my finding sleep. I would curl up on my side and nestle into my blankets, then I would count my blessings—all the things I had to be thankful for, even on my worst days. Even on the days where my anxiety told me that I didn't have a future, and that I'd never have a true friendship, a true *connection*, with another soul. I would picture the house I was laying in on a map, as if I was seeing the house, and its surroundings, from above. I would count the house, and Ma. Then, I would mentally pull away from the map, until I could also see the twins' house, and I'd count them. Then, I'd pull away more and see Anabel's house...then Ethan's, then Kara's, then Latrell's,...on and on with my small list of friends until I dozed off to sleep thinking I was the luckiest ghost in the world.

My stomach turns as I remember when, and why, I ever stopped counting blessings. Once the twins left, I decided that the world hated me and that, other than my Ma, I had no blessings at all.

Now, I'm blessed with friends again, but for how much longer? How much more time do I have before I don't have the ability to worry about sleep, or blessings, or *Existing* at all?

Okay, then. Counting blessings is out—I'm too emotionally exhausted to go down the road of worrying tonight.

I glance back at Ryden when inspiration strikes.

I've had to watch this lean, muscular Reaper, the epitome of peak health, hike through these godsforsaken mountains for days as if he's on a leisurely stroll down an artsy side street in Paris, while I sweat and struggle along like a pig, ending every day totally exhausted. But what if I were to...*borrow* some energy from a Reaper? Possession wouldn't deplete his own energy stores at all, but it may give me enough energy to not feel so tired that I can barely function every evening.

Unzipping my sleeping bag takes what feels like a decade—I have to move the zipper slowly, tooth-by-tooth, so that it doesn't make a sound. I pull my legs out then quickly feign sleep, squinting one eye open to see if Ryden moves. He doesn't, and I breathe a sigh of relief. I snap into my invisible form, so that if he wakes and doesn't find me in my bedroll, he'll assume I've gone behind a tree to relieve myself.

I crouch down before him and instinctively reach for the teres major. I find it and clasp my hand around it, thrilled that this is actually going to work. Then...nothing.

Nothing?

Where there has been give every other time, with every other Possession, Ryden's teres major does not budge. It's like it's just a muscle, functioning as a muscle should, and not opening a portal into one's entire being.

Is he closed off to Possession?

I gape. This is...a new development I hadn't expected, but obviously should have. He's a Reaper for God's sake. Ryden sniffs and I panic, sure he's about to wake up and catch me in this...betrayal?

Is this a betrayal?

Have I crossed a line?

I internally debate briefly before deciding that I haven't, because I'm only *pretending* that I trust Ryden—pretending that he can trust me.

I rise and pivot at the same time, snapping back into my solid form. I'm standing between our bedrolls, but facing my own, when he says dreamily, "Abby? Love, are you alright?" He sits up on his elbows and looks up at me, eyes still clouded in sleep. His hair is a tousled mess and my heart does this weird *tha-tha-thump*ing thing at the sight.

That's weird, and I need to stop looking at him.

I shake my head to clear thoughts of Ryden being beautiful and sleep mussed out of my mind.

"I'm alright, just had to...you know," I point nonchalantly at a random tree. "Go back to sleep."

He nods and closes his eyes. Within thirty seconds, his breathing slows and I know he's truly asleep again.

My breathing, on the other hand, can't slow. Not with this new information I've gleaned.

Reapers can't be Possessed.

30

"Abby, wake up."

Ryden is shaking me. Hard. "Abby, you've got to get up right now."

I'd been dreaming. I'd been on a yacht in the Mediterranean with Tom Hiddleston. We were admiring the Amalfi Coast in the distance, our skin and hair glimmering from the salt spray of the water, draining Aperol Spritzes like they were going out of style; this interruption is most unwelcome.

"Unnnnghhh." I swat at my shoulder where Ryden's firm grip is quickly becoming painful and stretch to pull out of his grasp.

I reluctantly open my eyes as he grabs my other shoulder and pulls me up into a sitting position.

"Wha—" I try to yell before he clamps a hand over my mouth to silence me. He presses one finger to his lips and makes a ragged shushing noise.

"You've got to listen to me," he mouths, barely making a sound.

I want to argue, to tell him to go to hell so that I can roll over and get back to Tom, but the words dissolve on my tongue when I notice his eyes: they are sleep hazy but *wild*.

Wild with both thrill and a slight glimmer of...fear? Concern? It catches me so off guard that I nod as we stand together.

"I want you to go invisible, then I want you to get behind me. Okay?" He chances a glance over his shoulder and bristles, clearly sensing something that I can't.

"What's going on?" I try to match his breathy whispers, but mine feel like shouts.

He gently places a hand over my mouth again, those wild eyes almost feral as they bore into mine. His breath tickles my eyelashes, making them flutter. He releases me after a heartbeat and spins, his back now pressed to me.

"Abby, there isn't time for your games," he barks low over his shoulder. "You've just got to *trust me*. Go invisible and stay behind me, no matter what happens."

I comply, winking into invisibility.

For several moments, we just stand there—Ryden, a warrior poised for battle, and me, a sleep-addled, invisible ghost girl crouching to peer under his arm at whatever threat he seems to have detected. The minutes drag on and I'm beginning to think that this was all an elaborate prank, that he's going to turn around and shout "gotcha!" before telling me it's time to start walking again, but then I hear the crunching of twigs that signifies someone—or something—approaching our campsite.

"This is impossible," I breathe, knowing instinctively that it isn't Jaali. "Your wards."

"Abby, please. You cannot make a sound," his mouth barely moves at the words, and his entire body is thrumming, as if he's gearing for battle. Ryden's response to a threat is all fight to my learned tendency of flight. Imperceptibly, Ryden tenses, pressing me firmly between a tree behind us and the hard planes of his back.

I begrudgingly admit that this isn't exactly unpleasant, and may be worth leaving Tom and the yacht for...until I hear the growling.

My entire body tenses when the black bear steps into the clearing.

It is *massive*, easily the size of Ryden's SUV, and ten feet tall when it stands upright. It growls again before falling back to all fours and approaching our makeshift campsite.

We stand in tense silence as it sniffs through our bedrolls and rips into our packs, shredding most of our belongings and devouring all of our remaining food. Since Ryden can flit to a store to replenish our supplies, this isn't exactly worrisome; it's inconvenient.

I'm most worried about my phone, my last tether to the outside world. If the bear crushes it, I won't have a way to contact anyone if I finally break free of whatever game Ryden is playing.

Once the bear has sniffed out all of the food in our packs, it turns and rises to cross the clearing and, blessedly, leave. From the glow of the fire Ryden had stoked before we slept, I can see its teeth, each one nearly the size of my fingers and razor sharp. This beast is so huge and terrifying that I can't help the gurgled gasp that rasps out of my throat.

The bear, who had begun to plod away, turns to face us, hackles raised. Because, of course, it *would* hear me.

Before I can even scream, Ryden pounces from our place in the shadows, a long blade I hadn't noticed before in hand.

Before I can blink, the blade protrudes from the bear's chest.

Before I can feel the cold washing over my front where Ryden's warmth had just been, the bear lies Dead at my feet.

"How...how did you do that?" I ask.

We're sitting by the fire Ryden had stoked back to Life. He's eyeing me warily as my adrenaline wears off, giving way to shock.

"I'm a Reaper and it was one bear." He's smug, riding the high of the kill, the thrill of the fight. Not that there was much of a fight.

"Yeah," I scoff, "a bear the size of a mid-size vehicle."

"Love," he grins that devilish grin that I've grown to hate that I find attractive, "one bear isn't going to take out a Reaper. Not one worth their salt, anyways."

I laugh freely, for once. "Yeah, I mean I guess you're all basically gods of Death. You have to have superhuman strength to be able to do all the killing all the time."

Ryden tenses beside me and sucks in a breath. There's an anguished look in his eyes that I haven't seen before, and I know instantly that I've said something horribly wrong.

"Is that truly what you think of me?" Ryden whispers coldly.

"Ryden...wha—" I stutter. "If I said something wrong, I'm truly sor —" he puts a hand up and the words fade on my lips.

"I won't insult you by asking if you know what it feels like to be a pariah, because I know that you do," he rasps, his fury palpable. "And I hate that you know that feeling. That *loneliness*. Truly, I desperately hate it for you. But I wish you could extend me—extend *Reapers*—that same courtesy. Reapers, as a general rule, do not kill people, Abby. Death...Death is what kills people. And Reapers are the poor fools who have to pick up the pieces once Death comes knocking."

I'm stunned, shamed, into silence.

"Can you imagine," he lifts a shaky finger, "just for one moment, what it's like to be surrounded by nothing but *Death* for most of your Existence? To have to be the one accompanying souls to the Unknown? Souls that are lost, scared, and alone? For your place of work to be sickbeds of those that will never heal, crime scenes of those that will never rise again, sites of horrific accidents that blindsided a soul on an idle Tuesday? Every day of this near miserable Existence, I wake up surrounded by the grief of yet another soul, yet another family, torn apart by Death. I tend to the soul. I comfort them, and I stay with them as long as I need to until they are ready to go into the Unknown. Regardless of whatever prejudices you have created about Reapers, what we do is a *kindness*, Abby, and I'd appreciate you to not so callously mock who and what I am in the future."

He rises before I can collect my thoughts enough to say a word.

Stupid, stupid, stupid!

How could I have been so cold?

How did I not think about how difficult—how *lonely*—the Life of a Reaper must be? Especially after hearing something so similar from Jaali just days ago. Especially knowing such an aching loneliness myself.

Even though my goal is to trick him into trusting me, I'm not completely heartless. I feel true guilt, true regret for my words, and for my causing him pain. It was, as he said, callous of me, and incredibly rude and offensive to assume that Reapers are murderers.

I turn to say just that to him at the same time that he reaches to thrust something into my hand.

My phone.

"I know you were probably worried about that, but the bear didn't maul it. I'm going to flit away to replace the food the bear ate and cool my head. You'll be alright? My wards will still be present, and I've fortified them to protect against predatory animals now, too, since I hadn't thought that much of a risk before. They will only allow me or Jaali in."

I nod.

"Ryden, I'm so, so—" He's gone before I can say more.

Maybe that's for the best. We don't need to be friends. He has whatever his job is, and I have mine: to get him to trust me and find out what it is he wants with me, and the twins, and any other Born ghosts out there before it's too late.

31

After Ryden's exit, I decide to take advantage of the moment and poke around at his wards.

When he'd set wards around me for the first time, the day of the fateful swim, I remember feeling a whisper of wind brush past me. Now, I'm determined to find the edge. Am I under an invisible dome? Fenced in by an electric current?

I stroll through the woods, marveling at how comfortable I've gotten here. I'm sure by this point that there are trees surrounding me for miles on all sides, but it's much more peaceful than I thought it would be. The only sounds are the occasional chirp of a cricket and the leaves crunching under my feet.

I marvel at my own bravery. A month ago I'd never have believed that I'd be out strolling in the middle of the woods, *alone*, in the middle of the night. It's still pitch black outside, but it's still and peaceful. The silence is calming, even after this latest fight with Ryden. If you can call it a fight. I feel like an idiot.

I trek for a few more minutes when a new sound joins the cacophony of nature: the same whispering sound of wind I'd heard when Ryden first cast his wards. It grows louder as I keep walking, then as I take one more step, the sound disappears entirely. I take a step backwards, and the wind is back.

I guess I found the ward line. I hopscotch across it a few times like an eight year old on the playground, but eventually get bored. I think at one point I hear someone calling my name, but chalk it up to my just hearing things. I'm out in the middle of forests on the Appalachian mountains alone, of course my mind will do everything in its power to freak me out—and certainly there's no one out here calling to me. I turn to head back to the campsite, and Ryden is suddenly standing in front of me, eyes wide in...*fear*?

"What now?" I breathe as I quickly step toward him and grab his arm. "Is there another bear?!"

He hunches over, hands on his knees, in what seems to be an

attempt to catch his breath.

"Woman, you are maddening!" he wheezes.

Huh?!

"What did I do?" I ask. I have no idea, but add it to the list.

"There I am in the middle of a Costco in northern California, trying to find us new bedrolls when all that was on the shelves was a single Queen sized blow up mattress..."

My heart stutters a bit at how close we'd apparently been to the "one bed" trope before I remember I should be listening to Ryden's story.

"...when I feel *someone* cross my wards."

I gasp. "Someone crossed the wards? How?!" I spin around, hoping to see who it might have been, trying to locate the threat.

He slowly places a hand to his forehead and rubs his temple.

"You, Abby. *You* crossed my wards." I feel the color drain from my face.

"Wait—what?"

"How could you possibly be confused about what I'm saying?" I can feel the annoyance radiating from him.

"How did you know *I* crossed your wards?" Do his wards have a creepy catalog system? Can he see his wards in his mind like some weird mental security camera? Does he have mental CCTV?

"Be...cause you and I are the only beings that are able to cross it." He says it like that's the most obvious, most natural thing in the world.

"I'm able to cross your wards?"

This is...news. Pretty important news, I'd say.

He scoffs at me, utterly bewildered. "Of course you are."

"But I'm your...prisoner? You'd just let me freely walk through your wards?"

For one second, just the blink of an eye, he looks pained.

"I truly hope, by the end of this," he muses, "that you won't feel like you've been a prisoner." He smiles softly, almost wistfully, before straightening. "But Abby, you must not cross my wards at night. Especially out here."

"What do you mean?" I ask.

Why would I be allowed to cross his wards if I'm not actually supposed to cross them?

"You're in Appalachia, love," he levels a gaze at me, his eyes going wide when I have no reaction. "Have you not...heard the legends?" He quirks an eyebrow, amused, as if he's talking to a precocious child.

"No...?" I ask, dumbfounded. *What is he on about?*

He sighs, stretching an arm out to guide me back to our campsite.

Could his anger with me have fizzled out that quickly?

"Come on, let's go back to the campsite. My bedroll didn't take too much damage, so you can use it tonight, and I'll go replenish our supplies tomorrow. You aren't going to want me to leave again tonight after I tell you about Appalachia."

I burrow so deep into Ryden's bedroll that only my eyes are visible to him from his perch on a nearby log.

We'd returned to our campsite quickly—mostly because I was utterly spooked. Whatever Ryden knows about these woods seems sinister, and I'm not sure that I'm ready to hear the tales. I know I'm a ghost and all, but *ghost stories* have always really creeped me out.

I nestle slightly deeper into the bedroll, oddly comforted by that leathery, woodsy scent that is so Ryden, and I have to roll my eyes. Why am I every girl in every book, swooning at *scents* now?

Gross.

I glance Ryden's way and see that he's looking at me, because *of course he is*.

"What are you smiling at?" I snap as I notice the slight grin tugging at his mouth.

"You," he says softly, but doesn't elaborate. A shiver tickles its way up my spine, and I'm not sure if it's nerves or something else entirely.

Rather than forcing myself to think about *that*, I feign impatience.

"I was told there would be stories," I sigh haughtily and Ryden chuckles.

"Very well," he agrees. "Where to begin?" He pretends to think, stroking his chin, and I throw his pillow at him. "Alright, alright," he laughs, handing it back to me as I settle in once again.

"Do you remember when I told you about these mountains?" He glances up at the trees towering over us, their silhouettes barely visible against the black of the sky.

"I do," I reply. "They're older than bones, and Reapers used to hide here."

"That's true. These are some of the oldest mountains on Earth, and because of that, have been home to all number of," he pauses to find the appropriate word, "...*beings* over the millennia."

As much as I love to make Ryden feel unimportant, I'm hanging on his every word.

"There are entities that roam these woods, Abby, that you do not want to cross."

"*Entities*? Seriously? I'm a ghost in case you missed the memo..." I'm all bravado, and I hope he doesn't realize it.

"*Entities*," he sneers animatedly, making it clear that he's teasing me and not being truly condescending, "are more than just *ghosts*, Abby." He reaches across the space between us to nudge my shoulder playfully, even as I feel a pit opening in my stomach.

"Okay, but what does that mean? Because now I'm slightly terrified."

He grimaces. "I can't even tell you that you *shouldn't* be terrified, honestly."

He looks down at his hands as he fidgets, clearly lost in thought.

"I'm afraid that I can't do many of the stories justice, as they aren't my stories to tell; the Appalachian lore is based off of ancient legends. For you, I will generalize, and I hope that someday, you'll hear these stories in their fullest glory, as they were meant to be told: handed down across generations from those who lived the stories to their descendants."

"For thousands of years before European colonizers appeared bearing laughable arms but civilization-devastating diseases, Indigenous tribes Existed alongside the occasional Reaper in these and so many other lands. The vast majority of these people were peaceful, except for when violence was necessary for protection or food. But every so often, evil would take over the spirit of a person, and they would be changed into something else entirely: a beast fueled by greed and insatiable hunger."

"H-hunger?" I ask through chattering teeth.

"Yes, and I hope that I don't need to elaborate on that further," he says, face stern but still kind. "These spirits, for lack of a better word, are master manipulators, and can mimic any sound or voice in the world. They can sound like your own mother, they can call your name... anything to lure you in."

My heart drops into my butt and I sit bolt upright, glancing wildly around in all directions.

If I weren't so utterly terrified, Ryden's reaction to my sudden movement would be comical: he nearly falls backwards over the log he's sitting on. Of course, being Ryden, he recovers and makes it graceful: in one fluid movement, he somehow twists from falling backwards, into landing into a crouch on the ground in front of me. His eyes dart around, a mirror of mine, searching for the threat.

I have to admit, *again*, that the man is *breathtaking*.

"What?! Abby, what is it?!" he hisses, a warrior ready to strike.

"S-something called my name," I breathe.

"What?" he twists to look at me, wild eyed and slightly exasperated. "Nothing called your name, love. I've been right here."

"No! Not now! Before! When you were gone. When I crossed your wards...I swear I heard someone calling my name, and then you were back and so flustered and I just put it out of my mind, but it was out there! Whatever this *entity* is, it was out there tracking me!"

His features soften in understanding then, and his gaze is almost pitying.

"I know what I heard. Please don't try and make me feel like I'm crazy."

His brows raise. "Oh, you're certainly not crazy. I don't doubt something called out to you—they likely sensed a single soul, out alone in these woods, and saw you as an easy target."

I can't help the whimper that escapes my lips.

"Abby, love," he chuckles as he kneels beside the bedroll and scoops me up into his arms as tears pour down my face uncontrollably. "Why do you cry?" He presses a thumb to my cheek and catches them as they fall before wiping them away.

"You're telling me that *something* was out there and saw me as a target and you have to ask why I'm afraid?" I can feel his heartbeat, strong and steady through his shirt, and I try to slow my racing pulse to match his.

"Ah," he whispers. "I see."

He shifts my weight easily so that his eyes meet mine, and the tenderness, the eagerness in them nearly cracks my heart in two.

"I know that I haven't given you the best of reasons to trust me yet, but Abby, I swear to you that *you are safe with me.* So long as you are with me, or with Jaali, or within either of our wards, nothing will harm you." He pulls me into his chest, and I can feel him gently stroking my hair.

It's weird, but...also kind of nice.

I want to believe him, especially given how quickly he rushed back to my aid the moment he sensed that I might be in trouble. The shame I'd felt over our earlier fight comes rushing back and threatens to knock me out cold.

"Ryden?" I whisper. He starts, almost imperceptibly.

"Mmm?" I can feel his chest rumble, but it's as if he'd been somewhere else; lost in his thoughts as his fingers lazily trace up and down the curve of my spine.

"I'm sorry about what I said earlier—before."

He sighs as his hand stills. "I know you are."

"I shouldn't have presumed to know anything about...what you do. About what your Life has been. I was ignorant."

"My reaction wasn't the best, I'll admit."

I sit up, twisting to look at him. "No, your reaction was normal—empathetic, even. Even when you were angry, you weren't cruel like I was. You left your wards up to protect me, even though I'd hurt you."

"You didn't mean to hurt me, love. I know that."

"That doesn't make it okay that I did. And I'm sorry." Gods, apologizing is always so uncomfortable—but necessary.

He gapes at me for a brief moment, losing himself to his thoughts again, before he smiles sadly and pulls me close once more.

"Perhaps not. But I hope that you'll begin to see that I *am* someone that you can trust. Someone that you'll *want* to trust. Even if I'm angry, or hurt," he whispers into my hair, "I will *never* leave you in danger."

In spite of every fiber of my being screaming that I can't trust him, I may be starting to believe him.

32

The following morning, I wake to organized chaos.

It's humid and sticky already, and the Sun is bright even though it can't be later than eight in the morning.

Ryden has set up...*something*, and he has his back to me surveying his work. I rub my eyes to clear the haze of sleep and sit up, cringing as I feel the crust of drool on my cheek. *Guess I slept well?* I frantically wipe it off before Ryden can see, then stretch more exaggeratedly than I need to so he'll realize I'm awake.

As predicted, he glances over his shoulder. "Ah, you're up!"

"What on earth are you *doing*?" I ask as more and more of the scene around me comes into focus.

There's a leather knife pack, unrolled to reveal several daggers of varying levels of intimidating, and he's set up a makeshift circle of fallen logs with one towering oak tree filling in about three feet of its perimeter. The entire circle looks to be about nine feet across, through the center.

"Well, as I mentioned, I've fortified my wards after last night's, ah— *incident*," I bristle, remembering the black bear mauling our campsite, "to keep out most animals, too. Any animals that could be considered predators, anyways," he smirks, "I thought you might not like me banishing wild bunnies from the area."

"Agree," I smirk back, "I'd never forgive you for *that*."

My words surprise both of us: Ryden stands up straighter, and I have to stop myself from slapping my hand over my mouth.

Did I just...insinuate that there are things I *could* forgive Ryden for? Surely not...

Sometimes I wish I could think before my mouth just lets words fall out. My Existence would be so much easier if I could be a little more in control of myself.

"So..." I press on, choosing to shove the elephant in the campsite outside of the wards, where all things I don't want to think about belong. "You fortified the wards, and made a...circle with that tree and those logs? And blades?" I chance another glance towards the daggers, which are still there glinting in the early morning Sun.

He smiles, and is that what's making the daggers shimmer? Suddenly the Sun seems dull in comparison.

No! No, we are not sitting here thinking about this Reaper's smile, Abby. Pull yourself together!

"Well," his grin turns sheepish, "as much as I wish you'd trust *me*, I'm glad that you at least trust my wards. They *will* keep you safe." The truth rings in every word, and I believe him wholeheartedly. His wards will not fail to protect me.

"But..." I let the word draw out, urging him to finish the sentence.

"But...," he sneers teasingly, "I thought that you knowing how to protect yourself, even to some degree, might prove to be, ah—beneficial? For you?"

My anxiety spikes. "Protect myself from *what*?" I can't help but dart a glance around the clearing. It's just us here, no one or nothing else. He notices and takes a step towards me. I flinch, only for a second, but he notices that, too, and holds his hands up in mock surrender.

"There's nothing for you to worry about. I just thought that *you* might feel better if you were comfortable with a blade?" He flushes and rubs the back of his neck awkwardly. "But we don't have to. You don't have—"

"No," I stand from the bedroll. "No, that sounds...okay."

I'm not going to shy away from learning to defend myself, even if my teacher is someone I don't trust. Who knows? Maybe I'll pick up some tips today that I can use against *him*, if it ever comes to that. Plus, if we're training, we're not walking, which puts us getting to the mystery destination off until later—and that's totally fine by me.

If Ryden is here with me, then he is *not* Reaping the twins.

I take a step towards him before I feel a throb behind my temple. I reach a hand up to massage my forehead and suck in a gasp. He's instantly in front of me.

"What's wrong?" he asks, laser focused on me. He clutches my arms behind my elbows and gently pulls me closer, as if his attention will threaten the ailment enough that it will leave.

"I can't do another thing without caffeine," I admit, still massaging my temples. "My head is already pounding at the thought."

Ryden had flitted away without another word and returned moments later with an iced coffee, two breakfast protein boxes, and several bottles of water in tow.

Once my caffeine headache is gone and our bellies are full, Ryden stands and steps into the center of his makeshift circle. He turns on his heels to face me and my stomach gives another one of those annoying swoops.

Why couldn't he at least be ugly? I think for the thousandth time.

But, alas, he's tall and lithe, and when he leans into what can only be described as a fighting crouch he looks purely lethal—like something out of a beautiful nightmare. I think idly that I'd never want to be on the receiving end of Ryden's wrath before remembering that I'm about to do just that: I'm about to learn to *fight* Ryden—the only other person here *to* fight.

"Our first lesson," he's all business now, "is balance. You have to be sure in your footing before you can expect to be able to hold your own in a brawl."

We then spend what feels like an eternity on balance training exercises.

This was *not* what I expected when I agreed to defense training.

He has me stand on one foot, then the other, in 30 second intervals. Over and over again. Then we move on to standing on one foot and *stretching the lifted leg out in front of me* over and over again until I think I might lose my mind. Then, I have to step up onto a log on one leg, then the other. Finally, he runs me through a few yoga poses. Just when I think I'm going to Die (pun intended) of boredom, he gently (and unexpectedly) shoves me on the arm. I topple over but manage to catch myself before completely falling.

"What was that for?!" I hiss as I rise to face him.

"To show you that your indifference toward balance is misguided. We're going to do balance exercises every morning from here on out, so that you're not so easily pushed around."

I roll my eyes. *Asshole.* He could have led with that little tidbit, so I'd have known to expect more than just exercises.

As if he's read my mind, he continues, "I want keeping your balance to be second nature, not something you have to be constantly on alert to maintain."

"Fine," I mutter. "Can we do something else now, though?"

His eyes shine and his smile is positively feral.

"I thought you'd never ask."

I was naive. I was foolish.

I miss walking mindlessly.

Sparring with Ryden is exhausting. He's taught me how to properly hold daggers, how to anticipate my opponents' next moves, and how to fight both offensively and defensively.

I know better than to think I'm going to be some fighting prodigy.

That's one thing I never understood about the books Em and I love: the main character always starts off thinking she's nothing and no one, has one fighting lesson, and BOOM! She kicks ass and takes names and all her enemies end up vanquished in the end. She starts the book weak and ends it able to brawl for hours without breaking a sweat. How?! That kind of athleticism takes months, *years* even.

No, I don't expect to best Ryden, or any Reaper, any time soon. But, anything I can learn is something I didn't know before, so I'm game.

We're circling each other, neither making an offensive move, so

Ryden idly reaches a hand up to scratch his bicep: the one with the Reaper tattoo. He's usually wearing t-shirts with sleeves long enough to cover most of it, so I've never gotten the chance to focus much attention on it, but I can now. Just like all of the other Reapers, he has the skull hourglass tattoo on his right arm, but the base he selected is a large chrysanthemum.

Maybe distraction will provide me an *in* to take him down.

"What's with the chrysanthemum?" I ask, feigning nonchalance even though I am genuinely curious. "Did they make you get that?"

"What? No," he glances down at his tattoo, but it's too fast—too little time for me to pounce. "We have to have the hourglass with the skull as the top bulb for our sigil—what officially awakens the Reaper's full power after training—but the base is left to the individual Reaper to choose."

I wait a beat to see if he will continue, and when he doesn't, I ask, "So, the chrysanthemum? You chose it?"

"I did," he confirms. "Because chrysanthemums have many meanings. In Japanese mythology, they represent courage and bravery, they are a symbol of the Sun goddess Amaterasu's warmth, and they're present in Japanese creation myths surrounding the god Izanagi. In Chinese lore, they represent longevity and good fortune. They're also sometimes referenced in relation to Demeter in Greek mythology, as a symbol of the cycles of Life. And in Europe, white chrysanthemums represent Death and mourning."

We're both lost in our thoughts for a moment before I break the silence, "So it means a lot of conflicting things, then."

"You could say that," he smiles wistfully, "I just like the idea of something that is ancient, that means something to people spanning different cultures, is a tie-in to Death, but also represents Life. It's like," he almost seems bashful, which does odd things to my stomach, "it's like it represents me, but it also represents everyone? That may sound silly..." he trails off.

"I don't think it's silly," I promise. "Thank you for sharing it with me."

He nods. "Now stop trying to distract me."

Busted.

We circle each other for several more minutes before he lunges at me. I jump to the side and he falls backwards, but I know he could have easily grabbed me had he wanted to. *He's playing with me.*

And that is...well, that is quite frankly annoying--but I let him do it a few more times as I track his movements, his stance, searching everything for any hint of a pattern. Any hint of a deviation from said pattern.

And...

Wait.

There's a slight shift in Ryden's fighting style. We've been circling each other for a while, each of us occasionally trying to get a strike in.

We'd agreed at the start that we wouldn't draw any blood—a "strike" would just be touching our dagger to our opponent's body. He stepped on a loose stone a few minutes ago, causing him to topple slightly, and now he's just barely favoring his left side.

I feel the grin overtake my face as I go in for the metaphorical kill.

Suddenly, I'm against a tree. I can feel the bark bite into my back through my t-shirt: Ryden has me pinned. He's got one hand pressed gently to my waist and the other is above my head, holding the wrist with the dagger I managed to keep in hand. I look up to meet his blue eyes only to see them darken slightly.

This is it, I think, *this is the moment that every girl in every book reaches for her thigh dagger—while he's drunk on her scent or drunk on power.*

Too bad I reek of sweat and Ryden doesn't strike me as the toxic masculinity type. Sure, he's strong and driven and could easily take anyone in a fight, but he doesn't seem to be one I'd consider power hungry.

"Where's my thigh dagger when I need it?" I joke.

He quirks a brow, but otherwise remains impossibly still, so I go on. "All of the coolest heroines in all of the best books have a thigh dagger they'd whip out with their free hand and press to your throat right about now."

He huffs out a laugh, and his face is so close to mine that his breath tickles my cheek.

"I've read some of those books. You're not wrong."

That dangerous, devilish grin is back. *The dimples.*

Remember you hate him, some weak, fading voice in my brain tries to remind me.

He's one of them.

"Which one is your favorite?" I whisper. I'm apparently just as frozen in this moment as he is.

"Which what?" he asks, eyes boring into mine.

Why does he have to be so intense?

And so freaking hot?

"Which book heroine is your favorite?"

His eyes drop to my lips for one, two heartbeats.

He coughs roughly, averting his eyes and immediately steps back from me.

"I think that's enough practice for today." He bends to pick up the roll of daggers, flexing his hand a few times before reaching to take the dagger I'm holding. I hand it over and he rolls the pack up and snaps its clasp closed.

"We'll get back on our trail in about twenty minutes, can you be ready then?"

33

The lecture is long, but I might deserve it.

We're back to hiking, having cleaned up both ourselves and the campsite and scarfed down sandwiches after our first training session. My bones feel heavier and my muscles are more sore than usual, which is to be expected: I added way more physical activity this morning than my body is used to, even knowing that I've been hiking day in and day out for the past...who knows how many days.

"So what do *you* think you did wrong?" Ryden asks with a smug smile plastered across his face.

I roll my eyes for what feels like the millionth time since he bested me.

"Well, for starters I, a novice, was sparring with a trained warrior, so the odds were stacked against me." I hold up a hand and exaggeratedly count off on my fingers. "Then my instructor didn't remind me to stretch before sparring, and..." he twists to walk backwards ahead of me so that he's facing me, "I honestly think it was the teacher, not the student." I wink at him, all sarcastic bravado.

His eyes darken and his grin turns nearly feral.

"Much as I love watching those excuses roll off of your tongue," he croons, spinning once more with the grace of a dancer to walk with his back to me again. "This is why balance is so important, don't you see?"

I *saw* the second he pointed out that he, the same person who spent what felt like hours emphasizing the importance of mastering the art of keeping your balance, wouldn't ever stumble over one tiny stone. It was so obvious! He'd faked losing his balance, and I'd played right into his hands.

"You always have to be three steps ahead of your opponent," he hasn't stopped talking since we've been hiking. He's like a teacher that knows his student is going to fail a test, but he's going to repeat the lesson a dozen times anyways. "And you can't expect everyone to be honorable."

"Yeah, you made that *very* clear," I snort.

"To be fair, I *never* said I play fair, love," he croons, turning to face me while walking backwards again. I know he's teasing, but frankly it pisses me off. I'm cranky and sore and it's hot and I'm uncomfortable. I'm tired of walking, I'm extremely tired of nature, and for the trillionth time, I wish I was home with my roommates.

"Can you stop talking now?" I ask, my tone full of bite. "Your silence is *always* appreciated."

He lifts both hands to his heart and mouths, "you wound me," before winking and spinning his back to me to continue up the trail.

It's hours before we speak again, when the Sun has begun its descent towards the horizon and both of our stomachs have started loudly grumbling.

Ryden replaces his bear-destroyed bedroll by doing the fastest Costco flit on record. Thankfully (I'm pretty sure), he landed on a different Costco that carried sleeping bags, so we don't end up in a one-bed trope tonight.

I'd been reluctant—okay, absolutely horrified—to let Ryden leave me alone after dark after the "someone calling my name in the woods" fiasco, but he promised that he'd be back before the Sun set and assured me that his wards would hold for the twenty minutes he'd be gone.

He was back in fifteen. With poke bowls.

We sit in silence around the small fire Ryden had made while we eat our dinner, and I take in our surroundings. Tonight, there's a barely-there creek winding to one side of our campsite. It's small enough that you can step over it, but the waterflow is strong enough that there's plenty of water for drinking, tooth brushing, and maybe even hair washing if I got creative.

I don't have the energy to consider washing my hair right now, so I push that task off as future me's problem.

Once we've had our fill of poke, Ryden gets to work setting out our bedrolls while I clear away our food. We don't have to worry about bears anymore thanks to Ryden getting more specific with his wards, but we don't want to be *those* people: the garbage people—pun intended—who go out into nature and leave their trash everywhere.

At least we can agree on something...even if that something is environmental protection.

Once dinner is cleaned up, I rifle through my pack until I find my toothbrush and the travel-sized tube of toothpaste. It's almost gone, and I make a mental note to ask Ryden to replenish my toiletries the next time he goes on a supply run. I crouch by the stream to brush my teeth, dipping my hands in and relishing the cool water on my still overheated skin. Once my teeth are clean, I rise, turning on my heels, and bump right into Ryden's chest.

"Ooooof," I gracefully let out as he reaches out, clutching my forearms to steady me.

"Sorry about that, I—I thought you heard me," he stammers as he holds up his own toothbrush in explanation. "I was only..."

My eyes meet his and the words seem to die on his tongue. I realize that we're still pressed chest-to-chest, but my body isn't listening to my brain as it whispers (that little voice even quieter than before) for me to *back up back up back uppp*.

At 5'9", I'm not short, but Ryden is still easily a head taller than me. My gaze locks with his and what I see in them makes me ache.

His eyes are hollow; the eyes of a starved and Dying man.

The voice in my head goes completely silent, like even she knows that I could no more back away from this moment than I could drill a hole through my own soul. Once again, I'm all but frozen in time, in a moment with Ryden.

I don't move as his hand reaches up, tentatively at first and so, *so* gently, to cup my cheek as his other hand tracks around my waist, pulling me almost imperceptibly closer to him. His eyes drop to my lips as if they're some lifeline I didn't know about—something that could save him, somehow.

I bite my lower lip instinctually and his carefully contained control snaps at the same second as a twig to my left.

My breathing won't even out, and I can't decide if I'm thankful for or devastated by the interruption—maybe both.

Ryden was about to *kiss me*—and I was about to *let him*.

But the second that twig snapped, the spell was broken. Ryden had turned and stepped several paces away from me just as Jaali stepped into the small clearing where we'd made camp.

"Jaali, hi," I call, much too loudly and awkwardly, and his steps falter.

"Am I interrupting something?" he smirks. His eyes dart between me and Ryden and I can feel the blush as it crawls up my chest and paints my face.

"Nope!" I yell, still too loudly. I hold up my toothbrush, which is apparently now my iron-clad alibi. "Just finished brushing my teeth before bed!"

"Uh huh..." Jaali nods as a knowing grin spreads across his face.

"Nice to see you, Jaali," Ryden calls at a normal decibel.

Ugh. Why is he so calm and collected? Did what almost happened between us not affect him as much as it did me?

"I had a Reaping in Waynesboro, so I thought I'd pop in and see how things were going with you two. But if this is a bad time..." his words trail off.

I'm finally coming down off of the high of *almost* being kissed by a devastatingly handsome man and force myself to listen to the rational side of my brain—the one that remembers that I *like* Jaali, and that I feel safer when he's around.

The one that remembers that my roommates trust him.

"No, of course not, Jaali. I'm glad to see you." I smile up at him and the tension dissipates from the campsite.

Twenty minutes later, we're around a campfire laughing hysterically.

Jaali has been regaling us with a story about the first time he'd met Amarie. It involved the ghost of a wily bus driver, a goat, and a five gallon bucket of pickles—and ended in a bar with everyone (except the goat) doing dill pickle shots.

Once there's a lull in the conversation, Jaali leans back comfortably, so at ease out here in the middle of nowhere in a campsite he's not familiar with at all. I envy that about him—that he can be comfortable in any situation. I'm wondering what that might be like when Jaali's voice interrupts my thoughts.

"I'm glad you two are getting along so well. I guess you finally told her about that fake abduction plot, huh?" Jaali asks, jovially elbowing Ryden in the ribs.

Ryden goes impossibly still.

My throat goes dry.

"What?" I breathe, suddenly hot all over.

Ryden is still frozen, and Jaali looks like he may have swallowed his own tongue. "Wait—you..." he turns to gape at Ryden, "you haven't told her?"

Ryden finally moves, shaking his head slowly.

"No," he mutters, barely a whisper. He coughs before continuing, and when he does, his voice is almost back to normal. "No, Jaali, I haven't told her. I was hoping to get her to trust me on her own. Although now," he laughs humorlessly, staring at his hands where they're loosely clasped between his knees, "I fear I may have just taken a few major steps back on that endeavor."

"Ryden, I—I'm sorry," Jaali sputters. "You guys just seem so comfortable around each other now that I just...I assumed she—"

"*She*," I snap, "would *love* to be spoken *to*, instead of *around* as if *she* isn't *sitting right here*." Jaali and Ryden turn their heads to look at me. Jaali looks mortified, and Ryden looks *terrified*.

Panic travels up and down my spine. *Fake* abduction plot.

Fake. What does that mean? The abduction wasn't real?

Of course it was real, I have the trauma to prove it,

Ryden coughs awkwardly, then begins his explanation. "Abby," he rasps, shifting his position so that he is facing me head-on. "Do you remember the night that you came home and found your apartment ransacked?"

I cut him off. "You mean the night that you destroyed my home and abducted me? The single most terrifying night of my Existence? The one where I barely escaped, but that was futile in the end?" I can feel tears burning my eyes already. "Yeah, haven't quite forgotten that yet, thanks."

I fold my arms across my chest as if they can hold me together—as if

I can wrap myself up so tight that the memory of that trauma won't take over.

"What if I told you..." he pauses, searching for the right words to say, "that that's *exactly* what I wanted you to feel?"

I rear back as if I've been slapped. I *knew* that Ryden wanted me terrified that night—he said as much as he was taking me from my apartment. But to hear him say it now, after so many days of the walls I built between us starting to slowly show wear? As if someday they might begin to crumble and fall?

It rips the wounds open again, only they're larger this time.

"That's obvious, Ryden," I snarl, "I don't think there are many kidnappers out there who want their victim to get the warm and fuzzies." I roll my eyes to feign strength and indifference, while also trying to subtly clutch my sides even tighter.

Don't cry, don't cry, don't cry. Not in front of them. It's what he wants.

He flinches, which gives me at least a little satisfaction.

"No, Abby, love, you misunderstand. I need you to really think back on that night. What do you remember?"

"You destroyed my apartment." I really, really don't want to relive this. Especially not in front of two Reapers.

"Was anything truly destroyed?" he quirks a brow. I think back, and I guess not. It had taken Amarie's magic no more than two minutes to clean and repair everything.

"No, I guess—I guess not, thanks to Amarie," I begrudgingly admit.

"And then what happened next?" I feel like he's a lawyer, like I'm on trial. Or, like he's a shepherd, leading this lamb to her slaughter. But his eyes are earnest, so I oblige.

"You loaded me up into your car, and told me not to bother fighting the ropes because they were warded." The memory of that panic, of being bound and tumbling around the back of a vehicle with no idea of what would come next, claws its way up my throat. Every breath I take is a struggle as I relive the nightmare.

He nods, looking pained, "I did say that. And then?"

"You stopped at an abandoned warehouse, and dumped me out of the car."

"If I remember correctly," he raises a finger as if he has to make a point," I opened the door to *help* you out, and you tumbled out on your own." I see red.

Who does he think he is?! But before I can say as much, he's speaking again.

"But that's beside the point. How did the ropes you were bound in feel then?"

I think back to that moment, and remember that they weren't as tight as they'd been in the vehicle. "They were...slightly looser, I guess," I say.

Where is he going with this?

"Interesting," his eyes haven't left mine. "And then what happened?"

And I know that this is it. This is the pinnacle of the conversation. The point Ryden is getting to. The lie being revealed.

All three of us have stopped breathing.

"And then, before you could—" then I gasp and sit bolt upright.

"Theeeere it is!" Jaali laughs nervously.

"What happened, Abby?" Ryden's eyes bore into mine, glittering, intense, and desperate.

I can't look away.

"Tell me what happened next."

"Jaali showed up."

34

I think I'm going to be sick.

No, I *know* I'm going to be sick. "Excuse me," I mutter as I rise and flee to the tree line.

I'm such an *idiot*! Of course it was Jaali. The entire thing, the entire *kidnapping* was staged. I'd never *actually* been in any danger; Ryden literally had Jaali there waiting to "distract" him so that I could get away.

But *why*?

Once I've heaved up every bit of my poke bowl, I realize that there's a gentle hand on my back. I tense, because if it's Ryden I don't know what I'll do.

"Hey," the owner of the hand whispers and I relax at Jaali's smooth timbre. "I just thought I would come check on you."

"I'm—I'm not okay," I hiccup.

"I know you're not," he nods sympathetically. "And I hate that. You *can* trust him, you know."

"I don't even know why I trust *you*, Jaali," I laugh without humor. "I've spent so much more time with him than I have with you." I survey him, noting his kind eyes and non-threatening posture (even though I'm pretty sure he could match even Ryden in a fight). "But after everything he's done, I don't know how I ever *could* trust him. I was starting to, I think, but...it's all been a lie."

I drop my face into my hands. I'm so tired, and so defeated. And okay, I'm hurt, too. So, so hurt.

"You should cut him some slack," Jaali suggests. "He's in a pretty impossible situation here." Jaali gestures at nothing in particular, but that nothing includes me and the campsite. His meaning is clear.

I scoff. "You make that sound so easy, Jaali. Why didn't I think of that? *Just cut him some slack*," I repeat in a deep, and admittedly terrible, mockery of Jaali's voice.

He nudges my shoulder playfully and laughs, the sound rich and deep. "I'm not saying it's going to be easy, you little terror," he teases.

"I'm just saying that I know that Ryden is a good man. I'm not saying he's perfect," he speeds up, putting his arms up defensively. "I'm just saying that he tries. He tries so hard and puts so much impossible pressure on himself. I don't know how he doesn't implode under the weight of it, if I'm honest."

"What kind of pressure?" I ask nonchalantly, hoping that I can get some more information out of Jaali. "What's he going through that's so bad?"

"I know I messed up once tonight, Abby," Jaali acknowledges. "Please don't try to trick me into doing it again."

His words hit their mark, and the shame starts to rise in me. *What am I doing*? Trying to manipulate Jaali now, too?

"I'm sorry," I whisper. "I'm just scared."

"I know you are," Jaali snakes an arm around me, pulling me into his warmth. Even on this balmy summer night, it's welcome; he has such a comforting presence. "And Ryden knows you are, and I can see it eating my friend alive. He doesn't want you to be afraid of him, and I think it kills him that you are."

Anger spikes, hot and fast within me. I pull quickly out of Jaali's reach.

"He literally just confirmed as much," I say, gesturing over my shoulder towards the clearing where I'm sure Ryden is listening to all of this. "He agreed that he told me he wanted me afraid."

"Ah," Jaali raises a finger in the air, like a professor whose student is about to get to the point of the lesson. "Context, my dear friend."

"What is that supposed to mean?" I'm baffled. Are these two ever going to stop speaking in riddles?!

"He wanted you scared *then* Abby. He wanted you afraid *then*. Why do you think that could be?"

I chew on the inside of my cheek as I mull over Jaali's words. "I honestly don't know?"

He releases a heavy breath and I can feel his disappointment.

"Who 'kidnapped' you, Abby?" he asks, raising air quotes around "kidnapped."

"Ryden did?" Seriously, where is he going with this?

"Less specifically," he presses. I can tell he's getting agitated. Well, that makes two of us.

"Why can't you just tell meeee," I whine. "I'm not getting whatever it is you're trying to tell me."

He clenches his fists. "Because of the code."

I suck in a gasp. "That's right! You have like...magical rules keeping you from saying some things!" I lean in closer, my interest reinvigorated. He only nods in reply. "Wait, is this why you told me and the roommates that you didn't know if Ryden was on your side when you did? Because you were in on the fake kidnapping from the start?" I squeal. "It's because you're *both* defecting from their official cause!"

I see the veins in his neck begin to pop as he strains against the invisible tethers that this code is clearly inflicting and abandon that question, because I'm pretty sure the answer is yes...I hope.

"Okay, so...less specific than Ryden. Um—a man?"

He rolls his eyes. "You're *so* close, Abby. Come on, you've got this. Less specific than his name, but more specific than his gender."

"Um..." I think for a few more seconds. "A Reaper?"

Jaali's smile could shatter the earth. "And why might Ryden want you to feel fear after an encounter with," he winces and presses a palm to his forehead. "...*one of those*," he grunts through clenched teeth. He must be getting close to saying too much.

"Because he...wanted me afraid of *Reapers*?"

Jaali doesn't say anything...just stands and returns to the campsite. Before he steps back into the clearing, though, he turns to me for a split second and I'd swear I see him wink.

Ryden and I really, really need to have a conversation, but if I know us, we'll put it off as long as we can.

35

I'm asleep, but even in my dreams the flickering is visible.

It's a half moon of shimmery glowing lights that stretches out in front of my eyes, dancing as if it's a celestial show I want to see. Just like I've done every other time it's happened, I will it to just be a dream.

It's never a dream.

I open my eyes to the hazy sunlight of sunrise filtering through the trees, far too bright for my sensitive eyes. I hiss, doing my best impression of a vampire, and lift my arms to shelter my eyes. The motion sends nausea ricocheting through every fiber of my being.

"Love, are you alright?" Ryden steps up from somewhere to my left; what he was doing, I can't see, because the tunnel vision has started.

"Migraine," I sigh. "You'd think being a ghost would have advantages like *not* having stupid medical things like this, but alas, being Born made me susceptible to Living's bullshit." I explain.

Normally I try not to be so negative but damnit I do *not* want to deal with this today. Or ever.

"Do these happen often?" he asks, brows furrowed anxiously.

"Maybe two to three times a year," I explain. "I'll be fine, I'm just not going to be able to move much, if at all, today."

He doesn't seem bothered, and instead goes directly into caregiver mode.

"What do you need?" he starts moving around the campsite, and I know a flit is coming. "I can go get any meds, comfort items, anything. Just say the word."

I can't move having finally found a position that curbed the nausea, so I whisper, trying to move my mouth as little as possible. "I'm not in pain yet. My migraines have what's called an aura, which blocks out a big part of my vision, makes my tongue feel dull and flat, and starts the intense nausea," I notice Ryden grimace and can tell he's sympathetic. "But the aura is my warning. I have about twenty minutes before the pain will hit, and it'll feel like someone has stabbed an ice pick through my skull and is constantly hammering it—but it's stuck in my brain matter so it just ricochets terrible pain through my skull."

"That sounds awful, love," he says, stooping to catch my wrist ever so gently. He rubs lazy circles in my palm, doing what he can to be comforting. "What can I do?"

"Could you go get some Excedrin Migraine, some bottled caffeine, and some anti-nausea pills?" I request. "Then, once the pain part is over, I'll be ravenous and want a smorgasbord of food, but that will be hours from now."

"Will you be alright if I leave? Jaali left early this morning but I can call him back." I can see him warring with himself, so I quickly reassure him.

"I'll be fine, I just need meds and sleep. Once the headache itself is over, I'll have aftershocks of pain for a few days, but they're manageable," I promise.

"I'm not worried about the next few days," he waves a hand, "I just don't want you to suffer."

"I'm going to suffer more if you keep talking and not flitting," I try to smile but the nausea ramps back up, eliciting a hiss.

"Say less," he rises from his crouched position before me. "I'll be back in ten minutes."

Ryden is back with the meds faster than I would have believed.

I dry heave as I sit up and choke down the meds he'd brought back and chug a Diet Coke. Somehow, in the mere minutes he was gone, he also found a face mask that can be frozen or heated and blocks out all light...and bought three, so that I could have options for cold or hot, or no additional temperature changes. I opt for neither temperature for now, but promise that I'll let him know if I need ice or heat.

I burrow deeply into my bedroll and lay the face mask over my eyes. I'd worried that the pressure on my face would exacerbate the pain, but whoever designed it was clearly also a migraine sufferer—it weighs next to nothing, has indentations for eyelids, and totally blocks out all light.

The aura has dissipated and the pain has come. It's present and overwhelming even after taking medication, but would be drastically worse without meds. I lie as still as a statue, focusing on my breathing. I'm not sure what Ryden is doing, other than making absolutely no noise. He may be taking this opportunity to get a little rest himself.

I'll ask him when I resurface.

Eventually, after what feels like hours of stabbing pain, I finally fall into a fitful sleep. Sleep during a migraine helps in that it makes me less aware of the pain, but it is not restful in the slightest—if anything, sleeping during a migraine is even more of an energy drain. In the moment, though, sleep is the only thing that can keep me sane when the pain feels unbearable.

My sleep is briefly interrupted when the numbness starts. It starts as a tingling on my tongue and the tips of my fingers, working its way down my body until my whole left side is pins and needles. I don't dare move, not wanting to risk making the searing pain in my head or the roiling in my gut worse. I lie there and breathe through it, and slowly, gradually, the tingling recedes back into nonexistence, allowing me to fade back into sleep.

I wake at dusk to find that the worst of the pain has passed. The nausea has been replaced by ravenous hunger, as usual, and I tentatively pull off the mask. The light of evening is still a shock to my sensitive eyes, but before I can blink, Ryden is there.

"Love? Are you alright?" he whispers, clearly trying to be as quiet as possible.

"I'm good," I assure him as I sit up. "Hungry, but good. The worst is over."

I stretch and it feels incredible. "Did you at least get some rest today?" I ask, curious about what he got into on this unexpected day off.

"No," he breathes. "I watched over you all day. I wanted—I wanted to be there for you at a second's notice if you needed anything. If you needed me," he coughs awkwardly, embarrassed.

"You just sat there and watched me sleep all day? That had to have been soooo boring," I sigh, rubbing my temples.

"No," his smile is soft, sweet, so very tender as he gently swipes errant hair from my forehead. "It wasn't boring at all," he whispers. "Now," he slaps his hands to his knees, his voice returning to a normal decibel, "you don't get up. You lie there and relax. I was told you'd need a smorgasbord and I do not plan to disappoint."

He flits away before I can protest, or even feel guilty that he's apparently spent the whole day tending to me.

When he returns twenty minutes later with bags from three different fast food restaurants, a pre-made charcuterie board, and several two liters of various caffeinated beverages, I understand what people mean when they talk about what it means to feel *seen*.

36

The next few days are lost in a blur of pine trees.

We hike, day in and day out. It's exhausting, especially dealing with migraine aftershocks, but we've found a companionable groove. Ryden doesn't push me too hard, knowing that while I've mostly recovered, I'll still experience random shooting pains through my skull that could bring me to my knees if I let them.

One warm afternoon once I'm fully back to normal, we sit on a rock near the base of a small waterfall, eating sandwiches and exchanging small talk, and for the first time in my Existence I truly marvel at *nature*. I have to admit that it is really, really gorgeous out in these woods. Warm sunlight filters through the tree trunks that surround us casting everything in such a bright, cheery glow. The air is clean and my lungs don't have to filter out the pollution of the real world. The water in the stream at the base of the waterfall is sparkling and clear, free of any impurities you'd find closer to civilization. I sigh, content, and appreciate a moment of peace amidst so much uncertainty about my future.

I occasionally hear (or, think I hear) my name being called, or a random, "hey!" or phantom whistling, but every time I bring it up, Ryden loudly replies with a, "no, you didn't!" coupled with a stern look.

"Love, you're in Appalachia," he reminds me. "You can't give these things attention."

"What is that supposed to mean?" I'm defensive, but it's because I'm afraid, and he knows it. His face softens.

"It means that if you hear something, no you didn't. You pretend that you didn't. You don't whistle back, or turn towards the voices you may hear, or call back to them. And you never look into the trees at night—for they may be looking back."

As if that isn't enough to send permanent chills down a spine.

We spend most of our days sparring and hiking, and at night, Ryden tells stories by the firelight surrounding our bedrolls. Each night, those bedrolls inexplicably inch closer together. I still haven't mustered up the courage to ask Ryden where we're going again, but I'm beginning to feel an inkling of rightness in the state of things.

Am I meant to be here, on this journey?

Will my being here save me?

And more importantly, will it save Eya and Wana?

I'm sitting alone in our campsite late one night watching the fire dwindle to embers.

Ryden isn't here. He's probably flitted off somewhere—I just can't remember where.

Keeping up with his schedule is getting too difficult; on top of his supply runs for us, he occasionally has to flit away for Reapings, which I can't let myself think too closely about. Thankfully (*thankfully?! What has become of me, being thankful for anything from a Reaper?*) Ryden returned from a recent supply flit with an e-reader, preloaded with several books he thought I might enjoy, so I don't usually have to even care when he flits away.

I honestly look forward to it: there's no hiking, no sparring. No pressure to fill a silence. There's a peace to being out in the middle of nowhere, totally alone.

Well, there *was* peace in this solitude.

The wind whistles through the trees, catching on leaves and branches and causing a cacophony of sound; howling cries that send shivers racing up and down my spine.

I pull the blankets from the bedroll beneath me up around my shoulders to ward off the chill and sneak a glance around. In my periphery I can see the trees closest to the fire. It's pitch darkness past them, but I know not to look directly into the trees. Anything at all could be out there, just waiti—*no*. Ryden's wards are here. I know that. He wouldn't let anything get to me, whether he's here or not. And whether he plans to deliver me to evil or save my Existence.

The wind shifts, and I could swear it's speaking.

"*Abbbbbbyyyy....Aaaaaabbbbbbyyyy,*" it whispers, gently at first as if it's testing the waters to see if I'll acknowledge it—which I promptly do. I cover my head with the blankets like a six-year-old having a nightmare.

The wind almost snickers before Dying down entirely. *Thank the gods.* I like to pretend I don't scare easily, but tonight has me utterly spooked. I pick up my e-reader to distract myself and calm my racing heart when a cry cuts through the night.

"Abby!" a female voice screams. "Abby, where are you?!"

I'd know that voice anywhere. I rocket out of the bedroll, my legs tangling in the blankets and causing me to fall. "Zelie?!" I call as I kick my legs to free myself from this temporary fabric prison.

"Zelie, is that you? What are you doing here?!" After a few more leg thrusts, I'm freed and on my feet, scrambling towards the source of the sound.

"Abby, we're here to take you home!" she calls. "Hurry, before he gets back!"

"Zelie! It isn't safe for you out there alone! I can't see you!" I shout as I reach the edge of the light from the fire.

"Hold on!" Her voice is closer now. It echoes off of the trees, causing an indignant hoot from an owl and a bird to shoot from her nest in outrage.

Why is her voice that loud?

I step back a few feet, closer to the fire and the safety net of the little light it's still producing.

Zelie bursts into the clearing, stopping for a moment to crouch and catch her breath. My unease from earlier is still present. Even though relief at seeing her crashes over me in waves, I don't make a move toward her just yet.

"Abby," she breathes, and her voice is barely a whisper, but still echoes—it's as if hundreds of different voices lurk just beneath the surface of her one.

Instinctively, I take another step backwards. She rises to her full height, and the moment our eyes meet, I know that this isn't Zelie.

This is someone—no, some*thing*—else entirely.

Ryden's words from a few nights ago spear through my head and heart: "*these spirits, for lack of a better word, are master manipulators, and can mimic any sound or voice in the world. They can sound like your own mother, they can call your name...anything to lure you in.*"

Anything to lure you in.

A sickening, grotesque grin spreads across its mouth, and keeps spreading as its face melts into a Living nightmare. Its jaw elongates, its eye sockets deepen, and suddenly, there are no eyes in them at all, only voids that are blacker than black. A squelching sound ricochets through the clearing as its form continues this odd and terrifying melting dance. It's as if it doesn't have a form itself, so it's trying to mimic the shape of others. Wings appear at its back before disappearing, hooves appear where hands had been, a rat's snout snivels and sniffs, antlers sprout where I assume its head is—it's an endless pattern of forms that it can't hold for more than the blink of an eye.

Slowly, it starts to slink toward me and all of Ryden's training goes completely out the window.

I do the only thing I know how to do, even though I know it can't possibly save me: I throw my head back and scream.

I scream and tumble backwards, legs once again tangling in the blankets of my bedroll. I fall, landing in a rough heap, the blankets wrapping tighter around me as I writhe and scream, doing everything in my power to get away from the *thing* in front of me.

"Abby?!" I hear Ryden call from a distance. I keep shrieking, hoping he'll make it to me in time. Strong arms grab at me from beside me on the ground and I lash out even harder, adding my arms to the battle I'm fighting against the blankets and phantom hands.

"Abby!" he calls again, and I'm so engulfed in terror that my body begins to rock back and forth, even as the hands that have grasped both of my shoulders tighten. I close my eyes tight, because if Death is coming for me, I don't want to witness it.

"Abby, what's wrong?!" Ryden shouts and the panicked desperation in his voice scares me enough to open my eyes—if Ryden is scared, I'm absolutely not surviving this.

He's kneeling over me, his hair wildly unkempt and his eyes wide and utterly terrified. "Abby, please," he begs, "what's happening?"

I freeze and take in my surroundings.

Ryden is breathing raggedly, his bare chest rising and falling as if he'd just run a marathon. He's leaning towards me from his own bedroll, clutching my shoulders as if they're a lifeline. His or mine, I'm not entirely sure. Beyond that, I can see our campsite. The fire is higher than it had been moments ago. I see my pack, with my e-reader peeking out of a pocket, and the *not-Zelie* is gone.

"Abby, you've got to take a breath for me," Ryden demands. "Please Abby, breathe." He clutches my shoulders and shakes me. "Love, you've got to breathe." His voice turns frantic. "You're in some sort of shock but I need you to please just breathe. Breathe, love!"

His tone is calm but commanding, and it helps to soothe me enough that I suck in a breath.

He looses one in a burst.

"I'm sorry," I whisper.

I'm completely mortified.

"What happened?" he asks. "One second we were both sleeping soundly, then the next, you were screaming as if you were being murdered but there was nothing here..." He trails off and releases another harsh breath.

He takes one hand off of me to clutch his chest as he works to regulate his own breathing. "And you scared the shit out of me."

"I'm sorry," I repeat, "truly. I guess I had a nightmare." My cheeks heat as I duck my head in shame. I'm a grown woman, I shouldn't be letting *bad dreams* rattle me so easily.

"Do you want to tell me about it?" he asks, and there's no pressure behind his tone. He's offering me a listening ear if retelling the dream will drive the monsters away, but won't force me to tell him if rehashing it will make it worse for me.

I nod. "I was here, and you were gone. You'd flitted somewhere. I was reading and then...and then..." Tears well in my eyes. I clasp my hands and drop them into my lap. "And then I heard Zelie calling my name."

We sit in silence for a few minutes, Ryden letting me process the rest of the dream before he coaxes, "And then?"

"She said she was here to take me home," I continue, even though my words feel like some sort of betrayal, which is absurd. "And I told her it wasn't safe for her out there, and then she got to me, and..." I crumple into sobs. They shudder through my body until I'm back to gasping for air.

"And you wanted to go with her," he whispers, a muscle in his jaw feathering as he glances away from me. He sounds so heartbroken that I have to clarify. I sit up slightly.

"No! No, I didn't want to go with her. Or," I reconsider, "or I don't *think* I did. I really didn't think about what she was saying...all I could think about was those things you told me about getting to her. So my focus was on her safety, on her getting *to me* safely. Which," I smack my forehead, because there was one clear tell that it had been a dream. One that I'd totally overlooked. "I should have known it was a dream. She couldn't have made it through your wards if it was real."

His look is equal parts pity and understanding.

"Unfortunately," he smiles, reaching up idly to tuck a stray lock of hair behind my ear before letting his hand fall away, "our dream selves are far less logical than our waking selves. That isn't your fault." I pick his hand back up and hold it in mine.

His eyes dart to mine, surprised.

"Sorry," I apologize. I drop his hand, mortified anew at what I'd just done. "I think...it just...helped to feel that you're real. That that was a nightmare, but that this is real."

"This *is* real," he whispers, leaning closer, so close that we're sharing breath. He picks my hand back up and clutches it to his chest. "This is real, love."

I try to suck in a deep lungful of air, but I'm still so shaky from fear and adrenaline that it remains uneven.

"It," Ryden starts, then pauses, waging some mental battle over what he wants to say. After a few seconds, he wins out against himself and continues. "It doesn't have to mean anything, but..." my cheeks flush again, "but if human contact will drive the nightmare away tonight...we can...I wouldn't mind if we...*erm...*"

The embarrassed awkwardness written all over his face is so endearing that I think I might burst. I put him out of his misery by dropping his hand, freeing my legs from my mess of blankets, rising, and stepping the whole foot over to his bedroll where I gently push his chest. He inches backwards and stares up at me, something like awe written across his face when I crouch down into the space he's made for me. I nestle my back into his front, gently laying my head on his bicep.

"Is this okay?" I ask, zipping us into his bedroll.

The silence is so loud and long that I reach back toward the zipper, ready to abort mission and dive back into my own bedroll, when an ever so soft whisper tickles my ear.

"*This*...is more than okay, love." A strong arm comes around me, pulling me gently, cradling me deeper into his chest. It's the most comfortable I've been in months—maybe ever—but I force myself to utter the words I need to remind myself:

"This doesn't mean anything."

"Mmm," Ryden acknowledges, clearly already almost asleep again.

"And it's just for tonight."

His arm flexes slightly and I'm pulled even closer into the delirium that is Ryden's scent.

"*Juss tuhny*," he mumbles into my hair. "*Iss nice for tuhny.*"

He's not wrong.

This *is* nice.

Then I'm tumbling into the deepest, most restful dreamless sleep I've ever had.

37

"Spar with me," Ryden says as we're finishing up breakfast the next morning.

We haven't discussed last night.

We woke tangled up in each other, warm despite the chill of the early morning mountain air. I could feel the steady beat of Ryden's heart against my own chest, having clearly rolled over towards him in the night, and for the first time in months, I felt peaceful. Our legs were as intertwined as our breaths, and any thought of fear was vanquished by Ryden's sheer proximity. For once in my Existence, I was grateful for the fact that I can sleep like the Living, for my not being like other ghosts. I hadn't wanted to leave the moment, the quiet perfection that was me and Ryden, curled up in his bedroll, but eventually, the moment had broken when nature called.

I'd awkwardly risen and stepped off into the trees to ready myself, and when I came back, Ryden was up, our bedrolls were packed, and it was time to start the day.

It didn't have to mean anything, after all.

"Okay," I agree dreamily, still sleep hazy.

That lazy, warm feeling dissipates quickly once we begin fight training.

"Remember your balance," Ryden calls from somewhere in the trees.

I roll my eyes, because even after such a blissful night's sleep (well, after the whole nightmare, that is), it is still far too early to be sparring.

But, "*learning to protect yourself waits for no one, love,*" so here I am, right after a quick breakfast of Burger King croissan'wiches and orange juice, weaving through the woods in an attempt to silently track Ryden's movements, since he wants me to not only learn to defend myself, but also how to go on the offensive with potential foes.

Not that I see myself seeking out a fight, but...who knows.

Maybe future me is vengeful.

Something crashes into the leaves to my left, but I turn right on instinct—I've been around Ryden long enough to know that he absolutely would throw a rock in the wrong direction to avert my attention so that he can pounce.

My instinct was correct, because there he is, a mere ten feet from where I stand, grinning like a Devil.

Ryden lets out a joyful whoop, looking so blissfully happy that it might crack my heart a little.

Out of nowhere, a dozen or so birds shoot out of a treetop above us, echoing a loud *whoosh*ing sound throughout our makeshift training pitch and startling us both.

I react almost unconsciously. When Ryden glances up to assess the potential for an actual threat, I pounce, hook my foot behind his calf, grab him by the shoulders, and slam all my weight into him. Miraculously, it works. The breath knocks out of Ryden in the clearing's second *whoosh* of the morning as his back hits the forest floor. I land on top of him and let out a victory screech.

He's still working to catch his breath, resting one hand on his chest as the other lands on my thigh and tightens infinitesimally.

I know it's poor sportsmanship to gloat, but I just can't help it.

Still straddling Ryden, I lean over until my lips are a mere inch from his ear and whisper, *"This is why balance is so important, don't you see? You always have to be three steps ahead of your opponent."*

I lean back only slightly, hovering above Ryden so we're nearly nose-to-nose. His breathing is back to normal, and he offers me a rare, genuine smile with those damned dimples.

"You're making all of my dreams come true," he whispers as he reaches up to tuck a stray lock of hair behind my ear, letting his hand linger at the back of my neck. "Every single one of them."

His face is an open book, upon which I can read every single thing he's currently thinking, and I have to admit, I'm thinking the same things.

How easy it would be for me to close the distance between us.

To press my lips to his.

To become the Stockholm Syndrome stereotype I've read in so many books.

To decide that I'm going to be his, whatever that may mean.

I know it'll have to be me—he won't make this choice, won't take this step, for us.

I only let my mind race a second more, but that's enough time for the moment to be ruined.

Just when I've decided that knowing what kissing Ryden is like is worth whatever problems could befall future me, Ryden's head snaps to the side. His pupils dilate in predatory focus, and he slowly rises, lifting both of us until we're in a standing position. He sets me down gently and picks up our packs, handing mine to me before lifting his own onto his back.

"Ryden?" I ask in a whisper, afraid there's another bear, or something worse.

"Everything's alright, Abby, but I think it's time we start hiking for today."

Then he heads straight towards the source of whatever called his attention.

38

"How much longer until we get there?" I ask Ryden as I follow him through the trees.

I'm grumpy, having not had coffee before our sparring match this morning.

About a half an hour into our hike, I'd needled Ryden to go on a Seven Brew run, but he'd put me off.

"I'll go get you coffee and a Gatorade," he promises in a rushed whisper, "but let's make a little more progress first."

Has he not learned by now that I simply cannot function without my caffeine? Did the migraine I had, where caffeine was a direct and immediate need, not sink in? Does he not understand my Existence's dependence on the it? This morning's training was an irregular occurrence that I'm chalking up to a *really* good night's sleep.

He takes me by the hand, and I let him.

This is new.

We trudge on for a few more moments in silence and I take in our surroundings while Ryden stalks slightly ahead of me—but not far enough to let go of my hand. We've found a weathered hiking path that is only slightly overgrown, but my knees and ankles rejoice at the more even terrain. Even coffee-less, I have to admit that there are worse settings to be in: the Sun is high and bright, filtering flecks of light through the canopy of leaves above us and warming the air while a mountain breeze keeps us comfortable. Birdsong echoes from the trees overhead, all playful and happy...I think. They could be insulting each other's mothers for all I know.

I chuckle at the idea of birds beefing with each other as I snap up a wildflower along the path and place it in my hair above my ear.

Ick.

My hair feels *disgusting*. It's oily from being unwashed while also frizzy and full of tiny leaves and twigs. I look down to appraise the rest of me and I have to admit I'm impressed: several days of walking mostly uphill in the woods has added some definition to my legs.

They're covered in so much dirt and so many bug bites (despite the bug spray Ryden had eventually brought back from a supply run that I've been using religiously) that I can barely see my skin, but I mentally thank them for being strong enough to quite literally carry me through mountains. I secretly hope that Ryden's trying to get us to a nearby spring or creek or any body of fresh water where we can clean up.

Wait.

Do I smell?

Was sleeping so close to me last night so bad that he's risking having to experience Abby Without Coffee to get me somewhere where I can *bathe*?

When a noise ahead makes Ryden drop my hand and take a few more steps ahead to investigate, I chance a sniff at my armpit, and while it's not the best, it could *definitely* be worse. Crisis averted—I think.

We're still firmly in the middle of nowhere, at least from what I can tell, and I'm not convinced that we aren't hiking in circles; everything has looked exactly the same for days on end.

Trees. Brush. Dirt.

"Not too much longer now," Ryden promises as we crest a small hill between two mountains. There's something off with his voice, though. I jog the few paces between us to catch up with him and notice his body language.

He's got a slight smile on his face, but I've spent enough time with him over the last few days that I can see through the facade. He's uneasy. His shoulders are tense, his pace is just too fast to be normal, and he's scanning our surroundings even more than he usually does.

I stop in my tracks. "What's wrong?"

He doesn't stop, but bristles and glances over his shoulder at me. "What?"

I stay put. "I said, 'what's wrong?' Why are you so tense?"

He sighs and turns, stepping back to me quickly. "Nothing is wrong, something is just...off."

"What do you mean 'off'?" I ask, fear tightening my throat.

He smiles, stepping back toward and takes my hand again. Again, I let him.

"Something is just...*different*. I don't know how to explain it. But my senses have picked up on something, and I'd like to see what it is."

"That's ominous..." I breathe, glancing around for whatever entities Ryden had told me about before.

He flashes that devilish grin again. "Love, I've told you before. You're safe with me." My traitorous heart flutters.

My gods that smile should be illegal.

"If I thought there was any *risk*, I'd have you sat down on that log," he points as we pass it, "warded to hell and back," a smirk, "so that I could handle the threat with you out of harm's way."

"And if it was a threat that was too big for you?" I ask and he scoffs.

"Abby. I'm a Reaper. There's not much, short of Death, that is a threat to me. But..." he mulls over his words for a breath before continuing, "if I thought a threat was too significant, I'd call for Jaali and have him get you out."

I blink at him, stunned.

"What?" he asks, as if he's just read me his grocery list.

"You'd have Jaali get me out but you'd stay?"

"'Course I would," he says as if it's the most natural thing in the world. "What am I going to do, risk your safety?" He huffs a breath. "Not hardly."

This is...another interesting development.

I stop in my tracks again. "Why?"

"Why what?" he asks, but he's still distracted by whatever is "off."

"Why do you care? About my safety. About my Existence."

I see his jaw tense and eyes darken the slightest bit before he fully turns towards me. "Because I'd like to think that we're...that we could be...*friends*," he says before turning to continue up the path into a small meadow.

I don't have time to let the words sink in, or to consider why I don't like the word *friends*, because Ryden pivots to snag my wrist, pulling me down into a crouch beside him in the tall grass.

"*What the hell is your problem*?!" I hiss, feeling a knee pop at the sudden and unexpected motion.

My eyes follow his gaze across the meadow to land on a girl, no more than 15 years old or so, and Ryden is right...something is *definitely* off.

She's flickering in and out of view, and once her eyes fall on us, her mouth falls open into a blood-curdling scream.

"What the hell?" I gasp, covering my mouth as bile rises in my throat.

"Damnit," Ryden swears under his breath, "she's stuck."

"*Whatdoyoumeanshe'sstuck*?" I squeak, the question jumbled into one long word.

He turns to me, and his eyes are sorrowful for one heartbeat, then the mask of the hardened Reaper melts any emotions away.

He stands, glancing back over his shoulder to me. "This may be upsetting for you, love. You are safe, but I'd suggest you go back, find that log we talked about, and wait for me there."

No way in hell.

I can't pull my eyes away, not even when the air around Ryden begins to shimmer. Where he stood seconds ago wearing jogging shorts, a tank top, and sneakers, he's now in those odd fighting leathers I'd seen in Halcyon Hall. They feature a hood, which he pulls up over his head before reaching out his right arm where an honest-to-gods scythe appears in his hand.

He approaches her slowly and to her credit, she stands her ground. She's in a flowy white top that forms a halo around her shoulders and cascades down over her blue denim bell-bottoms and tawny boots. Her brown hair is long and loose, parted in the middle and cascading around her shoulders to cover most of her face, but I can see her eyes.

They're eyes that will haunt me for the rest of my Existence.

They are both empty and overflowing, full of despair, fear, and pain. The hollowness of hopelessness. Voids between stars.

Her screams continue endlessly, as if she's stuck in a time loop. She's still flickering in and out of vision, as if there's some glitch in the world or my eyes are malfunctioning.

Ryden approaches her cautiously, but with the confidence of a decorated soldier heading into a battle they know they'll win. He's significantly taller than she is, so he stoops, speaking words to her that I can't hear. There is no cruelty in his ministrations, and I wish I could hear what he's saying. Is he trying to calm her down? Whatever he's doing isn't helping.

She doesn't stop screaming. I see Ryden's head drop, as if he's disappointed, before he rises, resolute.

He looks to the sky for a breath, then places both of his hands on her cheeks, caressing and calm. The world goes quiet as her screams cease, and she gasps in a deep breath. I can see her eyes meet Ryden's, and there's a glimmer of hope in them that wasn't there before. She smiles and closes her eyes, lifting her chin toward the Sun in supplication.

There's a rush of wind and then she's gone. Ryden's clothes return to normal, the scythe disappearing into the thin air it'd come from.

"What the HELL?" I repeat my words from moments ago, only louder this time. "What just happened?!"

Ryden trudges back to me, and I notice that some of the confidence has leached out of him—he's clearly dreading this conversation.

"She was stuck," he also repeats words from earlier. His sad smile doesn't reach his eyes.

"What does that mean?" I whisper, almost afraid to hear his answer.

"Sometimes," he speaks softly as if he's telling a child that their pet hamster died, "very rarely, a soul fights itself for what it wants. They want to go into the Unknown, but they're afraid, and they want to stay here to avoid facing that fear." He chews the inside of his cheek for a moment and I give him time to choose his next words. "Some souls that are here too long turn into Poltergeists, where they can't control their actions anymore. And others just...get stuck." He shrugs as if that's the most clear answer in the world.

"So she was...Dead?"

"She was, yes. I'd say she's been Dead for a while."

"Then what was she doing out here?"

That sad smile is plastered to his face. "I'm not sure. She could have been a ghost for decades," his brow furrows and he turns back to glance over his shoulder to where she'd been standing. "Although it is a bit odd. Ghosts can—" he stops himself, "*should* be able to—Exist for hundreds of years before their soul grows restless. Of course ghosts can change their clothes, but—she didn't *seem* hundreds of years old. She seemed so..." he sniffs, "so *young*."

My heart claws its way up into my throat.

"Ryden, what just happened to her?" Ice cold fear washes over my whole body and I break out in goosebumps.

He looks at me through his lashes and the pain and...fear? in his eyes nearly takes my breath away. He bounces one foot and sucks part of his bottom lip through his teeth—actions that I would call nervous ticks on anyone else, but *Ryden*? Ryden doesn't get *nervous*. He looses one long breath before answering me.

"That was a Reaping, Abby," he breathes. "Her soul was stuck, and it was endless agony for her, and I—I had to help her."

He catches me as my knees give out, gently dropping us both to the ground.

"I'm so...I never, *never* wanted you to witness...never wanted you to *see*...so, so sorry, love." I only hear snatches of the words he's saying as I try to catch my breath.

"Abby, look at me. Look at me, love," he grabs my face in both of his hands until his eyes have mine, and if I weren't mid-panic attack I'd find it ironic; he's holding my face as gently as he'd just held that ghost's.

"You have to know that that was *mercy*. She would have been stuck like that, *screaming* like that, until the end of time unless another Reaper happened upon her. I swear to you, to everything I've ever held dear, that I would never Reap a soul without their consent unless, and only when, they are so far gone that they can no longer *ask* to go on."

I know that Ryden is waiting for a response, but I can't give one yet.

He takes one of my hands in his and I realize that he's on his knees before me, both of us now fully caked in dirt. "Please, Abby," he whispers so low that I can barely hear, "I can't go back to you cowering every time I move. I'm begging, love. I'm begging you..."

All I can do is stare at him; the shock has frozen all of my faculties enough that I don't even pull my hand away when he presses my fingers to his lips.

We sit in the meadow for another twenty minutes before I can speak.

"It was..." I whisper, voice slightly hoarse, and Ryden bolts upright, "oddly beautiful—considering."

The sigh he heaves could shatter every mountain for miles.

"It's usually more peaceful," he admits, "since situations like this are rare, and—"

My stomach roils.

"Wait," I have to cut him off. He obliges immediately.

"I don't want to...I *can't*...talk about *Reaping* with you. Hers was beautiful and I'm glad you were able to help her, but," I choke on a sob as it rips its way from my body, "I don't *want* to go, but I don't feel like I will have a choice in the matter and I just...I can't, Ryden. Please respect that."

His lips disappear into a tight line and I know there's so much he wants to say, but he only nods. "Okay. We won't talk about—*that*."

We sit in tense silence for a while, listening to the wild breeze and birdsong that continue as if a soul hasn't just left this world right here. We're high enough on a mountain that I can see for miles and miles and it's utterly breathtaking. From this vantage point I can see tiny towns below, streams snaking their way through the mountains across from us, and the ominous smoke that is ever-present in this area. The entire image before me exudes tranquility, but nothing can stop the chill still seeping into my bones.

"I do have...just one question," I admit, barely above a whisper. I hate myself for even asking, but something has been gnawing at me for a while, and I've never been brave enough to bring it up.

"You can ask me anything, love," Ryden encourages me to continue.

"Do you—do *Reapers*—do you know when someone is going to Die?" I whisper. I can't meet Ryden's eyes, instead choosing to feign serious interest in a caterpillar that has crawled onto the toe of my shoe.

"Yes," Ryden breathes, and for some reason the admission feels like a betrayal.

"What if it's an accident?" I continue. "Like, someone is the victim of a freak accident. Do you know about those Deaths beforehand?"

"Yes," Ryden whispers again. He clears his throat then mercifully continues. "Reapers know, or could find out, the date and time of Death of any Living person between now and...well, essentially the end of Time if we wanted, I suppose. Not that I ever look at future Deaths. I find it..." he trails off when he sees my face as I balk and feel the ever-present rage roaring to Life within me.

"Seriously?" I snap, glaring at him. "You know people—GOOD people—will Die, and you do *nothing*? That's...it's despicable."

Ryden's eyes tighten infinitesimally, the only sign that my words have wounded him, before he responds.

"We can't interfere, Abby. Who am I to go against nature?" I know the question is rhetorical, so I silently seethe while he goes on. "We don't get to decide when someone passes. Heartless as you still seem to think Reapers are, we're often just as outraged by Death as you are right now. Especially when it's accidental or unexpected, and even more especially when it's a child. It seems, *and is*, cruel and unfair. But we don't make the call. We don't decide who lives and who Dies. And when it's unexpected, or a child, or a *good* person, the best thing we—I —can do is my job. I can help them transition either into their new Existence as a ghost, or into the Unknown, with patience and understanding."

"So you can just let someone *Die*, rather than tell them *not* to take the freeway to work on Tuesday?" I balk. "Your conscience is totally clear knowing that you could *save* people and you choose not to?"

He bristles. "Abby, I *can't* interfere. Even if I wanted to. There are rules..."

"Damn your rules!" I scream, rising from the ground to my full height. "And what happened to that poor girl back there, huh? Did her Reaper just forget she Died?"

"Hundreds of thousands of people Die every day!" Ryden yells, rising to meet me. "Hundreds of thousands of families destroyed, hundreds of thousands of confused souls, and it's our job to do WHAT WE CAN to help them! But we aren't miracle workers! There will *always* be ghosts that slip through the cracks, ones that lay so low under the radar that they end up falling off of it, and become the scenario that you just witnessed. I think we can both agree that it isn't ideal!"

He stalks away into the trees while I fall back onto the meadow floor, working to steady my own breathing.

I've gotten too friendly with this man, this *Reaper*, while all the while he's luring me closer and closer to my mysterious end—which he's just proven he won't warn me is coming. There's no way that this ghost's fate isn't my own, to some extent.

I'm sure the Brotherhood won't make my Reaping as quick, and they likely won't comfort me like Ryden did this girl, but he's obviously complicit in all of it.

I've listened to my heart far too much, and she is a traitorous fool.

It's time to start listening to my brain.

She's screaming that something is very, very wrong.

39

The next few days are tense, mostly because Ryden is walking on eggshells around me.

We walk, then we walk. And after that? We walk some more.

Ryden knows that my witnessing a Reaping has broken something in me, and I can tell that he's trying to right it—right things between us, even a little bit.

He succeeds in getting me to at least acknowledge him when he suggests a campfire and s'mores.

"Why," I ask, "do you suddenly want to have a traditional campfire? We've had fires at our campsites nearly every night."

"Because, I don't think you've ever experienced an *actual* campfire, the right way," he guesses correctly. "And I want to remedy that. And I can teach you how to make the perfect s'more."

"You act like it's a science," I roll my eyes.

"That's because it is," he says, eyes glinting with mischief.

He checks his wards, something I think he makes a show of for my benefit and not out of actual necessity, before making a Kroger run just as the moon peaks in the night sky. He's back in a flash with two grocery bags in tow. He spends a few minutes amassing the perfect collection of twigs and branches from the forest floor as I watch, doing exactly nothing to help since I'm not a s'more scientist...yet.

Once he has a roaring fire raging, Ryden gestures to a stump he'd set by the fire as a makeshift seat. I sit, and he makes a show of pulling the accoutrements from his bags.

"I had to rob a dry cleaners for these," he winks, pulling out wire hangers.

"How very morally grey of you," I gasp sarcastically, clutching invisible pearls.

He puts a marshmallow on the end of each hanger before handing one to me.

"There are two secrets to a perfect s'more," he begins, a teacher reciting facts to a pupil. "First, you *must* char your marshmallow. It needs to be all but a blackened husk, like so," he gestures to his marshmallow which is currently on fire. He twists his hanger a few times, letting the flames engulf the whole marshmallow before blowing it out in a huff.

I repeat his actions with my own marshmallow, then look to him for the next step.

"Then," he continues, "you assemble. You start with a graham cracker on the bottom, a few squares of Hershey's chocolate, the marshmallow, then," he pauses for dramatic effect, reaching around behind himself to the forgotten grocery bag. With a flourish, he pulls out a bag of Lucky Charms marshmallows. "You add a sprinkling of *these*," he says as he tops his charred marshmallow with the mini cereal marshmallows. "Put your other graham cracker on top and voila! You have the perfect s'more."

He takes a bite and closes his eyes, clearly lost in the perfection of his creation. I expect him to polish off the rest of it, but he hands it to me, instead, taking my hanger and assembling another.

I take a bite and...*ugh*.

"Okay, you're right," I begrudgingly admit. "I mean, I've never had a s'more before, but I can't imagine any scenario where it's better than this." I hold up the last bite of the s'more in a "cheers" gesture before finishing it and he chuckles.

"I'm glad you enjoyed it," he smiles before starting to set up our campsite for the night. I rise to help him, but he holds up a hand, urging me to sit back down.

Once the bedrolls are laid out, he checks his phone and grimaces before turning to me.

"I need to flit away for a bit. Will you be alright? I'll triple check my wards first."

I want to question him on where he's going, or what we could possibly need at this hour, but after days of walking and sparring lessons I'm too exhausted to care.

"I'll be fine," I assure him before a yawn sneaks out. "I'm actually really tired, so I'll probably just pass out."

He insists on checking his wards, and waits until I'm fully encased in my bedroll with my blankets up to my chin before he finally departs.

I drift off to sleep under a canopy of stars, the ever-present blanket of unease, and a new, tiny layer of hope.

The next morning dawns brighter and earlier than I'd have hoped, but I slept well, so I can't complain.

Truthfully, I've slept well enough lately that I can't remember the last time I needed a Trance.

The same can't be said for Ryden, who is, surprisingly, still asleep.

I never heard him return from wherever he'd flitted last night, so it must have been really late. Then again, Ryden moves with a predatory grace and I never really hear him coming or going at all, so he could've been gone and back within seconds and I wouldn't have known.

But I do know that he rarely sleeps, so I move around the campsite as quietly as possible to give him as much time as he needs. I dig into his pack for the stash of granola bars I know that he always keeps, and also find a Dunkin' Iced Coffee can. I send up a silent prayer of thanks for this smallest of miracles, chugging the coffee in seconds. I chase it with two granola bars and then decide to use this "free" time to get some stretching in.

We've been hiking *a lot*, and sparring, and my muscles are screaming in protest. I figure it's only fair to show them some love. I spend the next half hour stretching out my arms, legs, neck, and back via some of Amarie's favorite yoga poses, and I'm just settling into "corpse pose" when Ryden begins to stir.

He sits upright abruptly, eyes scanning the campsite before they land on me and for the briefest second, they look devastated—no, utterly heartbroken—before he blinks the pain away so quickly that I question whether it had been there at all.

"Good morning?" I say, unsure.

"Morning," he responds, still shaking the sleep, or whatever that was, from his head.

"I...had a canned coffee and some granola bars. Figured I'd let you sleep, you seemed tired."

"Yeah, uh, thanks," he responds almost robotically.

Oh-kay. It's gonna be one of those days, then.

One of the days where we hike and don't speak.

This one is odd, though, since the not-speaking isn't my doing.

I'm right, though. Once Ryden rises and we wrap up our bedrolls, put out the remaining embers of the fire, and clean the area of any trash, he utters a, "let's go," before walking away from me and not turning back.

40

I chalk Ryden's bad mood up to a rough night of sleep, which I can empathize with, and try not to take it personally, but I do.

I don't like this version of Ryden. This closed off, cold, heartless Reaper mask he's donned for whatever reason. But it's probably for the best. He's shown me that I can't trust him. How anyone could be so cold, so heartless as to let people just *Die*...I just can't understand. He could literally save people, and he chooses not to.

We hike the whole day, snacking on granola bars when we normally would have stopped to eat lunch, but he's in such a foul mood that I don't want to break the silence. I leave him alone with his thoughts, struggling to keep up with his pace.

Another few hours go by, the Sun has fully set, and the moon has risen before he flits for dinner, which we eat in awkward silence. I try to start a conversation, break the ice, make a joke, *anything* a few times, but he barely acknowledges me.

And his *eyes*.

There's something wrong.

But he won't tell me and I know asking will only close him off the more.

Once we finish eating, he tells me he needs to flit again and that he'll be gone a few hours.

That is *fine* by me—I would love nothing more than for him to take his bad vibes somewhere far from me for a while, because they're putting a pit in my stomach. Am I turning into Em, able to read the feelings of people around me? No, he's just being *that weird* today.

Once he's gone I set up the campsite and flop into my bedroll before it hits me: I'm alone with my phone. Ryden isn't here hovering, which means I might, if the cell-service gods smile upon me, be able to reach my roommates. I could update them on the fact that I'm still on this side of the Unknown, and check in with them.

Why didn't I think of this last night?!

I power up my phone and wait for the service to attempt to connect.

Mercifully, I have two bars, which means there must be a town somewhere nearby. I sit and wait as random notifications fill the screen: Instagram, StoryGraph, a torrent of emails from Xeta wanting to start work back up, and several alerts from the security camera at Ma's.

Seeing Ma always comforts me, so I decide to check in on her first.

It's late at night and calling her is out of the question without scaring her—she'd think there's an emergency. It's no matter. Simply seeing her on the security camera will have to do for now.

I pull open the app and see a thumbnail for the last motion recorded. It's from yesterday.

My mind filters through all the things that have happened to me since the timestamp on this video, which is about the time Ryden left after we'd finished our s'mores.

My stomach drops when I think of the turn things have taken; how we'd been almost companionable and how easily his willingness, his complicity, in letting innocent people Die had ruined it.

The drop of my stomach is nothing to the free fall my heart takes when I watch the security footage.

My mother steps out the door, silently weeping. It's late at night and clearly very gloomy—so dark that it casts an ominous haze around her.

Oddly, she doesn't pull the door closed behind herself. She's not wearing scrubs, which is strange, and she doesn't rush to a waiting Uber, or walk off out of the camera's field of vision.

She doesn't go invisible.

She just stands there, like the definition of the ghost that she is.

The construction crew working on the house she's haunting have clearly begun working on the front porch at some point: the railing has been demolished, but this was very obviously a rush job. Part of the porch still stands, as if they took a sledgehammer to the sections of railing immediately in front of the door, then decided to work on a different part of the house instead and left the porch floor intact. The jagged edges of wood from the parts of the porch railing still standing perfectly frame my mother's sides.

She pulls out her phone and scrolls, then begins frantically typing. It's clear that she's trying to type quickly, but keeps making errors... she types, then rolls her eyes skyward and backspaces, then starts over again. She continues to cry, constantly dabbing her eyes. She heaves a sigh, clearly struggling to find the words for whatever she's typing. She pauses, dropping her phone to her side, and glances over her shoulder.

A shadow appears in the door behind her, looming over her small frame. She wipes at her eyes again, a handkerchief balled in her fist. She straightens, then puts out a hand and nods once before glancing back down at her phone and finishing whatever she'd been typing.

She looks up and nods again.

Ryden *steps abruptly through the doorway behind her and takes her arm as the camera's timer kills the recording.*

As the clip finishes, a text from Ma, dated yesterday, appears at the top of my screen.

I love you so, so much. Forever.

And I collapse.

41

I wake in my bedroll the next afternoon.

My eyes are nearly glued shut thanks to sleep dust and the salt of my tears from the night before—tears I shed while I slept. I couldn't escape what I'd seen, even in dreams.

Ryden Reaped my mother.

My mother is *gone*.

My one constant in this Existence, snuffed out like a candle flame. Why?

Why?

I chance a glance in Ryden's direction and let out a sigh of relief to see that he's not here. He's been here; his bedroll is laid out near mine. I'm glad to see that it's a reasonable distance from mine this time—not close enough to reach out and touch as it had been just a few nights before.

I throw an arm over my face, as if covering my eyes will cover the memories of what I'd seen. I'd been such an *idiot*. I had myself begin to *trust* him! He played his part so well, acting as if he was worthy of that trust—even through all of our fights. Then he goes off and Reaps my mother?!

I'm going to be sick. I barely make it out of my bedroll before everything I've eaten over the last few days ejects itself from me. I throw up until there's nothing left, then I dry heave as sweat and tears fall freely. Once my body is spent, I crawl back to my bedroll to strategize.

I'm thankful that Ryden hasn't returned, because I'm not ready to face him, but I do begrudgingly note that it's odd...he's never left for this long without letting me know.

Relax, I think to myself, *he's probably just in your apartment slaughtering your roommates so that he can take* them *from you, too.*

That's not a road I can go down though, so I force myself to focus and shoot off a group text. I have to play nonchalant so that they don't suspect that anything is wrong—I can't make any rash moves that could endanger them. *If they're still alive...* that nagging voice whispers, causing new tears to prick my eyes.

Me: **Just checking in. On a mountain somewhere. Still un-Reaped for now. All good at home?**

Home. My heart falters at the word. Text bubbles appear...someone is typing.

Amarie: **Been Dying to hear from u...we miss u so much!**

Zelie: **Miss you love you! Everything is fine here, but we're so worried! Where are you?**

Em: **Any signs you're close to whatever he wanted? When can you come home? xx**

I release the breath I'd consciously been holding waiting on each of their replies. Each of them responds, so I know that for now, at least, they're fine.

I consider rifling through Ryden's pack in search of something to eat, but I know I couldn't keep it down. I settle for an early dinner of a bottle of water and a few ibuprofens to combat the blinding headache that is rapidly spreading across my forehead. I should feel grateful that my being a Born ghost means that at least painkillers work on me, but I'd never thought to ask Ma is she ever even *gets* headaches. Did she ever even need meds? Did she ever feel physical pain?

She'd nursed me through what felt like hundreds of migraines, but I never once asked her if she'd had one herself.

There are so many things I never thought to—never *got to*—ask her, and now I never will.

I slept through the night, but it was the sleep of sorrow... fitful and useless, offering no rest or respite. I've gotten too used to acting like a Living since Ryden is one. I've slept when he slept, risen when he rose, and I'm realizing now what a mistake that's been. My body may be in decent shape, but I haven't Tranced in weeks, and I feel the exhaustion deep in my soul.

I drop into my bedroll and finally sink into the oblivion of the Trance I desperately need.

42

I jolt out of the Trance to Ryden shaking me.

He doesn't meet my eyes, and I'm Trance hazy and confused. It's the middle of the night, and I feel the whispers of a memory tugging at my mind, but the pull of the Trance is too strong. Wisps of memories are there, and try as I might to grasp at them, they fade like smoke on the wind. My eyes flutter closed and Ryden shakes me again.

"We have another situation," he whispers. I force my stubborn eyes open and he's still refusing to look at me. I still can't remember why.

"Remember the bear?" he asks quietly. I nod, mostly to get him to let me close my eyes again. "Just like then, I need you to go invisible and stay behind me, love."

He turns to place me at his back as we both rise to standing positions, but I'm not fully alert until I hear crunching leaves.

The footsteps are leisurely, as if their feet are taking their time getting to us...as if they know we're here. Finally, (*finally?*) the source of the sounds steps into the clearing. I want to laugh, mercifully remembering how dangerous that was with the bear and clamp a hand over my mouth to stop myself.

The noise appears to be caused by a man, wearing those same, odd fighting leathers that Ryden has. That isn't what makes me want to giggle, though. It's the fact that he is, for all that I can see, totally ordinary. He's on the shorter side, maybe five foot six, with blonde hair cut high-and-tight.

Everything about the newcomer exudes 1950s "golly gee!" attitude; a goody-two-shoes if I'd ever seen one. I want nothing more than to step around Ryden and give this dude a wedgie, but Ryden's reaction makes me pause.

He hasn't calmed down *at all*. If anything, he's even more tense than he was before Captain America stepped into view.

"Evening, Ryden," the newcomer croons, raising his hand as if he's tipping an imaginary hat.

"Adam," Ryden nods. "What do you want?"

The newcomer—Adam's—eyebrows furrow. "Now, is that any way to greet your brother-in-arms?"

"It's the middle of the night, Adam, and I'd like to go back to sleep, so I ask again—what do you want?"

"I was just in the area and sensed that another Reaper was close. I hadn't heard of any pending Deaths around here, so I thought I'd come and see what reason that Reaper might have for being here."

"I'm off duty, and enjoy camping in solitude." He enunciates the last word, making it clear to Adam that he wants to be left alone.

"You can do that," Adam croons, "but you also could have invited some of your Brothers. So many of us like to camp," he says, kicking over a water bottle and watching the liquid trail tiny tracks across the dirt.

What a wasteful asshole.

Adam surveys our campsite then and I freeze, noticing at the same time that he does that in his haste to get rid of this guy, Ryden overlooked something vital. I'm frantically trying to think of a way to signal to him, settling on clasping the back of his arm at the same moment that Adam begins to laugh—a menacing, awful sound. "Solitude, huh? You need two bedrolls for yourself? And two packs?"

Ryden growls, his voice absolutely lethal as he commands that Adam, "Leave. Now."

As much as I don't want to, I have to give Adam credit; he doesn't seem worried at all. In fact, Ryden's clear threat of violence only entices him as he steps towards Ryden and grunts, "No, I don't think I will."

They begin to circle, each assessing their opponent. At first, I try to stay behind Ryden, but I realize that if they actually do begin to brawl, Ryden could step back into me and cause us more issues. I slowly begin to step backwards towards the treeline, taking care to only place my foot on the ground at the same time one of the Reapers does, so that the sound of my footfalls are masked.

"What's your problem, Ryden?" Adam sneers. "We're allowed to have romantic escapades. Where's your little girlfriend? I'd love to meet her."

It's as if Ryden can sense when I'm a safe distance away, because his entire demeanor turns even more deadly. He stands taller, more confident, and offers Adam a dazzling smile that promises that pain and suffering will follow.

"This is your last warning, Adam. Leave."

Realization sets in Adam's eyes then, and his face turns awestruck. "You found it," he breathes. "You found the..."

"Another word," Ryden cuts him off, "and I will remove your head from your body." He's practically vibrating with fury.

"Why?! This is wonderful! Wait until Raelle hears that you got her!" Adam is beaming, the brilliant white of his teeth glowing in the moonlight. "She'll promote you, you know. Whatever rank you want. Hell, she'd probably let you *retire* on this. Why would you want *my* head over it?"

It?

Is he talking about *me*?

I'm going to be sick.

Ryden is still glaring at Adam, and Adam is struck dumb over it.

"What is going on with you, Brot—*oh*. Oh my gods!" He giggles, and it's exactly the sound you'd expect from a nine-year-old little girl.

"Don't tell me," he reaches out, as if he plans to clap a hand to Ryden's shoulder. He thinks better of it and instead places both hands on his own knees, doubled over in a fit of laughter.

"Don't tell me you think you've *fallen* for her. Ryden, tell me you haven't. You can't *fall* for the *Primo Natus*. She's playing you! You know that, right? There is no future with her, or any of the rest of them."

Adam straightens, stepping toward Ryden until they are face to face. Or, as face to face as they can be with nearly a foot of height difference between them.

"Ryden, you know what you have to do, right? You have to hand her over to Raelle." He sneers. "You can't love the *Primo Natus*. She's nothing more than chattel...a means to an en-"

Adam can't finish his last word before he's relieved of his head.

I honest to gods don't know how he did it.

One second, Adam was standing there mocking Ryden, and the next, his head and his body were separated by a few feet. I notice that Adam's head, which had unfortunately rolled in my direction, still shows the echoes of laughter; his face will be forever etched with crinkles around his eyes and a mocking sneer on his mouth.

I register all of this in the two seconds that I have before reality crashes into me and I lose my entire mind.

I open my mouth and wail. The screams rack my entire body, and every creature for miles hears—knows that something is here and something is *wrong*.

Ryden whirls and attempts to step towards me, but the blood pouring down both of his arms is enough that I double down, and double over, promptly vomiting all over my shoes. He throws his hands up in front of himself then, a gesture of peace, and slowly backs away. He reaches into his pocket, whips out his phone, taps the screen twice, and presses it to his ear.

If he says anything, I don't hear it, but within a moment, I feel strong, comforting arms wrapping around mine, and a kind, familiar face is in front of my own.

"Jaali," I sob and crumple—my knees can't hold my body up anymore. He catches me, holding me upright and letting me cry it out.

"Shh," he soothes. "It's alright, Abby. It's going to be alright." He presses his cheek into the top of my head, and I can feel him wince. "I'm sorry you had to see this, okay?"

I vaguely notice that Ryden disappears, reappearing a few moments later with wet hair, different clothes, and clean arms. He glances our way, clearly wanting to approach, and this time, I nod.

His face is a mask of desperate sorrow, and I can't decide why.

Is it because he just murdered a man in cold blood? Or is it because I heard the things Adam said about my being something to hand over?

About Ryden *falling*...

"Abby," he breathes, my name a prayer on his lips.

"Why?" I demand.

"I'll explain everything, I swear," he's speaking low and fast, his gaze darting back and forth across our campsite. "I just...I need some time." His eyes are pleading, but he backs away and calls, "Jaali."

Jaali releases me gently and steps towards Ryden, where the two share a few tense words that I can't hear over the ringing in my ears. It drowns out any thought I could have.

Is this shock? Is this what true shock feels like?

I look down to see that my hands are shaking, and I've gone cold all over. My breaths come in ragged gasps, and I know that if I don't get a good gulp of air soon, I'll pass out.

I sit down on a fallen tree trunk and bend to dip my head between my knees, promptly kneeing myself in the face because I can't stop myself from bouncing my feet. I have so much nervous energy that I need to move, but if I move, I'll faint, and if I faint, I'll...what?

The realization that Ryden and Jaali are here calms me down enough to sit up. If I faint, they'll be here until I wake up.

They won't let anything happen to me.

Well, Jaali won't. Adam's words are still ringing in my head, but it could have all been for show. Jaali already told me, back in the apartment, that the Reapers' ranks are utter chaos. That they don't know who is going to be loyal to Raelle...and who already is. Maybe Ryden and Adam had staged it all somehow, to trick me into dropping my guard.

Or, maybe Ryden had just killed a member of his Brotherhood, who could have been on his side, merely because that Brother threatened *me*.

This is all too much.

I glance up and towards the Reapers' direction and am surprised to see that only Ryden remains. He's staring at me, brows knit, as if he's worried that I'm about to break.

"Well, don't just stand there," I snap. I instantly regret it as hurt splashes across his face. I amend my tone. "Where did Jaali go?"

"Jaali had to—ah," he steps towards me tentatively. I let him approach and take a seat on the tree trunk beside me. "Jaali needed to go...make sure that Adam goes quickly. Before anyone else realizes. He needs to get to the Unknown before he can...communicate with anyone."

"Wait, do Reapers have to be Reaped?" I gape.

"We have souls too, Abby," he smiles sadly, "just like anyone else."

I prop my head up in my hands. "So, what was that all about?" I don't have any fight left in me; I just want answers.

"I," he breathes. He turns abruptly towards me. "Abby, I need to tell you the truth."

43

I sit in anxious silence waiting for Ryden to begin.

He sucks in one long, deep breath, and it's clear that he isn't prepared for this conversation, this revelation to me, *about* me. He runs a rough hand over his face before gazing up at the stars, losing himself in his thoughts for a moment before shaking himself out of the reverie.

"I'm sorry," he laughs nervously, although there's no humor in the air. "I'm just not sure where to begin." He's seated beside me on a fallen tree trunk, putting a respectful distance between us because he knows I'm utterly spooked. He rests an elbow on his knee, cradling his head in his hand and for the first time, I see the ravages of stress that have wreaked havoc across his skin. His eyes are heavy and tired, and there are lines on his face that haven't been there before; he looks defeated.

A million questions race through my mind, but I can't bring myself to ask any of them. I'm afraid of what I'll learn, but also afraid that if I ask a question, it will derail his thoughts and he won't tell me anything. I wring my hands nervously as I stare at the ground between my feet, waiting for Ryden to speak.

He coughs, then begins. "The Brotherhood of the Reapers is an ancient organization, as I've mentioned before. As far back in human history as you can reach, as we were evolving from primates, Reapers have Existed—even before that. As long as there has been Life on this planet, Reapers have Existed. We, whether anyone," a glance at me, "likes it or not, play a necessary role in human Existence especially. All things Living must eventually Die, and in that transition into Death, Reapers step in to ah—assist in the process."

He meets my eyes as if he's expecting me to respond, so I nod, encouraging him to continue.

"Naturally, as it was with the evolution of humanity, over the ages we assembled, forming what is now known as the Brotherhood of Reapers. While we, of course, do not engage in any active warfare, our ranks mimic that of any military organization. We mobilize during times of great wars, of course, as there are more," he winces, trying to find the right word before settling on, "*casualties* to be tended to. But other than that, the Brotherhood is a formality, a way to organize which Reaper will attend to which Deaths, which Reapers have specific talents—"

"*Talents*?" I ask, unable to stop myself.

Again, he takes a moment, choosing his words carefully, "Perhaps 'talents' wasn't the best word. Take Jaali, for example. You've been around Jaali enough now that you can likely sense his...aura. The calming presence that he offers?"

I nod, because I have definitely experienced Jaali's, well, *Jaali-ness*.

"Jaali, and others like him, are the better Reapers for those who are passing young, or alone, or afraid. Whereas, for example, *Adam*," he says the name like a curse, and I can feel the rage radiating off of him again, "would be more successful with someone who is too tough to admit to *feelings*, even as they cross from Life to...after. Do you understand?"

I nod again, because I do: humans are similar, I guess. Some people have excellent bedside manner, and others don't. It would track that Reapers could be the same.

"Excellent," he whispers, though there's no joy or pride in his expression. He still looks fearful. Sad.

"Reapers know, from the second the Reaper gene awakens, what their Life's purpose is. We're trained, almost like the Spartans of old, once we join the ranks of the Brotherhood and fulfill our destinies. We swear oaths. Part of those oaths include a vow of secrecy, which has made telling you—giving you—*too* specific of information, difficult" he struggles, "but please know I'm trying. I think," his voice drops to a whisper so low I can barely hear him right next to me, "that I may have found a loophole. *Your* Lif—er—*Existence*," he amends, "can't be kept secret from you, and I don't think she—I didn't, even—realizes."

"She?" I ask, even though I of course already know the answer.

Raelle.

The new leader.

The Commander who wants me gone.

"Now for the awkward bit," he smiles sheepishly. "I'm sure you've realized by now that I didn't just happen upon you," he admits, flushing, and I nod. It would make sense that he was told about me.

Even though I know that, his next words sting.

"I was tasked to locate you, collect you, and turn you into the Brotherhood of the Reapers' new Commander, Raelle."

My eyes close involuntarily as the feeling of betrayal—*betrayal*, which is so absurd—rocks through me. I can't speak, so I nod again.

"Because of the Order, I found you. I found you at Halcyon Hall, and again when you moved to your apartment, which, might I add, was a surprising turn of events. It was my job to know, to anticipate, your every movement. I spent days following you, lurking outside windows and in alleyways, waiting for the perfect opportunity to strike. To fulfill my duty to my Commander. To *do my job*."

I hate the tears I can feel lining my eyes.

Pathetic. I'm pathetic.

He continues, "I rarely left my post for weeks, learning you, your movements, trying to find the best, easiest *in*. But I quickly found that I was more focused on," an awkward pause, "well, *you* and less on the task I'd been assigned."

"So you've been...watching me?" I ask tentatively.

"I have." He hangs his head in shame. "At first it was the job, but then—I don't know," he shrugs, the corners of his mouth lifting sadly. "I realized that I couldn't look away. I couldn't not be near you, like moth to flame. You drew me in, Abby."

I know from every rom-com I've ever read that this is supposed to be the moment that I take him into my arms, so overcome with appreciation for his attention, but I can't muster any warmth; all I feel is white hot *rage*.

"So you watched me at Halcyon, and out with Zelie, and in the apartment." He nods. "Were you—" I blanch, "did you watch me in the *shower*?" I feel a flush rising up my neck, covering my whole face in red splotches.

"No!" he balks, clearly affronted by the question. "Abby, no. I would never have violated your privacy like that." He straightens, doing the most to appear the chivalrous warrior, simply head over heels in love with a girl who's honor he'd Die to protect.

Garbage.

"I am so, *so* sorry," I seethe, inflamed. "You simply *must* forgive me for struggling to believe that you suddenly grew honor after literally stalking me for months."

"Abby, it wasn't like that, I swe—"

"Save it," I hold my hand up to silence him. I don't want to hear another word, I *can't* hear another word, answers to my questions be damned. "I can't do it, Ryden. I can't hear any more lies from you." He rubs his hand over his face, clearly trying to think of a way to talk himself out of this.

"Abby," he whispers, as soft as a prayer on the wind.

I've been such a fool. I'd totally dropped my guard without meaning to...without even realizing it. I had been letting him in, bit by bit. I'd thought that I might even be able to actually trust him one day, if I made it out of this ordeal. I thought that I'd eventually even be able to forgive him for...

A stone drops in my soul, deepening my anger into the endless pit of fury and despair.

Ma.

How quickly I'd forgotten in the chaos of the last few moments.

I rise to my feet quickly, stomach roiling, and Ryden follows suit. He stands in front of me with the most hopeful, most dumbfounded look on his face.

"You took my mother from me! You—you bastard!" I scream, slamming my fist against his chest. The words are out before I have time to even think about keeping them. But fine. *Fine.* I let out the sob I've been holding deep in my gut since the moment I realized that my mother stepped away from me and into the Unknown.

He stumbles—literally *stumbles*—backwards, as if my frantic fists have actually moved him. Impossible, but his face is different than I've ever seen it. *Is that*—no, it couldn't be.

Anguish?

Regret?

A heart, cracking in two?

"You don't have any idea what you're talking about," he mutters, straightening. His voice is devoid of any emotion. He sniffs and makes to turn away, stalking towards his bedroll.

I can't help the anger building inside of me. I'm past caring whether my words cut him—I *want* them to hurt him. I want him to feel a fraction of what I felt—what I still feel—losing Ma.

"Yes, I do. I had a mother! I had a mother, then *you* took her away!" The tears that spill from my eyes burn hot against my skin. "Seems pretty easy to understand."

He whirls, looming over me, ever the threatening warrior. "No, Abby, you don't understand. You don't understand at all. And do you want to know the worst part of all of it?" he asks, a vein in his neck pulsing wildly. "The worst thing is that I thought you would. I thought you *did*."

Is he really trying to act like he hadn't been the one to take her? Like *he* was some victim?

Of all the gaslighting bullshit I've ever heard...

"*Are you serious?*" I bark, barely a whisper.

"Not everyone is free to do whatever they want at a moment's notice. Contrary to what you might think, I don't exactly have a choice in what souls I'm assigned to *escort* to the Unknown—and I certainly don't have any say in when they *choose* to go."

Those last three words steal my breath.

"I certainly don't have any say in when they choose *to go."*

"What is that supposed to mean?" The words come out in a single, pained breath. I know I should put more malice behind them, but all the air has gone out of the world.

There's no way.

She wouldn't have chosen to leave...they took her. *He* took her.

Right?

"Look," his eyes are a deeper blue than I've ever seen them before, "I know it's hard to hear, and no matter what you might think of me, I'm not—," he sighs, raking a hand through his hair and stopping himself from whatever he'd been about to say. "This isn't how I wanted you to find out. But your mother *chose* to go, quite willingly."

"*Bullshit*," I breathe. Ma wouldn't—she *couldn't*—have chosen to go, especially not without at least talking to me. "You are a *liar*." He stiffens, clearly impacted by my words. "Do you really think I would believe that my mother chose to go willingly, when I am literally your *unwilling* prisoner?"

He falls backwards again, visibly wounded. "You cannot be serious." He starts to pace, rubbing his palm over his chin, clearly choosing his next words carefully. "You are not a prisoner, Abby. Everything I'm doing, everything I've *done*, has been to *protect* you!"

"*Protect* me from what, Ryden?" I sneer. "Egotistical soldiers who kidnap you and threaten your friends and roommates to force your hand? Self-impressed men who steal you away from your home to trek you through gods-forsaken mountain ranges before they do gods-know-what to you or hand you over to gods-know-who? Is that what you're *protecting me* from? Because if so, I'm sorry to tell you but you've done a *really* shitty job so far because here I am," I gesture around wildly, "in the middle of fucking nowhere with a monster masquerading as a knight in shining armor."

I drop onto a nearby rock and cradle my head in my hands. I want to sob, or scream, or hit something, but I don't want to give him the satisfaction.

"Thank you *so much* for protecting me from *you*." I can taste the venom of my words and I don't care. On the contrary, I hope that they finds their mark; I hope my words course through him, ripping and tearing and bleeding and paralyzing, until he hurts the way I do. I hope the pain festers inside him until he feels the same agony that his words, and his *actions*, have caused me.

His face hardens into the stone mask he'd worn in the days I'd first seen him at Halcyon, at the Skull: the heartless Reaper with black, soulless eyes.

"You don't know a godsdamned thing about me, Abby. You are free to think whatever you will of me. Your mother *chose* to go on—that is a fact. Past that, if you need me to be your villain, then so be it. I am your villain. Since you clearly can't let yourself trust me, there's no point in me telling you the truth—you won't believe it, or worse, you'll twist it around to *make* me the bad guy...again! So, unfortunately for me there will be no coming clean, no getting all the secrets out into the open, no relief. We will continue on the last leg of this little quest, and you can see for yourself what I've been trying to prove to you: that no matter how much you don't *want* to see it, *all* of my actions—every single one —have been to protect you. From there, we can go our separate ways and you won't have to be burdened by such a *monster* any longer."

I open my mouth and close it several times, as if I'm a fish suddenly out of water. I don't know what I want to say, other than to ask what he meant by "our separate ways." Would my being forced to go "on," or becoming some experiment on Born ghosts be something he'd consider "our own ways," or does he truly intend to allow me to go back to my home and my friends and my, for lack of a better word, *Life* when this ridiculous quest is all said and done?

And why does the thought of "our separate ways" cause a different, painful ache to bloom in my heart, even now, after this fight? After learning that my mother is gone?

And what does he mean by "no relief"?

"Fine," I finally force through gritted teeth. "Let's pack up our shit then you can lead the way."

44

The next days are tense.

I weep constantly. There's never a moment that tears don't leak from my eyes. My cheeks are blistered and my nose is raw, but there's nothing I can do to stop it; they continue to pour from my eyes day and night.

Ma is *gone*.

She's gone, and I don't know how to get to her.

She's gone and I don't know that I'll ever see her again.

How are we still breathing? How are birds still chirping? How is the Sun still able to shine when she's not here anymore? Time should have stopped the moment she did, because this world suddenly seems so hollow, so empty, so unnecessary.

Ryden and I don't speak past basic *"we'll stop here for the night"*s and *"I'm flitting away for supplies, don't wait up"*s. Even after our fight, he dutifully makes sure that my basic needs are met: there are three good meals every day, I have a hot cup of coffee every morning, and he *never* drops his wards. Not that any of that matters.

I hate him more desperately than I've ever hated another being in my entire Existence.

I hate him almost as much as I hate myself.

I hate myself for taking what time I had with her for granted. I hate myself for avoiding her calls, for resenting her as a shitty teenager, for hiding my roommates from her. I hate that I wasn't with her. I hate that I ever left. I want more than anything to call her, to complain about Ryden and about my fickle heart, to tell her everything that's going on, to ask for her advice. I want her to tell me how I should handle this impossible situation I've found myself in. I want to hear her voice.

I hate him for taking her from me.

Almost as deep as my grief is the desperate sorrow and brutal betrayal that Ryden delivered when he suggested that my mother left me *willingly*. I don't want to believe it, don't want to give it a second of my energy, but there's a tiny voice in the back of my mind that won't stop whispering, *"what if it's true? Could she have chosen to leave you? Would she have chosen to go?"*

Did I mean so little to her that leaving me behind was easy? Did she even consider me before she just...left? Did I ever matter to her at all?

I filter through the memories I have of my entire Existence, and can't find anything that suggests, even for a moment, that my mother didn't love me, but...

A text.

She sent me a text, and walked away from me forever.

45

I torture myself by watching my mother's final moments on replay every time Ryden flits somewhere.

I relive them over and over and over again, clinging to the stupid hope that if I watch it just one more time, something will be revealed. Some clue will appear, some proof that she's not gone.

Maybe if I watch it just one more time, she'll turn to the camera.

She'll turn to the camera and wink.

She'll mouth that it isn't real. That she's still at the house.

That I'm crazy for ever thinking she could leave me.

Of course, that never happens. I've spent countless hours dissecting the clip, and nothing has ever changed. Nothing *will* ever change.

I'm sitting alone in our latest campsite late one evening. Ryden has flitted off once again, probably to Reap someone's kitten. He's been replacing our battery backups anytime he flitted somewhere that sold them, so my phone's battery stays nearly full.

I sigh and drop my phone between my feet to cradle my head in my hands. The impact of my phone hitting the ground triggers the security app's "go back" feature, displaying all video footage from the selected date.

For the first time, I notice that there are more than just *that* video in the security app on the day my mother *left*.

There are two more videos.

I snatch my phone up, greedy for anything left of my mother. I don't care if it'll hurt. I need to see her. I need to see how she spent her last day. I need it all, welcoming the pain I know is coming.

I scroll back to the earliest video from that day and hold my breath as I click play.

Ryden flits onto the porch and gingerly presses the doorbell. I've spent enough time with him over the last few weeks to tell that he's nervous: he looks down towards his hands and fidgets as he waits for the door to open.

When it does, he smiles politely, almost shyly, at the answerer, obviously my mother although she's off camera. His mouth moves but there's no audio. He presses a hand to his chest, and it's clear that he's introducing himself. His movements are slow but confident; he doesn't want to scare the person that he's just met...he wants to gain their trust by exuding strength and surety in himself, but also sympathy and gentleness towards them.

My stomach roils as he is beckoned inside.

The next video, taken almost exactly three minutes later, according to the timestamp, plays immediately.

The door bursts open and Ryden steps out. His shoulders heave repeatedly as if he's trying to catch his breath, or calm a racing heart. He leans forward placing his elbows on what's left of the porch's bannister, then raises his face to the sky and screams. There's no audio, but the rage and anguish is clear. My mother's silhouette appears as a shadow in the light cast by the open door, and it's haunting. Her shadow over Ryden's Living, physical form is every bit the ghost story people think that we are.

Ryden spins on his heels and glares at her. She says something that causes him to bark out a laugh, but anyone with vision can tell that it's a sarcastic laugh, overflowing with malice. She says something else and the smile instantly falls from his face, replaced by nothing short of rage. He screams again, no words, just the roar that comes with this level of anger. The release forced by the body when the emotion can no longer be contained.

I know this rage. It's the same level of anger I felt seeing Ryden there to Reap my mother.

She shifts, and the light glows on Ryden's face. It catches in the shine around his eyes as tears spring there. His body shakes with emotion and adrenaline as he falls to his knees before the shadow I know to be my mother.

He utters a few words then desperately waits for a response.

No response comes. He glares up at her, eyes shining with unshed tears and with his lower lip trembling, and says two more words.

Whatever words she says, they aren't the ones he wants to hear. His head falls and he runs his fingers through his hair, hands shaking. Once again, he laughs like a madman, pinching the bridge of his nose. When he finally rises, defeat is etched into every line of his face.

His eyes are hollow, and he stares at her in pure desperation.

He looks like a man who has fallen victim to fate.

Who's realized that fate won't fall in his favor.

He steps back into my mother's house with the eyes of a man who has just guaranteed his own execution.

My mind spins.

The world spins.

My heart is racing and I feel like I can't catch a breath and my stomach knots until it's all too much. Once again, my body heaves out everything I've eaten—which admittedly isn't much this time.

The tears fall, and I scream, mirror image to Ryden on the video. The Ryden who was so full of rage and anguish.

The Ryden who, at least from what the video shows, *fought* my mother before her Reaping.

I can't do this.

I can't survive another revelation.

News of my mother's Reaping broke me in ways that I'll never recover from. I've hated Ryden, hated myself. Hated the Brotherhood of Reapers. Hated Death. Hated the Unknown. Hated every single force that drove my mother to do this. The hate has rotted away in me, leaving me a broken, bleeding husk. I'm battered and bruised, my emotions so disordered that I can barely string together a coherent thought.

I cry myself to sleep right there on the forest floor, watching the Sun set as I replay what the security footage revealed over and over and over again in my head.

In the moments before I finally drift off, one thought forces its way to the surface: if I didn't know better, I would *swear* that the words that Ryden screamed at my mother after dropping to his knees before her were "*please,* " and "*stay,*" before the final, fleeting, trembling plea of, "*your daughter.*"

46

I wake and, of course, Ryden is already gone.

He's definitely been here because there's a pillow under my head and the blanket from my bedroll is draped over me—when I know I'd fallen asleep in the middle of the clearing away from everything.

I stretch, wiping the sleep from my chronically sore, swollen eyes, and sit up, peering around the campsite. There's a bottle of water and a small bag of strawberry donuts beside my pillow, as well as a scrap of paper with the words, "back by 10" scrawled in Ryden's neat handwriting.

I glance at my phone, which Ryden has left with me, after plugging it into a portable battery. It's 8:30, which gives me time to wash off, change my clothes, and Exist without Ryden hovering; his proximity makes everything harder.

Everything is harder after seeing the second video.

Ryden *Reaped* my mother. Ryden Reaped my mother, but he begged her to stay. Begged for *me*. He begged her not to do this to me.

I don't know enough about Reaper laws to know whether he could have refused her, but I know now what an impossible situation he was in.

But none of that changes the fact that my mother is gone, because of Ryden.

It's all too confusing and I don't know how to process any of my emotions. I grab up all of my toiletries and stumble to the small stream we'd stopped beside last night.

The water is icy, but I welcome the sting. I can feel my eyes returning to some semblance of normalcy after days of being swollen with tears. It's almost cathartic in a sick way—the water is in no way washing the grief of my mother away, because that will quite literally never leave me. But the brisk water washes away some of the weight—or makes it easier to hold.

I'm dressed and towel drying my hair when I hear a twig snap behind me.

Angry at him or not, I have to admit that Ryden would be proud: I'm up and across the clearing to his pack in seconds. The dagger is out of its roll and in my hand before I have time to think about it. I'm still nowhere close to being as lethal as a Reaper, but I could hold my own against a regular person, and even not knowing what snapped the twig, I feel better with a blade in my hand.

I spin to face the source of the sound, stumbling backwards when I see who is approaching Ryden's wards.

"A...Anabel?" I stutter.

I remember terrorizing Middletown kids with Anabel anytime our parents would let us out of their sight. She was often part of the usual gang of misfits.

What I can't fathom is what she could possibly be doing here. Sheer terror interrupts my confusion because I have no proof that she isn't one of those things Ryden warned me about.

I take several quick steps back, and Anabel holds her arms up in front of her.

"Hey, Abby, long time no see!" She chuckles awkwardly. She tries to take a step towards me when she walks directly into thin air and bounces backwards.

Oh, thank the gods, the wards.

"How do I know you're really Anabel?" I demand. I'm still clutching the dagger, afraid that I'll have to use it on someone that looks like an old friend.

An old*er* friend, because this version of Anabel definitely isn't a teenager anymore.

"It's the wildest thing, isn't it?" She backs away from the wards and sits, palms still held up, on a log. "I didn't believe it when my...when my dad..." then she bursts into tears.

Unless these mountain monsters are creative enough to craft an older version of my childhood friend, and add to the drama by making her *cry*, I feel fairly confident that this truly is Anabel, but I still stay firmly within the wards, conceding only by leaning closer to her.

"Anabel, what's wrong? What happened?"

"We don't have much time, he'll be back soon," and I know she means Ryden but I don't like how ominous she's being.

"Then tell me! What is going on?"

The words tumble out of her in a rush. "Something happened to our parents. My dad came to talk to me, and he asked me to give you this letter," she pulls a sealed white envelope out of her pocket. "I was trying to figure out how he even possibly remembered that a kid that I knew fifteen years ago Existed, and how he could possibly have a *letter* for you, when suddenly there was a Reaper in my backyard telling me that my dad was gone."

My blood turns to ice.

"What?"

"Abby, I'm so sorry, but I think they got to your mom, too." And even though I already *knew* she was gone, the words still feel like a Death blow.

"I—I know," I whisper, afraid that if I say it too loud, it'll be real. I've watched the video for days, and I still cling to the hope it's not real.

"You...*know*?"

"I saw something on the Ring camera where she's staying," I admit, and I can feel Anabel's sympathy, our shared grief, even through the wards.

"I'm sorry about your dad," I breathe.

"I'm sorry about your mom," she returns.

"How did you find me?" I ask, needing to change the subject because I won't be able to hold myself together much longer.

Needing something to think about because Anabel's dad and my Ma suddenly going into the Unknown out of nowhere is strange. Seeing Anabel *aging*, just like the twins and me, is strange.

All of this is just *strange*.

After her dad's Reaping, Anabel started looking into our old crew, and discovered that so many of us had been Born. Ethan Matheson, Latrell Thomason, Anabel, the twins, me, and so many others.

We'd all been Born, and we'd all thought we were alone in that.

She explains how she found the twins, and the wild goose chase that led her here—something about Location Services through Zelie's phone plan—before we fall into an awkward silence.

"Abby, I don't," I can see her trying to find her resolve, which she does, thrusting the envelope towards me near the ward line. "I don't know what this letter says, but I think it's important that you read it, like, now."

I reach out, the letter bridging the warded space between us, and watch in amazement as it passes through the wards easily. I shouldn't be surprised; a letter is just a piece of paper, but I still find myself in awe as I tear the seal, unfold the paper, and begin reading.

47

Abby,

I know you probably know by now what I've done. You know that I've gone on, into the Unknown.

When you were Born, I was terrified. Even though I'd been on this earth for several hundred years, I still felt like a child, totally unprepared to have a child myself. I barely knew how to take care of myself, how could I plan to care for you? Even more worrisome: how could you Exist? I'd met enough ghosts in my time to know that you shouldn't have been possible. I expected to either wake up one day without my bump, because the Fates recognized this impossibility, or to give birth to you only for you to disappear into the ether because you couldn't possibly be real.

But then, you were here, and my soul found everything I hadn't even known I was missing. Mon coeur, you are every dream I've ever had and then some. You're better than anything I could have imagined as a young girl in France, and you altered my Existence so completely, so irrevocably, that I truly don't know how I Existed without you. Every giggle, every cry, every single sound that you made was the most perfect sound I'd ever heard, and I knew that I would do anything, everything, for you.

Then you started to grow! Oh, Abby, you were, you are, such a miracle. I thought that we would be frozen in time, me and my newborn baby girl, forever, and that would have been fine with me! But then you were crawling, then walking, and before I knew it I could talk to you—I could have full conversations with you!—and you were the most fascinating thing I'd ever encountered in my Life. Until my soul leaves this realm, I could listen to you talk every moment and be content.

When you grew up and wanted to spend time on your own, I mourned. I was so, so proud of you and didn't want to get in the way of your Existence, your happiness, but oh, Abby, how I missed you. I felt so lonely. Other than my work and my calls with you, I felt like I had nowhere to turn. I couldn't ever truly make friends, because how could I? How could I form bonds with anyone when I couldn't tell them about the best, about the most important, part of my Life?

One afternoon at the hospital, however, a fellow ghost RN slipped up and mentioned her infant son. At first, I assumed she meant that she'd left behind a baby when she'd Died, but I could tell by her expression that she'd said something she hadn't meant to. I pressed her, and found out that she'd also given birth to a ghost child.

My first instinct was to call you, to find you, to fall at your feet and beg you to forgive me for your upbringing. I know that I was hard on you, Abby, and I know that I sheltered you. I was selfish, and couldn't fathom how I could go on, either by continuing to Exist, or by entering the Unknown, without you were something to happen to you—were someone to find out about you and try to take you. Both options felt impossible, so I did what I knew: I hid you, I lied, I all but locked you away. When you started to make friends, I isolated you from them, or made us relocate like thieves in the night.

This RN, Lita, and I worked tirelessly to find more parents of Born ghosts and Abby there are hundreds of children like you. I haven't found any children older than you, but there are so many around your age and so many babies Born after you that we all openly wept with joy. We all felt so foolish! We'd hidden our babies away, sheltering you as best we could, thinking we were protecting you.

We formed a club of sorts, meeting every few days, and I've never felt so seen, so understood, in my entire Existence! We even scheduled a huge meetup, for parents of Born ghosts not near Wilmington, to travel here for a weekend. We snuck into the ballroom of a hotel that was being refurbished and spent the entire weekend gushing about our babies, and about all the things we'd kept secret for so long. It was truly a miracle!

On the last day, a new face joined us. She told us that she'd realized that ghosts were being Born and had originally hoped to conceive herself—she'd Died in childbirth before fulfilling her lifelong dream of raising children. She also told us about a few Born ghosts she'd been watching, and about how the Universe expects balance. Some of these children suddenly, with no warning whatsoever, winked out of Existence, never to be heard from again. Her theory was that Born ghosts couldn't Exist on the same plane as the ones they came from— their ghostly parents. She brought proof—videos of these children ceasing to be out of nowhere.

Abby, I can't let that happen to you. In that moment, myself and the other parents knew what we had to do to protect you, our children. We gave ourselves a few days to tie up any loose ends, but decided to undergo the Reaping and go into the Unknown to save you. To save all of you.

I know that I should go to you instead of writing this letter, but Abby, I can't. I can't face you. Even though I know what I'm doing is *right, if I see your face I will lose my nerve and I* will *stay with you until one or both of us fades from Existence. I can't survive with the possibility that it could be you to go. I can't Exist if you don't.*

I'm more sorry than I could ever convey to you with words for leaving you this way. I wanted us to have lifetimes, but if I have a chance, any chance, no matter how small, to save you, Abby I will choose to take that chance every time. You have to Exist, Abby. You have to Live.

As painful as it is to leave you here, I'm so thankful that Raelle found us, and told us what we needed to do.

I love you more than you could ever know, Abby. To the moon and back, more than all the stars in all the galaxies, to infinity, beyond, and back again.

Je t'adore, mon coeur,

Ma

P. S. - Ryden Pengrave being my Reaper was not, under any circumstances, a coincidence. Raelle mentioned that she was "in" with the Reapers and knew that Ryden had been assigned to protect you, specifically, so when it was time to call for my Reaping, I requested him. Raelle was very adamant that we not discuss what we knew with anyone, lest that upset the balance, but I want it to be him so that I can be one degree away from you as I leave this world behind.

The timing couldn't be more perfect if I'd called out for him.

As soon as I find my resolve to speak to Ryden, he flits into the path in front of me bearing a bag of what looks to be Greek takeout for lunch. His eyes immediately narrow and his shoulders tense when he sees Anabel standing behind me.

Faster than I can blink, the food is on the ground and Ryden is between Anabel and me, glowering down at her.

"Who are you? Who are you and how are you here?" he demands. I pull on his shoulder, trying to move him, but he's all but made of stone. He doesn't move even a millimeter, and he's laser-focused on Anabel, assessing.

Readying to strike.

"Ryden!" I shout, and he glances over his shoulder at me before doing a double take when he realizes that I'm actually speaking to him.

"Ryden," I repeat, catching my breath after the adrenaline rush of the last few moments catch up to me. "This is Anabel. She's...like me."

He relaxes even more when he confirms that his wards held—that neither Anabel nor anyone else, had crossed them while he was gone.

That I was safe.

"I need to talk to you, alone," I whisper, and the relief that flashes across his face could break my heart.

48

Gods this is going to be a hard conversation.

Anabel graciously agreed to give us some time to speak alone. She wandered off into the trees, promising that she'll be "out of eavesdropping distance, but close enough to scream if she needs help," which calmed my nerves a bit.

"So," I start.

"I'm so, *so* sorry, love," he whispers.

"I...am too?"

He laughs humorlessly. "Are you?" he asks, brows furrowed in confusion. "What on earth could you have to be sorry for?" and he's so genuine that I could throw up.

"I was so hateful to you," I admit. "I was just in a blind rage, and I—I don't think you deserved it."

"You'd just lost your mother, Abby. You could've said anything to me and I wouldn't hold it against you. Honestly, you could say anything to me whenever and I..." he cuts himself off by clamping his jaw shut tight. Like he'll let more words than he'd like to spill out if he's not careful.

"I just don't understand how she could go like that. I don't understand why she left me."

Ryden doesn't speak, so I look up to meet his gaze. What I find there is a pain that mirrors my own.

"I begged for you, Abby," he coughs past a lump in his throat. "I didn't want you to know this hurt." His eyes shine, tearful once again. Tearful for *me*. "I didn't want to be what *made* you hurt like this."

He looks away, shaking his head, as if he can shake his own actions from Existence. Like he can shake the memories away from ever occurring.

"I know," I whisper.

"I went to my knees for you, Abby. I begged her not to do this. I begged her to stay, here, for you. But she," he pauses briefly to catch his breath, his lower lip quivering. Once he's able, he continues, "But her mind was made up. She was convinced that what she was doing was *for* you. I can't...I couldn't..." he sniffs. "Nothing would change her mind, and I could *see* her soul wavering."

My stomach drops. I want him to be able to deal with the trauma that this whole endeavor has caused him, but I also have to protect my own peace—even if that peace is hanging on by an ever-fraying thread. My emotions war: do I sacrifice, opening myself up to more torment to allow someone else to heal? Do I stop him and send him to Jaali for a trauma dump?

He draws a correct conclusion from my silence and from the mental aerobics he likely sees on my face, tentatively reaching a hand out to press to my shoulder. When I don't immediately draw back, the tension radiating from him eases slightly and he continues.

"I swear to you, Abby," his solemn eyes meet mine, "I will never give you details of that night unless you expressly ask me for them—other than to tell you that I fought for you to keep your mother. And that your mother loved you to the very, very last. And that it was," he hesitates before rushing to finish his sentence, "it was peaceful and I just needed you to know that."

"*Why did you have to take her from me, though?*" I whisper. I hate myself for asking the question, especially of a person so obviously trying to heal from a traumatic experience. But I have to know.

He closes his eyes as the words find their mark, and a tear finally falls down his cheek. He lifts a hand up to clutch his chest, as if he can *feel* the wound I knew the question would inflict, but he's too far in to give up on this conversation now.

He takes a moment, fidgeting with his fingers, then once again meets my eye. "*How could I let anyone else?*" he whispers back at me. "She was your *mother*, Abby. Short of Jaali, who else could I have trusted to be there for her?"

Now I'm the one feeling wounds inflicted by words. But this time, my wound is the sour shame that fills my chest. I hadn't for a single second thought about my mother's Reaping in this way.

She was a ghost. She Died hundreds of years ago. And she was ready to go on. *Nothing* could have stopped her. I don't know the rules and regulations of the Brotherhood of Reapers, but I do know that a soul ready to leave this earth will summon the nearest Reaper, if a Reaper hasn't already been assigned to that soul. I saw it myself with the ghost Ryden and I found wandering that hilltop. The one he Reaped in front of me after the night his mere presence around me in his bedroll chased off my nightmares.

If Ryden had refused her, would another Reaper have been assigned to her? Would just anyone have shown up? Would it have been someone like Ryden, someone like Jaali?

Or someone like Adam? The thought alone sends shivers up my spine.

The tears sting my eyes as the brutal truth punches into me: if I could have anyone escort my mother to the Unknown, I would want it to be Ryden, just like she had.

I know that with unwavering certainty. The same certainty that knows that I will also never be able to fully forgive him for it.

And I'm not sure where that leaves us.

We both need a minute before we can continue the conversation.

I have to tell him about Raelle being the reason my mother thought she was protecting me by going through with the Reaping, and I'm sure he'll have plenty to say about it.

Ryden steps towards the edge of the small stream a few paces away from where we'd been standing, and stoops, cupping both hands full of water and splashing it across his face.

I stay put, trying to take control of my breathing. I dig back through my memories for every Yoga class that was ever on screen in the apartment—*in through the nose, out through the mouth.*

In through the nose, out through the mouth.

In through the nose, out through the mouth.

In through the nose, out through the mouth.

Finally, my breathing evens and my heart rate slows.

I turn to Ryden to find him watching me, hollow eyed and still looking like a broken man.

I hate this.

I hate that I want to hold him just as desperately as I want to rip him apart. I want to console him and I want to banish him from my presence. I never want to leave his side, and I never want to see him again. My heart rate ratchets up, only this time, it's the reminder that I need. This fury and anguish and confusion and betrayal has a source. Instead of fighting it, I need to *feel* it. I need to feel it all.

I need to funnel it to where it's deserved.

My rage is an arrow poised to strike Raelle through.

"So, will you tell me about Anabel?" Ryden asks gently. "Because I've got to be honest, Abby, when I got here and found someone here, I..." he chokes. "I thought I was having a heart attack." The joke is an olive branch that I gingerly accept.

"Yeah, sorry about that," I admit. "Anabel and I—knew each other when we were kids." I hope he sees that my trusting him with this information—that Anabel is another Born ghost—as the olive branch that *I'm* extending to *him*. His response will tell me if I'll ever be able to attempt to trust him again, and I clench my fists waiting as he lets the words sink in.

"And how did she find you all the way out here?" he asks. Good. He doesn't pry for more details about her.

I smirk. "Anabel got some information, which I'll tell you in a few minutes," I rush as he raises his eyebrows, clearly wanting to ask more questions. "So she started tracking down the other ghosts she—we—

knew as kids. She found the twins," I stiffen at the mention of them. The threat of harm against them is what brought me here. Talking to Ryden about them seems cruel.

"Abby," he breathes. He reaches for me, but at the last moment, thinks better of it and lets his hand fall. "I was never, *never* going to harm your friends. I'd hoped you'd have seen that by now."

"Why would I believe that, though, Ryden? When you literally showed me pictures of them in a cell..." I trail off, the memory twisting my insides.

"Love, they're not in a cell. They were *never* in a cell."

I blanche.

"But...the photo," I demand. "You showed me a photo of them in a cell."

He sighs. "I'm so ashamed of that," he whispers. "I did show you a photo...a heavily doctored photo."

"What do you mean?"

"The photo I had of the twins was of them huddled together waiting for a Uber—they were sitting so close because it was about to start raining. I used an app to change their surroundings and make it look, well, pretty dire I guess," he admits.

He pulls out his phone and shows me the original photo, then the photo I'd seen.

"I can't believe I fell for this. I'm *such* an idiot!" I stamp my foot, not even caring that it feels childish.

"You're not," he promises. "You believed me because you believed I was capable of harming them, and you're the kind of person who would do anything for those you love. That's nothing to be ashamed of."

Once I'd gotten to know Ryden, I wanted to believe that he wouldn't harm the twins. And maybe I'd even started to without realizing it. But then everything happened with my mother, and...that's a route I can't go down right now. I nod, once again choosing to attempt to trust him.

What do I have to lose at this point?

I pivot back to Anabel's story.

"Anabel found the twins, and together they found Zelie. And because they found Zelie, of course they found Em and Amarie too."

"She's persistent," Ryden admits, seeming impressed.

"She is that, and it's a good thing she is, too. So then, Amarie had found a way to turn on Location Tracking on my phone remotely. I'm sure it was fairly easy since I'm on Zelie's phone plan, but anyways..." *why* am I choosing *this moment* to ramble?! "Apparently we are close to a highway, so Anabel snagged this morning's coordinates from Amarie, hauled ass to get as close as possible, left Amarie's car parked on the side of the road, and has just been wandering around in the woods ever since."

Begrudgingly, Ryden laughs. It's stilted and still so full of pain that it barely counts, but it's a laugh nonetheless. Some of my tension eases at the sound.

"And you found her at the ward line," he pieces together.

"I did...I heard a twig snap and grabbed this," I hold up the dagger and his brows rise in surprise, "then turned to find her there."

"So our training was good for something then," he nods. "That's good."

"Yes, it was. *She* wasn't able to cross the wards, but she brought this, which was..."

I pull the letter from Ma out and hand it over. Ryden takes it gently, as if it's made of glass, and unfolds it. He notices who it's from, smiles up at me sadly, and hands it back over to me.

"I shouldn't read this," he whispers, eyes shining again.

"Yes, you should. You should absolutely read it," I press the paper back into his palm, holding it there this time. "Because Raelle is mobilizing. And she's convincing the parents of Born ghosts to off themselves."

Ryden sucks in a breath and begins to read Ma's letter.

49

We stop moving to Ryden's original destination.

After reading Ma's letter, after realizing that Raelle has *killed off* so many of the Born ghosts' parents, he'd sent Anabel home with instructions to keep her mouth shut, and has put his entire plan on hold, adamant that my combat training is his top priority. He's convinced that if I can be fast enough, that if I know how to fight, I'll somehow be able to take on Raelle and the entire Brotherhood of the Reapers—or at least those Reapers that are loyal to her.

I think that he's delusional, but I'm in no hurry to get anywhere other than back to my friends and civilization.

We train, day in and day out, only stopping for meals and sleep.

We spar so much that it's seeped into my dreams. I wake with new moves in mind, new ways to get past the opponent's defenses.

Ryden is relentless. He's no longer gentle with me when it comes to my training. He holds nothing back. There's no letting me win. Nothing but me being beaten, time and again, and him correcting my actions for the next round.

"So," I cough out after a particularly brutal sparring match, the side of my face currently pressed into the mossy forest floor. I spit out the bits of grass and dirt that found their way into my mouth when I'd fallen after Ryden kicked the legs out from under me. I roll to the side and push myself back into a standing position before continuing. "Are you going to tell me *why* we're doing all this?" I wave my hand between the two of us before using the back of my arm to wipe the sweat from my brow.

I'm breathing heavily and try the *in-through-the-nose-out-through-the-mouth* method to try and slow my racing heart.

Ryden huffs out a laugh, almost equally as winded. He uses the bottom of his shirt to wipe the sweat from his face, and I'm again struck completely dumb at the perfection that is his chest. It's nice without being showy—there's no "pack" of abdominal muscles proudly on display—but he's clearly strong. As his shirt drops, my gaze flits to his arms, strong enough to best any man I've ever encountered, yet gentle enough to hold me the night my nightmares wouldn't let me sleep.

I blink away that memory and meet his eyes, which are already on mine.

Fantastic.

The man misses nothing.

"What, love," he asks, eyes shining with amusement, "you don't enjoy sparring with me?"

"I would *enjoy*," I retort, "some information. Please."

He must sense the level of anxiety I have, that I've had this whole time, because for once he takes pity on me.

"Let's clean ourselves up, I'll flit for some lunch..." He must notice my jaw tense because he quickly adds, "then I will tell you what I know, and what theories I've come up with."

I begrudgingly agree, even though I want to stamp my foot and demand answers *now*.

Mercifully, we're near a stream, so we're able to take turns bathing. It's been weeks since I've been able to wash my hair, and I can feel my body relax infinitesimally as the suds work through the matted strands. Ryden stayed at the campsite, which is a respectful distance away yet close enough for him to be here in seconds if I need him.

It hits me, yet again, how safe I feel with him, and how long I've felt that relative safety. Even when I thought he was guiding me to my demise, I knew I was safe from anything these woods could throw at me. I knew no harm would come to me until we reached Ryden's destination.

I towel dry off and throw on the cleanest clothes I have, which happen to be biker shorts and an oversized Taking Back Sunday tee. I take a blissful extra minute to brush my teeth and apply deodorant before I step back into the clearing to find Ryden, freshly showered and with a brown paper bag with "Jim N' Nick's Barbecue" stamped on the side.

"*How...?*" I trail off, knowing that there's no way he could have bathed in the same stream.

"I triple checked my wards, then flitted to a truck stop shower stall, hosed off, then grabbed lunch," he holds up the bag as if he's presenting evidence. "I didn't think you'd want to wait much longer."

"You thought right," I smile. "Thank you."

As if it's seen the bag, my stomach grumbles. I finally notice that it's twilight—no wonder I'm starved.

I plop down on top of my bedroll, which has stayed in the same spot since we've been sparring here for days. Ryden hands me a chicken taco and a small container of sliced lime.

"I noticed when I brought back burritos, you searched around in the bag for the one lime wedge the restaurant gave us, so I thought you might want more this time."

My heart tightens at the thoughtfulness, even as my brain screeches that the bar is on the earthen floor beneath me.

"Thank you," I whisper, meaning it.

We dig into the food, and it's absolutely delicious, especially doused in the lime juice.

"So," Ryden begins, and I feel my whole body tense. It's equal parts dread and excitement, because while I desperately want to know what Ryden knows and what his plans are, I'm still terrified that they'll end with me, or the twins, or Anabel, or any other Born ghosts being sent into the Unknown against their will—or worse.

I can't let fear get in my way, though.

"So..." I reply.

"Raelle has known about you for years," he offers. "From what I can gather, especially after your mother's letter," he swallows, "she's closer to her goals than I thought."

I blanche. "What are her goals?!"

"I think," he searches for the right words, "that she wants to take you. You are the *Primo Natus Exspiravit*, the First Born Ghost. Before you were conceived, a ghost being Born was unheard of. So I think she wants you, not to Reap you, but to...test you. She wants to know *why* the prophecy triggered. Why *your* birth happened. Why *you* Exist. And obviously she wants to stop the prophecy, you bringing down the Brotherhood of Reapers, from coming true. She doesn't want to lose her power and will do anything to stop it. And if she can get you—can torture you—all the better in her mind."

I can't help the shiver that skates down my spine, and Ryden, of course, notices.

"Abby, she will get to you over my Dead body," he vows. "I will not let her take you."

"So what is your plan?"

He opens his mouth to finally, *finally* tell me his plan when the ground begins to shake beneath us.

We're running before I even have time to register the movement, Ryden near dragging me behind him.

The ground beneath us vibrates in rhythm, as if the Earth itself is pulsing in time. It makes crashing through the trees while staying upright that much more difficult. Trees race past us in a blur, and even in the terror and uncertainty I'm feeling in the moment, one thought surfaces above all the rest: I couldn't have run like this a month ago.

I have to begrudgingly admit that this entire experience, my "kidnapping" and being forced into the wilds of Appalachia with a Reaper I was certain would see to my demise, has forced me to be stronger. All the hiking, day in and day out, all the sparring lessons, every single bit of it has changed my body for the better.

It's made me able to run for my Existence.

Ryden shows no signs of slowing, and it's clear that he's got a destination in mind—one that I won't know, being totally unfamiliar with where we're going.

I throw one hand out in front of me, desperate to protect my face from the brutal onslaught of branches that whip against us as we twist and turn through gnarled trees, my other hand still clutched in Ryden's —the contact the only anchor I have. The only assurance that I'll be safe.

Just as I'm starting to feel an aching begin to burn deep in my calves, he releases my hand to scramble up a nearby pile of rocks that forms a makeshift overlook to the mountain pass below. I stagger up behind him, desperately trying to catch my breath, and skid to a halt beside him. I overcorrect and nearly topple over the other side of the rock edge, but Ryden throws his arm out and catches me, keeping me from falling.

He turns to face me for the length of a heartbeat, his breathing ragged as he holds a finger to his lips and mouths, "Don't make a sound. Not one sound."

I nod my understanding before I peek over the edge of the rock ledge, and am grateful for Ryden's arm as it comes around me, his hand as it gently covers my mouth, the way it catches the gasp I involuntarily let out.

I shift into my invisible form and feel Ryden sigh, but unfortunately, it's not a sigh of relief.

"It's too late for that, love," he whispers against my ear, barely a breath.

And I know, deep in my bones, that he's right. Because a hundred feet below our secret ledge, hundreds of Reapers march in formation.

"They already know we're close."

His words send ice ricocheting through my veins.

50

"Before we go any further," Ryden whispers, gently grasping my arm, "I need you to know something."

I brace for impact. I peek over the ledge again, terrified that the Reapers will hear him, but the sounds of their marching feet winding through the trees and brush below muffle the hushed whisper that is Ryden's voice. I turn back to face him, and he pulls us slowly down the rock formation to its base, seating us on a boulder on the earthen floor just inside the treeline.

"I've been Living in Hell, Abby," he chuckles humorlessly.

That—isn't what I expected.

I quirk a brow at him, unsure of what he means. But since Raelle has mobilized her forces and time isn't on our side, there's no room for anything but listening, and getting out those famous last words as the moon rises for what could be the last time for me.

"I tried to tell you this before, and it didn't go so well," he smiles sadly, not yet meeting my gaze. "But Abby, I'm so, *so* disgustingly in love with you."

My eyes meet his and all I can see is truth and...*something*, something *more*, shining there.

I'm utterly frozen.

"Do you have any idea what that's like? Looking at another person and feeling like you're Dying? Like you're already Dead? It's like you're starving, starving for even one second with them, as if that one second could satiate you for the rest of your Existence. But instead of telling them, you have to keep them at arm's length. You have to lie. You have to make every attempt to intimidate them, because you hope to the gods that they fear you. Because if they fear you, they'll fear anyone *like* you, and they might somehow make it out of this and return to their happy Existence and friends and forget you while you know you'll never be the same again." His hands begin to shake where he holds them between his parted knees.

"I can barely eat, I don't sleep for shit, *all* I can think about, day in and day out, is you and the best outcome possible for you. And how I can make that possibility into a reality...into your future. Because Abby," he gasps out a sob, taking a breath before continuing. "Abby, I *desperately* want you to have a future. More than I've ever wanted anything in my Life. More even than I want you. We've been through enough that I couldn't ever expect, or even dream, for that future to be with me, but that matters far less to me than you getting to experience everything you've ever wanted without this looming threat over you at all times. I want you to just *be*. I want you to be happy, and spontaneous, and free. I want you to spend as many years as you wish to have doing every single thing you want to do, and when you finally decide that you're ready to go on, I hope beyond all hope that it's me you'll remember, me you'll want to call. Me you'll want there with you as you leave from this place and step into the Unknown. Because Abby, as all the gods that ever were as my witness, I would be there, and if you'd have me, I would follow you past the veil of Death and into whatever comes after. And I would do it gladly, without so much as a second thought. I would leave every single bit of this wretched, beautiful world behind and go into the Unknown at your side."

He glances down at his hands before his eyes meet mine, so bright and blue and honest that I could willingly drown in their depths.

"That, Abby, is how desperately I love you."

"*You*," I whisper, tears glistening in my own eyes so much that I can barely see his face inches from mine, "*you want me to survive this.*"

It's not so much a question, but he huffs a laugh and answers anyways. "Love, that's all I've wanted this whole time."

I don't have time to process his words, let alone react to them, before the rumbling of hundreds of feet below us suddenly ceases.

51

He grabs my hand, giving me no choice but to follow him as he silently winds through the trees. We're no longer running, because running causes sound.

No. Now, we're slinking. We're moving as quickly as possible while making no noise, stepping swiftly from tree to tree, their thick trunks providing cover.

The ground underfoot goes from soft, packed earth to hard and unforgiving stone as we follow Ryden's path downward.

"Nearly there, love," he mouths and I'm called back to the countless times he's called me "love" over the last month. I thought it was torment, a way to tease and irritate me, and not the confession that it's been this whole time.

Ryden Pengrave is in love with me.

My feelings for him are messy and muddled, and since we're kind of on the run from a horde of Reapers of unknown allegiance, I don't have time to even think about beginning to unpack them.

We slide down a boulder that is mercifully not steep and find ourselves at the mouth of a dark cave. In any other scenario, I would outright refuse to step one toe inside, but if it comes down to our upsetting a bear in its den or seeing how Ryden and I can hold up against hundreds of Reapers, I choose the bear.

Ryden has already proven he can handle the bear.

"Trust me, love," Ryden breathes, holding out his hand.

And I finally know in my very soul that I can. That I do.

I trust Ryden. Nearly implicitly.

I twine my fingers with his and revel in the warmth that radiates from his hand through my very being.

I have exactly one second to register his smile, the *dimples*, before he jerks me into the cave and we're running again.

We skid to a halt in a cavern several hundred feet from the cave mouth.

Since the Sun has fully set, our surroundings are nearly pitch black—

illuminated by the smallest sliver of moonlight peeking through from a slice in the cavern ceiling fifty feet up. I wait for a fit of claustrophobia to claw its way up my throat, but there isn't time for fear, anxiety, or panic.

I want to hope that Ryden's plan is for us to ride out the Reapers. Maybe this is a perfect hiding place. Maybe they won't even see the cave mouth and we'll wait until they think we've fled, or slipped from their grasps, and then we'll go back to our bedrolls and sparring and...

"I wanted to take you to an abandoned, long forgotten Reaper cabin," Ryden admits in a rushed whisper, interrupting my thoughts. "It's another few days' hike from here. I wanted to show you the Brotherhood's methods of record keeping, which can still be accessed from there," his breath tickles my cheek, "and Abby, I wanted to watch you destroy *your* records. I wanted to wipe you from their databases. You and any other Born ghosts that you knew of—*that* is why I needed you here. So you could see it done yourself, so you could be a part of it. So you could help me help you, and all of the other Born ghosts we know of. I wanted you to know how to do it, so that if anything happened to me, you were safe. You were protected, and could do everything to protect others, too, even if I was...found out. Then," he presses a kiss to my temple, as if he can't stop himself. As if he can't continue his confession until his lips have touched me, marked me in some way. "Then, I wanted to return you to your apartment and your friends and your future, so that I could spend the rest of mine killing any Reaper who still had knowledge of you...any who may have still sought to harm you."

"Can—can you do that?" I ask. "Isn't there, like, a Reaper's code against...*murder*?"

There has to be, right?

"How could I care about that?" he laughs humorlessly. "I would've spent the rest of my Life loving you, and killing anyone who even casually posed any threat to you, Reaper regulations be damned. Nothing, *nothing* matters to me more than you do, love. There isn't a single Existence that I wouldn't end if it ensured your happiness. I would destroy this entire world, and everyone on it for you—I'd lay waste to it all and drop it at your feet."

I only feel the tears pouring from my eyes as they glide gently over my cheeks because this is all so devastatingly unfair. Ryden's words are so much, *too* much, but also nowhere near enough and I'm greedy. Greedy to get out of this cave, greedy for a future with him, greedy to fight with him and kiss him and have years that *mean something*, even if we don't know when and how my years may come to an end. *Primo* and all that.

But I want every second of that future.

52

"*Possess me.*"

It's barely above a whisper, but I snap my head to meet Ryden's eyes.

"W-what?" I rasp, unable to breathe after those two words. We're pressed against each other, nose to nose and chest to chest in the back of the cavern, trying to make ourselves as small, as *invisible*, as possible with Ryden not actually having an invisible form like I do. Our shared breaths create whorls in the dark air, which is unseasonably cold and an omen I can't think about. I shake my head, trying to make sense of his words.

"Possess me, Abby," he quietly demands, twisting the end of my hair idly in one hand as if it's the most magical thing he's ever felt.

"I—I can't." I don't want to tell him that I'd tried to Possess him before those weeks ago, searching for energy for the grueling hikes we had ahead of us. I don't want him to know that I'd violated the little trust he'd placed in me when he was willing to sleep in my presence.

"Abby, " he repeats, cupping my face in one hand like he can't stop himself from touching me. "Possess me."

I heave a sigh. He's going to *make* me admit it.

"Ryden, I can't. I can't Possess you. I've tried. I'm so sorry," I say, hot, anxious, angry tears bubbling over my lashes and streaking down my cheeks. "I shouldn't have even tried, and I should have told you before now, but it was such a violation and I was just scared and ashamed and I—"

"Abby," he cuts me off. "I *know*. You couldn't Possess me before. I'm a Reaper, remember? Special abilities and all that. We don't have time for me to explain how now, but I'm asking you—" he straightens his back, setting his jaw and boring his earnest eyes into mine, "I'm *begging* you, Abby. Try again. Possess me now, love. *Please.*"

Something about the eagerness in his gaze takes me completely out of this moment, at least temporarily. I reach up tentatively, gliding my fingers across his strong brow, down his cheekbones, and across his lips, memorizing every line and shadow. The stubble of his skin rubs against my fingertips in a peculiar—but not uncomfortable—way. His blue eyes are a sea that I'd have wanted to swim in, if Life and Death had allowed it.

But that isn't going to be my fate.

"Can I—can a ghost even Possess a Reaper?" I ask, and Ryden looses the breath he'd been holding while waiting for my answer.

I can hear the Brotherhood of Reapers cresting the hill just above the cave mouth.

We're out of time.

Ryden grabs my hand, pressing my fingertips gently to his lips, then against his chest for the span of one heartbeat before slamming it into the crook under his left arm. I feel the teres major, and instinctively close my hand around it. He swiftly jerks my arm down, opening his side to Possession, and I gasp. It's—it's beautiful. An array of deepest blues and shimmering golds that remind me of his eyes glows from under his arm. Before I can do more than blink my owneyes in wonder, his right arm comes around me and I'm thrust into my invisible form on instinct. He shoves me into his side and into *him*.

This Possession is earth shatteringly different. I feel fire and electricity flood every vein, every pore, every single part of me. It's like I've been electrocuted, am being electrocuted, and I lose every one of my senses to the flames that are racing through me. They lick up my arms, down my legs, until I'm totally engulfed in him.

The vision that blasts to light before my eyes is different than any other Possession, too. In the past, I've seen glimpses of my host's Life: memories they've had and now long for, their hopes and dreams for their future, all the places they wish to go. Now, I just see...*myself*?

Me, laughing with my roommates, joyous tears pouring from all of our eyes.

Me, smiling in the passenger seat of a car, the wind whipping my hair through an open window with the Sun filtering through the palm trees lining the road.

Me, toasting a glass of wine with an older couple I don't recognize.

Me, sighing, tangled in a sea of sheets and pillows.

Me, wiping away a tear standing over a headstone.

Me, with deeper laugh lines and crow's feet.

Me, with silver hair and wizened hands.

Me, me, *me*.

Every new image is colored in rose, like I hung the Sun in the godsdamned sky. Like it only hangs because I will it to.

The electric fire racing through me goes molten, changing in an instant from burning heat to simmering...something. It's just on the edge of my consciousness, the ability to put it to words...

I have never felt so alive in my entire Existence, and I never want this feeling to end. It's exhilarating and overwhelming and so devastatingly *right*, until...

Until I feel Ryden's body begin to break around me.

"No..." I whisper, trying to end the Possession. I reach for the space under his arm, but Ryden's hand presses over it so firmly that I can't get out. I've been in here too long. I know Ma and Mr. Byrne assured us all those years ago that Possession couldn't harm a Living, but could they have been wrong? Does his being a Reaper change that? I can feel his energy depleting at a dangerously high speed, but can do nothing to stop it as I hear the bone-chilling laugh that means that the Reapers have made it into the cave.

They're here.

Ryden is surrounded.

Ryden is outnumbered.

Ryden is weakened...*because of me.*

And there is absolutely nothing I can do to stop it as Raelle steps in front of him with her sword raised.

53

"No!" I scream, realizing as I hit the dirt floor of the cavern that he's finally released me.

It feels like time both stands still and speeds up; everything is in slow motion, but happening too fast for me to stop it. Raelle brings the blade down over Ryden and runs it straight through his chest in one clean swipe.

I swear that the action takes a thousand years.

How could it not? Even as I scramble to rise from the ground, to do something—anything—to stop what is happening before my eyes, I still have time to notice how ragged his breathing is. How his eyes are locked onto my face. How his hair is ruffled ever so slightly by the breeze that her whipping the sword down causes. How none of them, not a damned one of his so-called *Brotherhood* lifts a finger to stop her. How his mouth forms the word "run...run...*run*" over and over again, a silent plea for me to use his Death—his *Death*—to escape and save myself.

How he thinks that I ever could.

Then, I'm beside him. I don't care about Raelle, about her plans, or about the fact that my back is now exposed to her and an entire horde of Reapers that are loyal to her. They could Reap me before I even have time to tell him.

I grab his hand in mine, marveling at how pleasantly rough it feels against mine. His breathing is growing shallow, and blood tinges the corners of his lips. He's fading, but he has to know.

"Ryden. Ryden you have to listen to me, okay?" I try to keep my voice steady even though every part of me is breaking. I pull his hand up to me, cradling it against my chest as the tears pour down my face.

His eyes begin to flutter, and I know I'm running out of time. Mercifully, through whatever force of will he has left in his body, they stay open.

"Ryden, I...I'm beginning to love you too. I think I might have loved you this whole time, and that terrified me so I fought it—I made myself hate you. But even more important than that," I choke. I have to get this out, and have to do it before he's gone, but I can feel myself sinking into the pain. I can't feel anything but the agony of the loss I know will happen any second now.

I know now that I can bear the loss of my mother. As painful as losing her is, it's the natural order of things. Children are *supposed* to lose their parents, and grieve them for the rest of their days. But *this*?

This is utterly unbearable, as if my own soul is cracking in two.

I swallow down the torture, because I can't let him see it. I don't want him to have any fear in his last moments. I suck in a breath, square my shoulders, and continue.

"Ryden, you've got to come find me, okay? I am going to be fine, and I don't want you to worry about me, but I need you to promise me that you'll come back to me...*after*."

For the briefest second, his eyes meet mine and I feel a pulse shock through my chest. Without his having to say a word, I know that he understands. That he will fight his way, through however long Death takes him, to find me. Whatever it takes, and for however long it takes. He will find me, and we will get time, too much of which is being robbed from us right now.

"I...would...do...it...again," he breathes.

One tear falls from the corner of his eye, then he is gone.

I finally let out the keening wail that I had been holding since Raelle had appeared with her sword.

I scream, and it's both pain and relief, determination and the overwhelming emptiness that is a world without Ryden in it. I take the smallest comfort in the knowledge that he'll likely already be with a Reaper, preparing his soul for the transition through Death and into becoming a ghost.

A memory tugs at me: a moment in the woods, me curled in Ryden's arms. A promise: "*even if I'm angry, or hurt, I will never leave you in danger.*"

And I know.

The power that I felt during the Possession. Ryden had planned this. He knew Raelle would come for us. He knew that he couldn't fight off the entirety of the Brotherhood alone. He knew that he alone was no match for Raelle.

He promised me that I would never be harmed inside his wards—but he didn't make the same promise of himself.

Ryden knowingly sacrificed himself to give me the chance to survive.

But *how*?

54

I refuse to turn from Ryden, not yet, but I can feel Raelle hovering feet away, convinced that she's won. And she has—without Ryden here, it's me versus Raelle and the hundreds of Reapers at her disposal. No amount of sparring or lectures on balance with Ryden could have prepared me for this.

I know my end is imminent—how could it *not* be? If Ryden's words were true, if he's truly *in love with me*, then he wanted me to make it out of this. With him gone, so is any chance of that.

But even more important than my own pending demise is the knowledge that Ryden's soul lingers here. I can still feel him here in the cave, still feel his power and energy and the *Ryden-ness* that is just *him*. And I know without a shadow of a doubt that I cannot let Raelle or her followers get to him in the moments he's becoming a ghost—becoming like me.

At least, I'm desperately clinging to the hope that he's going to be like me. The alternative is too devastating, too soul-crushing for me to even consider.

If I think about that possibility, I won't be able to do anything more than lie down on this cold stone floor and let Raelle take me.

Ryden wouldn't want that.

Ryden *Died* trying to prevent that.

So after I've screamed until it feels like my vocal cords have to have snapped, I slowly rise and turn to Raelle, and let her see the maniacal grin that rivals her own as it spreads over my face.

Of course she's going to want to make a speech.

"I started out as a Reaper *with a heart*," she mocks in sing song, stirring up laughter from the Reapers behind her. "I wanted to *help* new ghost children learn how to navigate their new Existence, post-Death. I wanted to start a *school*." She makes a gagging noise, and points a finger at her tongue. More laughter follows from her adoring public. I roll my eyes.

"I never got my school," an exaggerated pout, followed by *boos* from the crowd, "but I did start to study ghost children...and imagine my surprise when children started showing signs of *more*." She shrugs her shoulders, really putting on a show for her Reapers.

"First it was little Lukas, who grew an inch in the three months his family haunted the house next door. Then, it was Rebecca, the girl who played in the park I jogged through, who needed a training bra overnight. Tiny little details that no one else seemed to notice, but every time, after one of these 'milestones,' the child's family had a 'reason' for them to move away. It was interesting enough that I took it back to Headquarters. And the fools there cast my findings aside." She balls her hands into fists and her Reapers scream in outrage on her behalf.

"Yes!" she shouts, turning to her adoring public, empowered by their attention. "Yes, they didn't want to hear from little old me. They all but patted me on the head with directions to 'just leave them be,' and 'it doesn't matter,' but it did matter!" She's screaming now, her voice magnified by the acoustics of the cave. "It does matter! These Born ghosts," she jabs her sword, the sword coated in *Ryden's blood Ryden's blood Ryden's blood*, towards me, "they're an abomination and they must be stopped! *All ghosts must be stopped!*"

Her Reapers' screams reach a crescendo, and I can feel their hatred for me radiating off of them in waves.

"So," she turns to me and croons, once again sing-songing. "What happens next, is we're going to the Reapers Headquarters in Augusta where we can find out if you *can* Die. Truly Die. Can an abomination like you, a Born ghost go into the Unknown? Don't worry, dear, we'll figure out just what. makes. you. *tick*." She emphasizes every word with another jab of her sword. "We'll spend a few decades testing your blood, your marrow, your body's reaction to...*extreme conditions*." A maniacal grin spreads back on her face. "Then, we'll send you into the Unknown, and bring you back as many times as is necessary, so that we can see just how much the *Primo* can survive. But it doesn't stop there!" Her eyes are bright and promise more misery. "Because we'll be doing the same to all of the Born ghosts that we can get our hands on. I'm tired of just killing them—I want to *study* them now."

My blood runs cold as her words hit home. My fate, I can handle, as miserable as it will be. But I cannot, I *will not* allow that for the twins, or Anabel, or any of the other Born ghosts out there. I will fight with every breath I have until then.

Even if they take me.

Even if they torture me.

Even if they send me into the Unknown.

I will fight.

I will fight for Born ghosts until I'm left in the Unknown.

I can't give myself time to even react to Raelle's suggestion that people can be brought *back* from the Unknown. Nothing matters to me now except standing in her way, and stopping her from her ridiculous obsession with Born ghosts.

If I'm going down, I'm going down swinging, and I'm taking as many of Raelle's lackeys with me as I can.

55

"No one touch her!" Raelle commands. "*This* one is mine."

Her emphasis on "this" sends shivers down my spine, though I can't show it. Does that mean that other Born ghosts have been found and taken?

"Make it last, Raelle!" one Reaper who closely resembles a bridge troll grunts. The guffaws and cheers his words earn from the others turns my stomach.

I glance around the cavern and note that the crowd of Reapers, at least inside, is smaller than I thought. There's maybe twenty Reapers backing Raelle.

That doesn't mean that hundreds aren't just outside of the cave.

"So how are we going to do this, then?" I ask Raelle. "Are you so afraid of me that you need me utterly defenseless while you have your legion of," I glance around, "goons?"

She laughs humorlessly. I know it's bold to challenge her, but I hope she still takes the bait.

She does.

"You," she gestures to one of the smaller Reapers in the front line. "Toss her your sword."

He balks and she raises a brow. "Insolence will never be rewarded, Daniel. Besides, look at her. She isn't going to know what to do with a *sword.*"

He laughs before hurling his sword at my feet.

I bend to snap it up before taking a defensive stance in front of Raelle, keeping myself between her and Ryden's body.

She jolts toward me and I stand my ground, which surprises her enough for me to swing my sword down. Unfortunately for me, she's a Reaper with years of training. She swings her sword up to meet mine with ease.

I'm clumsy and inadequate, given that Ryden and I had never been able to spar with actual swords—only daggers so far. But his training did teach me balance, and how to be quick on my feet. I dart back and forth, parrying any shots she might have to actually land a blow.

Raelle and I circle each other in this fatal dance. If she moves right, I go left. I mirror every step of hers, keeping myself just out of her reach.

I hold my own and keep my distance long enough to piss her off, and Raelle finally shouts, "Enough! I tire of this!" before tossing her sword aside and lifting her boot, landing a kick in the middle of my chest before I have time to register what's happening.

I fall in what feels like slow motion, seeing the glee on the Reapers' faces as their leader bests me.

I land in a heap beside Ryden, and I know that this will be the moment. Raelle will order her minions to grab me, I'll be taken, and I'll be pulled from him.

And I can't bear it.

I turn, crawling to Ryden. If these are my last seconds of freedom, I want to see him one more time, even if it's just his corpse.

"I love you," I whisper as I take his cold hand in mine. "I love you and I'm so, *so* sorry."

"Seize her," Raelle commands cooly, and I brace for rough hands that never come.

I look up to two dumbfounded Reapers looming over me, both trying to charge at me, but neither of whom seems to be able to come within three feet of me. It's like they've hit a glass wall.

They can't move another inch in my direction.

Because I'm still warded.

56

I bolt upright and jump to my tip toes, searching the cavern for Ryden's form.

If the wards are intact, that means he's here somewhere, now in his ghost form.

My scan of all of the faces surrounding me doesn't find him, but that must mean he's in his invisible form, which is smart.

It's odd that none of the Reapers have considered that he could come back so quickly, but I don't exactly expect much from the grunts in front of me.

Before I can decide what to do next, something I can only describe as a war cry shrieks out from my left, and Jaali appears with Em, Amarie, and Zelie.

My blood turns to ice when I see my roommates, because this is the last place that I want them—right here, in the line of fire, and in Raelle's clutches.

I must think some form of that at Zelie, because I hear *AS IF WE COULD BE ANYWHERE ELSE* ring through my head in her voice.

Jaali, with a stereotypical Reapers' scythe, hacks his way through Reapers like a farmer cutting down wheat, blood splattering in his wake. As he passes them, Reapers fall and don't rise again.

My roommates branch out: Zelie rushes to Ryden, checking for the pulse I know isn't there, then scanning the room as I had so that she might communicate with him, wherever he is.

Amarie throws spell after spell. They're not visible, but where she points, Reapers bleed. There had only been a handful of Reapers in the room moments ago, but sensing the bloodshed my friends are causing, the hundreds outside are pouring in anywhere they can fit.

The Reapers start fighting each other, too, as if this moment is the catalyst for allegiances to be revealed...for Brother to turn on Brother. Swinging sword sounds ricochet through the cavern, clinking and clanging in a grotesque song as Reapers fall left and right.

Even with some of the Reapers fighting on our side we're still outnumbered.

Raelle has been lost in the chaos, so I dive into the mayhem in hopes of finding her. I'm not foolish enough to think that I can end her myself, but my friends being here has empowered me in ways I would never have expected. And at the very least, maybe I can incapacitate her, holding her long enough that Jaali can help me.

As I move to take another step, ten Reapers fall before my feet. They're all still Living, but they've all fallen to the ground, eyes wide in terror and despair.

I glance around and spot Em staring at us. I quirk a brow, and she shouts, "their moods just quickly switched to terrified," and winks at me. A dark, wet spot appears on the pants of one of the Reapers before me.

Gods, Em is *good*.

She whirls, and where her gaze lands, more Reapers fall, giving Jaali and Amarie time to dispatch them. Zelie is still helplessly searching the room for Ryden, and when I see the panicked look on her face, it feels like all of the sound and movement in the room stops.

More Reapers appear behind Jaali, and in slow motion, it sounds like their shouts are a chorus of, "protect the *Primo*!" but none of it truly registers.

All I can hear is the thumping of my own heartbeat.

All I can see is the look of anguish and *sympathy* on Zelie's face as her eyes meet mine.

I'm paralyzed.

I'm in agony.

Is this what Death feels like?

Because if Zelie can't communicate with Ryden...

...then Ryden isn't here.

57

The battle against Raelle's faction of the Reapers wages on, and though I know that I've near-immediately become some de facto symbol of the rebellion, I can't find it in me to care about anything.

Ryden is gone.

Ryden is gone, and he hasn't come back.

I'm not much use in the battle that surrounds me. Even after weeks of training with Ryden, I'm no match for the Reapers that have had years to hone their skills, to become these lethal soldiers for—I shudder.

This.

This is the warfare that Reapers engage in. This is why their leadership wants them to be militant brutes.

So that they can crush any spark of resistance that may arise before it becomes a flame that could burn them all.

I'm jerked out of my reverie by a cry to my right, and I glance that way to see Jaali. He's been holding his own, but he's one Reaper against dozens. He's lost the element of surprise and is no longer laying waste to the Reapers before him; now, they're fighting back.

I pick up a fallen sword, clutching the hilt tight and charge towards him. Jaali is here because of me. *Everyone* is here because of me. I can't, I *won't*, let my friends die here.

I collide with Em, who is also rushing to Jaali's aid. She skids to a halt beside him, glaring at the Reapers before him, and once again, they begin to fall, but fewer fall than before. Em is exhausting her body.

"We have to go!" I yell to them, and Jaali nods his agreement. Beads of sweat pour down the sides of his face as he continues swinging his scythe.

"Where are Amarie and Zelie?" Em screams. I rise back up on my tip toes searching for them.

"Right here!" Amarie whizzes past me clutching Zelie's hand.

"How do we get out?" I scream.

The cavern is completely full of Reapers, both fallen and still fighting, and more still pour in from the mouth of the cave.

"Stay behind me!" Amarie directs, placing herself at the point of our group with Jaali guarding her side. My friends form a triangle behind them, with me at its center, protected, and begin to herd us toward the cavern exit, through the mass of Reapers that somehow keep coming in an endless wave.

"Keep moving!" he shouts above the din. "I'll get Ryden."

As fast as lightning, Jaali flits to Ryden's body and hoists him over his shoulder before flitting back into our triangle.

Another rush of grief slams into me as I recall Ryden's words when he'd explained flitting to me. "*We can only flit ourselves and whatever items are on our person at the time.*"

I know, I *knew* that Ryden the Living Reaper was gone, but my subconscious didn't get the memo. I was foolishly clinging to the hope that it was all a mistake. That the blade missed his heart. That the blow just knocked him out. That blood loss was real but the end of his Life was not.

But no. Ryden's body is now an *item* that can flit with Jaali.

We're about halfway through the cavern and it just feels like too much. We're so outnumbered and there's just no way possible for us to win this. I'm defeated, and ready to throw in the towel. Let them have me, if that's what they want. It would be far, far easier than whatever lies ahead. I don't have it in me to be some pathetic leader of a resistance that has no chance of winning.

I can't ask these people, my friends, to put their lives on the line for me every single day for the unforeseeable future. I can't expect them to risk everything.

But...

If I don't, who will?

This isn't just about me. This is about the twins. It's about Anabel, and Ethan, and Latrell, and all of the other ghost children I grew up with, who just happened to have been Born that way. If I don't fight for them, will anyone?

Will the rest of their existences be in hiding? Forever running from Raelle and her twisted views on who has the right to Exist as they are? Or, worse, will she find them, and use them like she wants to use me?

That outcome is more than I can stomach.

Our progress through the cave has slowed, but we still press on, inch by miserable inch.

Jaali's arms are shaking uncontrollably, and Amarie's spells are slowing. Em wipes the sweat from her brow, and every time she uses her power, less and less Reapers fall.

"*They're coming,*" Zelie breathes, and it sounds like relief. "Just hold on!"

I don't even have time to demand to know who *they* are before a blinding white light stops everyone in our tracks. Raelle's Reapers and our group alike, everyone freezes in search of the source of it.

"'Ello, love," a voice whispers from behind me. I whirl to face it and find Nels standing there, hair wild and windswept with a knowing grin on their face.

"If everyone could touch me, please, we'll be off," they instruct, and everyone instinctively obeys. I cling to their wrist like a lifeline before the entire world goes black.

58

I'm the most physically uncomfortable I've ever been in my entire Existence.

It's like every particle of me, every particle of my entire Existence, is being taken apart and put back together in an infinite loop. There's no beginning or end, no stop to the discomfort. Time seems to speed up and slow down at the same time; like it ceases to be entirely. I'm acutely aware that I should have a body, but I can't sense anything but the pins-and-needles-on-steroids feeling that comes with not having a corporeal, *or* an invisible, soul form. Every atom that has ever formed me has been pulled apart, every thought I've ever had has vaporized, every sense of self vanished entirely.

I am everything, and I am nothing.

Just as my will to *be* begins to shrivel to dust, I'm thrust back into my solid form and land in a pile on a hard wood floor. It sends pain radiating through my body, but nothing breaks.

I gasp for air before slowly opening my eyes.

We're in the apartment.

We're *home*.

I sit bolt upright, searching for Nels, and when my eyes meet theirs, I projectile vomit onto the floor between us.

"There, darling. That's it, let it all out," Nels coos somewhere to my left.

"You too, Jaali. S'going to be alright." Their voice is farther away now, and I can hear the sounds of multiple people retching.

"Right then, remind me never to take you lot on a roller coaster," Nels jokes and is met with multiple moans.

"What," Em breathes, her face a shade of green I hope to never see again, "was," she breathes again, "that?"

"Oh, that? I just brought you all home." Nels grins.

I have so many questions, but the room won't stop spinning and my stomach is trying to deliver my intestines into the bucket in front of me.

I choke on bile but finally get out a quick, "how?" before burying my head back in the bucket Nels clearly provided for me.

"What are you?" Amarie demands before doing the same in the mixing bowl she's claimed.

"This isn't exactly how I expected this to go down," Nels admits nervously. They meet Zelie's eyes and she nods before retching again.

"So, I'm a Weaver," they announce, throwing out exaggerated spirit fingers like they're a magician who's just done a particularly neat sleight of hand.

"A what?" I ask at the same time that Amarie hisses, "Of course!"

"I'm a Weaver," Nels explains.

Em gasps and brings a hand up to cover her mouth.

"I didn't think Weavers were real!" she squeals. "I thought you were just, like, a fairy tale!"

"'Fraid not, darling," Nels grins at her. "I'm a real Life Weaver."

"WHAT DOES THAT MEAN?" I shout. I should feel bad, because Nels just saved us, but I'm so tired of being left out of the loop.

"I'm a Weaver," Nels repeats and I am very nearly going to explode when they quickly continue, "I can weave through...*anything*, really. Many of the constraints of time, space, and physics don't really apply to me."

I glare at them long enough that they go on.

"I was here yesterday when everyone left to save you and Ryden." Just his name sends me searching the room for him. My eyes land on the couch where Jaali has carefully placed his body. I relax, but only slightly.

"Yesterday?" I ask. Why would they have left yesterday?

"I can only flit myself," Jaali reminds me from his place sprawled on the floor by the TV. He's resting his head on the side of the coffee table, but fortunately all of our combined nausea seems to be slowly passing. "I wanted to flit to you and Ryden immediately, but I knew that we could use Amarie and Em's powers, and Zelie's ability to communicate, if we had any chance at all of getting you two out."

My brows furrow. "But how did you know *yesterday* that we needed help today? It's only been—" I trail off, because it can't have been more than an hour. My stomach lurches at the reminder that Ryden was alive, alive and breathing and confessing his love for me *an hour ago*. And the fact that he still isn't here means he may never be alive, or breathing, or confessing anything ever again.

I vomit again.

"I'm still in the Brotherhood, and Raelle doesn't—or didn't—know that I've defected from her cause," he breathes through a burp but continues, "so yesterday, she put out an all hands on deck call for today in the general area of the mountains I knew you and Ryden to be in. I immediately called the group together, and we all agreed that getting to you and Ryden was our priority. So we got in the car and drove to the nearest trailhead, then Zelie and Em went to work."

"I used my power to seek out anyone nearby," Em offers, "if I can feel a mood, it means a person is nearby. If the moods were sharp and angry, I knew it was Raelle's Reapers, and not you two. When I found some..." her face reddens, "*other* moods, I knew it was you and Ryden."

My cheeks heat to match her own. She must have felt Ryden's and my emotions during his final moments. The hope, the earnestness, the love that was so new and fragile and precious...

I fight back the tears that threaten to start and never stop again.

"Then I," Zelie inserts, "communicated with spirits in the forest that helped us navigate closer to the cave you were in, while also avoiding Raelle. It was a pretty tedious thing, but they eventually brought us to a huge rock overlooking the cave."

"Then I felt..." Em gasps and tears pour down her face, "...then it was only *your* emotions there and they were so devastated and hopeless that we just ran."

"It was so chaotic outside, and Jaali was in front of us," Zelie sobs, "so they just didn't notice that there were three non-Reapers trailing him until we got inside and...well, you know the rest."

My mind is racing. "So then how did Nels get there so fast?"

"I was meant to hear from at least one of our group every hour on the hour. When I didn't hear from anyone at the last check-in time, I knew something had gone wrong. I Weaved to the last coordinates I had from you lot," they glance around at our friends, "then told Zelie I was coming and—"

"But," I interject. "I thought flitting can only happen with non-Living things. How did you get us all out?"

"I'm not a Reaper, darling, I'm a Weaver. Reaper's limitations don't apply to me. I can Weave anyone with me, whenever I need to, wherever I want to go."

A thought hits me then, and I crawl the few feet between my bucket and where Nels sits cross-legged on the floor. I grab their hands, ready to beg.

"So you can bring him back?" I pull their hand to my chest. "You said you can Weave through time, right?" I'm frenzied, I know it, but I can't help it. The thought of having Ryden here is too appealing. "You can Weave back and get us before Raelle stabs him!"

I let the tears pour freely now, because everything is about to be solved.

Well, not everything, but...Ryden will be here.

I've been so lost in my thoughts that I haven't noticed the anguished look on Nels' face. In my periphery I see Zelie press her face into her hands to let the sobs pour out of her.

"I'm so sorry," Nels whispers, "I'm *so* sorry, darling, but I can't do that."

I snatch my hand away.

"But you said!" I scream, rising to my feet. "You *just* said that rules don't apply to you!" The tears that mar my cheeks are as white-hot as my anger.

"I said *most* rules don't apply to me. Death is still Death, darling. It's the one thing I can't bring anyone back from."

"Then what use are you?" I hiss, knowing deep down that I'm ashamed of the words, knowing I'll have to apologize later, but too angry to care.

I don't have time to watch them hit their mark before I spin on my heels, march to my bedroom, and slam the door.

59

I feel his presence before I see him.

I'm sitting on my bed, back in my apartment, staring at the wall but seeing nothing.

The mattress dips beneath him as Jaali sits beside me, wordless. We stay this way for a moment, and while I've vowed to never feel again, knowing that he's here grieving with me does help. In the silence, with Jaali at my side in such similar pain makes me feel seen and understood on a soul-deep level.

"They were your wards, weren't they?" I ask in a whisper. Tears still spill over and down my cheeks, and I haven't had the energy, the emotional capacity, to even try and stop them.

Jaali smiles sadly before slowly nodding.

"Ryden," he breathes, reaching over to take my hand in his, "he thought that this might be a possible outcome. So, he asked me to cast wards around you, just in case. He wanted you protected, Abby. At all costs. So I cast them, not only for him, but for you, too." Tears fall from his eyes now, too. "At first I didn't want to, because," he reaches his free hand up to pinch the bridge of his nose before swiping at his eyes, "I didn't want to give Life to the theory. I thought that if I didn't cast my wards, then this couldn't be what came next. That fate would find another way, and that my friend would stay."

He releases a long breath.

"But I knew I had to honor my friend's wishes, and even more, I *wanted* you to be protected. I don't know if you realize this," he says as he playfully nudges my shoulder with his own, "but you are quite likable, Abby. I also wanted, and still want, you to survive the storm that's coming."

"Why didn't he come back?" I whisper. I'm ashamed to ask the question, but it's haunted my every second since he fell. "I...I thought he would come back." I can't control the sobs as they crash out of me in waves.

"I think," Jaali starts before loosing a sob himself. "I think Raelle did something."

My spine straightens and I drop his hand. "What do you mean, you think she did something?"

Rage, hot and swift barrels through my body again.

"I think that the blade she stabbed him with," we both wince, "could have had something on it that could delay his soul's transition process."

"What does that mean?" I demand.

"I think that his soul is in a limbo state, where he isn't aware that his physical body has Died."

"Like—like the souls that sometimes get lost?!" I gasp, horrorstruck.

"Yes, exactly like that." Jaali chews on his lip, lost in thought.

"What could do that?"

"I'm not sure, but I would wager that many of the Death herbs everyone knows about could have that effect on a Reaper if they were given in the right way and dosage. Oleander, hemlock, belladonna...if she mixed up a concoction with any of those plants, I think it *could* result in soul delays—although this is just a guess. I know none of this to be true."

"But you do think there's a chance he's coming back?" I ask, terrified to hope.

"I think that I'm glad that *we* have his body," Jaali turns to face me, "and I think that *nothing,* not even Death, will stop him from finding his way back to you."

EPILOGUE

Three Months Later

Our rebellion is gaining traction.

Jaali has taken up the painstakingly tedious process of finding Reapers that would be sympathetic to our cause and recruiting them, without word getting back to Raelle.

Or so we hope.

Eya, Wana, and Anabel moved into the apartment next door, the one the International Super Spy who was actually just a guy name Randall had conveniently vacated, and much of our floor has become Born-ghost headquarters. Em's dad graciously allowed us to use any empty apartments to house as many Born ghosts as we can—although he doesn't know the details. Just that his daughter needed space for friends.

I war with myself daily over allowing them all to stay here. Part of me wants them close so that I know they're okay. That they're safe and well and as happy as anyone can be when your Existence is threatened every second of every day.

But the other part of me is screaming that having all of us in one place is asking for trouble. What if Raelle shows up here? What if someone tips her off? What if one of the Reapers Jaali has recruited decides they'd rather have brownie points with Raelle and sells us out?

She could show up and find all of us.

Part of me hopes she does. Because that part of me wants nothing more than to look into her eyes as I kill her.

I want my face to be the last thing she sees before she's sent into the Unknown.

I want to be her demise, for what she did to the world when she took Ryden from it.

I want to be his vengeance.

And I will be.

ACKNOWLEDGEMENTS

This is probably going to read like some sappy, Academy Awards-style list of "thank you"s and dedications, but this book (this *book!*) would not be possible without the following people:

Joshy: thank you for always pushing me to be my best self, showering me in all the books I could ever want, and for building me the library, and Life, of my dreams. The day we met, for dinner at China Palace, my fortune cookie said that I would, "be coming into a fortune," and the night we got engaged, at that same tiny Chinese restaurant almost a year later, it said, "Life is a series of choices. Today, yours are good ones." Neither has proven to be wrong so far, and it has been the privilege of my Life to raise dogs and nieces with you. I love building our (eventual) empire together.

I get my love of books from my Mama (the Rory to my Lorelai, my forever Disney partner, and my Christmas co-conspirator). Thank you for always encouraging my love of reading, for being just as excited as I am for every used book sale we can find, for bestowing upon me your love of a black and white movie, for always encouraging me in everything I do, and for raising me to be capable of anything—including writing a freaking book. You are everything to so many of us —I cannot put into the right words how profoundly lucky I am to have gotten you as my mother, but just know that *I* know how lucky I am. *Yeah, luckily!* Thank yer, ladies and gentlemen.

I get my hard headed tenacity from my Daddy. It has served me well, and I am so thankful. Thank you for a childhood spent playing Barbies on caskets and tag and hide and seek at midnight in funeral homes. Those years of removal and transport have absolutely contributed to this book, and made sure that I have a backup career path as a mortician if the world goes sideways—even if I had to spend my teenaged years with a hearse and a police car in the driveway effectively scaring boys away. I promise to pick my friends, and pick my nose, but never to pick my friends' nose.

To my grandparents: I am honored to be your granddaughter. All that you've taught me is with me in everything that I do, and I could not be more grateful. Grandaddy and Mammy: How I got to be so lucky as to be yours, I'll never know or understand but I could never put into words how thankful I am for it. Your steadfast and unwavering love has made me who I am. Every time I'm told that I'm like the Cole side of my family I shriek with pride—how could I want to be like anyone or anything else? Grama and Grampa: Our countless trips to Cherokee and Maggie Valley are engrained in my very soul and made this book what it is. My childhood was magic because of you, and I'm forever grateful.

Ariel, Josh, and Logan: you are all terrors, but as the oldest, I am your leader (if you didn't read that in a robot voice, I revoke your sibling status). Antagonizing all of you throughout our childhoods are some of my fondest memories. I love you all so very much and I regret all of the years I didn't always act like it but being your sister is truly an honor and a privilege. I'm the luckiest eldest daughter in the world. Ariel, I've known you since the very beginning of your life and you started mine when you came into this world. Matt and Serena: I have no idea why you would willingly choose to join this chaotic family, but we wouldn't be complete without either of you and I'm endlessly grateful that you love my siblings the way you do. Rena, the creatures below wanted me to tell you how much they love you, too.

George Bailey, Tallulah Claire, Zuzu Grace, Harry Potter, Pirate "Poochie" Rover, and our dearly departed Daisy Mae and Maisy Day: I may not have human babies, but I love you fiercely. You've brought light and joy to my Life in ways I could never explain.

To Georgie, especially: this book was written, 100% of the time, with you snuggled up on my chest. WE wrote this book. You are my very soul, the absolute love of my Life, and I will love you until the day I Die. (Then after, but we both know that we find each other in every lifetime.)

To the Johns, both D and P: you are shining examples of love, hard work, and dedication. Thank you for including me in your circles and for loving me like your own.

To my Existing and future nieces and nephews, my A's, E's, L's, and T's: one of my favorite of the hats that I wear is the one of auntie. I am so incredibly proud of each and every one of you, and I cannot wait to see what you become. Mimi/Aunt Mandy loves you so much more than you could understand.

Brandy: You have ALWAYS encouraged me, especially in my writing. I'll never forget YALLFest 2022 when you saw an author's handler who was opening books for them to sign, greeting people in line, and overall being the best, pointed to them and said, "that's what I'm gonna do for you one day." And I'm going to do it for you right back—don't think I've forgotten about your story! I'm so thankful for you and every dinner, every vacation, every text gushing over a book...gods I love you, my Crackhead.

Karin: I'm so glad that I somehow got lucky enough to find the same corner of the Internet as you. Thank you for being my sounding board, and for writing a book at the same time as me so that we could bounce ideas and frustration off of each other. IFG truly changed my Life for the better, you (and Tiny Human) are incredible, and I can't wait for our next Disneyland date.

Nikki: you're my beautiful and majestic tropical fish forever. My emo heart saw your emo heart and just knew, when you "friend-posed," that we were destined to love each other, to be concert buddies, and have the same taste in, well...pretty much everything. I'm so grateful for you.

BJ, my forever Code 3: Your steadfast mentorship, friendship, and love over the years has been invaluable. I couldn't have been more lucky to find you and to get to be in your orbit.

Alisha and Amanda: there is a 100% chance that spending our middle school years writing stories about Ashley Parker Angel, Lance Bass, and Freddie Prinze Jr. falling in love with us directly contributed to my love of writing, and, subsequently, this book. I love you both forever.

Finn, you took a chance on me by diving in headfirst and becoming the Editor that Abby and I absolutely needed. Your feedback made Abby's story so much better and I'm more grateful to you than I could ever put into words.

Castro: This COVER, though. Thank you for taking a *terrible* sketch and a girl with an unhealthy reliance on Canva and turning her ideas into magic.

Autumn, Angie, and Shella, the world's absolute best Beta readers. Thank you for your steadfast support and your honest feedback—yall made this book better and I'm so, so grateful. Autumn, your unwavering dedication to supporting your friends is incredible and I'm so, so glad to get to count myself in those lucky ranks. Angie, my "meet you somewhere on the east coast" travel buddy—you are such a loving, gentle, loyal human and I can't wait for our next adventure! Shella, goodness you are one of the kindest, most selfless people I have ever had the privilege of encountering and I am eternally blessed to know and love you.

To the friends I made in TFP: the group may have been a cult, but I'm still thankful for it every day because it brought so many incredible, loving, supportive people into my Life.

To BookTok: I have gotten so many writing and publishing tips, countless book recommendations, and endless encouragement from you. You are all incredible and such a blessing.

To the best teachers I ever had (in alphabetical order because there is no hierarchy—you were all amazing): Mr. Alan Bowers, Mme. Jennifer Bowers, Mr. J. Altos Godfrey, Mrs. Carla King, Mrs. Cathy Murphy, Mrs. Rebecca Staines. I truly don't think that this book could have been what it was without the impression that all of you made on me.

I will be forever grateful to the random NaNoWriMo ad email I got on June 30, 2021, about the NaNoWriMo "Summer Camp" that was starting the next day. That email was the kick-start that I needed to sit down with my laptop and write more than the hundred "Abby Gale" sticky notes I'd covered my Life in, so that I would randomly find them and not forget about her.

To celebrities I love, because when else am I going to get the opportunity to permanently tell them that I think they're great?! My celebrity crushes: Milo Ventimiglia, Tom Hiddleston, Adam Lazzara, Ben Barnes, and Adam Driver (thank you for Existing, this fangirl appreciates it greatly), Meghan Markle (you are a dream and an inspiration and I truly treasure your Existence), Lizzo (you taught me to actually have confidence in myself), Stassi Schroeder-Clark (you helped me embrace the fact that being my basic bitch self is totally fine), Mark Ruffalo (I can't explain how much I adore you, you gift to humanity, you), Harry Styles (I'm not sure this world deserves you, but thank you for healing so many things you didn't break), Andrew Hozier-Byrne (HOW do you write like that? How do you just *know*? And what did I do to deserve to be on the Earth at the same time as you?), and Ed Sheeran (you sing directly to our souls and it's a profound blessing to experience).

To authors that inspire me on the daily (alphabetically, again, because I can't play favorites here!): Victoria Aveyard, Stephen Chbosky, Robbie Couch, Jason B. Dutton, Rebekah Faubion, Lauren Kung Jessen, Amber D. Lewis, Hannah Nicole Maehrer, Tahereh Mafi, A. K. Mulford, Breanne Randall, Finnely Ray, Adam Silvera, and Rebecca Yarros. Thank you for sharing your worlds with us.

To Aaron Warner. My raison d'etre. Because, duh.

To Nerds Gummy Clusters, and Favorite Day Gummy Sharks. I developed an allergy to my beloved, go-to writing snack of Hot Tamales, and you immediately stepped in in their stead. I'm profoundly grateful for you.

To you, for reading this book. I truly thought that like, my mom and I would be the only ones to read this, so thank you for taking a chance on me. Now please, go tell Goodreads and StoryGraph how much you liked it!

And last, but certainly not least, to Abby Gale. Thank you for showing up in my dreams so many years ago, and for trusting me with your story. I hope I've begun to do it justice, even if you crushed my soul when you told me that book one had to end like *that*.

Abby and Co. will return.

ABOUT THE AUTHOR

A. E. Purvis grew up with her nose pressed between the pages of books and her heart in faraway places. She currently lives under a pile of five rotten dogs with her husband and twin nieces and could not be happier about it. When she's not reading or working on the endless stream of stories filtering through her head at any given moment, A. E. can be found in her library whispering to her beloved books, chattering away to the bookish communities on TikTok and Threads, or spending time with an endless array of dogs, nieces, and nephews.

To follow along on A. E. Purvis' journey, visit www.aepurvis.com, or follow @mandypurv pretty much everywhere.